"Hostin's debut novel is aspirational escapism at its best, balancing an idyllic setting and lush, evocative language with emotional heft and adroit social commentary. . . . Hostin's story is a vast, intricate, and ultimately rewarding one about love, family, and self-fulfillment. . . . In short, this book is summer incarnate."

—*New York Times Book Review*

"A complicated, memorable tale of family, allegiances, secrets, and summertime."

—*Good Morning America*

"The Emmy Award–winning lawyer and journalist invites readers to the exclusive Black beach community of Oak Bluffs, Martha's Vineyard, where the money is old, the secrets are deadly, and summer is more of a sport than a season. . . . Think *The Undoing* with a hint of melanin, where everyone's wearing $300 sandals."

—*Essence*

"*Summer on the Bluffs* by the Emmy Award–winning Sunny Hostin is a delicious, shimmering novel about the lives of Amelia Vaux Tanner and her three grown-up godchildren. I was riveted by these fascinating, complicated women, and looked forward every day to opening Hostin's luminous novel and escaping, through its pages, to the golden dunes of Martha's Vineyard."

—Amanda Eyre Ward, *New York Times* bestselling author of *The Jetsetters*

"Everybody needs a fairy godmother and a glorious summer read. Treat yourself to both with the magnificent Sunny Hostin's *Summer on the Bluffs*. . . . This beautiful novel will have you turning the pages long into a summer night."

—Adriana Trigiani, *New York Times* bestselling author

"*Summer on the Bluffs* is a thoroughly enjoyable escape. . . . A revealing glimpse into the lives of the Black bourgeoisie and the Vineyard as told by someone who understands the complex nuances of our sisters. Sunny Hostin is an elegant yet contemporary voice that daughters, mothers, and matriarchs alike will enjoy!"

—Rita Ewing, author of *Homecourt Advantage* and *Brickhouse*

"The highly anticipated summer must-read from the talented cohost of *The View* is finally here. . . . No one, including the reader, is prepared for the feelings and secrets exchanged in this novel about love, family, and the courage to make the hardest of decisions."

—Shondaland

"Bestselling author and *The View* cohost Sunny Hostin has penned the ultimate beach read in *Summer on the Bluffs*."

—PopSugar

"*The View* cohost, an Emmy award–winning journalist, has written her first novel about a dramatic, romantic season on Martha's Vineyard. It's an entertaining beach read set in Oak Bluffs, a real-life affluent black beach community on Martha's Vineyard (where Barack and Michelle vacation) during one life-altering summer."

—AARP The Magazine

ALSO BY SUNNY HOSTIN

I Am These Truths

Summer on the Bluffs

A NOVEL

SUNNY HOSTIN

with Veronica Chambers

WILLIAM MORROW
An Imprint of HARPERCOLLINS*Publishers*

To my Summer Vineyard Sisters, Kathy and Regina,

and my "writers room,"

*Kathy, Regina, Floyd, Farah, Jill, Pierre, Linsey, Therese,
and, of course, Manny.*

See you on the Bluffs.

P.S.™ is a trademark of HarperCollins Publishers

SUMMER ON THE BLUFFS. Copyright © 2021 by Asunción Hostin. All rights reserved. Printed in the United States of America. No part of this book may be used or reproduced in any manner whatsoever without written permission except in the case of brief quotations embodied in critical articles and reviews. For information, address HarperCollins Publishers, 195 Broadway, New York, NY 10007.

HarperCollins books may be purchased for educational, business, or sales promotional use. For information, please email the Special Markets Department at SPsales@harpercollins.com.

A hardcover edition of this book was published in 2021 by William Morrow, an imprint of HarperCollins Publishers.

FIRST WILLIAM MORROW PAPERBACK EDITION PUBLISHED 2022.

Designed by Bonni Leon-Berman

Library of Congress Cataloging-in-Publication Data has been applied for.

ISBN 978-0-06-299418-9

22 23 24 25 26 LSC 10 9 8 7 6 5 4 3 2 1

PROLOGUE:

AN INVITATION

MARCH 21, 2019

Amelia Vaux Tanner, rich, glamorous, beautiful, was one of the first Black women to have a seat on the New York Stock Exchange. She had been married, until his death, to Omar Tanner, a quiet man who looked good in suits and who was content to let his wife shine.

Amelia never had children. She always thought she would, then she looked up one day and she was forty. Her career was in full swing, and she and Omar had everything they needed and wanted. She thought about having a baby, as her doctor kindly pointed out to her, "before it's too late." But truth be told, she didn't feel like it.

It wasn't that Amelia didn't like children, she did. She was godmother to three girls. She loved taking them to Europe on their birthdays and swooping them up for summers on Martha's Vineyard. It was like a dream. But she also realized that the beauty of loving other people's children is that you get the best of them and then you get to give them back.

Now all three girls were grown up, but they remained close to Amelia. She was more than a fairy godmother, she was their Ama, their second mom. With her support and generous financial gifts through the years, they had all excelled. Perry Soto, almost twenty-eight, was on the partner track at one of New York's top law firms. Olivia Jones, twenty-six, followed her Ama onto Wall Street and was shaping up to be a gifted analyst. Billie Hayden, twenty-five, was a marine biologist, currently serving as an assistant director of the Marine Biological Laboratory at Woods Hole in Massachusetts.

Each summer, the girls, now women, came to Oak Bluffs to spend time with Ama at the house she and her late husband had built nearly thirty years before. It was customary in the Vineyard to humbly refer to a luxurious summer home as a "cottage." But Ama was having none of that. She boldly christened the house, her most prized possession, Chateau Laveau, named after the New Orleans voodoo priestess herself, Marie Laveau.

Ama's picturesque home sat high on the Bluffs. It had five bedrooms, a chef's kitchen, a pool, three French-country-style beehives, a pool house with three additional guest bedrooms, and steps that led down to a private beach. Her grandmother died shortly after she married Omar and she rarely visited New Orleans except when it was convenient to stop on trips to the coast. Oak Bluffs had become home. Over the years, the house had played host to American presidents and African royalty, movie stars and Wall Street titans, Nobel Prize winners and MacArthur Fellows. It was a stunning piece of property, but most importantly, it was the backdrop for a rich slice of cultural history.

On the eve of her sixty-sixth birthday, Ama was sitting at her desk, her monogrammed Mrs. John L. Strong notecards laid out in front of her. She had decided to send each of her three goddaughters an invitation. Within each invitation, she enclosed a small gold bee pendant. "Come spend the entire summer with me, the way you did as schoolgirls." It was time for the bees to come back to the hive. At the end of the summer, she planned to give one of them the keys to Chateau Laveau.

Although Ama promised that none of her goddaughters would leave the summer empty-handed, for each of them their beloved Chateau Laveau was the only prize. Each young woman wanted the house desperately.

But as the old folks used to say, "Every shut eye ain't sleep and every goodbye ain't gone." By the end of the summer, new bonds were created and others torn apart. It turned out there was very little Ama didn't know and no limit to how far she would go to protect her girls. And in the end, the three found sisters discovered that they weren't the only ones with something to hide. Ama had a few secrets of her own. What she had to gift them was far more than property. There was a reason she entered each of their lives all those years ago. This was her season to tell them everything they never knew they needed to know.

CHAPTER 1

THE WITCH OF
WALL STREET

Amelia Vaux Tanner arrived in New York City on June 22, 1972. She had a diploma from Southern University, a junior college in Shreveport, Louisiana, and a patent leather purse with forty-five dollars in cash and a bank check from her grandmother for three hundred more. Amelia traveled by one train from New Orleans to Chicago and then another from Chicago to New York. The journey was long but worth the trouble. On a warm summer morning, her train finally breezed into Grand Central Station with her set of matching luggage. She can still remember the thrill of it, how she stood in the main concourse, staring up at the starry silhouette of Orion in the bright blue celestial ceiling. Just getting to New York was everything she had ever dreamed of, all that came after was just gravy. It was two P.M. in the afternoon, hours away from rush hour, and still the hall was packed. Men in suits and trench coats, ladies in smart dresses and perfectly coiffed hair. They zoomed by her so fast, she had to check that they weren't wearing roller skates. Would she ever move so fast? She doubted it.

She stepped out of the station, oriented herself, and headed south. On West Thirty-Fourth Street, she entered the Webster Apartments. It was an integrated boardinghouse for single women over the age of eighteen, regardless of race, nationality, or religious belief. To qualify, a woman must show proof of employment, at least thirty hours a week. Amelia had, through her college career office, landed a position as an executive secretary at Mayflower Advisors, a financial services firm on Wall Street.

Dorothy Hadley, the boardinghouse director, was a prim woman with skin so pale that Amelia could see the veins in her hands. Mrs. Hadley went over the strict house rules. No ironing in the bedrooms. Irons were only allowed in the laundry. No male guests on the upper floors. Men were allowed only in the dining room, the drawing room, and the garden. Beds were to be made once a day. A housekeeper did a thorough cleaning once a week on Fridays. Two meals per day were provided, breakfast and dinner. Beverages and small snacks, such as yogurt or cottage cheese, could be kept in the pantry refrigerator. No alcoholic beverages were allowed on the upper floors. Once a week, on Saturdays, there was a coed cocktail social. Each resident would be given two tickets a week, which entitled them to a glass of wine for themselves and a guest. The cost of the room was $150 a month, payable on the first.

Amelia signed the lease agreement and took the key to her room on the eighth floor. It was tiny, no bigger than a garret, but from it she could see—or so it seemed—every rooftop in Manhattan. From the eighth floor, there was a staircase that led up to the roof deck.

There she encountered two blond women in oversized sunglasses, laying out in their bathing suits. "Hi," the first one said, "I'm Libby and this is Blythe."

Blythe took her sunglasses off and beamed. "Welcome to the club, new girl."

"Come sun with us," Libby said, oblivious to the fact that the tan Amelia was sporting was from heritage, not sunbathing.

"Oh honey," Amelia said, with a wink. "I was born with a tan, but you know what they say, the darker the berry, the sweeter the juice, so let me change and I'll be right back to join you."

Amelia never let people think she was white—though she was lighter than Lena Horne, with green eyes and bone-straight hair. She carried her Blackness up front. She was a proud Black woman, and if people didn't guess that right away, she threw a little cayenne into her perfectly phrased English to make it clear. She couldn't help it if her ability to blend in made white people more comfortable. Within minutes, Libby and Blythe knew they had made their first Black friend.

By 1977, Amelia had worked as an executive assistant to Benjamin Walsh for five long years. Walsh was in his forties, with Robert Redford hair and a similarly chiseled jaw. He was wealthy, connected, and a vice president at Mayflower Advisors. What he was not, was bright.

He'd tried to make a move on her, inviting her out for drinks, letting his hand rest too long on her shoulder. Then when he thought her silence was permission, he closed the door to his office and put his arms around her waist. Then one afternoon when he came back from lunch, he found her in his office, chatting away on his phone to what appeared to be a girlfriend. "Get off the phone," he said. "Get out of my office." He couldn't believe her. The cheekiness it took to make a personal call at his desk. She smiled at him and said into the phone, "Sure thing, Mrs. Walsh. I will certainly get you my grandmother's recipe for étouffée. I think your husband will love it."

Then, after wishing her boss's wife a good day, she hung up the phone.

Benjamin Walsh stood silent, fuming, at his desk.

"Watch yourself, sugar," she said. "Or the next call I make to your wife will not be about recipes."

After that, he turned his attention to the other secretaries on the floor.

The 1970s were a terrible time not just for the business, but for the country. Watergate and the oil crisis had sent the economy into a tailspin, the market nose-dived 45 percent in one year, and it seemed to the brokers, who had once believed that trading stocks was just a means of printing money, that everything they touched turned to dust.

Benjamin Walsh managed a mutual fund and his clients were protected only by the relatively low percentage of risky stocks in the portfolio. Walsh followed the industry trends and took long, three-martini lunches with colleagues in the name of "research."

Every night at dinner, the young women around the

Webster Apartments dining table complained about how they were practically doing their bosses' jobs for them. Over plates of poached salmon and wedges of iceberg lettuce, they passed around copies of *Ms.* magazine, strategized, and made plans. Some planned to marry their way into prosperity, but even that seemed fraught with pitfalls.

"Married women still have to get their husband's signature to get a credit card," Libby said. "That's bullshit."

"Language!" Mrs. Hadley said, from the butler's pantry. She did not even need to be in the room to sense when the young women were falling out of line. Feminism she could tolerate. Boorish behavior she could not.

"You know, Amelia," Blythe said from across the table. "I read a story in the paper that Black men are much more enlightened when it comes to women's rights than white men. Apparently, the sentiment is linked to the civil rights movement and the shared struggle."

"That's probably true," Amelia concurred.

"I don't want an *M-R-S*," Libby said. "I want an *M-B-A*. And I'm going to get my company to pay for it."

Over the next few weeks, a path began to open up for Amelia. One she had never imagined.

It turned out that Libby was on to something. Amelia already had an associate's degree. She realized it was entirely possible to get her bachelor's, and then a master's, by taking courses in the evenings. Amelia couldn't believe that a graduate degree was suddenly within reach—paid for by the company. All she needed was to get her boss to sign the papers.

She could've forged Ben's signature. She signed his name

all the time to form letters he was too bored to deal with. But she was proud of her Southern ethics and she wanted her tuition reimbursement to be on the up-and-up.

The day she approached his office, she wore one of her favorite outfits, a camel-colored sleeveless dress with a belt that matched and a pair of black-heeled Mary Janes.

"Can you sign this benefits form for me?" she said, casually handing the form to Ben. She hoped he wouldn't look at it too closely. But he did.

"Why do you need to go back to school?" he asked. "A looker like you could be married tomorrow."

It was true. She had a boyfriend, Carter. But he was, to put it lightly, hard to pin down. She wanted something more. Something harder to achieve.

"What are you going to study?" Ben asked.

Amelia smiled and said, "Art history. I'd like to work in a museum someday."

She didn't know why she lied. Maybe because she was afraid of telling him the truth, which was: I'm getting an MBA because I could do your job better than you can. Ben sighed, perused the document, then signed his name on the form. Amelia gently retrieved the paper and walked swiftly out of his office ready to secure the life she wanted.

It took a long time. Eight years of part-time study in total, but Amelia got her MBA. Then she passed her security sales supervisor exams and became one of the first Black women to wear the trading jacket on the floor of the New York Stock Exchange.

In 1985, becoming one of the first Black women on the New York Stock Exchange floor was a proud historical moment for Amelia's community, but the rest of the world can be cruel to the "firsts" and she was not immune to their insults. The hazing was quick and brutal. One Monday morning in December, she came in to find that the drawers of her desk had been filled with what she hoped was horse manure but could very well have been human excrement. Someone had turned the heat off that weekend to ensure that the cold temperatures would freeze the manure rock solid and make it impossible to remove. You could smell the shit from fifteen feet away. Maintenance workers had to break down the desk, remove it, and bring in a new one. Amelia lost a whole week on the floor because of that prank, but she persevered.

The next month, her phone lines were cut. In the decades before the invention of cell phones the landline was the stockbroker's most valuable tool. Two days and hundreds of thousands in trades were put on hold as a result of what the supervisory board called a "non-malicious" prank.

In the first few years, Amelia was audited by her supervisors every three months. A process that required hours and hours of preparation as she opened her books and proved the legitimacy of her trades.

She watched other women quit the floor, but she held strong. Every time she put on her forest-green blazer and pinned on her badge she felt a rush of excitement. She had a sixth sense for undervalued stocks and was well placed and experienced enough to ride the waves of risk assessment to a level of success few women on Wall Street had ever achieved.

The media called her "the Witch of Wall Street" and joked that she used her Creole heritage to cast a spell on the market. Ironically, she wasn't a nonbeliever. She believed in spirits, lighting candles to saints and friends on the other side. But that wasn't anything she brought into the workplace. She was whip smart and did not need magic to make money. She had instinct, insight, and a well-honed ability to make split-second decisions when millions of dollars were on the line. Still, she thought, it was just like men to look to magic or luck as an explanation, when the simple answer was that she was a woman who happened to be very, very good at her job.

CHAPTER 2

WEST TISBURY

One summer after they had graduated from college, Libby Brooks invited Amelia to visit her family home in West Tisbury on Martha's Vineyard. New Orleans born and raised, Amelia had never been to New England, but summer in New York City was almost as hot and relentless as Louisiana, so she said yes.

What Libby said exactly was, "Come stay at our cottage." She then explained that West Tisbury was at least five hours away by car. "You should do what I'm doing," Libby said. "Take Friday off and the Monday and Tuesday before the Fourth of July. That way we'll get a whole five days on Martha's Vineyard. I promise it'll be worth it."

As it had been Libby's idea for both of them to enroll in college, Amelia trusted her instincts. Libby seemed to move through the world with a confidence that things would work out, and they usually did.

Libby had grown up in Manhattan, on affluent Sutton Place. When they met, that address meant nothing to Amelia. She was still new to New York, and her world consisted of downtown, where she worked and went to school; midtown, where she lived; and uptown, in Harlem, where she went for dates and to eat in restaurants that reminded her of the food back home. The rest of the city was a mystery to Amelia, and she assumed that, as the city was on a grid system with a few distinctions of ethnic makeup and architectural style, each neighborhood in New York was pretty much the same.

The night before their trip, the girls began to pack. Libby knocked on the door of Amelia's room and said, "Hey, I have something for you."

She handed Amelia a dress. It was bright pink with green flowers on it. "It's Lilly Pulitzer. Brand new. My stepmother bought it for me. I have one, too," Libby said. "I thought it would be fun if we dressed like twins for our road trip."

No one would mistake the women for twins. They were both beautiful and on the tall side—Libby was five-seven, Amelia was almost five-nine—but the similarities ended there. Libby was white with pale, rose-colored skin, blond curls that fell, in their natural state, in Shirley Temple–like spirals around her head. She washed her hair each night and set it diligently in giant rollers that produced the elegant waves she preferred. Amelia was just a shade tanner than Libby with straight brunette hair that she had pressed once a week at a salon in Harlem.

Amelia thought the dress seemed a little bright—she usually dressed in muted colors: black, white, and tans. The palette calmed her mind and made mixing and matching a cinch.

Libby read her friend's expression and said, "You don't have to wear it. I promise I won't be offended."

Libby never pushed her. Theirs was a friendship that had grown slowly over time. In Pontchartrain Park, the neighborhood where she'd grown up in New Orleans, Amelia never had a white friend. Even though she had grown up nearly a hundred years after the end of slavery, New Orleans was a place where time felt fluid and history felt like a layer of grass that stayed alive, green, and unruly under your feet. What was the thing that Faulkner had said? Something about the past never being dead, it wasn't even past.

Being friends with a white girl in New Orleans was like being friends with all those women who had owned her grandmothers' grandmothers as slaves and all the terrible history that lay within. The tales the elders in her family shared, stretching back through the ages, still frightened and unsettled her. She would see white girls her age in shops and restaurants and she would smile politely, silently admiring their hats and dresses. But she would never invite one of those girls to her home. Would never consider breaking bread with the granddaughter of slave owners. It would be like setting the table for ghosts and a revival of evil.

For all she knew, Libby's family might have had slaves; maybe her history was also tainted. But there was something about the *new* in New York that made Amelia more comfortable with crossing the racial divide. It felt safer here to give relations with white people a go.

With all that in mind, Amelia smiled politely, thanked Libby for the dress, and resolved to wear it the next day.

That morning, at the breakfast table, Libby beamed when she saw Amelia in the dress that called to mind a pitcher of pink lemonade studded with slices of lemons. Libby was wearing a complimentary sheath; hers was yellow with green vines and pink flowers. On her head, she wore a bright yellow kerchief. Amelia was glad her friend hadn't asked her to wear a scarf, too. She wouldn't have done it. Too much of an Aunt Jemima vibe.

Libby kept a car in the city, a 1968 Chevy Nova convertible. "A hand-me-down from my dad," she explained. But to Amelia's eyes, the red coupe looked brand new.

They tossed their bags in the trunk. Libby's was a white canvas weekender with her initials embroidered on it in bright pink thread. Amelia had packed the smallest bag in the three-piece luggage set her grandmother had given her when she'd graduated from college.

They were about to get in the car when Libby said, "We should get someone to take our picture!"

She ran into the apartment building and returned with a sour-faced Mrs. Hadley.

"Make it quick, ladies. I do not have all day," the woman said.

Libby handed Mrs. Hadley her Polaroid camera. "Take two," she said. "That way Amelia and I can both have one."

The two young women posed in front of the car. Amelia realized they were quite the sight in their decidedly non–New York City summer dresses, posing on Thirty-Fourth Street in front of a convertible.

Mrs. Hadley said "Say cheese" in a grumpy tone of voice that made the girls laugh. She might as well have been saying, "Eat rocks."

She took two photos, as instructed. And the girls held

them in their hands, shaking them in the summer breeze, waiting for the image to appear.

Then there they were. Two girls of different hues. Wearing similar dresses. Ready to rock and roll.

It would remain, as long as she lived, one of Amelia's favorite photos. Not just because it depicted her and the woman who would become her beloved friend, but because it seemed like a missive from her future self that said, "Amelia, you can trust this white woman. The world is changing in ways you can't even imagine."

In the car, Libby encouraged Amelia to pick a radio station. Amelia turned the dial until she heard the voice of Diana Ross. It was an all-Supremes set, and the coupe roared up the West Side Highway as the two young women sang along to all the groups' greatest hits: "Stop! In the Name of Love," "You Can't Hurry Love," "Come See About Me."

When they lost the FM radio signal, they started playing eight-track tapes. Amelia listened to groups she had never paid attention to, like the Rolling Stones, Simon and Garfunkel, Fleetwood Mac. Somehow, as the car made its way along the Connecticut highways, the music sounded better and different than the snippets she'd caught before. The songs felt like the ultimate summer road trip soundtrack, a perfect fit.

Paul Simon was singing about him and Julio down by the schoolyard when Libby's car arrived at the ferry in Woods Hole, Massachusetts. "My stepmother prepaid our ticket," Libby explained. "This is the only car ferry to the Vineyard and you have to pay months in advance."

From the moment they boarded the ferry, Amelia knew

that something in her life had changed. The ride was less than an hour, but it was not the length of the journey that shook her. It seemed to her that driving onto the ferry was the equivalent of Alice falling down the rabbit hole. Everything seemed different on the other side. Never before had she seen such a dramatic shift between the sun and the sky.

In New Orleans, Amelia had grown up in a family of Black Catholics. Mixed into that was a healthy respect for the African religions and influences that darted in and out of the Big Easy—the love spells; the potions and incantations for prosperity in a land that knew more than its fair share of injustice.

In New York, Amelia attended Sunday services at St. Charles Borromeo on 141st Street, the oldest Black Catholic church in New York City. Amelia loved the way they threw just a touch of the Holy Spirit into the gospel music, and she admired the way the Black, middle-class congregation shared a commitment to social justice issues. She went to church, she gave thanks, but she couldn't really say what it was she truly believed.

But out on the Atlantic, nothing but sun and sky before her, she felt the simple truth that would become the bedrock of her adult life: God is. Only a higher power could create a vista like this.

It was a short trip from the ferry landing in Vineyard Haven to Libby's family home in West Tisbury. As the stones crunched beneath the wheels on the long gravel driveway, Amelia began to grasp that her friend Libby was more than just city savvy, she was also very, very wealthy. Because what

Libby had coyly referred to as the family's "summer cottage" was actually an eighteenth-century center hall colonial that sat on twenty-five private acres. The salt-gray clapboard had been weathered by time, but also lovingly maintained. A delicate greenish blue covered the doors and windowsills as if the ocean had splashed its ethereal color against each point of entry. Lush white and blue hydrangeas lined the gravel driveway.

Libby explained that the main house had been in her family for generations, and that over the years her father had shrewdly added to the estate by buying neighboring properties when they went up for sale. Hence there was the Stratham House, a four-bedroom house where her older brother and his family stayed when they came to town, and the Barn—which had once been an actual barn but now served as a dining room with a double-height ceiling and indoor entertaining space, with three small loft bedrooms and a chef's kitchen for entertaining.

"We'll stay in the Barn," Libby said, leading the way.

If Libby's father and stepmother were not used to having a Black person as a houseguest, they did not show it. Libby's father, Chris, was an executive at an airline, but out on the Vineyard, he dressed the part of a casual local: all Lacoste polos and brightly colored chino pants. Her stepmother, a beautiful French woman named Anne-Marie, wore simple dresses in black and white, but Amelia could see that the materials were what distinguished the woman's clothing; they fell with the precision of the most luxurious linens and silks. The only person who seemed slightly uncomfortable around Amelia was the family's live-in cook, Aileen. She was, Libby explained, a local, one of the fifteen thousand people who lived on the island year-round.

The second day, after breakfast, Libby asked Amelia if she wanted to go for a drive.

"I have something to show you," she said. "My favorite place on the island."

Together they drove to the Flying Horses Carousel. Libby parked and excitedly purchased two tickets.

"Don't you think we're a little old for this?" Amelia asked.

"Never!" Libby said. "This place is Vineyard history. I've been coming here for as long as I can remember. It's actually the oldest platform carousel in America. It was moved to the Bluffs from Coney Island. So a little bit of New York, right here on Martha's Vineyard."

Amelia raised an eyebrow and made her way to one of the benches on the ride.

"Oh no," Libby said. "You have to ride a horse. They say the tails have real horsehair."

Amelia was wearing a miniskirt, and awkwardly maneuvered herself onto a horse behind Libby, who had mounted the wooden beast with the grace of an accomplished equestrian. Amelia tried to avoid the real old horsehair.

It really was lovely. She felt like a little kid as the carousel slowly turned and the carnival music played from giant speakers on the wall.

"Now as we go around, you've got to go for the brass ring," Libby said.

She pointed overhead. "The brass ring comes out of the slot and only one rider on one of the horses can grab it."

They went around and around, each girl going after the ring and missing it. Until finally, on the last go-round, Amelia reached up and felt the brass circle in her hand. The ring was hers.

When they got off the ride, Amelia purchased a brass ring necklace, a reminder to herself that in life, there are certain rings that only come your way once; if you hesitate, you'll miss your chance. You must grab it and hold on for dear life.

After the carousel ride, Libby suggested they have lunch in Oak Bluffs. She showed Libby the rows of what were called gingerbread houses. "There are three hundred and eighteen in total, each unique in its detail and coloring," Libby said.

They looked like the kind of houses you might see in fairy-tale books, Amelia thought. Each intricate dwelling was peaked with a triangle on top, a small balcony, and a darling little front porch. They sat, side by side by side, as if they were arranged in a child's game. The orange-and-yellow house, next to the green-and-blue house, next to the pink-and-lavender one. Each roofline and porch was trimmed with bargeboard, cut by hand into delicate, elaborate shapes.

Suddenly Amelia realized that everywhere she looked, she saw well-heeled Black folk. Often when she watched films, she imagined what it would be like to buy a ticket, sit in a darkened theater, and spend two hours watching beautiful, successful people falling in love, going off on adventures, having parties, with no regard to race or racism. Noticing Amelia's smile, Libby offered, "It used to be known as Cottage City in the late 1800s." Libby continued, "The town incorporated as Oak Bluffs in 1907. This is one of the oldest Black beach communities in the United States."

They spent the rest of the afternoon driving around the island, taking in the fancy houses and estates. Libby had no shortage of stories about the people who lived behind the privacy hedges and the dramas that raged behind closed doors.

It was clear that in Oak Bluffs, the Black people weren't there as guests of white friends as she was with Libby. These people *owned* the palatial houses, they had the wealth to acquire a second residence, a place where they could go, not to work or make a living, but to simply enjoy. For Amelia, the very concept of such leisure and freedom was mind-blowing.

In Oak Bluffs, she felt a sense of belonging that exceeded anything she had ever felt, even in her native New Orleans. Here, where God had painted this ever-changing landscape of sun and sea and sky, she would make a home.

CHAPTER 3

JUMPING THE BROOM

Omar Tanner never had much growing up. He graduated high school in 1958 and got a job in the bookkeeping department of a button factory in the Garment District of New York. Working there, watching how clothes were made, gave him a lifelong appreciation for design and fashion.

His supervisor at the factory was an Italian immigrant named Milo. Milo saw the changes that were happening in the country at the time and believed that all Americans would be helped if African Americans weren't left behind. Milo watched how quickly Omar's mind worked, how swiftly he did sums in his head, his capacity for remembering even the tiniest details. He encouraged Omar to go to night school to earn his associate's degree. Omar listened to Milo's advice and kept going. It took him a decade and a half of going to school part-time, but he continued on to his BA and then to law school. Omar worked in the button factory until the day he passed the bar exam in 1975.

As a gift for his triumph, Milo gave Omar his first custom-made suit. It was a fourteen-gauge, mid-gray, worsted wool suit with a silk-lined jacket and vest. That suit was sharp.

Omar was top of his class in law school, clerked for an appellate judge, and upon graduation had his choice of big national law firms. Omar, however, had only one destination in mind: Cravath, Swaine & Moore. Cravath, Swaine & Moore had a special place in the hearts of civil rights–minded Black law students. Cravath lawyers wrote the US Supreme Court brief on behalf of the Congress of Racial Equality, crafting language that would change the laws of segregation. Those lawyers, all white, most of them older and the furthest things from activists, became powerful allies to the Freedom Riders of the civil rights movement.

It was the same firm that President John F. Kennedy had turned to for help when creating the Lawyers' Committee for Civil Rights Under Law. While many lawyers went right into a specialty, Omar and his class of young lawyers trained in the Cravath method, rotating through each department for six-month stints so they would gain a solid footing in all the firm had to offer, from family law and intellectual property to mergers and acquisitions.

Omar never lost the quiet humility of the boy who spent most of his twenties working in a button factory. He gained a reputation for being unpretentious, honest, and loyal. CEOs trusted him, and in the 1980s, when conglomerates were built and antitrust cases exploded, he was often called upon for his Solomon-like ability to make sure all sides felt they had been heard and were respected.

He was thirty-four when he graduated law school, more than a decade older than most of his peers. For the next five years, he lived the life of a happy bachelor. He spent his summers on the Vineyard, where he cultivated a circle of

Black men of means who cared about uplifting the race. Together, they golfed and sailed, planned fundraisers for major political candidates, and mentored young Black men.

During the winter, he traveled to Vail with his colleagues from the firm. The company owned several houses for entertaining. He learned to ski and, to his surprise, loved it almost as much as he did swimming and sailing.

As an eligible Black man, he was constantly set up on dates, but he cared little for being matched with a Black woman of the "right" pedigree. The ideal that so many of the Black elite clung to—that of "our kind of people"—made him shudder. What did that mean? Even when his net worth crossed into the millions, he didn't think of himself as "our kind of people." He was Omar Tanner from Bed-Stuy, Brooklyn, who had worked in a button factory and caught a few lucky breaks.

He was so careful and measured in most parts of his life, but the thing he told no one was this: he had no interest in being part of a *power couple*—the new term that was being bandied about in the 1980s. He wanted to fall head over heels in love. He decided he wouldn't settle down until he met a woman who stopped his heart at first glance. He had worked hard, he had done the right thing by his mother, his sister, his colleagues, and his race. He would allow himself this one indulgence—he would wait for a woman to knock him off his feet.

The first time Omar saw Amelia Vaux, she was tooling down Peases Point Way in Edgartown, Massachusetts, with a white girl in a red convertible. He'd just stepped out of the Old Whaling Church where Gloria Naylor had read a short story that would become a chapter of her landmark book *The Women of Brewster Place*. He'd been thinking about how the women in the novel reminded him of his mother and sister.

He loved the Vineyard because it was a counter-narrative to the things he read about Black people in books and saw on the screen. Diahann Carroll had as much glamour as Princess Grace, but in the movies she still dated sanitation workers and wore sensible shoes. He had decided to walk over to the Right Fork Diner; it was late afternoon and he could enjoy a fried fish sandwich while watching the planes take off from the private airstrip nearby. He was walking back to his car when she whizzed by him, the very opposite of the armies of long-suffering Black women in brick cities. She seemed carefree, but more than that, buoyant, as if nothing and no one could keep her down. Her hair was flying and the way she smiled, he thought, I want to be the one who makes her smile like that. I want to spend my life with a woman capable of such joy. His life was steady, peaceful, and he liked it that way. But he knew in that instant he would turn his whole world upside down to be with her. All the things he had worked so hard to earn and achieve seemed like fake treasures compared to the luminosity of that golden woman.

The next summer, Omar returned to the Vineyard with one purpose and one purpose only: to find her, the beautiful Black woman in the red convertible. As luck would have it, she was back, too. He found out from the most reliable gossips on the Bluffs that there was a pretty Black woman staying with an old moneyed white Vineyard family on the other side of the island in West Tisbury. Determined to meet this mystery woman, he borrowed his friend's car and drove right up to their front door. When Libby answered, he was soft-spoken and direct. "I'm Omar Tanner and I'd like to meet your friend."

They were married the following summer, in 1982, in Libby's backyard. They shared sweet wedding vows, a ring, and a kiss, then to honor the tradition of their ancestors, Omar and Amelia held hands and jumped over a broom with colorful cloth wrapped around its stick.

The party was small. Just Omar's mother, sister, and a handful of his friends. Just Amelia's grandmother from New Orleans and her cousin Rogene, who served as her maid of honor. Libby and Blythe from the boardinghouse were her bridesmaids. When the photo of the bridal party ran in the *Vineyard Gazette*, the whole of Oak Bluffs buzzed over the Black woman with the all-white bridal party. Rogene was light-skinned Black, but you couldn't tell from the black-and-white pictures.

In the decades that followed, people would hold Amelia and Omar up as the ultimate Oak Bluffs couple. They were beautiful, wealthy, and powerful. It seemed they wanted for nothing, except children, an emptiness that was eventually filled by their three goddaughters. But nobody knows what goes on behind closed doors in a marriage. Nobody ever really knew all that Omar and Amelia had faced.

One thing was for sure, God had blessed Omar more than he could have imagined that August day when he and Amelia had jumped the broom. He would come to see that Amelia was more than a wife. She was a warrior.

CHAPTER 4

THE HOUSE

From her very first visit to the Vineyard, Amelia loved the slow pace of the island. It reminded her of New Orleans. Many people thought of New Orleans as a party town of jazz, gumbo, colorful beads, and the ruckus and mayhem of Mardi Gras. The N'awlins that Amelia loved was slow and green and lush, a dreamy world of Spanish moss and oak trees, a never-ending watery maze of rivers and bayous. The Vineyard, she discovered, mimicked the pace, the fullness, the peace she felt back at home.

When she and Omar first found the site where they would build their house, the home she lovingly called Chateau Laveau, they remembered driving through what seemed like an endless stretch of woods. Then, finally, they were there, an expanse of grass, high atop a bluff, overlooking Vineyard Sound. Amelia remembered standing back in awe and thinking it was as if she were looking at a painting, rather than something out of real life.

Together with their architect, Charlotte Kemp, they built a home that would straddle the old and the new. On the outside, they wanted a mix of the classic Greek revival details that were popular "down island," while still cloaking the house in the more relaxed, wood-shingle cottage aesthetic of "up island." Inside, they longed for a home that would serve as a living gallery for the collection of African American art that was quickly taking over their New York City duplex. Pieces by Woodrow Nash, Leroy Campbell, Charly Palmer, and so many more. In the interior of the house, skylighted hallways with cathedral ceilings served as the gallery walls for the art. The public rooms boasted floor-to-ceiling windows, and the L shape of the house meant there was a water view from almost every room.

The walls were painted a creamy white so that the real stars of the house remained the pieces of art that Amelia loved so very much. Custom-made sofas and chairs of cream, tan, and white with throw pillows the colors of the Vineyard waters graced the sitting room. Driftwood tables anchored the space, while limed-wood ceilings made it seem as if the house might float upward like a hot-air balloon.

Each of her goddaughters had a bedroom with a specific mood and a masterpiece. Perry's room was a vision of blue and white. China-blue fabric made the walls soft to the touch, while navy-blue-and-white floral patterns covered the headboard and a mannequin torso that sat sentry in the corner. The room was filled with her favorite books, all custom covered in black-and-white jackets Ama had designed so that when they were grouped together on the shelves they made a map of Oak Bluffs.

Lorna Simpson's *Waterbearer* was the central piece of artwork in Perry's room: the ebony skin of the model, clothed in a white linen dress, her back turned to the camera, water pouring out of the pitchers she held in either hand. It was a photograph Perry never grew tired of; for her, it was rife with possibility. In the artwork, the jars were always half-full, there was always more to pour.

Olivia's room was golden. The walls were covered in a sunshine yellow fabric that Farrow & Ball called Babouche because it mirrored the color of the leather slippers of that name worn by men in Morocco. The headboard was covered in a fuchsia-and-marigold Mexican print and there were pops of fuchsia around the room in pillows and on the bookcases. It was a room that Olivia loved so much that when she got her first apartment, she asked Ama's interior designer to decorate it in the same color schemes. One of Carrie Mae Weems's *Kitchen Table* series hung in Olivia's room. In it, the artist applies makeup in the mirror, while an Afro-puffed little girl looks on and does the same. It always reminded Olivia of her and Ama, how much they were alike. While Ama would never say it, Olivia couldn't help but feel that she was Ama's favorite.

Billie's room was a study in black and white, a tiny little alcove that sat on the third floor, the attic level of the house. For years, Billie thought she had been slighted. The room was small, with just one window, round like a porthole on a ship. But by the time she graduated high school, Billie had come to love it. It wasn't until she entered college that she realized the tiny painting of the woman with a mustache was a bona fide Frida Kahlo *autorretrato*.

Ama's suite had several museum-quality pieces, including a cheeky little Basquiat that she kept in her dressing room. But the one the girls liked best was called *Mayflowers Long*

Forgotten, also by Carrie Mae Weems. It featured three girls, much the same age as Perry, Olivia, and Billie were when they first started visiting Ama.

Now, all these years later, salt air had softened the shingles into a café au lait patina. It was, Ama knew, a house that would only grow more beautiful with time.

Omar Tanner died in 2015. It had been a long, hard four years without him for Ama. She had mourned him with the patience that had been the hallmark of their marriage. In the first months, she'd carefully edited, then digitized, all their photo albums. She wanted her girls, and the children they would have someday, to know what Black love looked like in the twentieth century when the world was changing so fast and so slow at the same damn time. She often felt that one of the problems with "Black history" as a rubric was that between Februarys, so much was lost. It always seemed like people were so caught up in the first—first Black astronaut, first Black president, first Black artist to exhibit at this museum or that—that they lost the glory of a life on a continuum. Ama thought it didn't matter that she was one of the first Black women on the floor of the stock exchange; what mattered was how she felt every time she rang the bell or closed a multimillion-dollar deal. It mattered all the times her hunches paid off in spades and all the times when she'd nearly lost her shirt, and somehow summoned the courage to get out there and risk boldly again.

When she looked at pictures of Omar, what she loved wasn't remembering the first time they went to Paris or Tokyo, but the tenth and the twentieth, when the city seemed as familiar to them as their hometowns and they could make their way back to a favorite restaurant down the back alleys, never needing to consult a map.

She wanted the pictures to show all the life they had lived—the travel and adventures, the quiet moments and the appreciation. Omar had not been much of a talker, but his heart was pried open in a way that his mouth was not. He loved art and music and people. Ama loved to give dinner parties at the Vineyard, and he encouraged her. "As much as I'd like to, I can't keep all this beauty and genius to myself," he'd say when she'd rattled off the guest list for a Saturday supper.

She took a year to just go through the pictures, to organize them, to inhabit them, to let the memories wash over her.

The next year, in 2017, she went through his letters. Omar was a fine one for courting by letters.

She felt bad that her girls would likely never know the incomparable pleasure of opening up the mailbox and seeing a letter from a lover, the script as familiar as his hands. Emails! Whoever fell in love over emails? Texts were worse. Dating apps, the very bottom of civilized society. Ama sucked her teeth and shook her head, enjoying the internal rant that was building. She thought it was a wonder people were still getting married, still falling in love, still having babies. The modes of connection were so quick, so soulless and cold.

In the third year, 2018, she sorted through Omar's clothes. Many widows do this first, but she hadn't been able to bear it. His walk-in closet in their Central Park apartment smelled so much like him that she could hardly bear to open the door for the first year. Every time she did, she would be hit by a wave of tobacco and his aftershave scented with patchouli and vanilla. She kept the door closed that whole first year, and maybe that's why the scent stayed so strong. His closet was a tomb of his scent, a scent that she loved more than she'd realized.

It wasn't until the second year that she opened the door and took out a single item. Omar's black turtleneck. The one that made him look like the Black Panther he never actually was. It was cashmere, Ralph Lauren, and he wore it with jeans every time they went to Paris. He never wore jeans in New York. Even on the weekends, in the city, he wore slacks or khakis. But something about Paris made him gravitate toward American denim. Ama wore his turtleneck to sleep sometimes. For an entire winter, she curled up in it while she watched movies or fell asleep late at night, watching the news. She had one serious love affair before Omar, but that seemed like a blip compared to the thirty-three years she'd spent with Omar. He was more than her partner and best friend; he was her mirror. She looked at him and she saw her whole adult life.

Every New Year's Day, she wrote each girl a letter. After breakfast, she changed into his turtleneck and a pair of silk pajama pants and curled up on her couch with its Central Park views. These letters she kept in a safe-deposit box at her office, only to be opened after she passed away. Emails and texts be damned. She wanted the girls to know her handwriting. She wanted to tell them all she'd learned in this life, about how to love a man—and what she'd learned, after his death, about how to slowly and lovingly let him go.

CHAPTER 5

THE BEEKEEPER

Ama first saw an urban beehive on a rooftop in Queens in the nineties. The boroughs were on the come up and she was intrigued with the idea of becoming a beekeeper. The expression "you catch more flies with honey than vinegar" had been a cornerstone of her upbringing and one of the keys to her success on Wall Street. The idea of an apiary of her own felt not just good for the planet, but good for her soul.

When she mentioned the idea to her husband one night over dinner, Omar was intrigued.

"Beekeeping on the Vineyard would be perfect," he said. "They'll pollinate the gardens on our grounds."

It was years before Google was a thing, so that Saturday Omar headed off to the New York Public Library. Ama kissed him on the lips in front of their apartment building and went off to shop for dinner.

❋

Omar strolled from their Central Park apartment to Bryant Park. He always got a thrill when he stood in front of the main branch of the library with the stone statues of lions as sentries out front. The library was massive and impressive with its marble fixtures, ornate detailing, and dark wood walls. It was second in size only to the Library of Congress. He spent the whole afternoon doing research.

While Omar was at the library, Ama walked over to Second Avenue on the Upper East Side, to Schaller & Weber, the best butcher in the city.

When she walked in, Leo, the head butcher, called out to her over the long line of customers that crowded the store. "Bonjour, Madame Tanner, we'll be right with you."

"Bonjour, Leo! I'm in no rush. Take your time."

When she got to the front of the line, she blew Leo a kiss. "How are the wife and kids? Everyone good?"

Leo threw his arms wide open and looked up at the sky, "Thank God, Madame Tanner. We are good and we thank God. What are you making tonight?"

"Jambalaya."

Leo beamed. "Someday, I will taste your cooking, Madame Tanner! So you will need some tasso. We've got the perfect piece, just allow us to dice it for you."

As he walked to the back, Ama remembered how her grandmother made tasso back home in New Orleans. They would drive out to the Covey family farm and her grandmother would buy a whole pork shoulder. She'd cure the meat with salt and sugar, then season it with herbs and spices, going heavy on garlic and red pepper. Then she would hardwood smoke it in the little shed in the back of the house.

She thanked Leo when he handed her the tasso. It wasn't

the same as shopping from a farm and smoking it yourself, but she liked knowing the people she bought her meat from, liked knowing that they knew her, too.

That evening, as she put the final touches on the jambalaya, Omar returned from the library.

He held up a book: "*The ABC & XYZ of Bee Culture*. Some bedside reading."

Ama put the pan on a trivet on the dining table and set the table with her favorite dishes. In one day, Omar had become a bee expert, and he started explaining the intricacies of that part of the insect world.

"It's all so interesting," he said. "There are records on beekeeping up and down the Nile River in ancient Egypt. Exodus 3:8 refers to Canaan as the 'land of milk and honey.' We're talking 2000 BC! . . . Did you know that ninety percent of all plants rely on pollinators like bees, birds, bats, and butterflies to survive? There's a reason they call it the birds and the bees; they're intrinsic to our survival."

Ama smiled. "That's fascinating, honey."

Omar looked as excited as a kid who'd just been handed a very elaborate Lego set. "Oh, we'll get to the honey, honey," he quipped. "Bees are such a huge part of the grand design of this planet, you have no idea. The plants they pollinate don't just give us fruits and vegetables, they prevent soil erosion, provide the raw material for so many of our medicines, it just goes on and on. How many flowers do you think a bee can hit in one day?"

"I'm going to guess a lot."

"Give me a number."

"Eight hundred?"

"More."

"A thousand?"

Omar shook his head. "*Two thousand.* Can you believe it? Now this is going to blow your mind. How much do you think crops pollinated by honeybees contribute to the US economy?"

Ama served Omar an extra helping of jambalaya. He hadn't even noticed that he'd cleaned his plate.

"It's a big number."

"A hundred million."

Omar gave her a look.

"You know I'm a bad guesser," Ama said.

"Okay, I'll tell you," Omar said, tearing into his second helping of jambalaya. "Fifteen billion. Bees are directly related to fifteen billion dollars' worth of crops for American farmers."

"*Billion*, wow." Ama was impressed.

"Do you know that in 1940, the year I was born, there were twice as many bee colonies in the US then there are today? We've gone from more than six million bees to just three million today."

"Sounds like we're going to build ourselves a hive," Ama said.

"I'll do all the work."

"Thank you, baby."

One thing Ama always loved about Omar was that he was a doer.

He smiled and said, "But the first thing we need to do is

to get tested to make sure that we don't have a deadly bee allergy."

※

When they went up to open the house on the Bluffs that May, Omar had the trunk packed to the gills with all the supplies he needed to build a home for the bees that would soon be arriving on the island. Omar hadn't heard of or seen any other beekeepers on the Bluffs, but Ama and Omar were used to being firsts and onlys.

Ama handed him mason jar after mason jar of sweet tea, as it was an unseasonably warm day on the island when Omar decided to build the hive.

He explained as he went along, "There's a bottom board and a super box—this is for the queen and the brood. Then there's a shallow box, that's where the honey will be collected. There's an outer cover and an entrance reducer to keep the hive warm in the winter."

The day the bees arrived in the mail was like Christmas. Their mail carrier, a woman named Dolores, handed them over like they were explosives. "Ugh, I don't like bees."

Omar took the boxes from her gladly. "They're good for the planet. And the honey is going to be so sweet. I'm naming the queen after my wife."

Omar had chosen the site of the hive very carefully. Although bees are survivors—they date back millions of years on the planet—they needed a food source. They would forage over a mile easily and up to five miles if necessary.

Their bees would need wind protection, so the hive couldn't be too close to the water. And the hive needed to face the morning sun but shouldn't get overheated. Omar decided to start their hive with thousands of honeybees called Italians. "They're supposed to be gentle and easy to work with. I've read that beekeeping can be hard work. The bees must be able to work in almost perfect harmony for a hive to be successful. Swarms could be deadly to the health of a hive. If bees are uncomfortable in their designated roles, the entire hive can die."

He was devastated to learn that nearly three hundred bees had died in the shipping process. Yet another thousand died while they were setting up house.

"I'm so frustrated," he said to Ama, after the bees had been in their hives for a few days. "There are bees dying every day. The queen comes separately in her own cage."

"Royal life has its downsides," Ama deadpanned.

"The worker bees are supposed to release her," he said. "I called the apiary society and they said I have to go in and release her myself." What was fascinating to Omar was that the queen's DNA was no different from that of her worker bee sisters. The only difference was environmental. The queen was fed extra rations of royal jelly, a secretion produced by the workers and fed to all the larvae for a short time, but extra rations were fed to the larvae who would become queens. It was poetic to Omar. He knew environment was everything and that Ama and he were providing the jelly to make their girls queens. This was serious business.

The next day, Omar drove to Boston to purchase the protective gear for the task of liberating the queen. Ama couldn't help but laugh when she saw Omar put on the full white bee suit, with the hat and protective veil. But when he came in for lunch that day, he said, "The queen is free and no dead bees today. I think we're going to make it."

They did more than make it. Beekeeping became a part of their lives, like riding their bikes to the beach, or walking into town to watch the sunset on a bench at Inkwell Beach after dinner. One hive became two, which became three.

The hives produced no honey for bottling that first season. Omar read that it was better not to harvest the first year, so the hive could get stronger and store food over the winter. He hired a local guy to make sure the hive had the proper stores and was healthy enough to make it through the Vineyard January and February.

The next year, they couldn't believe it, the hive produced *twenty-five* pounds of honey. Omar printed bespoke labels that read: *Queen Ama's Honey.* They gave jars to all of their friends and favorite clients for Christmas.

Every summer, right before Labor Day, Ama's goddaughters helped Omar harvest the honey. Billie, in particular, took to beekeeping so much that by her senior year of high school, she'd set up a little stand at the farmers market on East Chop Drive. She wrote her college admission essay on the growing phenomenon of bees abandoning their hives and how she was excited to go to a college where they were exploring solutions in sustainability.

Billie perched on the window seat in the kitchen as Ama cooked.

"Ama, did you know that pesticides give bees a kind of Alzheimer's?" Billie asked, her crystal-blue eyes welling with tears. "They go crazy and forget how to get home. They call it 'Colony Collapse Disorder.' It's really simple, Ama. If the bees die out, then humans go next. It would be years, not decades."

Ama shivered. Billie's long legs were folded underneath her. She'd cut her hair into a bob that summer and she reminded Ama of a very chic flapper.

Billie looked at her plaintively and said, "Ama, no offense. But I blame your generation. You all were the *worst* when it came to protecting the planet. They say the 1970s were when we began to lose it all."

Ama sighed. "*Cher*, do you know what a struggle the seventies were for Black people? The bees are dying and it's bad, and we've got to do better. But I was ten when those four little girls were killed in Birmingham. I was sixteen when the FBI assassinated Fred Hampton. Not to mention all the slain whose names are hardly known. The years after all that wreckage, the seventies were a time of constant injustice and unrest. Do you know who Lamar Smith was?"

Billie shook her head no.

"He was a civil rights activist in Mississippi. All the man was trying to do was register Black voters. For that, he was shot in front of the town courthouse, in the middle of the day, by a white man who never served a minute of jail time. Maybe Black people could've done more to save the earth in the 1970s, but I will tell you because I was there, most of us were just trying to save ourselves, our families, and hold this country to the promise it made to our people the century before."

It became a regular thing with Billie and Ama. On Sunday afternoons while Ama cooked supper, Billie sat in the window seat and they talked about the environment.

"Have you heard of Dr. Rose Brewer?" Ama remembered that Billie had asked last summer when they'd all gathered at the house to hear what mystery compelled Ama to formally invite each of them to the Vineyard.

"She's a fierce sister," Billie said, her voice full of admiration. "She's a professor at the University of Minnesota and has written these fire papers on environmental justice."

Ama had learned to keep a pad next to the stove, where she discreetly wrote down the names that Billie mentioned. She shared them with her friends who served on the boards of foundations and other organizations that gave grants for important research.

Ama was making a court bouillon, a New Orleans seafood stew that was the Big Easy's take on bouillabaisse. The kitchen filled with the smell of seafood simmering in a rich, garlicky, tomato broth.

Billie was grown, but Ama could see the girl she was, as she sat there, cross-legged, by the bay window that looked out onto the sea. Joan Didion once wrote, "I have already lost touch with a couple of people I used to be." Ama didn't know it until the girls came into her life, but that was the glue that made family, at least her family, so powerful. We sometimes forget who we were. But the ones who have journeyed with us longest—our parents, our siblings—they remember. They always see not just who we are but all the selves we used to be.

CHAPTER 6

SUMMER SISTERS

The Castle Hill neighborhood of the Bronx didn't have a castle, but it had everything else a kid could desire. The local Y had indoor and outdoor swimming pools, basketball courts, and a baseball field. Castle Hill Point Park had boat ramps and fishing piers for the summer. And the Kips Bay Boys & Girls Club had an ice-skating rink where everyone hung out during the winter.

It was a Saturday in December 2000 and Perry Soto, then nine, was hanging out at the rink with a bunch of friends from PS 110. They had pooled the change in their pockets for fifty-cent cups of hot cocoa. The cocoa was made with water, not milk, so it was a little thin. But Tia Lucia, who made it, always put a splash of evaporated milk in each cup so the drink was hot and sweet.

Perry sat with her friends in the bleachers, her hands wrapped around the hot cup. They were all in the fourth grade, but this was the Bronx, where kids grew up fast. Perry winced a little when someone brought up the subject of writing a letter to Santa. A tall girl named Dana said, "Negro, please. Picture me sitting on some old white man's lap, telling him all about my hopes and dreams." Marisa, who was widely acknowledged as the smartest girl in their class, nodded in agreement. "Santa is just a perv dressed up in a tacky-ass red suit." It was the year that *perv* had overtaken *weirdo* as the biggest insult in their circle.

Perry glanced over at Layla, her best friend. Layla lived down the hall from Perry in Jamie Towers. Layla was white with dark hair and catlike green eyes. Her whiteness was something she denied on the regular. "Look, kid," she'd say with a scoff. "We're all from Africa. Lucy is the mother of civilization. Look that shit up."

Layla was the only one at their school who knew that not only did Perry still believe in Santa Claus, but every year, her mother took her to Macy's so she could mail her letter in the official mailbox and, yes, sit on the perv's lap.

As they walked home from the ice-skating rink, Perry tried to explain. "It's not that I really hundred percent believe," Perry said. "It's more that . . ."

Layla smiled. "You like tradition. I get it. But don't you think you ought to give up on the fat white guy/stand-in for Jesus bringing all the gifts?"

Perry said, "Way to kill the magic, Layla."

Layla smiled. "Yo, that's how I do. Speaking truth to power since 1991."

Perry looked confused. "But we were born in 1991. You weren't talking then."

Layla was unfazed. "I've always been about the truth. Even in the womb."

Perry smiled. "You're . . . unique."

Layla grinned. "I'm a unicorn, baby. Only one of me in the whole wide world."

✳

The girls parted ways at the elevator and Perry reached for the key to her apartment.

She knew she was lucky. Her parents, who'd adopted her when she was a baby, lived in a spacious two-bedroom apartment they owned. Perry was an only child, so although her folks weren't rich, she never wanted for anything. Her mother was a hairdresser at a salon for white women with curly hair in Manhattan. Her father drove trains for the MTA. The apartment was clean and well put together, like something out of a magazine. But her parents were more like exhausted roommates than a loving married couple. Her father cooked. Her mother cleaned. After dinner and on the weekends, her mother watched hours of TV and her father sat in the armchair in their bedroom reading thick presidential biographies. It was a quiet house and the air was thick with all that was unspoken.

After she arrived home, Perry finished her homework, then went to the dining room to join her parents for dinner. Perry would remember that night for many reasons, one being it was the first time her father had made a recipe he'd seen on TV—grilled steak with blue cheese mashed potatoes. The potatoes were buttery and salty with flecks of blue from the cheese. They were also delicious.

Once they were done eating, Perry cleared the table and

her father laid out the Junior's cheesecake, which they would eat in tiny slivers, throughout the week, until it was done. Over dessert, Perry announced, "I don't believe in Santa anymore. I'm not a little kid. You don't have to pretend."

But even as the words came out of her mouth, she wanted to take them back. She was still, very much, a little kid. She wanted, with all of her heart, to keep pretending.

Her parents exchanged glances. Then her mother spoke. "Maybe this year, instead of Macy's, we can go to Rockefeller Center for the lighting of the tree."

Her father agreed. "That sounds nice."

The following Saturday afternoon, Perry came home from the ice-skating rink to find the most beautiful woman she'd ever seen, sitting in their living room. The woman was wearing a black wool dress that revealed her collarbone—what Perry would later learn was called a sweetheart neckline. The dress was cinched with a wide, black leather belt. She wore knee-high, burgundy suede boots and her purse was the same rich shade of dark red.

Perry's mother explained that the woman, Amelia Vaux, was a family friend who had taken an interest in Perry and her education.

This seemed strange to Perry. Her parents didn't seem to have many friends outside of the aunts and uncles who visited once or twice a year. They were reserved and simple people. Where they would have met a glamorous woman like Amelia was a mystery.

Amelia offered to take Perry out to high tea the following Sunday after church. "I'll send a car to collect you," she said, beaming at the girl.

It was just seven simple words: I'll. Send. A. Car. To. Collect. You. But the phrase would change Perry's life. For the rest of the school year, every other week, a black town car, driven by Virgil, Amelia's personal driver, would show up at her school or her apartment building and whisk her into Manhattan, into Amelia's dream world. Amelia took her to tea at the Plaza and to see all the latest Broadway shows. They went to see the Alvin Ailey American Dance Theater on New Year's Eve and to see a Romare Bearden retrospective at the Metropolitan Museum of Art.

Layla would stand in front of the building, waving as the car drove Perry away to her other life. "You're so lucky," Layla would say wistfully. "She's like your real-life fairy godmother."

Perry knew that her friend was right. She always wondered about the timing. Was it the act of giving up Santa, who was of course not real, that made it possible for Amelia, a real fairy godmother, to enter her life?

The following summer, Perry spent four weeks on the Vineyard with Amelia and her husband, Omar.

The next summer, Amelia announced that she had a surprise. "Another one of my young charges is going to join us. Her name is Olivia and she's a year younger than you."

Olivia lived in Montclair, New Jersey, with her mother, Cindy, who was a schoolteacher in Newark. Whereas Perry had light, honey-hued skin the color of cocoa butter, Olivia was her opposite. Her skin was a rich gingerbread brown, and her hair was jet black; her mother straightened it herself every week.

That second summer at Chateau Laveau, when it was just

Olivia and Perry, was like a slumber party that never ended. The girls each had their own rooms, but they spent most nights together, in the guest bedroom that had two double beds. That school year, Perry was going into sixth grade and Olivia was entering fifth.

Neither girl played a sport so Ama arranged for tennis lessons. They spent four hours a day taking private instruction with a top-ranked coach who had worked with the Williams sisters early in their careers. Lunch was usually made by Ama's cook, Bette, who had come from Ama's hometown of New Orleans. The afternoons were for swimming and reading. Twice a week, on Tuesdays and Thursdays, a tutor came by to make sure the girls were well prepared for the coursework that would be coming in the year ahead. Evenings were for sit-down dinners. During the week, it was just Ama, Omar, and the girls. But on weekends, Ama entertained. Dinner could range from an intimate gathering of eight to a backyard soiree that numbered fifty or more.

When the girls arrived that summer, the wardrobe and drawers were filled with new clothes, personally selected by Ama. She reminded them that anything that did not fit or suit could be returned. But the girls kept everything. They had never had so much luxury in their lives.

At the end of the summer, the week before they were to return to school, Ama announced that they would be taking a weekend trip to Montreal to do back-to-school shopping.

It was Ama in her element, speaking French, moving through the streets like the grande dame she had become. They stayed at a magnificent hotel in the Vieux Port, the old part of the city. Both girls decided, when it was time to choose a language, they would study French.

Both girls were also embarrassed to admit that they did not miss their parents very much or feel homesick. Ama insisted they stay in touch, so they wrote letters once a week. They called every other day, but the calls were short. Their parents seemed ever so slightly relieved to be untethered from the rigors of parenting.

"I don't think my mother misses me at all," Olivia said to Perry one evening after hanging up the phone.

"I don't think my mom does, either. She's so quiet, it's hard to tell what she's thinking."

Ama entered the room and did not pretend she hadn't overheard the conversation.

"Being a parent is hard," she said. "It's a twenty-four-hour, from cradle-to-grave kind of thing. If these trips give your parents a little reprieve, all the better. It doesn't mean they don't love you or miss you. Black parents do what they have to do to create opportunities for their kids."

Perry, who favored Ama most in looks and tone, said, "So what's the opportunity for you, Ama? Who would want a couple of rowdy kids in their house?"

Ama smiled. "You should know I do nothing that I don't truly want to do. That is the blessing of my situation. You are here because Omar and I feel deeply that you don't have to be blood related to become family."

Two summers later, another girl arrived. That year, Perry would turn thirteen, Olivia turned twelve, and Billie was ten. Whereas Perry and Olivia were girlie girls, content to blithely follow along with whatever Ama suggested, Billie was a rule breaker. She was curvy with pecan-colored skin, blue eyes, and a head full of braids. She lived in Queens with her father, who worked in a famous Manhattan comic book shop. Billie herself was like something out of a comic book. She was part Catwoman, part Storm from X-Men, and part Daredevil. Billie never saw a tree she didn't want to climb or a diving board she wouldn't go running toward, grinning broadly, her eyes wide open. At night, even though she was the youngest, she told the most chilling ghost stories. And when the girls played truth or dare, Billie always took the dare.

Perry wondered that first summer with Billie if this was going to be the way. Was this Ama's summer home for wayward girls? Would every summer bring a new cast of characters? Were they all just Ama's Fresh Air Fund kids?

But as if to assuage her fears, one Sunday evening Ama and Omar held hands and after grace, welcomed the girls to the family. "You are not ours by birth, but we are happy to step into the role of godparents and treat you as our own. Perry, Olivia, and Billie, you have made our hearts fuller than we thought possible. Thank you for being here. May we have many more summers together."

As the girls grew, they struggled to find the connection. How had they landed in the Vineyard with these wealthy benefactors? How did their parents, each of such modest means, meet Ama and Omar? Why them and not any of the thousands of girls, just like them, living in New York and New Jersey?

Ama was loquacious and secretive at the same time. "All will be revealed," she would say when they asked her anything—be it something as simple as what was for dinner or something more complicated, like how she ended up in New York City.

They say that whatever your dream was, God could dream bigger. She never asked them to worship, but they came to realize as they grew from girls to young women, that whatever they imagined for themselves, Ama held a greater vision.

And although they were not related by blood, it became clear that each girl had her own connection to Ama. Perry looked the most like Ama. She sounded the most like her. And if it is to be believed that nurture trumps nature, it was Perry who came to be the most like Ama, the godmother, the hostess, and the entertainer. Perry, like Ama, was a fierce protector of the ones she loved. She was incredibly book smart, but at the end of the day, her strongest muscle was her heart.

Olivia was a fine example that children don't always listen to what you say but they will often do what you do. Olivia was the one who rose early, like Ama. Often, while the rest of the household slept, it was Olivia who made her way into the kitchen, who turned the Nespresso machine on and made both her and Ama a perfect latte. She eventually learned how to time it so the coffee was sitting at Ama's chair, with swirly hearts drawn in foam, just as Ama entered the kitchen. Ama and Olivia would sit in happy silence for an hour or more, reading the papers. First the *Wall Street Journal*. Then the *New York Times*. And if the others slept in, it was on to the *Economist* or the weekend edition of the *Financial Times*. Olivia, like Ama, had perfected the art of seeking the single answer that would answer ten questions.

Maybe it was because her mother taught high school algebra that Olivia loved logic, mathematical problems, and anything that could be solved with an equation or an algorithm. Under Ama's guidance, Olivia purchased her first stock at the age of fourteen. By the time she graduated from high school, she had day-traded enough to sock away her first year's tuition. No one ever doubted that despite their physical differences, Olivia and Ama were almost intuitively, psychically linked. Olivia had Ama's mind. Her brain worked in the exact same way.

It was true that the youngest were often the most indulged, but Billie was not a girl who wanted or needed coddling. The most confident of all the girls, Billie never sought Ama's approval, which she had wisely observed was the quickest way to get it. Billie lived in her own world of comic books, superheroes, sci-fi, and video games. She was the first of the girls to smoke, to drink, to sneak out at night. But instead of getting in trouble, the more Billie bucked the rules, the more freedom she got. When she was sixteen, Ama moved her up into the attic bedroom, which had its own entrance. A decision that Perry, who had just started college, found to be absolutely stupefying. Why give a kid who sneaks out a door that made it easier for her to go out and act like she's a grown-up? But Ama was unconcerned. She saw in Billie the part of her own past that refused to be caged—not by segregationist Louisiana, not by the old white boys' club that was Wall Street, not even by the Bluffs and its cadre of Black elites. Nobody put Ama in a lane, and she saw it as her duty to make sure Billie remained as free as the spirit that roared within her. Billie had Ama's courage.

CHAPTER 7

SWIM

2010

It was Billie's junior year at the Mathilde Nelson School for Girls, where tuition was over thirty thousand dollars a year. Ama and Omar had arranged it all, from her application to the full scholarship ride to the wardrobe bag of crisp brand-new uniforms that had arrived at her house two weeks before school started. Unlike Perry and Olivia, at age seventeen, Billie couldn't care less about clothes. She read that Steve Jobs wore a black turtleneck and jeans every day and that the space it opened in his mind enabled him to create the iPhone. She wanted to be a scientist. She wanted to make sure there was plenty of room in her brain to create great things. The navy-blue turtleneck and charcoal-gray tartan skirts that were the Nelson school uniform weren't exactly Jobs worthy, but it felt like a start.

The Mathilde Nelson School had a heated Olympic-sized indoor swimming pool. Ama had suggested that Billie try out for the swim team. Billie loved to swim. She had learned to swim, like the rest of Ama's girls, during summers on the Vineyard. Omar would take them to the Inkwell, a beach whose name had begun as a slur in the 1890s as whites nicknamed the stretch of segregated beach allotted to Blacks. A century later, the Inkwell had kept its name but the world had changed. Black was beautiful, once and decidedly for all, and local residents used the name Inkwell as a point of pride—this stretch of beach and ocean was theirs, no milk was necessary for all that coffee.

It was there that Omar patiently and diligently taught each girl how to tread water, how to swim underwater, then how to dive. Perry didn't care much for ocean swimming, and Olivia was perpetually concerned about what the water might do to her hair. But for Billie, the ocean felt more like home than any place she'd ever been on land. Omar had promised that one day he'd take her scuba diving. She wanted to go to the depths of the ocean where the water went so dark you needed a light in order to see.

She met Whitney Bowen the first day of swim team practice. Billie was tall for her age with wiry muscles that wrapped like rope under her baby-soft skin. Whitney was shorter with more of a bust and more curves, but she was also strong. Billie admired the muscles in both her arms and legs.

The swim team was surprisingly diverse. Besides Billie and Whitney, there were two other Black girls: Josie, who was from the Bahamas and spoke with a lilting Caribbean accent, and Lindsey, who'd transferred in from Colorado. The four of them quickly formed a posse. They ate lunch together, they studied together, and five days a week, they practiced together. The swim team practice schedule was intense: Mondays, Wednesdays, and Fridays from three to five P.M.; Tuesdays and Thursdays from six to eight A.M.; and meets on Saturdays.

Often, on Friday nights, the four girls spent the night together so that only one parent had to drive them to the early-morning meet. The first weekend in May, Billie found herself alone at Whitney's. Josie's grandmother was visiting from the Bahamas, and Lindsey had caught the flu and wasn't going to compete.

Billie had never been alone with Whitney overnight before. And yet the minute she realized that the other two girls were not coming, she found herself hoping that something romantic might happen between the two of them, and the thought of it took her by surprise. She hadn't had any crushes on boys, but she thought that was a function of going to a girls' school. Her interactions with boys consisted mostly of awkward conversations at intramural mixers and the painfully shy boys who crowded the comic book shop where her father worked.

Perry and Olivia talked about boys all the time—who they had kissed, who they had let get to first or second base. Both of the older girls had made it clear that you couldn't let a boy slide into third, not in high school. Not if you were a good girl.

In their parlance, as much as Billie had understood it, boys were always on the offense and girls were on the defense. "A boy is always going to try," Perry said dramatically, swinging on one of the posts of her four-poster bed as if it were a ship's mast and she were a sail. "But you've got to hold your ground."

Perry and Olivia didn't discuss their own desire, the kind of longing for touch that Billie felt, it seemed, all the time. In their hands, it was much more a game of chess than seduction. The preferred balance of power was for a very handsome boy to like you much more than you liked him. If that was the case, then everything was golden.

No one ever asked Billie if she liked boys, if she wanted a boy to kiss her, or to try to get to first. They assumed her desires were the same as theirs. "You'll see," Oli said, with the slightly superior *tsk-tsk* voice that was her trademark. "It's all so tricky with boys."

Now, as she stood in the entryway of Whitney's apartment, she wondered, What about girls? Was it just as tricky? How did it work?

She pondered pretending to have forgotten something important—her goggles, her racing suit, flip-flops for the shower. Billie wanted to go home and google it: How do two girls make out? What's first base with two girls? What's second?

If she went home, she could buy a book online and download it to her Kindle. Her dad never supervised what she read. "As long as you're reading," he'd say. "All I ever read was comic books and look at me, I'm a . . ."

Then she would answer, "Bona fide genius."

Billie searched Whitney's face for some flash of recognition of what she was feeling. But her friend seemed unaware. Whit was her same, beautiful, bubbly self. "My mom says we can order from Grimaldi's for dinner."

"Cool, cool," Billie said.

"And I'm so behind on *Top Chef.*"

The show had quickly become popular among their circle of high school friends.

"Me, too," Billie said.

"Let's throw your stuff in my room," Whitney said, and Billie followed her down the long hallway to the bedroom at the end.

Whitney's parents, Yvonne and Ray, were having dinner two floors down at their neighbors' place.

Whitney's father was a contractor. He'd worked with the architect who'd designed the building they lived in. "Otherwise, we'd never be able to afford digs like this," he once said. And Billie was aware that Whitney's condo was like something out of a movie. Billie and her father lived in a tiny two-bedroom railroad flat in Queens. Their building was more than a hundred years old. Billie's father had grown up in an identical building, just a few blocks away.

Whitney's mother was a dermatologist, with a ton of celebrity clients. She and Whitney shared the same perfect, TV-commercial skin, and she was always giving the girls on the swim team samples of super-expensive moisturizers she got for free. "The pool is so drying on your skin!" she'd exclaim.

Billie noted that her dad could not care less about things like face cream. He kept Dr. Bronner's Pure-Castile Soap in the shower, a jar of Palmer's Cocoa Butter next to the toothpaste, and a bottle of Carol's Daughter Hair Milk next to the brush and comb in the bathroom. That was it for him and grooming.

That evening, Whitney's mother was dressed in a pretty cashmere sweater, leggings, and expensive-looking sneakers. Because Billie had never met her own mother, she studied other mothers wondering what her mother might have been like if she had lived. Her father told her it was less "studying" and more like "staring." Hearing his voice in her head, she shyly looked away.

"You girls have a fun night," Yvonne said. "Just text if you need us."

An hour later, the two girls were sitting cross-legged on the living room floor. They had agreed, without argument, on ordering the Colony, which was a red sauce pizza with pepperoni, pickled jalapeños, and honey that was delicious but not as good as Ama's. It didn't sound like it should be so tasty, but it was.

She had no idea why they all watched *The Great British Bake Off* on British TV. None of them actually baked. But it was fun to watch something so silly happening an ocean away. Billie especially loved the British accents. It might also have been true that watching the contestants fumble and fail took the edge off the competition that awaited them the next day. Mathilde Nelson was ranked number two in their division. It was a pressure-valve position. So many teams wanted to knock them off that vaunted perch. And yet, the gulf between their spot and the number-one-ranked school, High Tech, seemed insurmountable. It was like the difference between being number one and number two was greater than the distance between being number two and number twenty.

In her head, Billie pictured herself relaxing in the water.

She tried to picture every stroke and imagined her arms reaching even longer, her legs moving with greater and greater force. She was doing the two-hundred-yard freestyle. Their coach, Liz, was a big fan of visualizations.

After dinner, the girls cleaned up and went to Whitney's room. Whitney's phone buzzed and she looked at it. "My parents said we should go ahead and get ready for bed; they'll be out for a while."

Whitney had her own bathroom, attached to her bedroom. She called it an en suite. It was as fancy as it sounded. It had a rain forest shower, a slate-gray marble floor, and a little niche with a dressing table and light.

"Do you want to shower first?" Whitney asked.

They always showered the night before a meet. The next morning, they'd get up at five, quickly blend a smoothie, and be in the car by five forty-five.

"Sure," Billie said.

She took her overnight bag into the bathroom along with the giant plush bath sheet that Whitney's mother had laid out on the guest bed. She couldn't remember the last time her father had bought new towels. Theirs were so raggedy and thin. She'd have to try to convince him to get some new ones from Target. She turned on the shower, as hot as she could take it, and let the windows steam completely. She pictured herself in the pool the next morning. She needed to drown out the sounds of the room. She needed to pretend she was alone in the pool, that the only person she was racing was herself.

Her eyes were closed and the shower smelled of the fancy eucalyptus soap Whitney's family liked to use.

She stepped out of the shower, got into her pajamas, and opened the bathroom door. "It's all yours," she said.

"Thanks," Whitney said. Then she kissed Billie, ever so softly on the lips.

Billie instantly felt like she was back on the Vineyard, the first time she'd dived off the Jaws Bridge. She felt the same mix of joy and exhilaration when she felt herself suspended in midair.

Of course, she thought, as she kissed Whit back. It was so easy. So simple. So good. Her coach used to say, "A journey of a thousand miles starts with a single step." It only made sense that this journey of passion, of touch, of pleasure, would begin with a single kiss.

CHAPTER 8

RED BEANS AND RICE

May 2016

Their last semester at Harvard Law School, Perry and Layla still lived on campus in Story Hall. They'd often played with the idea of moving off campus, maybe to Somerville, or a great sublet in Cambridge, but Story Hall was easy. A perfect location, close to classes, plus they had each other. When they'd both found out they had gotten into Harvard Law School, they knew they would be roommates. Layla's biggest complaint when they were looking for housing: not enough Black people in the dorm.

"You know you're white, right?" Perry said, covering her mouth, as if sharing a secret.

"Don't test me, trick," Layla whispered back, through clenched teeth. It was funny because they were alone touring the campus. "I renounce my colonialist heritage."

Perry smiled. "Look, you're my girl. And you're cool with

me. But I don't want somebody to blow your shit up. That wouldn't be cool."

Layla shook her head. "One, that Rachel Dolezal chick took it way too far with the braids and the tanning. See, I just pretend that my straight hair is that expensive yaki weave."

Perry laughed. "You're going to get caught. Jay Leno's going to be telling jokes about you on national TV and there's not a thing I'll be able to do to help you."

Layla didn't look worried. "You just wait. One of these days, I'ma take a 23andMe, and I'm gonna bet you good money that I'm just as Black as you." Layla waved her hands, game show–girl style, around her hips and booty. "There's gotta be some Africa for me to be this blessed in my hips and thighs."

"Whatever," Perry said.

Layla took down a clipboard. Every week, they signed up to use the communal kitchen and hosted a get-together.

Perry took the sign-up sheet from her. "I think this week, we should do a red beans and rice dinner on Monday. And people can come through, grab a bowl, and get back to studying if they want."

Layla smiled. "You going to bring Ama's red rice and beans up to these Harvard types? They're not worthy. But I am. Don't leave out the pork, 'cause I ain't no Five Percenter."

That Monday, Perry made Ama's recipe and more than a dozen of their classmates came by. When Ama heard that Perry was cooking her signature dish for her classmates, she sent a box of bona fide New Orleans ingredients. "You've got to use the right beans. The right rice. The right hot sauce. The right seasoning. Or it'll all be wrong. And I don't want my name attached to some fake wannabe red beans and rice."

The following Monday there were even more students, and by the third Monday of the month, it was a tradition. Red beans and rice with Perry and Layla.

Perry was cooking in the kitchen, two Le Creuset stockpots simmering on the stove. The blue one had the vegetarian version of the dish, into which she now crumbled bits of veggie burger. The white pot had the original, made with pork per Layla's instructions. She was far away from the room entrance, but she could feel that the space was changing, the energy was palpable.

Perry turned the burners on the pots down low and went looking for Layla.

"Hey, what's going on?"

"The Plastics are here."

"Excuse me?"

"The Plastics. The very good-looking, very superficial med students who are specializing in plastic surgery."

Perry rolled her eyes and turned to go back to the kitchen, but Layla pulled her elbow.

"You've got to see them. They are *really* hot."

"What? Do they operate on themselves?"

She stepped away from the stove and looked at the far end of the room. There were five guys she'd never seen before, and one guy she couldn't stop staring at.

"Um, is something on the stove?" said a girl she knew from secured transactions class.

She ran back to the stove and lifted the lid. She was just in time to save the rice from burning. She let out a huge sigh of relief.

The Plastics had followed her into the kitchen. One of them, a freakishly tall basketball player–type, introduced himself. "Hey, I'm Jeremy."

Perry was unimpressed. "I'm Perry."

"Thanks for having us," Jeremy said. The British accent helped a little. But he wasn't her type.

"Who invited you?" Layla said flirtatiously. "This is a very select crowd."

Jeremy looked around and smiled. "There must be thirty mugs milling around. Not that select, innit?"

The one Perry had been eyeing stepped closer. "It smells really good. I haven't had a home-cooked meal in a long time. I'm Damon."

She took a step back. She couldn't stand so close to him because honestly he was so good-looking she didn't know what she might do. Everything about him was as if he had been made for her, crafted by the heavens to be everything she'd ever dreamed about. She didn't know what she was going to do, touch his shoulder, kiss his neck, invite him back to her place. She felt an emotion she rarely allowed herself to feel. She felt reckless.

When the red beans and rice were ready, she prepared a bowl and handed it to him. Then she made one for herself. He followed her to one of the sofas.

"This is a nice setup you got here," he said, looking around appreciatively.

"Not too bad for a dorm. It feels pretty homey at this point," she said.

Her mind was racing. She couldn't date a Plastic. A plastic surgeon. A guy so freakishly sculpted that he probably had a friend do surgery on him. But she also felt that whatever happened was inevitable. Ineffable.

"So where are you from?" she asked. She was down for whatever, but the least she could do was make an attempt at small talk.

"Queens," he said.

"Like Run-DMC said, from Queens come Kings," she said, referring to an old lyric her father used to sing along to. "My dad's from Queens, too."

"So did you grow up there, too? I feel like I would've met you before then."

She laughed. "Really? There are 2.278 million people living in Queens."

He smiled. "One, that number is kinda mad specific. Two, I just feel like if we were in the same place, we would've met. I would've found you. Like I did, here, tonight."

She thought he was going to kiss her then. She wanted him to kiss her. But instead, his friend, the human scarecrow, loudly dragged a metal chair across the stone and parked it next to them.

"Hey, bro," Jeremy said. "Don't you start pushing up on the girl I came here to meet."

Perry was flattered. And confused.

"Yeah, girl, I've seen you in the gym. Four P.M. Pilates. Tuesdays and Thursdays. I'm there lifting weights. You probably noticed me," Jeremy said, flexing a muscle.

"I started looking out for you in your little leotard and capri tights," he continued. "Looking so fine you could be my next ex. So I asked around and heard this is where to find you on Monday nights."

Perry put her head down. She was blushing, despite herself.

Luckily, Layla came to her rescue. The way Layla pulled up a chair all loud and abrupt made Perry think maybe she and Jeremy might hit it off.

"What's up, playa?" Layla said, winking at Jeremy.

Jeremy looked like he couldn't decide whether to keep pressing on Perry or to take a chance with Layla.

Layla said, "You know I haven't gotten into anything in a while. This one's a Latina from the Bronx. Straight-up altar girl."

Jeremy took the bait and said, "Should we go to a proper pub and grab a drink, Layla?"

Layla waved at Perry and mouthed, "You're welcome."

Damon said, "Altar girl?"

Perry flushed. "Something like that."

"I like a good girl," he said, leaning in to kiss her on the cheek. "How about you and me do the opposite of our friends? Why don't we take our time?"

That night, he stayed and helped her clean up the kitchen. That was always the worst part of Red Beans and Rice Mondays. People seemed to clear out en masse without cleaning up.

While she rinsed dishes and stacked the dishwasher, Damon synced his phone to the Bluetooth speakers in the room and started playing some French hip-hop.

"What's this?" Perry asked.

"Alliance Ethnik," Damon said.

Then he started rapping in French.

"Wait, what?" she said. Perry had to steady herself by gripping the kitchen counter. The urge to take off her panties and take him on the creepy kitchen couch was almost overwhelming. Black-light grossness be damned.

"How'd you learn to speak French like that?" she said.

Damon said, "My grandmother was from Haiti and she was always so disappointed that I couldn't really speak French. So I started listening to French hip-hop, watching the videos on YouTube. Voilà, I learned faster and I got a little of that Parisian *banlieue* flow in my accent, too."

Perry let out a sigh. "It's sexy."

He was walking around the room, picking up cans and bottles, putting them in recycling. "Your cooking—that's sexy."

Perry said, "So we agree. We find each other sexy."

Damon said, "And we're going to take it slow."

Perry said, "Why slow again?"

Damon smiled sweetly and held her at the small of her back. "Because you can't rush a forever thing."

He meant what he said about forever. That spring, when Perry graduated from law school and Damon graduated from medical school, he proposed.

CHAPTER 9

FIRST COMES LOVE, THEN COMES MARRIAGE . . .

Since she and Ama had planned every bit of the wedding, Damon had said, "Let me surprise you with the honeymoon." They flew to Thailand, which was beautiful. But the real surprise came three days later, when they boarded a plane to Indonesia. She could barely contain the tears when she heard the word *Bali*. In law school, she'd torn a page from a travel magazine of a beautiful bungalow over the water in Bali. She'd scrawled the words "You are here" on the picture and taped it to the corkboard in her room. She and Damon had never even discussed it. The photo was there for so long, most days Perry didn't even notice it. But when she was exhausted or worried that she was in over her head, she'd think about that image of crystal blue waters and say to herself, I'm there.

On the island, her husband had reserved a beachfront villa, with its own private pool and meditation pergola. A carpet of white, fragrant, melati putih flowers marked the path from the entrance of the villa to the bedroom. Perry took off her sandals and walked barefoot through the candlelit space. The stars beamed bright through the sky-light, and although she could not see the ocean, she could hear it and smell it.

"Damon," she whispered, as if they weren't alone. "How in the world can we afford this?"

He smiled. "You did good, girl. You married a surgeon with no student loans."

"No, seriously, look at this place," she said.

"We can't take another vacation for a while," he said more seriously. "But I figured we'll both be working so hard for the next few years, we might as well do it big." He took her hand and stepped onto the wooden deck that looked out onto an infinity pool that seemed to flow right into the ocean. "This is it," he said. "This is where we start being us."

In Bali, they were twelve hours ahead of New York time, so no one called; there was no need to check emails because they were up when everyone back home was asleep. For a week, a private chef prepared their meals when they called for her. There was nothing to do but sleep, eat, read, and . . . was *make love* even the right term? Alone in the villa, Perry stopped wearing underwear underneath her blousy sun-dresses. She wanted to be ready for him. She loved the free-dom of not having to fully cover up. She might be lying on the chaise longue, reading a mystery novel, and Damon would come up behind her and put his hands on her breasts. She was ready for him even when she didn't expect it. But the way he dove between her legs, bringing her almost to climax with his lips and his tongue, drove her insane. She'd find herself tugging hungrily at his pants, anxious for him to enter her, feeling both the familiarity of his manhood and knowing that each time would be just a little different. Would she come first? Would he? How long could she last, this time?

In the daytime, they eyed each other playfully, coming together and apart in unexpected moments. At night, after dinner, they soaped each other in the outdoor shower where sometimes Damon took her against the cedar wall, the smell of the wood and the Bulgari green tea soap mixing to form an intoxicating fragrance. And then they would walk naked to the pool, where they drifted lazily on the floating daybed as the sun set over the ocean, an explosion of warmth and color.

"This is what it must have been like for Adam and Eve," she said, on their last night in paradise.

"Before they got thrown out of the garden," Damon said, with a wry smile.

"Thank you for this," she said.

"Thank you for being my wife," he said, kissing her on her lips, then her shoulder, and moving on to her breasts.

She thought she'd never think of her body in the same way again, never not know how much pleasure she and Damon could find in each other. They were well matched.

Their trip to Bali had been so blissful that she had expected to come home pregnant with twins or triplets or maybe even more. Although she understood, intellectually, that the number of times you had sex was in no way related to how many babies you had, she had not come home pregnant. She thought she'd never want anything more than the heavenly equation of beauty and luxury, sex and pleasure that had been their time in Bali. But it was right, what they said, about the brain being a discounting mechanism.

Because what she wanted now, more than anything in the world, was not multiple orgasms in an infinity pool. What she wanted was a baby.

There was something about a fancy doctor's office that made Perry feel rich. She remembered all those years of visiting Dr. Martin's family practice office in Castle Hill. Everything was slightly run-down. The pale green paint on the wall looked tea stained after years of wear and tear. The wood paneling on the receptionists' desk was flimsy and showed clearly that the material had come from a factory, not an actual tree. The fluorescent lighting buzzed while casting its unforgiving glare.

In contrast, the office for the Bryant Park Women's Health Practice looked like a floor in a sleek hotel. Floor-to-ceiling windows flooded the room with natural light. She recognized the coffee table, with its curved wood base and glass top, as an iconic Isamu Noguchi. The charcoal-gray sofas were as crisp as tuxedos.

Perry admired the round walnut legs of the furniture. The magazines were all brand new and strategically placed; lamps cast soft, peaceful spheres of light around the room.

When the nurse called her name, Perry let out a quick exhale. She hoped the doctor had some answers for her. It had been two years since she and Damon had gotten married on a sunny September day in Ama's backyard on the Vineyard. Twenty-three months since their honeymoon when she'd pulled the goalie and stopped using birth control.

Perry's doctor, Aja King, was the kind of happy-go-lucky Black girl Perry found to be absolutely mystifying. Aja had grown up in Venice, California, the daughter of a professional surfer mom and a sound engineer dad. She was in a perpetual good mood and she spoke as if every word she uttered had been written in purple ink and bubble letters.

"Oh my God! You look great!" Aja said. "You have to tell me who made that dress."

"Ulla Johnson," Perry muttered. Among her godsisters, Perry was known as the cheery one. But she was like the before girl in an antidepressant commercial compared to Aja.

"So, I have good news!" Aja said.

Perry paused and wondered aloud, "Am I pregnant? I just had my period two weeks ago."

Aja made an "oh shucks" face. She said, "No, sorry, not that kind of good news. I mean that I've checked your eggs and Damon's sperm and you are both perfectly healthy. There's no reason you can't get pregnant."

Perry wanted to punch Aja in her cheerful face. Instead, she said quietly, "But I've been trying for two whole years."

She noticed that she said "I" instead of "we." She couldn't help it. The baby quest had started to feel like a personal quest. Like climbing Everest. Maybe Damon was essential to the mission, like the guide carrying the supplies, but she was the explorer. It was up to her to scale the mountain. Getting pregnant was something only she could do.

Aja clasped her hand over Perry's. "I know this is hard to hear, but try to relax. The human body is complex, but your body was literally built to do this. And as far as I can tell, there's no scientific reason for this not to happen for you. Just keep at it. And remember, orgasms release endorphins!"

Perry stared at Aja in disbelief.

"Come see me in two weeks," Aja said. "Remember, this is good news!"

Then she was out the door.

Perry walked out of the fancy doctor's office and up Sixth Avenue. She normally loved this part of the city. She hardly ever went, but she liked to see the marquee of upcoming performers at Radio City Music Hall. She liked to smell the cupcakes baking at Magnolia Bakery and window-shopping at Brooks Brothers. She needed a new go-to work dress, like the pleated navy jacquard piece that she saw in the window. That would be a one-and-done outfit on the days when she couldn't be bothered. Which was every day, these days, if she was being perfectly honest. But she wasn't in the mood for clothes shopping, so she made a mental note to check out the dress online and kept going.

As she approached their Central Park apartment building, she noticed their doorman, Eli, helping a woman put a car seat in the back of a taxi. She felt the familiar pang of jealousy. Why her? Why not me?

❋

That night, over dinner, Perry told Damon the not-great-but-not-bad good news.

"That is good news, honey," he said, looking at her, concerned.

"I know," she said glumly.

"Hey, listen," he said, "the American Society of Plastic Surgeons conference is next month in Turks and Caicos. Come with me. We can stay a few days after the conference is over. I'll find us a villa to rent, one with an infinity pool, and who knows . . ."

Perry shook her head and counteroffered flatly, "We can have sex here."

Damon whistled. "Wow. Way to sell it. I know we can have sex here, we can also have sex on a gorgeous Caribbean island. Sex here has become a little clinical, don't you think? All you think about is having a baby. What happened to romance? Love? Lust? I'm still a man, Perry."

"I'm too busy at work. I have that big case coming up. Maybe after," she said.

He looked at her in disbelief. "But the conference dates won't shift because of your case."

She sighed. "I know, baby. I know. You go ahead and maybe we can take a trip together around the holidays."

He said, "Okay, you know Jeremy will be there."

She sighed. "I figured. All I ask is that you try to behave like the married man you are."

Damon looked at her, hurt. "What the hell does that mean? Was that necessary? Sometimes I don't think you deserve me, Perry."

He went into the bedroom and turned on the football game, loud. She didn't think it would ever be like this with them: barbed threats in polite tones of voice, turning up the TV so loud that the apartment sounded like a sports bar; those were plays from her parents' so-so marriage handbook. She wanted to do better. She aspired to be better.

She loved him. She did. Lord knows they were compatible in bed. But if she was honest with herself, the skirmishes had started early. She thought back about how they hadn't even harmoniously agreed on what city they would live in. After graduation, her from law school, him from medical school, she'd always assumed that they'd move to New York. She was a Bronx baby with Manhattan dreams. She'd made no secret of that.

But at the end of their time at Harvard, Damon had gotten a job offer in Atlanta, to oversee medical tourism practices internationally, including plastic surgery, at the Centers for Disease Control and Prevention, a prestigious government agency. He asked Perry to fly down with him to check it out.

"Why?" she'd bristled. "I'm never going to live in Atlanta."

Damon had looked so hurt. She remembered the expression on his face. It still made her feel bad that she could have ever hurt him like that.

"It's kind of my dream job, Perry," he said. "I grew up reading books about bioterrorism and global health crises like *Contagion* by Robin Cook and *State of Fear* by Michael Crichton. I think the work the CDC does is fascinating—and important."

She'd gone with him to Atlanta for the weekend and Perry had been miserable the whole time.

Damon kept exclaiming about the size of the Black elite in Atlanta. "Black people run things here, baby," he kept saying. "This is the new Chocolate City." But Perry didn't need a chocolate city, not when she had the Bluffs, a seaside retreat filled with a community of sepia perfection.

When the CDC recruitment liaison took them around to see houses "for fun," Perry had been similarly underwhelmed. Even the houses that were technically within the city center felt as if they were deep in suburbia.

Damon fell in love with a mock Tudor four-bedroom house that had a basketball court and a swimming pool. The two-car garage had been converted into an in-law suite with a shower and a kitchenette.

"This is so dope," he kept saying. "This is my dream house."

But Perry couldn't see it. To her mind, the house was a McMansion. What was the charm of living in a mock Tudor in the suburbs of Georgia?

She hadn't said it, but it also felt a long way from the Vineyard and their beloved Chateau Laveau. She tried to go up every weekend during the summer and as much of the fall as she could manage. If they lived in Georgia, she'd be lucky if she made it to the Vineyard one week a year. That wasn't the life she imagined. That wasn't her dream.

She'd tried to reason with him on the commute front. "Baby, this house is forty-five minutes each way to the CDC. It's twenty minutes from the nearest grocery store."

The recruitment exec picked up on Perry's vibe and said, "They deliver groceries these days, honey."

Perry could've throttled the woman. Didn't she know this was an A and B conversation and she needed to C her Southern way out of it?

"I grew up in a bodega culture," Perry explained. "I like knowing that if I want a pint of ice cream, the store is just steps away."

"The service delivers ice cream too, honey," the recruitment exec said, and Perry thought if she called her *honey* one more time . . .

Damon said, "Honestly, Perry. I wouldn't mind the commute if I could ball out on the weekends in a place like this with my friends."

Perry didn't say it, but what she had been thinking was, Exactly. All this place is good for is balling out with your friends. This house is a glorified man cave.

She'd prevailed and they'd moved to New York. She'd hit a bit of luck when Damon's friends from med school, Jeremy and Sabrina, took jobs in New York, too. But the doctor crew was always traveling—to conferences and pharma junkets, which seemed to often be scheduled in places that Perry didn't want to go—Miami, Jackson Hole, Vegas.

Perry liked most cities but she loved the quiet elegance of Manhattan—walks in Central Park, rooftop drinks at the Peninsula and Soho House. She didn't really do clubs or casinos, big arena concerts and sporting events—all things that Damon and his friends loved. Her passions had been shaped by a childhood exploring the city with Ama and Omar, so it was probably unsurprising that what she loved was Broadway and the ballet. She liked live music but Cassandra Wilson at Lincoln Center was more her vibe than Rihanna on Governors Island.

For a long time, she thought it didn't matter. After all, didn't they say that opposites attract? But the longer she and Damon were on the outs, the more time she had to consider just how opposite they really were. And what she really wanted.

CHAPTER 10

8 SPRUCE STREET

Spring 2019

Olivia waited almost two years for an apartment to open up at 8 Spruce Street. An iconic Frank Gehry–designed building that rose seventy-six stories into the sky. It was an astounding glass and steel version of Jack's beanstalk. When she lived in Brooklyn Heights, she often walked over the bridge to work. And each morning, when she saw the Gehry building with its asymmetrical bay windows that seemed to undulate like an Alvin Ailey dancer, she was in a trance; she longed to live there.

When she made partner at Array Capital the previous spring, the first call she'd made was to Ama. Her godmother seemed unsurprised, and for an instant, Olivia wondered if her swift rise had been Ama's doing. It certainly helped that she had brought Amelia and Omar's estate planning to the firm. And once that deal had been set, it was only a matter of time before Olivia was handling the portfolios of a baker's dozen of the most prominent families on the Bluffs. But she worked hard and was hungry for success. Nothing had come easy for her. Not as easy as everything came for her godsisters. Perry seemed to have been born for the law— she had an almost innate sense of strategy; the understated dramatic flair that played so well in court, not to mention an almost photographic memory with an ability to recall the minute details in court documents that often swelled to include nearly a thousand pages.

Her godsister Billie had parlayed four years on the high school swim team and a silver medal in the Junior Olympics into a career as a marine biologist in Woods Hole. Ama liked to boast that Billie had ancestors from Atlantis—that explained how comfortable she seemed under the sea.

Olivia had always loved numbers and had aspired to be a broker since the day she'd understood what Ama did for a living. Every year she feared she would lose Ama, that the phone would not ring, that there would be no invitation to summer on the Bluffs. Of all the girls, Olivia was the most insecure about her relationship to her godmother. She got this sense of unsureness from her own mother. Cindy Jones was a teacher in Newark, New Jersey, where every day she saw how easy it was for Black boys and girls to get caught up in the system. She taught Olivia that there was no room for African Americans to make even the slightest mistake. Her way of loving Olivia was to insist that the girl reach for perfection in every aspect of her life.

"You're not white and you're not light, nobody's going to take care of you," Cindy told Olivia from the time the girl began elementary school.

Cindy insisted that Olivia's hair be dead straight at all times. "Don't you follow those girls with their naturals and their braids; nobody out there wants anything to do with your naps," she said as she ran the hot comb along Olivia's edges. When the hot comb occasionally slipped and she felt the pain of a new burn, Olivia always wondered if her singed skin wasn't her mother punishing her for having kinky hair.

As she grew up under Ama's tutelage, she followed the woman as closely as she could, holding back just a little lest Perry call her "creepy." She got up early because Ama rose early. She read the *Wall Street Journal* and the *Financial Times*, keeping a little diary of vocabulary words that she looked up in the afternoon when the other girls were splashing about in the pool. She taught herself how to read the S&P and made herself flash cards of the symbols: *EMR* was Emerson Electric Co., *SPGI* was S&P Global, *WBA* was Walgreens Boots Alliance.

She studied YouTube videos and taught herself how to make the perfect latte, which was the way Ama started each day. Then she learned how to make a heart in the foam, the way they did at Starbucks. Then she taught herself to make the initial *A* with steamed milk, which was something Ama loved.

Olivia went to Yale undergraduate because it was the first school to give Ama an honorary degree. Then she went to Wharton because Ama said she thought its MBA program was stronger than Harvard's.

All along, she'd had to work harder than it seemed her godsisters ever did. She needed tutors in every subject, except math. She went to every bonus seminar and wheedled her way into the best study groups.

She'd gone after the job at Array and then partnership with an archer's precision. But the apartment at the Gehry was the biggest prize yet. It was the thing she had done, not to impress Ama, not to gain Omar's praise, but solely for herself.

The two-bedroom apartment faced the Brooklyn Bridge, the "eighth wonder of the world." Olivia marveled at the bridge's steel cable suspensions leading up and away from the regal granite and limestone arches. She secured the most beautiful view in the building. All the interior finishes had been designed by Gehry himself, and her appreciation for its beauty never waned: the brushed stainless-steel hardware on the door, the custom cabinets made of the most exquisite amber wood, the mix of silver and charcoal gray in the appliances, the quartz countertops with their sparkling onyx patina.

The building offered weekly housekeeping and fresh flower delivery. There was a library, an Olympic-sized indoor pool with glass garage doors that opened in the summer, a fifty-seat screening room, a private dining room with a baby grand piano for entertaining, and a four-hundred-square-foot state-of-the-art fitness center with sauna and steam room.

One Sunday evening, Olivia was running on a treadmill when she met him, Nate Gordon. He jumped on the treadmill next to her and cranked it up to an eight-minute mile.

She had been jogging at an easy ten-minute-mile pace

and he turned to her, smiled, and said, "Are you walking or running?"

Never one to back down from a challenge, she upped her pace to a seven-minute mile. "On your left," she said, playfully quoting a line from *Captain America*.

He smiled. "You've got jokes, huh? I was just warming up." He reached down and quickened his pace to a six-minute mile.

Olivia looked down at her legs, said a quick "Feet don't fail me now," and went to a five-minute mile. It felt good to go so fast.

He reached for the pace button, then seemed to think better of it. Smiling, he said, "Let me quit before I hurt myself."

She slowed down and tried to be chill about it. She loved to win.

When they had both stopped their treadmills, he wiped his hand on his towel and reached out to shake hers. "I'm Nate Gordon."

She said, "I'm Olivia Jones."

They went back to their respective units and showered. They had agreed to meet up in the building's game room where the football game was playing on the big TV.

"I ordered Han Dynasty," Nate said. Olivia wondered: Am I on a date with this guy?

Over spicy dan dan noodles and ice-cold beers, Olivia fell for him. She always thought that living in the Gehry was her destiny. She didn't expect to fall in love, almost literally, with the boy next door.

For six whole months, the affair with Nate raged on. He walked her to work each morning before hopping the train to his job as a video game designer in the Flatiron District.

She began to fantasize about bringing him to Ama's that summer. Finally, Perry wouldn't be the only one with a fine-as-wine brother on her arm.

But shortly after the first day of spring, Nate started ghosting her. First, he stopped inviting her back to his place. Then he stopped walking her to work. He said that the new video game he was designing was going off the rails. "We've got to change the whole thing from wireframes on up," he said apologetically. "I've just got to focus right now. You understand, right?"

She did understand. How many times had she broken dates because work demanded it? She never wanted to be the needy kind.

Two weeks had gone by with only the briefest texts from Nate and she was beginning to believe that this thing she'd given her whole heart to was, in fact, too good to be true.

Then one morning she left for work later than usual. It was ten A.M., and as she walked out onto the covered driveway of the building, there was Nate, his arms wrapped around another woman, his tongue snaking down her throat.

She walked up to them and waited for him to notice her. She had a ten thirty meeting with her boss, but she was a partner, what were they going to do, fire her?

Nate turned around and squeaked a little too loudly, "Hey, neighbor! I wanted you to meet my fiancée, Kenyatta."

The girl was clearly biracial, with curly reddish-brown hair and freckles that dotted her heart-shaped face. She was light and bright and, as they used to say, damn near white. Her skin tone shouldn't have mattered so much to Olivia, but it did.

"Hi," Kenyatta said cheerfully. "Nice to meet you."

Olivia plastered a smile on her face, the never-show-weakness smile that her mother had taught her to perfection.

"I'm Olivia, I live in thirteen K." Immediately, she thought: Why would I give this girl my apartment number? What was I thinking?

"I'm a PhD student in linguistics," Kenyatta said. "I've spent the last six months in Papua New Guinea."

Everything in Olivia's brain said: Walk away, walk away, walk away. But she just stood there, chatting with this woman as if she hadn't until very recently been sleeping in Kenyatta and Nate's bed.

"Interesting," Olivia said.

"It is, actually," Kenyatta continued brightly. "Papua New Guinea is one of the most culturally diverse countries in the world. Eight hundred fifty-one languages are spoken there and eleven of them have no known native speakers. My thesis is about the death of languages and the psychological impact of lost dialects on ethnically diverse citizens."

"Fascinating," Olivia said. "Well, lovely to meet you. See you around."

❊

Nate never called her after that day. Never attempted to explain what he'd done and why he'd done it. She felt so stupid and used. Worse, she'd let this man play her and all she did was smile. Olivia was often reminded of her pain because she ran into Nate and Kenyatta more often than made sense. There were 904 apartments in the building, how could it be she kept running into the two people she most wanted to avoid? It got so bad that she considered moving, but she felt sure that eventually they'd move out and 8 Spruce Street would be her little slice of heaven once again.

Olivia was eating dan dan noodles from Han Dynasty by herself and stalking Nate and Kenyatta on Facebook when she came across a photo from Jeremy Adenuga's feed. She'd been a bridesmaid at Perry's wedding. Jeremy had been the best man. Olivia had tried a little fling with Jeremy. But who hadn't? It wasn't a big deal; she knew Jeremy was a dog.

The photo caught her interest because it was of Perry's husband, Damon, frolicking in the ocean with a woman who was definitely not Perry. She clicked on one photo after another. It was all more than she expected, then all that clicking led to something that made Olivia catch her breath. And she'd be a liar if she didn't say it provided a kind of solace. Apparently, Perry's picture-perfect life had been more photoshopped than Olivia realized.

CHAPTER 11

BABY, BABY, BABY

Perry's phone buzzed as she was walking through Whole Foods on Sixth Avenue near Times Square, wondering what had compelled her to go grocery shopping right after work when the supermarket was entirely packed. It was a text from Olivia, her godsister. Even though they both lived in New York, she hardly ever saw her in the off-season. Olivia lived downtown in a huge loft in the Financial District. She worked as a broker; she was the one who followed most closely in Ama's professional footsteps. Billie was consumed with her marine biology research and Perry never saw her either. They all visited Ama over the summer, on the Vineyard, but each on a different schedule. They exchanged birthday and Christmas cards and occasionally they got together for dinner at Ama's. But mostly they kept their distance: they were not best friends. They weren't the type to text. Perry looked at the phone and read the message—**Hey girl, gotta sec?**—and wondered what Olivia wanted.

Grocery shopping, Perry typed back. **Is it urgent?**

The text-in-progress bubble popped up instantly. Olivia was typing.

Uh, yeah. Call when you can.

Perry looked down at her empty cart and then glanced at the crowded market. She'd order in. Red Farm, the fancy farm-to-table Chinese restaurant, with outposts on Hudson Street and on the Upper West Side. Damon would like that. She put the cart away and walked across the street to Bryant Park. The city was doing its show-off, spring thing. All the trees were in bloom and the parks were lush, lively, and green.

She sat down on one of the green metal chairs near the Bryant Park lawn and hit redial.

"Hey, it's me," she said. "What's up?"

Olivia sounded happy to hear from her. "Girl, I'm so pleased you called me back. Are you sitting down?"

Perry felt a moment of panic. Had something happened to Ama? Was she sick? Omar, Ama's husband, had died four years before. It was too soon, he had only been seventy-five. His death had been devastating. Perry did not know what she would do if, then she corrected herself, *when* it was Ama's time. She was closer to Ama than her own mother. She talked to her on the phone almost every day. Often, it was just a quick hello and check-in, first thing in the morning when Perry got to work.

But it gave Perry a boost to hear her rich contralto say, "So, how's my girl, today?" No matter what went down at work, it always made the day better when she took a moment to remember that before anything, she was Ama's girl. The two women played Words with Friends throughout the week, and on Sunday they often worked on the *New*

York Times crossword puzzle together over the phone. Perry texted Ama photos of any significant purchase she was considering and Ama liked to send along inspiring quotes. Perry could feel her heart racing. Ama was in her mid-sixties. She wasn't old. But she wasn't that young. This was the age when things started to go off the rails.

"Is Ama okay?" she asked breathlessly.

She could hear Olivia chuckle, amused that she'd gotten a rise out of Perry. "Girl, that woman is fiiiine. Chances are good she'll outlive all of us."

Perry was annoyed at how flip Olivia was being. "So what's up?"

Olivia paused dramatically. "Look, I've got something I want to talk to you about. It's about you and Damon. Promise not to kill the messenger, okay?"

Perry was confused. She and her husband had hit a rough patch. What was for damn sure was that none of this was any of Olivia's business. She'd read in *Forbes* that the fund Olivia managed was worth $100 million. Didn't that mean she had other things to think about than Perry and Damon's marriage?

"We're okay," Perry said evenly. "What's up?"

She was beginning to regret having this conversation in a public place.

"Do you know a girl named Sabrina Cotton?"

Perry felt her heart sink. Sabrina Cotton was a Plastic. She was also one of Damon's friends from medical school. She had a list of celebrity clients, and her Instagram feed was full of pictures of herself walking the red carpet, hanging off the back of yachts, and generally being fabulous. She'd also just become a regular contributor to one of Perry's favorite morning talk shows and Perry had to stop watching it because she just couldn't take seeing Sabrina in the morning. Or really at any time, if she was being honest. Something about Sabrina had always made Perry uncomfortable.

"Yes," Perry said. "She's Damon's friend. They went to med school together."

"Well, I'm going to send you a video and you tell me what you think."

Perry wanted to say, "No, don't send it." Or "Don't send it now. Let me get home, take these damn heels off, and pour myself a glass of wine, *then* send it." But this conversation with Olivia was like a boulder rolling over the hill and heading right for her. She knew there was no way for her to outrun this. She was in it now.

She said, "Okay, send it. I'll call you back."

A minute later, a Facebook link showed up on her phone.

She clicked on it and it was a video of Sabrina Cotton, sitting on a rooftop in Manhattan. Perry was willing to bet it was the new Restoration Hardware rooftop restaurant in the Meatpacking District. Sabrina was clearly very, very pregnant. Perry guessed she was about six months along. And the setting was a party. A baby shower?

Sabrina was sitting in the seat of honor, surrounded by wrapped gifts and giant teddy bears.

Damon entered the frame and kissed her on the cheek. "Congratulations, pretty mama," he said.

Then he said, "So do we know, is it going to be a boy or a girl?"

She said, "It's definitely a boy."

Then he said, "Don't y'all think Damon is a great name for a boy?"

Then his asshole friend Jeremy entered the frame: "Yo, yo, Damon Jr. is where it's at. Bri, you gotta name the baby Damon J."

Perry felt the tears on her face before she knew they were coming.

She could feel the phone ringing in her hand and saw Olivia's face and name on the screen, but she couldn't answer.

She didn't trust herself to get home, couldn't even lift herself up off the park bench. She opened the phone to recent calls and hit a number. "Layla," she said, her voice barely above a whisper. "Can you come and get me?"

CHAPTER 12

LOVE DON'T LIVE
HERE ANYMORE

Perry held the invitation from Ama with trembling hands. She, Olivia, and Billie were cordially invited to spend the entire summer on the Vineyard. It was going to be an eight-week reunion with a very specific purpose. At the end of the eight weeks, Ama would decide which one of her three goddaughters would take over the deed to her Oak Bluffs home. The girls knew Ama had spent less and less time on the Bluffs since Omar had passed. They were sad but not surprised that she had decided she needed a new summer tradition, although it was hard to imagine what that could be. It was just like Ama to send a formal, engraved invitation out of the blue. Also very Ama to have cleared it with Perry's and Olivia's bosses. Sometimes, every once in a while, she forgot just how wealthy and connected Ama was. But then Ama did something like this; only a woman with tremendous power would call a major law firm, ask if her goddaughter could have the summer off, and expect that to fly. But with Ama, it always did. Making the impossible possible was Ama's superpower.

Work was a grind. A summer on the Vineyard would be the perfect reprieve. But Ama would expect Perry's husband to come up on the weekends. And therein lay the problem. Her husband, Damon, had, at Perry's request, moved out two weeks ago.

He had been outraged when she suggested that he was the father of Sabrina Cotton's baby. Sabrina, Damon's very single and very pregnant friend.

When Perry confronted Damon, he denied it emphatically, but she was still not sure. "Are you crazy?" he'd asked incredulously. "Have you lost your goddamn mind?"

She showed him the video and he groaned. "Come on now, can you not tell I'm kidding about the baby's name?"

She opened the calendar on the phone and pointed out that Sabrina had likely gotten pregnant when she and Damon were both at the Plastics convention in Turks and Caicos.

Damon paced the apartment nervously. "Come on, Perry. You're a smart woman. The smartest woman I know. Please don't come at me with this Wendy Williams gossip queen, don't know shit about shit, conjecture."

"I'm not crazy, D," Perry said, standing at their dining room table, leaning on it as she might a banister in court while presenting her case. "If it wasn't a big deal, why did you lie to me about the shower? I checked Sabrina's Facebook. Ms. No Privacy Settings Because My Life Is an Open Book. The night of her shower you told me you were going to a cigar bar with the guys then to Keens Steakhouse. Why would you make up such an elaborate lie?"

"You're right," Damon said. "I did lie about that. But only

because Sabrina is a friend and you can't seem to handle that. You've always had this weird problem with her. You've never liked her. I would have gotten cut from the med program if Sabrina, Dean, and Jeremy didn't have my back."

Perry was still in prosecuting attorney mode. "So who's the baby's father?"

Damon tried to hedge. "Is that your business, P?"

She wasn't having it. "Really, you're going to try that?"

He said, "I'll tell you the truth but don't act crazy."

She thought she was going to lose her mind. It was all too much. Just too damn much. Did he donate sperm to that bitch? Was he the baby's biological father?

Damon stammered, "Sabrina doesn't know who the baby's father is. Um, things got a little wild in Turks and Caicos and she slept with more than one guy that weekend. Everyone was pretty drunk."

What the hell did that mean? Perry wondered. "Everyone was pretty drunk? Would that include you, Damon?"

Damon looked away. She knew him. He seemed embarrassed. Ashamed.

Perry was done. "I want you to go."

Damon now looked confused. "Wait. What?"

Perry's voice was even, but firm. "Trial separation. Whatever you want to call it. I want you to move out."

Damon looked like he was going to cry. She'd never seen him so devastated and yet she couldn't reel it back. He begged her, "You're throwing me out? You're throwing us away? Are you for real, right now?"

She was silent.

A tear rolled down Damon's face. "I knew from the day I

saw you standing on that yellow linoleum floor, cooking red beans and rice, that you were the one. But if I'm not the one for you, I will go. Just know that if you ask me to go, you better mean it."

Perry walked out of the room and left him in the dining room, hands clenched, jaw clenched, eyes steely, more tears streaming down his face. She had never seen him cry.

She handed him an overnight bag into which she'd packed two days' worth of clothes.

Then she waited at the door until he walked through it.

He stood on the threshold of their apartment and said, "Are you done with this marriage, Perry? I'll go, but you better think long and hard about what you're doing and what you want. Because this is how you do it. This is how you break my heart. This is how you break us."

* * *

Damon spent the first week on his mother's couch. But a week was all he could take.

Then he'd found an affordable Airbnb near the Palisades, in New Jersey, near to where he often did surgery.

She wondered about his little buddy Sabrina. If he had cheated on her, could she get over it? If it wasn't his baby, could she forgive him? Was his cheating her fault? And if it was his baby, could she get past it? She was going to beat Sabrina's Botoxed pregnant ass! Deep down she realized she was more jealous that Sabrina was pregnant than anything else. Why did she get a baby—by accident—when Perry could not on purpose?

How was this going to end? She had no clue. Her parents had been married for forty years and were still holding on. They never fought. But they weren't love doves, either. It was like they seethed with anger and the way they punished each other was by never ever leaving.

Perry had watched Ama and Omar's marriage carefully for clues, but their relationship was equally mysterious. Ama was clearly queen to his consort, the head sista in charge. Omar wasn't docile, just quietly happy to hang back in the cut. If she was honest with herself, Perry thought Damon would've been her Omar. She could be the rock star. He'd be the strong, silent type. But this mess with Sabrina and his bad-influence bestie, Jeremy, threw a wrench in all of that. She had to stand up for herself, she did the right thing by asking him to go, right? Perry wasn't sure.

She started to miss Damon within days of him moving out. She needed answers, she wanted to fix it, to set up couples therapy, maybe a little weekend getaway to the Caribbean. If they could work it out, she would woo him back and figure out a way to keep Jeremy at an arm's distance. But she was leading a multidistrict securities litigation case and the firm had to submit a response in court in less than a week and she left each morning when it was still dark and came home every night, hungry and tired. Her boss had been in Alcoholics Anonymous and he told her that the most important thing he'd learned in the twelve-step program was to "HALT" before you made any big moves. You should stop and ask yourself, Are you Hungry? Angry? Lonely or Tired?

She had quickly come to suspect that she was Hungry, Angry, Lonely, and Tired when she asked Damon to move out. Now she was too Hungry, Angry, Lonely, and Tired to figure out how to properly fix things. To add insult to injury, if she asked him to come back now, he would think she was trying to save face with Ama.

She kicked off her high-heeled shoes and went to answer the door. She was expecting a delivery from Karma Café. Damon didn't like Indian food, so she'd been ordering up a storm since he'd moved out.

She opened the door and was surprised to see her friend Nikesh, the very handsome son of the restaurant's owner.

"Hey, it's good to see you, Nikesh, but what happened to Rahi?" she asked. Rahi was the delivery guy for the Karma Café.

"VIP service for a VIP customer; I saw the order was for you so I offered to bring it over," Nikesh said, handing her the bag. "My dad says this is your third time ordering this week, Perry. That's a new record for you."

"You know how I feel about your mom's chana masala," she said, smiling. "It's sooo good."

Nikesh paused and looked around. "How have you been?" he asked. "You haven't stopped in the restaurant in a minute. I miss our little chats over a glass of lassi." Perry blushed. They talked whenever she went to the restaurant, which was whenever Damon went out of town for work. She knew she went out of her way to flirt with him anytime he smiled at her. Then she sighed. "I've been better, not the best these days."

Nikesh smiled. "You look like you could use a friend, let me take you out. For a real meal."

Perry was tempted. She knew that Nikesh was in his third year at NYU Stern School of Business. He was a few years younger than her, but she didn't mind robbing the cradle. She wondered if Damon had been out on any dates during their "break." She did not want to think about Damon and Sabrina.

"I can't," she said. "It is a very tempting offer, but I can't." Then she said the words that every single person hates to hear: "It's complicated."

He looked disappointed. Which was a huge bump for her ego.

"Too bad," he said.

"You know," she said, suddenly thinking of Billie. "I have a little sister who is single."

He shook his head. "Thanks, but no thanks, Perry. I'm the oldest son of an oldest son. Every mother at our mosque wants to set me up with someone. I can pick my own dates. Believe it or not, I'm kind of a catch."

"I believe it," Perry said, slowly looking him up and down.

Sensing Perry's hesitation to say no, Nikesh leaned over and kissed her on the cheek. "Let me know if your situation gets . . . less complicated?"

"I will," she said, smiling.

She closed the door and subconsciously put her hand to her cheek. His lips felt nice against her skin. She'd spent a lot of time wondering if Jeremy had corrupted Damon during their many medical conferences and freebie pharma trips. She had been so preoccupied with whether he had crossed the line, even a little bit. Even if the baby wasn't his, it didn't mean he didn't sleep with her. Or kiss her. Or whatever with her. And here she was, in her own living room, and she'd just been pecked. And she liked it.

She took off her suit pants, ¡adiós pantalones!, and sat cross-legged on the carpet in front of her couch. She laid the roti out on the coffee table and poured herself a glass of shiraz. Then she turned on her favorite guilty pleasure, *The World's Most Extraordinary Homes.*

What would her and Damon's life be like if Ama gave them her house? They'd spend whole summers there, their future kids would get to grow up on the Inkwell, and they would be far, far away from Jeremy and his trashiness. It would be everything she'd ever dreamed of and more. She needed to be honest with Damon, and she hoped he'd understand. She wanted to try to figure things out. She also wanted Ama's house. The two were not mutually exclusive.

CHAPTER 13

THE INCREDIBLY TRUE ADVENTURES OF TWO GIRLS IN LOVE

Though each of the girls had their own way of staying close to Ama in the off-season, for Billie it was easier. The area around the Vineyard held a special sway. She spent summers during her undergraduate years there and then graduate school at the Marine Biological Lab at Woods Hole.

When she was offered a full-time job at Woods Hole, she jumped at the opportunity. Since the summers she spent with Ama on Oak Bluffs were the highlight of her year, she figured that living in Woods Hole would be like having summer all year round.

Billie loved her work at the lab. She was the point person for a multinational team conducting research on sustainability solutions. Ama had offered to let her live year-round in the house, but Oak Bluffs was a full hour away from Woods Hole in the fall and winter and the ferry ran infrequently.

She'd found a little cottage to rent, an old ferry station that had been renovated into a work/live space by an intrepid photographer. The cottage had floor-to-ceiling windows in the front, a full en suite on the main floor, and a loft bedroom with a giant skylight on the second floor where she could watch the stars at night. It was just a short walk to the Nobska Point Light, a lighthouse where you could take in the panorama from Vineyard Sound to Chappaquiddick and beyond.

She moved into the cottage in September and spent weekends at Ama's through October. After that, Ama closed the house for the season and the Vineyard population dwindled from the summertime high of a hundred thousand to the winter average of fifteen thousand. Very few of the year-round residents were African American. Outside of the scientists who worked at the lab, the majority of Billie's neighbors were white, working-class people who were conservative at best and, she feared, racist at worst.

Early during her first November, when it became clear that Billie was going to be a yearlong resident, her elderly neighbor, Leslie Cushing, knocked on the door. She introduced herself as "Mrs. Albert Cushing" and asked if she could come in. Mrs. Cushing was a petite woman, in her late sixties, who was dressed head to toe in L.L.Bean. Her jeans were sturdy and shapeless. And she wore a red plaid shirt over a garnet-red turtleneck, and an insulated parka ensured that she would never feel the cold.

Billie invited her in, and the older woman sat on the couch looking uncomfortable.

"We've never had an African American in the neighborhood before," Mrs. Cushing said.

She said the words as if it were a foreign term that she'd

looked up on Duolingo. It reminded Billie of the way so many Americans took a simple phrase like *Comment allez-vous?* and butchered it to *Commez tallez vous?* It wasn't that the way they said it was wrong, it was just that the way they said it wasn't right.

Mrs. Cushing continued, "I want you to know my husband has no experience with African Americans at all. But Albert's a good man. All I ask is if he uses the wrong words like *colored* you take a beat before calling the newspapers. He's a good man and we aim to be good neighbors to you."

Mrs. Cushing declined the cup of tea that Billie offered her but pressed a torn piece of paper into her hand. "This is our landline," she said. "And both of our cell phone numbers. If you get into any kind of trouble, you call us. Around here, we look out for our own."

Albert Cushing never did more than nod in Billie's direction. But whenever there was a snowstorm, she woke up to find that he'd shoveled her front steps and cleared the driveway. Her car was never blocked in. The week before Christmas, she came home to find a tin of sugared pecans in her mailbox. MERRY CHRISTMAS FROM THE CUSHINGS said the preprinted label on the tin. And the note inside read: "These are homemade. My mother's recipe. Season's greetings, Leslie."

❄

Provincetown was a full two hours away, but the parties were always worth the drive. When Akari, one of her friends from the UN, invited her to a New Year's Eve party in P-town, Billie decided to book an Airbnb and make a weekend of it.

She decided to dress sexy but casual in a cashmere cardigan and cashmere bralette, which peeked out from underneath, her favorite pair of flared jeans and black heeled booties.

She was standing with Akari and her friends, when a beautiful young Puerto Rican woman named Dulce came over to their circle.

Akari introduced her. "Billie, this is Dulce, she's actually a Vineyard girl like you."

Billie was intrigued. She was sure if she'd seen Dulce on the island, she would have remembered her full lips and the long chestnut brown hair that fell all over Dulce's curves.

Dulce said, "I'm a sous chef at Rockfish in Edgartown."

"I know the place," Billie said. "It's one of my godmother's faves."

"What do you do?"

"I work at the Marine Biological Lab in Woods Hole."

"So you're a scientist."

Billie nodded. "My work focuses on climate change and sustainability solutions."

Dulce made a face. "But wasn't the whole concept of 'climate change' created by the Chinese to make the US manufacturing sector less competitive?"

Billie almost spit out her drink.

"Seriously," Dulce said. "My dad works at the Toyota plant in San Antonio and he told me all about it. Besides, it's December thirty-first and it's eighteen degrees outside. How can global warming be real when it's so cold?"

Billie didn't know what to say. She'd never fallen in and out of love with someone so quickly. She hated it when the beautiful ones were so dumb.

She was looking at Dulce and trying to formulate a response when Dulce and Akari both burst out laughing.

"Dude," Dulce said. "I'm messing with you. Of course I know climate change is real. Akari had already told me what you do and I think it's really cool. People like you are going to save the planet."

Over the next few weeks, Billie and Dulce were inseparable. Dulce was gorgeous and funny, but mostly Billie was drawn to her creative energy and her propensity to see the positive in everything. Dulce listened, without rolling her eyes, to podcasts by "happiness experts" like Gretchen Rubin and Dr. Tal Ben-Shahar. She lit candles to Catholic saints and to African deities with equal fervor. Her favorite sleeping T-shirt was one that read MAGIC IS FUCKING REAL, COÑO. Billie hadn't realized how being a climate change scientist could take you to some dark places until she saw how much light Dulce brought into her life.

Billie had once dated a girl named Courtney who was a massage therapist. The girl refused to give her a massage, ever. "I hate to bring my work home, I'm sure you understand," Courtney said. Eventually Billie broke up with her—not just because she had been banking on some free massages. The way Courtney touched her—cold, disinterested, almost clinically—was so unappealing, Billie thought either Courtney was deeply asexual or she was actually the worst massage therapist ever.

In contrast, Dulce was a caretaker, always cooking. Even

when Billie said "You must be exhausted, let's go out, my treat," Dulce preferred to be in the kitchen.

"I became a chef because I love it," Dulce would say. "Plus there's nothing in this town as good as what I can whip up in thirty minutes or less."

She was, of course, right. In the morning, before work, they didn't just dash to the car with toast and coffee, which had been Billie's go-to forever and ever. On weekday mornings, Dulce made sriracha eggs with crispy kale; cauliflower and rainbow chard frittatas; apple, cacao, and coconut muffins.

Most evenings, Dulce worked late, but in the winter, she only worked on the weekends, and during the week she'd spend all afternoon in the kitchen trying out recipes she was considering adding to the restaurant menu: honey turmeric pork with watermelon radishes and rainbow-colored beets; slow-cooked pineapple pork ribs served with corn, lobster, chile, and cotija cheese.

One weekend in March, Dulce brought home a cotton candy machine. It was the dead of winter, but Billie's little house felt like a carnival because all around the kitchen there were tiny cones of cotton candy in all different colors and flavors.

She kept asking Dulce, "What are you making?"

But Dulce, who was dressed in a light blue jumpsuit that was zipped just low enough that Billie could see the curve of her breasts, winked and said, "You'll see . . ."

For dinner that night, Dulce served them a large bowl of steamed mussels with a giant dollop of cotton candy on top.

Billie was confused. "It's pretty. And you're a genius. But I really don't get it."

Dulce smiled and said, "I'll be right back." She returned with a small ceramic gravy boat of steaming soy and garlic broth. She poured the broth over the cotton candy and it melted into the mussels.

"It's ginger cotton candy, which, if I've got it right, should add a perfect mix of spicy sweetness to the broth," Dulce said, looking at the bowl with trepidation.

She was right. It did pair perfectly and the dish she'd experimented with at home became the most popular item on the restaurant's menu. Billie began to see how much cooking was science, how Dulce experimented with textures and flavors the way she used experiments to test sustainable solutions in oceanography in her work. It felt good to be with someone she was never bored with, who made her feel so satisfied, intellectually, emotionally, and physically.

In her field, Billie had learned that the best, most reliable results were comprised from broad-scale observations and detailed field experiments. That winter, it seemed to her she got to experience both with Dulce—the pleasure of observing her girlfriend, the way she carefully made the daily shopping list for the restaurant, the way she checked in on her team over texts and phone calls, urging people to stay home and take care of their sick kids or spend a day with their dying dogs. "It's not high season," Billie could hear Dulce say over the phone. "When service slows down, it's time for us to take care of ourselves and the ones we love." Dulce balanced the demands of a hectic job with the same grace that she balanced flavors in the kitchen. She didn't complain. She didn't go fishing for praise. She just got the job done.

As they sat in the living room of their little ferry house, watching the boats go by on cold winter evenings, drinking wine and eating delicious food, Billie felt like her grown-up life was beginning. This was love. This was her vision of marriage. This was what she wanted the rest of her life to be like.

Time seemed to slow down in the evenings when Dulce filled the space with candlelight and music. Dulce made the best playlists. She played artists that Billie had never heard before but loved at first beat: singer-songwriters like Ozuna, The Highway Women, and Wavy the Creator.

They didn't own a TV, but on Saturday nights they propped an iPad on their laps and watched a movie or a TV show. On the Saturday after Christmas, Dulce suggested they skip going out for dinner and instead she cooked up a skillet of spaghetti carbonara and they ate it, with two forks, right from the pan in bed. They drank a beautiful shiraz and binge-watched the entire first season of *The Crown*. Billie had always thought that the saying "Food is love" was a cliché, but life with Dulce made her think differently. Dulce was food, Dulce was love, and with Dulce, food was the adventure of a lifetime.

Mrs. Cushing took note that Dulce had gone from being a weekend visitor to moving in. "I see you've taken a roommate," Leslie said. "Makes sense. I cannot believe what Bernard Homes was charging for rent for that place. It's a wonder that regular people can even afford to live out here anymore."

Billie wondered if they'd think of her as "regular people" if they knew that she and Dulce were a couple. She thought of how Mrs. Cushing had said that out there in Woods Hole, they took care of their own. That had expanded to include her as a woman of color, but was it elastic enough to include a gay couple?

The more they talked about it, the more Billie and Dulce felt strongly that it didn't serve them to come out to the year-long residents of Woods Hole and Edgartown. They both worked late hours—Billie at the lab, Dulce at the restaurant. They both got their fair share of catcalls and harassment by local white boys who both longed to date them and cursed them for being uppity.

"It would be different if we were just here for the summer," Dulce said when they lay in bed together, listening to Ibeyi by candlelight. "But it doesn't feel comfortable for these kind of people to know all of our business."

"I couldn't agree more," Billie said, wrapping her arms around Dulce.

Billie was determined to tell Ama and her godsisters the minute they went back to the Bluffs this summer that she had met the love of her life. It would be the first time in years they would all be on the Vineyard together for a stretch, instead of long weekends here and there. She had decided. It was enough playing cloak-and-dagger with her godmother. She and Dulce were the real deal. She wanted everyone to know it.

CHAPTER 14

AN OLD FLAME

Ama hadn't planned on visiting Harlem on this particular day. She'd spent the afternoon in a midtown office building in a board meeting for an athletic apparel company she and Omar had invested in years before. The investment had proved to be a wise choice, and the brand was beloved by both pro athletes and young people all around the world. But the CEO, Logan Henkel, was Ama's least favorite kind of millennial. He was white, privileged, quoted Drake and Lil Wayne with the same aplomb that he name-dropped LeBron James and Steph Curry, yet he had filled the board with friends from his years in the bastions of white privilege. The board represented a mix of Henkel pals from boarding school, Harvard, and McKinsey, where he had spent the early part of his career. Ama was the only person of color on the board, which given the landscape of the country and the brand's clients, made no kind of sense.

Conor Hamilton, the company's founder, had been an old friend of Omar's, and Ama had taken the board seat after her husband's passing. But after a four-hour marathon of rich-boy bromancing and precious little innovation, Ama had had enough. She vowed to talk to Conor and remind him that diversity was good for all businesses, but especially important for a youth-focused retail brand influenced by Black culture, which had seen its market share slip considerably recently.

She walked out of the east side office tower to see that her driver, Virgil, was waiting for her. Billie had spoken to her about the environmental impact of keeping a car and driver in the city. "Your carbon footprint is off the hook, Ama," Billie had said the last time she had come over. "The car. The G5. None of this is sustainable." But Ama was sixty-six years young. She'd come a long way from Louisiana and red state politics. She wanted to be part of the solution when it came to global issues, but she was more than a little put off that just when she had acquired financial wealth, she was being told to dial it back for the good of the planet. It reminded her of all the hullabaloo around fur coats a few years back. Just when Black women could finally afford to have that luxurious, glamorous coat, it was declared cruel and out of fashion. Didn't matter if you bought a vintage one, all of a sudden this thing she'd craved her entire young life was déclassé.

When she'd first moved to New York, you couldn't open a magazine without seeing those ads: "What becomes a legend most?" And there would be a photo of the most beautiful women in the world, wearing nothing but a sexy fur coat. She could close her eyes and still see Diana Ross, rocking an exquisite bob, her eyelashes curled just so, her plum-colored lips brightened in a cat-who-ate-the-canary smile. She'd torn that picture out of the magazine. Pinned it to the bulletin board near her desk and covered it with a securities regulation memo, but it was always there for her to peek at any time she wanted. Everybody was in those ads, everybody: Faye Dunaway and Lauren Bacall, Elizabeth Taylor and Bianca Jagger.

One Christmas in the late eighties, Omar surprised her with the mink of her dreams, and just to show that the man knew her better than she knew herself, he'd had a custom wrapping paper fashioned out of the old Diana Ross Blackglama ads. Just seeing the paper made her smile. Omar never did things halfway. Everything about the careful way he presented himself and the things he gave was a gift.

She still remembers walking out of her office building, one winter day five years later. Virgil had just started driving her, and the expression on his face was what cued her to turn and see the young blond woman just as she tossed a bucket of red paint onto Ama's coat. "Murderer," the girl had screamed. "Monster!"

Virgil raced over, cloaked Ama in his arms, slipped the coat off her shoulders, and slid her into the backseat of the car in one smooth superhero sequence.

That night at dinner, she and Omar decided she would have to retire her coat. But damn it if it didn't seem that certain people got to be dramatic while others always had to keep things buttoned up. "How many Black kids are killed in the city every year?" she asked Omar. "What would happen to me if I stood outside the police commissioner's office or the mayor's office and threw a bucket of red paint on police officers screaming, 'Murderer! Monster!'"

Omar shook his head and smiled wryly. "They'd lock your Black ass up, Ama."

"Exactly," she said. "Everybody and everything has a champion except Black people. We've been turning the other cheek for more than three hundred years, and the one thing we're never supposed to do is express our outrage. I wouldn't mind all of these protests if I could take to the streets and scream and holler about all the dastardly deeds that have been committed against my people."

Sitting in the backseat of the Porsche hybrid she had purchased at Billie's suggestion, Ama wished she could go home and talk to Omar about the trifling board meeting she'd just attended. What she missed more than anything was her evening conversations with Omar. Somehow, sitting across from her husband in their kitchen, Oscar Peterson playing through the speakers, each of them sipping a beautiful glass of Argentinian malbec, it felt like they could conquer anything. Life was a giant puzzle that they took apart and put together each night. With Omar by her side, the pieces always fit, even if they had to jam them in there. Now he was gone and there were figurative buckets of red paint headed her way, she could feel it, and there was nothing for her to do but stand and face them alone.

On a whim, Ama asked Virgil to drive her to Harlem. She didn't want to go home, not yet. She decided to go up to

Lido, her favorite Italian restaurant. The place was packed, but she found a seat at the bar. She ate, solo, at the bar often in the years since Omar had passed. It made her feel a little less alone.

She was sitting at the bar, sipping a lovely cabernet and perusing the menu when someone sat down next to her. She turned and was surprised to see a face she had not seen in decades.

"Amelia Vaux," he said, chuckling. He always chuckled when he said her full name.

She smiled back and said, "Carter Morris, as I live and breathe."

Everything about Carter Morris was understated cool. His curly hair was tucked stylishly into a knit beanie. He wore a plaid shirt, an African beaded necklace that frankly very few men could pull off, a pair of dark denim jeans, and biker boots. Sitting next to him at the bar, Ama could smell that he was freshly showered and shaved. He had always been like that, smooth.

"What are you doing here?" he asked.

"This is one of my favorite spots," she said. "But I live in New York. I should be the one asking you, what are *you* doing here?"

"I'm meeting with my publisher about my next art book," he said.

There was silence then. She looked at his ring finger. Empty. He looked at hers. She was still wearing the Flintstones-sized, "Upgrade U" rock Omar had gotten her in Paris, ten years before he died. They looked at each other and it all came back—how good they had been together, how young they had been when they parted. Look at God, Ama thought. Look at God.

✳

1975

Amelia Vaux first met Carter Morris in Central Park. It was July, and Bob Marley and the Wailers were headlining a free concert in the park. Lavinia Fox, a British friend from school, had convinced her to go. The plan was that the two women would share a picnic lunch and a bottle of wine and check out the music and what was sure to be an array of cute, single guys. But within minutes of their arrival at the park, Lavinia took off with a Rastafarian wearing aviation sunglasses and a dashiki, declaring, "Back in a tick."

An hour later, Ama was sitting solo on her picnic blanket with the strong realization that she had been ditched. As the opening acts blared, slightly out of tune, Ama kept telling herself she'd leave after the next song. But she stayed on. Later, she would realize that a heavy-duty contact high had contributed mightily to her lethargy.

The performers onstage were all Black, but the crowd was mostly white. The cultural consumerism reminded her of stolen rock-and-roll riffs and the whitewashing of Motown. The masses loved the music, but did they care about the people and the communities that the music came from?

When the lead singer, Bob Marley, took the stage Ama

was mesmerized. He was so different than the artists Ama and her friends listened to when they went dancing. His vibe wasn't anything like the urban cool of artists such as Stevie Wonder or Marvin Gaye. He didn't display any of the disco sizzle that gave such a spark to singers like Donna Summer and Natalie Cole. Onstage, Marley talked about how all he'd heard since he arrived in New York was talk of a financial crisis—but it seemed to him that the city was in the throes of a *spiritual* crisis. The crowd roared and he broke into a stirring rendition of "No Woman, No Cry." Although Ama knew that she wasn't the only girl there to feel it, it felt in that moment he was singing directly to her. As Marley sang, Ama thought of all she had lost, how much she had risked to start a new life in New York just as the city seemed to be crumbling around her. But would she make it? She looked around at the thousands of people swaying to the reggae beat: Would any of them make it?

Ama had so many dreams. After work, on the nights when she didn't have school, she sat up for hours, listening to old Nina Simone albums, scribbling in her notebooks about what she imagined her life might be one day. She'd grown up in a time when colored girls weren't encouraged to dream. She knew if the folks back home ever got a peek at her diaries they would laugh harder than they would at a Richard Pryor comedy show. But Ama always believed in the gospel of Zora Neale Hurston—you had to jump at the sun if you ever wanted to get off the ground.

Bob Marley and the Wailers had just started singing "Get Up, Stand Up" when a little bit of sunshine beamed right at Ama. He was Billy Dee–handsome and he was more dressed up than most of the people on the Great Lawn. It was ninety-five degrees in the shade, but he looked cool as could be in a white linen shirt and a pair of perfectly flared jeans.

"I'm Carter," he said. "Mind if I join you?"

She didn't mind and told him so.

That night, she learned a lot about him. "My dad was a jazz musician," he told her. "Nobody famous. He took off before I was even born. My mom held it down. She's Swedish, she's a painter, and she lives upstate in a little town called Kingston. She teaches art, she makes art. She's a free spirit."

When he asked what she did, she mentioned that she worked for a brokerage firm. In that moment, she wanted to be a free spirit, too. So she said, "I've got a day job. I go to school at night."

"What are you studying?" he asked.

She didn't say "finance." She couldn't, not while Bob was singing "Rebel Music."

She looked up at the night sky and said, "Astronomy."

"That's cool," he said, and there was real admiration in his voice.

She looked across the park and said, "I'm hoping to get an internship at the Hayden Planetarium."

That was the thing about Carter Morris. From the beginning, he made her feel different than any man had before or since. The edges of what was possible always seemed to stretch a little further when Carter was around.

They spent the entire summer together. They visited tiny downtown galleries and all the big uptown museums. They went to see a show at the Whitney by Betye Saar, marveling at how her work mixed together African spiritualism, surrealist technique, and folk stereotype figures like Aunt Jemima and Uncle Ben. Ama read in an interview that Saar once said, "I'm the kind of person who recycles materials but I also recycle emotions and feelings." And Ama thought, Me too, Betye. Me too.

Carter was the first person Ama knew to truly embody the idea of six degrees of separation. He seemed just a few acquaintances away from anybody you might want to know. One night, they found themselves hanging out in a back room at Max's Kansas City with a crowd that included Mick Jagger and David Bowie.

Ama didn't know it then, but it was the beginning of everything in New York—the art, the music, the fortune, and the creativity—that would turn the city around. Recklessly, Ama, who was always careful with money, spent half a paycheck on two slinky jersey dresses and a pair of glittery heels that seemed to be the uniform of all the downtown girls. In those dresses, she and Carter did the hustle all around town. Her boyfriend was so good-looking. He was always impeccably dressed. He was the smoothest dancer. He reminded Ama of Bob Marley when he danced. Carter moved like the music was inside of him, not the other way around. It was beautiful to watch. It was even more electrifying to be in his arms when he moved like that.

Now there was one more thing Ama remembered as she sat at the Lido in Harlem, next to the man who had been her lover more than forty years before. Carter had a sweet tooth. After they'd been out dancing, he never wanted a slice of pizza or a chic steak frites the way so many of the other club goers did. They would go back to his apartment in Little Italy, which he rented from a friend of his mother, and they would eat vanilla and caramel gelato straight from the container. When he kissed her, his mouth was cool and sweet.

Ama thought that they were beginning a life together. But that September, Carter announced that he was moving to Rome. He had a friend who had an apartment with a spare bedroom. He planned to get a job, "In a gallery or as a waiter, it doesn't matter, it's Rome."

They were eating ice cream in Mount Morris Park. They'd walked all the way from Ama's building up to Harlem. Listening to Carter say he was leaving, Ama felt like she'd been dropped out of a plane and she was free-falling through the air.

"Come with me," he said as if he was asking her to take the subway from Manhattan to some cool dim sum spot way out in Queens.

She looked at him and knew it was over. She didn't need a suburban life and a white picket fence. But she didn't want to live a life that was filled with that free-falling feeling. She'd already spent too much of her life navigating through corridors of chaos. The mistakes of her youth that had almost cost her everything.

She had come to New York to plant herself firmly and, God willing, to bloom. Carter was built differently. He was somehow already complete. Everything he needed or seemingly wanted, he carried within the confines of his skin. It seemed like he could be at home anywhere and with anyone.

"You're not coming," he said, as if he thought in her silence she'd been seriously considering the idea.

She shook her head no.

"I'll come back for you," he said.

She had willed herself not to cry until she was back in her own bed, far from where he could see how much he had hurt her, a hurt from which she was sure she'd never fully recover.

Five years later she met Omar, who was the opposite of Carter in every way. And it was then, in the summer of 1981, when she was in the throes of falling in love with Omar, Carter returned. He showed up at Libby's house in West Tisbury as if he'd never left.

"Carter," she said, willing her heart not to leap as she came to the door.

"Come with me on a boat ride," he said. He looked as handsome as ever. He was wearing a sun-faded turquoise T-shirt, a pair of khaki pants, and loafers without socks.

"Today?" she asked incredulously. She wanted to kiss him. She wondered if he still tasted like gelato.

"Today, as in now," he said, smiling mysteriously.

She glanced at Libby, who motioned for her to go.

He leaned in and whispered to her, "Pack an overnight bag."

She did as she was told.

When she stepped out to the driveway, Carter held her in his arms and kissed her. Being in his arms felt like he'd been gone for days, not years. She still wanted him. She counted how many dates she'd been on with Omar. Five? Six? Certainly, this wouldn't count as cheating.

He was driving a classic Land Cruiser, borrowed, he explained, from a friend. She threw her monogrammed duffel bag in the backseat.

He drove to the dock at Vineyard Haven and they walked out to a beautiful sailboat.

"Ama, meet *Amazing Grace*," he said, beaming.

"Wow, what a beautiful boat," she said admiringly. Libby's family chartered a big boat every summer, which they sailed out to one of the little islands off the Vineyard and then prepared a giant clambake on the beach. But this was different. She'd never been out alone on a yacht with a guy before.

"When did you learn to boat?" she asked.

He said, "I spent the last year on the Dalmatian Coast. I was working for a cruise line there."

Ama was embarrassed. She didn't even know where the Dalmatian Coast was.

"It was while I was there, on these incredible boats, that I got the idea for this project," Carter explained. "It's called *Horizons*. I've been using this large-format camera to photograph the thin line where the sky meets the sea. We were boating off of Trieste and I looked out at the horizon and it reminded me of a Mark Rothko painting. You think, blue sky, blue water, it's all pretty much the same wherever you go. But when you photograph it, it's never the same. In Trieste, the sky photographed a pale white, almost like a bowl of milk, and the sea was a silvery gray."

He took out a few prints to show her. She was moved. They were so elegant and beautiful.

"I decided to do a series—I'm going to spend the next year photographing horizons all around the world."

"And what will you do for money?" The words came out of her mouth before she could stop herself.

He looked hurt. "Actually my grandfather in Sweden passed away earlier this year. My mother gave me part of the inheritance as a grant. She told me to stop waiting tables on the cruise line and go make some art."

Ama looked at him then and wondered how many Black men had ever heard those words: *Stop waiting tables. Go make some art.* Not enough. No matter the number, she was sure it was not enough. Someday she wanted to give someone that kind of inheritance. How many zeros would she have to put on a check for someone to feel that free?

She put her bag in the cabin underneath the stern. As a girl, she'd always wanted the kind of fancy store-bought dollhouse her grandmother could never afford. The cabin reminded her of those dollhouses. Everything was perfectly scaled down to fit the space: there was a tiny table with two barstools on either side, a miniature fridge, a two-burner stove, a small sink, and a little built-in loveseat.

Only the bedroom was out of scale—a big bed with no room to walk around it, just two small lamps on either side of the bed and a large skylight.

Carter pointed up and said, "Perfect for looking out at the stars." Ama gazed at the stars, and when she looked back at Carter he was already wrapping his arms around her waist. Pulling her close, Carter kissed Ama, but this time something was different between the two of them. After a smoldering kiss, his fingers immediately began searching her body, his tongue exploring her most sensitive, delicate places. Ama was hungry for him. His touch felt so good, necessary. Ama lost her breath, then began breathing faster. Her body quivered, she was on fire. She could smell his cologne and its scent of sandalwood, cardamom, and vanilla made her completely surrender. He was stiff, hard, and ready and she was soft and dripping wet between her legs. Ama moaned and with each touch, each taste, her moans increased. Before she could catch her breath, she threw her head back in complete surrender and Carter slipped inside her.

He froze, she froze. Now locked into each other, under the stars, he held her body tighter, pushed himself in deeper. Carter and Ama's eyes met and their souls began to speak as their bodies moved. The rhythm first mimicked the waves under the vessel, but in minutes the movement was a crescendo. The sex quickened in a way that felt dirty but so good. Ama's body responded with wanton lust. Carter fed her with his body and used his tongue to lick and taste Ama at the same time. As his rhythm hastened, she could feel a flutter inside, a release began. She was ready. She whispered in his ear, "I want you to come, Carter." He kissed her and continued thrusting until they both orgasmed. Ama felt completely satisfied, but slowly, she began to feel an ache in her soul. The ache took over the desire she'd felt just seconds before. They fell asleep in each other's arms, naked. Before long, they woke, dressed, and went back to the lounge on deck.

He pulled a speaker onto the deck and flipped a switch. Bob Marley started singing "No Woman, No Cry."

"Our song," he said. Then she watched as he expertly turned the engines on and steered them into the open water. The two lovers talked and laughed, as if nothing had happened just a few hours before. There was an unspoken understanding. Ama had no regrets. She loved Carter, but they were on two different journeys, worlds apart. Carter smiled at her and even though she now knew that he would never settle down, he was a forever kind of love, and she was happy he'd returned. The trip on the yacht felt like a gift. She had given a piece of her heart to Carter that she could never get back, and that was okay. She knew she could love more than one man. She knew this because she loved herself.

In the years to come, his *Horizon* series became the acclaim of the art world. In the early nineties, when the Museum of Modern Art did a retrospective, she went to see it alone. She and Omar had been married for ten years at that point, and they had very few secrets. But Carter was one of them. Walking into the low-lit rooms where Carter' photographs were displayed, she felt almost as if she were seasick. The images were so large, each covered an entire wall. Taken in as a whole, you felt like you were in the center of all the great bodies of water in the world. Through Carter's lens, the Arctic Ocean flowed into Lake Superior. The Atlantic poured into the South Pacific. In one small room, a film played. She recognized it immediately. She remembered being on the boat and Carter taking out the video camera.

She'd watched him steady himself, filming the sun setting into the sea. There had been a moment when he'd turned the camera on her. She had been wearing the white ruffled swimsuit, the one she wore after July fourth when she'd tanned enough that her skin had turned golden brown. She sat in the museum watching the film of the sunset on the Vineyard and nervously expected to see herself, laughing and gesturing for him to turn the camera back to the riot of pink and red that was the sky that night. But he had edited that bit out. He had kept their secret.

That had been nearly thirty years ago. She'd kept track of his career—amazed at how he moved from success to success. He'd not only become an acclaimed fine art photographer, he'd also directed a movie and opened up an architecture firm where he did everything from designing homes to making furniture. She knew he'd never married. He had one child, a daughter who lived in Berlin with her mother. He dated fashion models and actresses. Sometimes Ama saw a photo of him in a magazine, or a camera panned across his face at an awards show like the Oscars, and she wondered if anything they'd shared had been real. Had the piece of her heart been well cared for? Had it just been a fantasy—a dollhouse love on a dollhouse boat—that she'd made up in her head?

Now he was here, sitting next to her at Lido in Harlem. He still looked the same: a little gray in his beard and salt and pepper in his hair, but he was still so handsome. So much so that two thirty-something women at the bar kept looking back and forth from their phones to Carter as if to confirm that it was really him in person.

"You have some fans," she said.

"Please," he said. "Not a woman in this place can hold a candle to you."

He looked at her appreciatively. Ama knew she looked good for her age, but it had been a long while since a man had looked at her the way Carter was looking at her, with hunger in his eyes.

"I can't believe that I'm running into you here," she said.

"I can't believe that it's taken this long for us to reconnect," he said. "I was sorry to hear about your husband."

"Thank you," she said, wondering if Omar would be okay with this. They had never discussed the notion of life or love after their marriage. Even after his diagnosis, it never came up. Theirs was a true love. When Ama tried to imagine a life without Omar, all she saw was darkness. Then little by little, after his death, she realized how much she needed to do to sort her girls out. To make things right. To ask for forgiveness for the secrets she and Omar had kept.

She had never thought of Carter Morris as someone who would come back into her life. But now he was here and she knew right away that they were at the beginning of something. A reclamation. When the girls were younger, on rainy afternoons on the island, Omar liked to play board games. The Game of Life was his favorite. They'd all put their pieces at the beginning of the winding road—filling the space with degrees and babies and houses. Then at the end of the game, the big reward was retirement. Omar always winked at her when she landed at the retirement home seconds after he did. "Beans and cornbread," he'd say, referencing an old Louis Jordan song. He always said he and Ama went together like red beans and rice, or beans and cornbread.

But now Omar was gone. It seemed like God had lifted her out of the retirement village and put her car right back at the starting line and said, "How about it, Ama? Fancy another go around the board?"

Ama and Carter ordered a plate of squid ink linguini and ate it, *Lady and the Tramp*–style with two forks off one plate.

"So where have you been the last forty years?" she asked. "I know a little from the art magazines. But I want to hear it from you."

Carter smiled. "Well, I spent that whole year after I left you in the Vineyard on the *Horizons* project. After the Vineyard, I went to Mexico to the Sea of Cortez. Then I went to New Zealand because a girl I went to school with married a farmer there and they had a guesthouse where I could crash for free. I wrote a bunch of grant proposals. Got a few. Then I moved to Japan for a few years."

"Wow!" Ama exclaimed.

Carter ordered a bottle of wine and poured them both a glass. "Your turn. Somehow you went from astronomy to banking. I read all the articles about how they called you the Witch of Wall Street. They just keep thinking of inventive ways to be racist."

She should tell him she never was studying astronomy. Or maybe not. What did it matter now?

"How long were you married?" Carter asked.

Ama blushed. "Thirty-three years."

He raised a glass. "That's a long time. You deserved it. That kind of forever love is precious and rare."

"What about you? Are you in love?" she asked boldly.

"I have a daughter but I never settled down," Carter said.

"I think I had a different vision than a lot of people. I didn't so much want a wife as a coconspirator."

"And you never found that kind of woman?" Ama asked.

Carter leaned into her, his voice, sexy and just above a whisper. "To tell you the truth, I think I stopped looking. I shut the soul-mate part of my brain down. But seeing you here tonight, I can't help but wonder if God didn't have this in mind all along."

Ama could feel her heart beating faster. It was as if she were twenty-two again, standing on the lawn of Central Park, ready to fall down the rabbit hole of a crazy love.

Ama felt her face get hot.

"What are you saying exactly?" she asked him.

"I'm saying—do you have any interest in spending the rest of your life as a coconspirator with a vagabond artist who only took forty years to get it together?"

Ama didn't know what to say. "Carter Morris, you haven't seen me in forty years. Who knows if we're even compatible?"

She couldn't believe they were having this conversation in a public place.

Carter said, "Ama, I'm a grown man. You are beautiful, intelligent, and kind. You can't underestimate the importance of kindness. Do you remember after the boat ride when I asked you to come with me to Mexico? You turned me down for the second time. We stopped at the carousel in Oak Bluffs and you were like a little kid. You insisted that we both buy tickets and every time the ring came around you leapt at it. When you got the brass ring, your face lit up like Christmas. I'm looking at you now and I see that same girl, the one who got the ring. When I asked you to come with me to Rome, then to Mexico, I was asking you to marry me, to spend your life with me. But I didn't know how I was going to make a living from month to month. I couldn't figure out what was going on with my art and whether an 'artist' with air quotes was something I'd ever be. I was too cowardly then to ask you to bet on me, to roll with me through all that uncertainty. I was too afraid that without money or a plan, I'd be like my dad, the moody, creative brother who splits in the middle of the night when shit gets hectic. But I'm past all that now. I've made a life and I've made art and I've made more than a living. I walked into the restaurant tonight and saw you sitting there and it was like God was saying, 'One more ride on the carousel, Carter.' I'm not leaving here tonight without the brass ring. We can have a long engagement but I will not wait to propose. I love you, Ama. You've always had my heart. You still have it."

Then Carter Morris got on one knee and out of the corner of her eye she saw dozens of cell phones pop out to capture the moment.

"I think God is telling me that it's never too late to reclaim love. Amelia Vaux Tanner, will you marry me?"

Then, because Harlem restaurant managers are nice with their playlists, as if on cue, Luther Vandross's "Never Too Much" blared across the restaurant speakers.

Ama didn't know what to say. It was the last thing she was expecting when she took the ride to Harlem for an early supper on a Friday night.

"I won't get up until you say yes," Carter said flirtatiously.

Then not because she felt pressure—or because the whole restaurant was watching—Ama said yes because yes was what was in her heart.

Carter stood up and flashed his rock-star smile to the crowd that had their phones trained on him. "She said yes, y'all. Champagne for everybody. Or prosecco, a brother's not trying to break the bank before the wedding."

There was a round of applause as the restaurant settled down and Carter and Ama returned to their seats at the bar.

He asked the bartender to pour them two glasses of vin santo, the sweet Italian dessert wine.

Ama smiled when she heard Carter say, "Hey man, what kind of ice cream do you have?"

The bartender said, "We've got four types of gelato: vanilla, Turkish coffee, salted caramel, and strawberry with black pepper and balsamic vinegar."

Carter said, "Bring us two scoops of everything you've got."

She told Virgil he could call it a night. She would find her way home. If he was surprised, he was the soul of discretion and didn't show her.

It was after midnight when Carter dropped her in front of her apartment in an Uber. Before she got out of the car, he politely asked, "Would it be okay if I kissed you good night?"

Ama nodded yes.

It was just as she remembered from all those years ago. His kiss was both cool and sweet.

CHAPTER 15

A NOT-SO-SECRET REUNION

The next day, which was Saturday, Perry woke up to her cell phone buzzing long before her alarm was scheduled to go off.

She looked at the caller ID. Olivia.

She answered the phone groggily. "Hey, what's up?"

"Go to People.com."

"Why?" Perry asked. "It's Saturday morning. It's my one day to sleep in."

By this, she meant sleep in-ish. She and Layla had a standing date for a nine A.M. Peloton class. They worked out then went for breakfast at the NoMad hotel. No matter what kind of week she'd had, Layla never failed to make her laugh.

"Ama is on the *home page*," Olivia said, her voice tinged with shock.

Perry sat up; Olivia had her attention now.

"Hold on," Perry said.

She went to People.com on her phone, and in a tiny square crammed between news of the Kardashians and news about the first trans Bachelorette, there was a photo of Ama with a guy who Perry didn't recognize. He was on bended knee and he was clearly proposing.

Perry said, "Let me call you back."

She could hear Olivia protesting but she hung up anyway.

The headline said "Never Too Late for Love."

The article read:

> Last night at Harlem hotspot Lido, art world darling Carter Morris proposed to finance titan Ama Vaux Tanner. Ms. Tanner has a reported net worth of $750 million and was recently widowed.

The article included an embedded slideshow titled "The OG Bachelor. Past Paramours of Carter 'Love 'Em and Leave 'Em' Morris." Perry flipped through a slideshow of pictures of Carter with an array of famous-ish women: a woman who'd starred in *The Handmaid's Tale* and another who'd played a general in the Wakanda army in *Black Panther.* There was a model who'd starred in a Fenty Beauty makeup campaign and another who'd toured as a dancer with Beyoncé and Jay-Z. None of it squared with Perry as a suitable companion for Ama.

She FaceTimed Billie and Olivia, propping up the phone in her bathroom as she brushed her teeth and threw her hair into a ponytail.

"You guys," she said. "This all seems really weird."

Billie said, "He's a so-called successful artist. But what if he's blown it all on drugs and fast women? Now he's looking to Ama to bail him out."

Olivia rolled her eyes. "Who are you right now? Nobody uses the term 'fast women.'"

Billie said, "You know what I mean, okurrr?"

Perry said, "Has anybody talked to Ama this morning?"

Olivia looked terrified. "Do you think he drugged her?"

Perry had no patience for Olivia's dramatic flair. "Do you really think he drugged her after proposing to her in front of a hundred cell phone cameras? I don't think so."

Olivia said, "So you're not concerned about her safety?"

"I just think we should check on her."

Billie said, "I second that. Maybe her erratic behavior is because she had a ministroke or something."

Sometimes Perry hated the groupthink of her godsisters. "I'm sure she's fine. But clearly, there's something going on. I'll head over there now."

"I'll meet you there," Olivia said.

Billie groaned. "I hate being so far away. Somebody call me when you've got your eyes on the package."

Perry said, "Roger that."

She loved Olivia and Billie but sometimes she thought both of them had the blood type AB crazy town.

Perry texted Layla and said: It looks like Ama is eloping with some crazy artist dude. Can't make class today. Drinks instead?

Layla texted back: Escandalo!

Her friend's text included a Memoji that was two shades darker than her friend actually was. But that was Layla.

She was waiting for the elevator in Ama's building when Olivia came flying into the lobby.

"That was fast," Perry noted. Olivia lived all the way downtown.

"I know," Olivia said. "I took the subway and then I ran."

Perry looked confused. "Why? She's okay."

Olivia pointed to her wrist. "My Apple watch has me on this crazy schedule. It's got me doing a nine-mile-a-day jog or walk."

She looked at her watch as if squaring off against an enemy. "This is the tiniest, meanest trainer in the world."

Perry laughed. She sometimes had to remember that she and Olivia were close once and maybe they could be again.

❋

It was almost nine A.M. when they rang the doorbell to Ama's condo.

Ama answered, clearly surprised to see them. She was wearing a beautiful mint-green kimono with bees on it. It had been a gift from the girls the Christmas before.

Olivia poked her head into the apartment. "Ama, I never thought I'd be the one asking this, but do you have company?"

Ama's face, in that moment, was hard to read. Perry imagined she found the question both unexpected and offensive.

Ama said, "I'm sure you're not asking me what I think you're asking me?"

Their godmother padded to the kitchen in her ivory marabou slippers. How she managed to keep them so clean was a miracle. But that was Ama—everything in her house was pristine, from her magnolia-white sofas to the cloud-gray carpeting.

Ama gestured for the girls to sit at the kitchen table. "May I offer you some coffee to counteract that giggle juice that you've clearly been drinking?"

She poured each of the girls a cup and took a tray of scones out of the oven. Then she said, "Now, who would like to tell me what's going on?"

Perry and Olivia looked at each other. Olivia said, "I'll let Perry tell you all about it."

Perry felt sorry for Olivia then. She was so afraid of losing Ama's favor that she would never step into the fray unless absolutely necessary.

"Ama," Perry said, "are you getting married?"

Ama's face flushed then, in a way that the girls had never seen. She looked younger, so much younger than her sixty-six years. And in that moment, she looked more like Perry than ever.

Their always composed, elegant godmother cleared her throat and her voice dropped an octave. "What would give you that idea?"

Perry took out her phone and showed her. The article now included a link to a Facebook Live post.

The three of them watched the social media video. Carter proposing and Ama looking radiant. Both Olivia and Perry knew from the video that their godmother wasn't sick or out of it; their Ama was in love.

The doorbell rang. It was the building's concierge, Edgar. He handed Ama a package. "Someone dropped this off for you."

Inside there was a book that Ama had never seen. It had been published fifteen years before by the Mori Art Museum in Tokyo. It was the museum catalog for a show Carter had done called *American Carousels*. The exhibit and book featured images he'd shot of twenty-five of America's oldest carousels, including the Flying Horses Carousel in Oak Bluffs.. The book had a dedication from all those years before: "To A.V."

Along with the book, there was a Tiffany's box, and inside of the box was a carousel brass ring and a note that said, "Do you remember this?"

❋

Ama did remember it. She had given him a brass ring souvenir after the boat ride, when she'd told him no, she wouldn't go with him to Mexico. Sailing the Sea of Cortez sounded so enticing. There was a part of her that wanted to go with him, to spend the next year or ten. She could see herself walking away from New York and her corporate ambitions. She could close her eyes and picture herself—a head full of wild curls, dressed in a uniform of rainbow-colored sundresses and fisherman's sweaters. She wanted to be the kind of girl who could leap at a life of adventure. Lord knows she loved Carter with a Marley-worthy "Is this love?" kind of ardor.

But she knew that there would be no peace in her heart until she sought her own fortune, until she made art out of her own life. She had mistakes to fix and a future to craft and none of those dreams would be realized if she dropped out of school to globe-trot with Carter like a lovesick girl with no cares in the world. Ama was not that girl. She had cares.

She'd given him her brass ring and now it had come back to her. She'd hardly been able to sit with the magnitude of it all and it was out there in the world before she'd had time to fully process it herself.

Ama remembered the first time Omar held a smartphone. "This thing has a camera, email, GPS," he'd said, examining it carefully. He was not just a brilliant lawyer, he was at heart a born tinkerer. He'd held up the device that had more power than the supercomputers that had sent men to the moon and he said, "This is a miracle. It's also the end of privacy."

He had called it. Remembering his words, she went back to the kitchen and attempted to explain to her goddaughters who Carter Morris was, what he had been, and what he might still be to Ama.

CHAPTER 16

WELCOME TO MY WORLD

That Sunday, Carter came by Ama's apartment. He seemed to sense right away that a certain demureness was called for upon entering the home that she had shared with Omar. He kissed her on the cheek upon greeting, sighed when he took in the sight of her. It was spring and Ama was wearing a crisp white shirt, a camel-colored midi skirt, and a pair of light tan knee-high Prada boots. Her hair was in a high bun, and as she moved through the room Carter thought she had the grace of a ballet dancer. He noticed that age made some women jittery; they dealt with the inevitable changes in their body and the world around them with a low-grade hum of frustration that followed them around like a car that needed a tune-up. Ama was different. She carried the years lightly like a musician whose familiarity with the music gave them the confidence to improvise.

The foyer of her condo offered a glimpse into the living room and the rooms beyond. He could see, at a glance, that she had, in the years since they'd last met, become an art collector with a discerning eye. He admired the mix of old and new that animated the walls of her space. There was a nod to the old masters with classically wrought portraits by Kerry James Marshall and Barkley Hendricks. A rendering of the night sky by the Philadelphia-born artist Howardena Pindell. And he could see, in the living room, in a pride of place on the largest wall, a work that was a favorite of his, Glenn Ligon's *Negro Sunshine*.

He wondered, feeling ever so slightly competitive with the artists on her walls, if she had ever seen any of his work in museums or galleries? Had she ever come to any of his shows? Did she like his work? Did she think the gamble he had taken when he walked out of her life had paid off?

Carter realized how much he still wanted to impress Ama, to prove that he was worthy. He'd thrown down the gauntlet and said he wanted to spend the rest of his life with her, and he'd meant it. They were in their sixties, with a little good luck and a lot of green juice, it was possible they could have a full thirty-plus years together. He hoped, greedily, for decades that might balance the scale of all the years they had spent apart.

That spring day, they took off from Ama's Central Park apartment and headed downtown. They took Fifth Avenue, stopping for Korean food on Thirty-Second Street. When they were young, Koreatown hadn't even existed.

Over steaming bowls of bibimbap and warm cups of barley tea, they began to talk about the future.

"So how is this going to work?" Ama asked.

Carter had more experience with improvising a life plan than she did. But finally, she was ready to do what she couldn't all those years ago—go with the flow.

He said, "Let's take it day by day. It'll take time for us to intertwine our lives together. If in a year, you still feel the way I hope you do, then I'd like to invite you to come live with me in Europe. We can spend the summers at my place in San Sebastián, the winters at my apartment in Paris, and we can come back to your home in New York as often as you'd like."

Three weeks later, they traveled together to San Sebastián and then spent the entire month of May at his apartment in Paris. She hadn't been back to Paris since Omar had passed away. But Carter's Paris was different. She and Omar always stayed in the 7th, near the Eiffel Tower. Carter lived on the other side of the river, in the 12th arrondissement near the Gare de Lyon train station. His apartment faced a giant park that Ama had never visited called the Bois de Vincennes, and that locals called "the lungs of Paris."

While Ama and Omar sometimes traveled to Paris with friends and were well known at their favorite hotels, they did not have a circle of French friends. Everyone knew Carter in his neighborhood. He and Ama often went out for lunch, but most evenings they ate in. On Saturday nights, almost without arrangement, Carter's apartment turned into a bustling salon. Around eight in the evening, friends would arrive with flowers and wine and cheese. Carter would put out a platter of roast chickens he had picked up from the Moroccan market, spiced with flavors Ama had never tasted. As a soundtrack of Latin and African music played, Carter would deftly arrange platters of fresh fruit, cheeses, and meat with big bowls of sliced baguettes. People would stay until well after midnight, talking and drinking and smoking cigarettes (which Ama was surprised people still did).

Ama loved the way the conversation veered back and forth between French and English. She surprised herself with how much French she remembered from her childhood in New Orleans. Her Creole grandmother spoke French almost exclusively around the house, but once Ama came to New York, she hardly used it. But after a short time, it was back again. She found herself making jokes and jumping into conversations. She went to a French bookstore and purchased French graphic novels that she devoured with the energy of a kid who has discovered comic books for the first time. Her favorite was by a French African woman named Marguerite Abouet.

Abouet's Aya series centered on a trio of young West African women managing love, marriage, and motherhood for the first time. The characters reminded her both of herself as a young woman and of her girls. She devoured all of the books, in French, in quick fashion: *Aya, Aya of Yop City, Love in Yop City,* and the best one of all, *The Secrets Come Out.* Ama missed Perry, Olivia, and Billie more than she expected. But she also couldn't wait to bring them to Paris, to share with them the community Carter had created in that vaunted city.

CHAPTER 17

IT'S JUST LUNCH

It was late in May when Perry ran into Nikesh in her midtown office building.

She was standing in line at the expensive coffee shop with the fancy signage and sleek Scandinavian design. The lines were too long. The coffee was pedestrian. Every time she spent twenty minutes to be handed a not-hot-enough paper cup, she calculated her billable hours and vowed to brew and bring in her own.

She was thinking all of this through when she felt an arm on her shoulder. She turned. It was Nikesh. He was dressed as she'd never seen him—in a gray, slim-fit, checked jacket and matching pants. As it turned out, she was wearing an A.L.C. Prince of Wales tartan shift with a matching jacket.

"I see you got the memo," he said with a smile.

A woman standing behind, in line, looked at them and said, "So cute! I love couples that dress alike."

At the very same moment, Nikesh said, "Thanks" and Perry said quickly, "We're not a couple."

The woman looked confused. Then in typical busybody

fashion, she ignored the information being handed to her and said, "You are super-cute together."

Perry rolled her eyes.

Nikesh leaned down and whispered in her ear, "She's right, you know. We look good together."

Perry shivered a little. The way he said *good* sounded so dirty. How dare he flirt with her, looking so handsome, when she had four thousand pages of antitrust documents waiting for her on her desk.

Maybe it was the suit, Perry thought. But she'd never really looked at him that way before. She was glad he wasn't wearing a tie. She could see how fit he was from the close cut of his shirt.

"What are you doing here?" she said.

"Getting coffee," he said innocently.

"But this is my coffee shop," she said.

"You mean you own it?" he said. "Well done. The coffee's overpriced and mediocre so your profit margins must be through the roof."

"No," she said, smiling with a grin she couldn't dial down. "I mean that this is my office building."

"Come now," Nikesh said playfully. "I don't believe you own this office building!"

Perry laughed and looked to see that the cashier was frantically waving to her, as if saying, "You're next!"

After they'd both ordered, they moved to the waiting area.

"Just tell me what brings you to this neck of the woods," Perry said.

"I'm working with a new start-up called White Ops. It's a cybersecurity firm."

Perry was intrigued.

"The most complex bots can now mimic humans in the way they fill out forms, click on ads, and navigate all the sites you use every day. White Ops verifies whether there's a real human behind close to a billion online interactions every day. In layman's terms, the machines are getting smarter so our tech has to get better."

"It sounds like something out of a dystopian novel," Perry said.

"It's funny you should say that," Nikesh said. "The founders started the platform in a Brooklyn sci-fi bookstore. I'm on fifteen, where are you?"

"Oh, that's a different tower," Perry said as they walked to the elevator bank. "So I'm on thirty-six."

Nikesh looked at her wickedly. "I don't mind you being on top."

Perry felt herself flushing. "Will you stop?"

Nikesh looked at her and said, "If you have lunch with me."

She shook her head. "I would love to. Thank you for the invitation. But I'm in sad desk salad mode. I'm swamped this week."

"But you've got to eat," he said, looking genuinely concerned. "What if tomorrow I bring you lunch. We can sit at your desk and eat our sad salads together."

She looked at him, wanting him. It wasn't even nine o'clock in the morning and she could feel how hot she was for him. It was crazy.

But if they only met up at the office, then it would be easy for her to keep her horniness in check. She wasn't the "do it on the desk" type. She could count on herself to behave while at work.

"Okay," she said. "One P.M. We can meet on three. The company cafeteria. You don't have to bring lunch, we can get something there." Nikesh agreed and began walking to his elevator bank. As she moved to get on her elevator, she could see him turn and gaze at her. His attention made her quietly smile inside. When she reached her desk, she took out her phone and texted Damon: **Hey, how's it going?**

He didn't answer her for an hour. Sixty minutes in which she had to admit that she'd texted him mainly out of guilt.

When he wrote back, she could feel the coldness of his message.

I'm still in an Airbnb. That's how it's going.

Then he wrote, **Are you texting me to come back home?**

She looked out the window. As many times as she'd stared out at the skyline, it always made her happy. She held the phone in her hand and took a minute to gather her thoughts. Let him simmer, she thought.

All she had to do was say, "Yes, come home, let's fix this." But had Damon suffered enough? Had he felt any of the pain she was feeling? Not to mention, the minute she invited Damon home, this new thing—if it were a new thing—with Nikesh would be over. After this morning's run-in, she had to admit she did not want it to be over—not yet. She burned thinking about Damon's nerve. He had done what he felt like—hanging out too late with his friend Jeremy, cavorting in the Caribbean with that Plastic bitch Sabrina. He'd snuck off to Sabrina's baby shower and let himself be filmed, cavorting baby daddy–style with the mother to be. All the while, she thought, I had my feet in the ice-cold stirrups at the fertility doctor's office, trying to start our family. The more she thought about it, the more pissed she became. But in her heart she knew she did not want a divorce. She did not want to be a statistic. She believed in marriage, committed love, a two-parent household. For that dream, she wanted Damon home, in her house, in her bed. But not yet. She was still angry at him for lying about Sabrina's shower, for not getting how much she wanted to start a family with him. For not wanting it as much as she did. Let him suffer.

She texted him back, **Enjoy your Airbnb.**

The next day she found herself dressing carefully for work. Most days, she kept her hair in a simple ponytail and stuck to a uniform that Damon referred to jokingly as "Dark Sky." It was true that most of her suits were gray or black, evoking the feeling of a summer sky after a tumultuous rain.

But today she was having lunch with Nikesh. She reached into the back of her closet for a fuchsia dress that was so bright, it was almost tropical. She swiped a simple gloss on her lips and decided that to wear her voluminous curls loose would be too much. She didn't want to give the old white partners at the firm a heart attack.

The morning was jam-packed. Perry's work life was consumed with a high-profile securities litigation case. The case involved a cybersecurity firm named Glitch, a company worth over $100 billion. Glitch was headquartered in San Francisco, but had a rich Japanese parent company, Yamato. In 2010, computer scientists at Glitch developed an internet security algorithm that went beyond detecting malware on computer systems. The "super algorithm," as it was known, transformed to mimic and destroy any and all national and international hacking software. Perry was gifted and best equipped to break down complicated securities law to the public in a way that would shape a positive news story about the case. She thrived in this role.

At noon, Perry's Glitch case prep was interrupted by this year's law school student who arrived for an hour of scheduled mentoring. It was usually one of her favorite hours of the week. Her mentee, Sofia, was a lovely girl from Ghana. But today Perry found that she could not follow Sofia's stories. The words flew past her, like butterflies she had no energy to chase. When she saw that it was, at last, twelve fifty-five, she gathered the girl gently out of her seat and shooed her out of her office.

Nikesh met her in the cafeteria with two bags filled with tin containers.

"What is all this?" she asked.

"In Mumbai, where my parents are from, there's a system of lunch-box delivery. There are men, called *dabbawalas*, traveling on bicycles and by train who pick up hot lunches from homes and restaurants, then deliver them to office workers. Then in the afternoon they return them. Every day, two hundred thousand lunch boxes are delivered by five thousand *dabbawalas*. Today I'm your *dabbawala*."

She said, "I love that."

"It's the original Uber Eats," he explained. "So what we have here are curried king crab and prawns for our main course. Deep fried chickpeas with garam masala and ginger. Basmati rice with lima beans. Roti canai. And for dessert, fresh apples with my mother's own spice blend."

Perry smiled, noting Nikesh had brought some of her favorite menu items from his family's restaurant. They spent the lunch getting to know each other better. Perry learned about Nikesh's dreams. She had totally underestimated him.

"I'm finishing my MBA and working for this start-up," he said. "But my main thing is trying to solidify my parents' business. I plan to start a company of my own, which would compete with Seamless, Grubhub, and Uber Eats." He continued, "There is something to be said about the personal service of *dabbawalas*. Seamless and the like are largely powered by a service made up of people who deliver food as a side hustle. Let's face it, those companies are successful because American eating habits have changed and the demand for fast food and takeout is growing. I want to widen the choices and improve the quality of service, nationwide. My company will be called 'Walas' to pay homage to my Mumbai roots."

"That is a terrific idea. I really respect the hustle," Perry said, impressed. Putting her legal hat on, she then started asking him intricate questions about the competition. Now Nikesh was impressed. He pulled up some of the figures on his phone. Perry thought, Wow, he is really smart and thorough. This business is going to happen.

"Ultimately, I just want to make sure my parents don't

have to work so hard into their retirement as so many immigrant restaurant owners do. Then looking ahead, I hope to give my kids just enough financial freedom for them to have the space and support to create extraordinary things."

"But not so much loot that they are spoiled and directionless," Perry added.

"Exactly."

Perry was enthralled. The time flew by and then they both realized they had to go back to work.

"Can we do this again?" Nikesh asked hopefully when he realized he had shared so much.

She looked up at him. It couldn't hurt, she thought. It's just lunch.

"Yes," she said. "I'd love to."

CHAPTER 18

OPENING THE HOUSE

Every Memorial Day, the girls followed the same routine. Perry flew up with Ama the Monday before the season officially began. She always made it clear to her bosses she would be working remotely if necessary and that week was not negotiable.

Perry loved that solo time with Ama. She loved flying up on the fancy private jet, how they arrived at the island in just an hour and fifteen minutes. She remembered a whole childhood of six-hour car rides, longer when the traffic was bad.

Once they pulled up to the house, Ama always took a moment to stand in the front yard and take the house in. "Hello, old friend."

When they entered, the house would be icebox cold. Jonathan James, the caretaker, would turn the heat on periodically to make sure the pipes didn't freeze or burst. But May on the island was always chilly.

It was Perry's job to make a fire, while Ama scheduled visits from what she called the house's "glam squad." Kyle Manzo to clean the gutters and tend the grounds. Katherine

Pierre-Antoine, the summer housekeeper, to give the house a top-to-bottom cleaning and prepare all the beds with fresh linens.

That first night, Ama and Perry always had lobsters. They drove together to the pier and bought them right off the fisherman's boat. They'd bring fresh asparagus and beet greens from the Union Square farmers market in their carry-on bags. Sometimes they made a salad, or if Ama was feeling ambitious, she made a batch of her perfectly crispy matchstick fries. But there was always lobster and corn the first night. And ice-cold Veuve Clicquot.

Sometime on Thursday, Olivia or Billie would arrive. This signature year it was both of them. Ama had insisted. All three of the young women might have to put some face time in that summer at their respective offices, but the idea was that they would work mostly remotely—Ama had seen to it. She was either a client or a benefactor at all of their places of business. Her reach was formidable. Their employers offered little resistance. They simply knew better. The Bluffs was going to be their summer-long home base, for the first time in a long time. The first few weeks flew by pretty quickly. It almost felt like they were young girls getting to know each other again. They spent mornings eating breakfast in the kitchen with Ama, or in town after a brisk walk, jog, or swim, and spent some afternoons lounging around and generally just catching up or biking around the island. There were also many afternoons of shopping in Edgartown with Ama. It was especially nice to spend time with Ama. With Omar gone, she'd seemed a little out of her element on the Vineyard these last years.

One morning, as Billie was going to check on the bee-hives, Ama was already there. She saw Ama was removing a black cloth from one of the three hives. Billie asked, "Ama why the black cloth? I never saw Omar do that. Is it to protect the hive from the wind?" Ama replied, "Omar had learned so much about beekeeping, Billie. It almost seemed spiritual to him. He had become somewhat of an expert. He told me once that in his research he learned that when a beekeeper dies there is a tradition that the hive is covered with a black cloth. For one day, the bees remain in the hive and in mourning. It is because the lives of the beekeeper and the bees are so intimately intertwined that one should mark the loss of that connection. I have covered the hives for the winter every year. I suppose I wanted to honor our beekeeper."

Ama felt lonelier that summer than she ever had on the Bluffs. She missed her friend Libby, who had passed away decades before. She missed caring for the bees and the girls with Omar. But mostly, she missed Carter. More than she expected to. He had offered to visit, but she couldn't see it. There was just no way she could have another man in the house that she and Omar had built. She ate dinner with the girls, then went to her room early. She spent her nights watching movies that reminded her of her youth: *Claudine*, *Mahogany*, *Cooley High*—they were all on streaming now and they kept her company during the long nights by the sea.

The evenings had started becoming dull and the girls were getting on each other's nerves. One Friday night, the three decided to go out. They hadn't gone out dancing on the Vineyard together since they were teens. They sat on the back porch of the house, sipping watermelon mojitos and formulating a plan.

"I don't even know where to go," Perry said. "Damon and I mostly go to house parties when we come up to the Vineyard."

"I know a place," Billie said. "You all would be a little old for it, but the DJ is great. Classic hip-hop all night long."

"If it's classic hip-hop, how could we be too old?" Olivia wondered.

"I'm just saying," Billie said. "The crowd skews young."

Perry rolled her eyes, "I'm not even thirty. I can skew young, too."

That night, in an attempt to prove just how young she could pass for, Perry broke out her superlong clip-on ponytail with the blond highlights. She wore her shortest skirt and a pair of ridiculously high sparkly shoes.

She knocked on Billie's door. "So what do you think? Will I get carded tonight?"

Billie shook her head no. "You look like Beyoncé."

Perry grinned. "Why thank you."

Billie smirked and said, "You're not welcome. Beyoncé is an almost forty-year-old mother of three. Nobody's carding that woman."

Billie was dressed in a strapless black jumpsuit with a pair of gladiator sandals; her hair was slicked up into a tight bun.

Perry shook her head. "You look cute. And I'm glad you're

wearing shoes you can fight in. Because, just so you know, I'm not going to have your back when the Beyhive comes after you."

Billie shrugged. "I'm not concerned."

They knocked on Olivia's door. "Come on, sis. There are drinks to be drunk and lips to be kissed."

Olivia was dressed in a bodycon dress, and her hair fell in ringlets around her face.

"You look amazing," Perry said.

Olivia looked Perry up and down. "Really, with the blond ponytail that hangs down to your ass?"

Billie poked her head into Olivia's room. "She's trying to look like Auntie Yoncé."

Olivia looked annoyed. "So what else is new?"

❋

The three girls jumped into an Uber. First stop, Donovan's Reef for three painkillers. Then they walked past Jimmy Seas Pan Pasta, down some side streets to a block neither Olivia nor Perry ever remembered being on. Outside of what looked like an underground fried chicken shack there was a long line of what appeared to be college students, swaying along to LL singing about how he couldn't live without his radio.

"I love old school hip-hop!" Perry said.

Olivia looked down at the crew of very young, very casually dressed young people. "I think Billie may have been right. I am too old for this."

"No, no," Billie said. "Let's just get in, it'll be cool."

An hour later, they made their way into the tiniest night-club Perry had ever seen. "Was this somebody's garage?" she asked.

"Prolly," Billie said with a grin.

But the DJ was fire and the girls couldn't resist when he started playing Lizzo's "Truth Hurts."

Olivia smiled when a good-looking dude came over and started dancing near her. After finally getting over Mr. I Have a Secret Biracial PhD Candidate Fiancée Studying Shit in Papua New Guinea, maybe she was ready to give one of these brothers a shot. But when the dude elbowed her, it became clear that it was Perry he was trying to step to. The pattern repeated itself again and again all night. Here we go again, Olivia thought as she spent more time rolling her eyes than dancing.

When they got home, Perry could tell Olivia was mad at her. "Okay, out with it," she said.

"When you walk in the club, all the men see are your hair and skin."

Perry didn't know what to say. Was she supposed to apologize for the skin she was in and the weekend weave she used as an accessory?

"Look around," Olivia said plaintively. "This island is full of brown-skinned men who are color struck. I don't even know if I want this damn house. I'd rather be a black uni-corn in Montauk than spend my summers here putting up with this *School Daze* crap."

Perry looked around plaintively for an intermediary. But

Billie wasn't having it, looking out the window like, "I'm not going to get into it with you two."

Perry looked Olivia in the eye and decided that if Olivia was itching for a fight, she might as well get back in the ring. "Okay, O," she said. "The older generation definitely were on some brown paper bag test insanity. But it's changing. Beautiful brown-skinned women are all over the place. Hello? Michelle Obama, Kelly Rowland . . . Um, um . . ."

Olivia said, "See, you're stuttering. Because they don't put us on the screen. I'm the darkest in the house so I'm going to speak on this. If you're famous and you're dark, you get a pass. But I've been coming here my whole life and I've never met a guy who wanted me for anything more than dating rotation. You've got a man and you don't even appreciate him. Do you think I'd let stupid hearsay get to me if I found a brother who fell hard and just loved me for me?"

Perry muttered, "Maybe that's 'cause you've got to love yourself first."

Olivia looked like she wanted to throw her drink in Perry's face. "What did you say to me?!"

Perry took a deep breath. "I said, you've got to love yourself first. We all see your beauty, but it doesn't mean a damn thing unless you see it for yourself."

Olivia looked furious. Earrings off, Vaseline on the face, ready to throw down mad. "Perry, really. Stop talking. Just stop. Because you are too light to have the agency to tell me anything about looking in the mirror, in these United States, and loving myself."

Perry said, "Oh, is that why you sent me a video of Damon

at Sabrina's baby shower? Because you wanted to put me in my place? You are a self-hating bitch!"

Across the room, Billie gasped. This was getting ugly quickly.

Olivia's eyes narrowed and her voice got low and icy as she whispered, "Oh, you want to go that route, Perry? You want to call me a bitch? Well, maybe it's you that needs to stop pretending you live a perfect life, Perfect Perry. Your Instagram feed is just a highlight reel. You think we can't see through that shit? And for real, I was just trying to have your back. You wouldn't know anything about that because all you think about is yourself and your made-up perfect life while your man probably fucks every nurse that walks through the hospital corridors."

Billie mimed eating popcorn at the movies, trying to lighten things up before it went to a place they could never return from. "Are you two really gonna throw down? In Ama's house?"

"Back it up, Olivia," Perry said. "I'm willing to hear your truth but you don't get to attack me because of how I look. I'm not having it with your plantation-mentality victim bullshit."

Olivia looked like she wanted to cry. She yelled, "That's the thing you don't get. You never will. It's not plantation-era thinking. It's now. It's my reality. Every damn day!" Then she really did start crying, ugly crying. It was like the pressure of having to live in her skin was just too much that night. Too confining, not elastic enough.

Perry sat down on the sofa and reached her hand out to Olivia. Olivia desperately grabbed it. As Olivia entwined her fingers with her own, Perry let out a sigh of relief. Honestly, Olivia had never exposed her feelings before. She realized some of her anger at Perry had to do with Nate and the biracial fiancée traipsing in and out of her building daily.

And Perry had come dangerously, ratchetly close to punching O in the face. She was the oldest one. She was the married one. She did benefit from light-skinned privilege. Olivia's feelings were real and valid and shouldn't be dismissed. Olivia was right—she didn't have the agency.

"I wish I could build you a Lupita app," Perry said to Olivia. "Put it in your phone and deprogram you from the negativity that you are subjected to. And quite frankly, deprogram the damn world from what they do to you. How they see you."

Olivia rolled her eyes. "Seriously, P. Stop talking to me about famous dark-skinned girls. I want to hear about the regular/schmegular girls like me."

Perry looked her godsister in the face, taking in all of her beauty. "That's the problem right there, sis," she said. "You are extraordinary and extraordinarily beautiful. There isn't anything regular about you. I see it. You need to start seeing it, too. But I realize you are damaged and may never." Billie realized at that moment that try as she might, the three godsisters would never spend the entire summer on the Bluffs together as they did as children. As Ama had hoped for this summer. Somehow, there was too much between them. But what was it? What had happened?

CHAPTER 19

WHAT AMA KNOWS

The next morning Olivia took an early flight back to New York. "My mom needs me" was the excuse she used as she kissed Ama goodbye briskly.

"When will you be back?" Ama asked. She had meant to bring the girls together this summer. But it was probably to be expected that they would need to cycle through some of their old teenage drama before they felt at home again and were ready for all she needed to share with them.

"Soon," Olivia said, holding the woman in a tight embrace. "I love you."

"Love you too, *cher*," Ama said, blowing kisses at her middle girl. She remembered when Omar had brought home a book about birth order. She was an only child so these were not issues in her life. But damned if her husband had not been preternaturally wise. Perry had been the typical oldest child—fierce, independent, territorial, but a protector when outside forces intervened. Olivia was a typical middle—sensitive, a peacekeeper, but resentful, too, as if every bridge had been built on her back. Billie was a textbook youngest—she felt adored, and had blossomed from the benefit of being raised by parents, or in this case godparents, who had experience and years to develop patience.

An hour after Olivia's departure, Perry appeared at Ama's bedroom door. "I've got to go back to the city," she said, sitting by her godmother's bedside. "It's this case I'm working on. It could make the difference between making partner or not."

Ama nodded knowingly. "You've got to go out into the world and make your mark. I'd never deny you that. Not me, the Witch of Wall Street."

Perry laughed. "You're no witch, Ama."

Ama let the remark pass. The girls would learn soon enough the kind of spells she was capable of casting.

Perry wanted her godmother to know she would be back. She was still competing for the house. She was damned if she would let Olivia bully her because of the color of her skin.

Ama could have told Perry that her godsister had already left, that she'd just missed her and she might well bump into Olivia at the small Martha's Vineyard airport. But she didn't. Omar had always said, "You've got to give the girls a chance to be grown women. They're not as grown as they think. But they'll never bloom without the water of trust and the sunshine of independence."

He'd been smart, her husband, Ama thought. Smart enough to die before he had to deal with three hardheaded twenty-somethings. Their teenage years had been *nothing* compared to this, and Ama knew what lay ahead once she'd given each of them their inheritances.

"I'm going to take the ferry to Woods Hole," Perry said. "The boat ride will help me clear my head. Then a shuttle to Boston airport and I'll be home in time for work tomorrow. My high-maintenance boss and the other partners can wait."

Ama held her eldest girl's hand. "Come back as soon as you can. I did arrange for you to spend the summer here. I don't want your firm to disappoint me."

Perry promised that she would.

When Billie woke up, she was surprised to find the house half-empty. She checked her phone. There was a text from Olivia saying, **Paper bag test time, I'm out. See you when I see you.**

Billie found this a little cruel, since she was light-skinned but she'd never pulled skin privilege.

The next text was from Perry: **Gotta go back to the city. Back in a few. Love you, B.**

Billie walked down to the kitchen and then out to the pool. Ama was doing her laps. "Her morning constitutional," she called it. Even in her late sixties, Ama was elegant and Lena Horne beautiful. Her body was long and lean in her plain black one-piece. Billie changed into her swimsuit and went to join her.

The two women swam in silence for a few minutes. Billie always felt the urge to race when she got into the pool, muscle memory from her days on the swim team. But it felt good to go slow, to match the older woman's easy pace. Ama turned to smile at her and they swam together in silence for the better part of an hour. It was one of the things that Billie loved about Ama. She was comfortable with silence. She never felt the need to fill every space with conversation.

When they were done, Billie climbed out of the pool first.

Then Ama followed behind her. They each reached for a towel from a stack that sat in the outdoor cabinet near the chaise longues. Billie reached into the outdoor fridge near the grill and took out a pitcher of water, pouring it into a cup the color of sea glass and handing it to Ama. Then she poured one for herself. She thought then of telling Ama her secret, that she was gay, that she was in a relationship that not even Perry and Olivia knew about. But she kept silent.

Ama carried the water to the railing that led down to the private beach. She looked out at the ocean, letting the breadth and depth of it serve as a reminder of how small she really was. She knew that her kind of wealth, the kind of money that made it so you could go on a spending spree every day of your life and still never spend it all, could make you feel like you were sitting on a giant throne. But she never wanted to set herself above anyone, most of all, her girls. She wanted to use what she had worked so hard to earn to lift them up. But damn it if these girls kept tugging away from her helping hand.

Human nature, she supposed. Her grandmother used to say there's a difference between heart knowledge and head knowledge. Head knowledge is what people tell you is true. Heart knowledge is what you went out there in the big, bad world and learned for yourself—in the end, that's the only unshakable truth any of us can ever have.

Ama opened her arms and Billie drifted toward her, pulled into her embrace. "My dear, dear, girl. You are my youngest. And my most stubborn. I didn't invite you and your sisters here for a *Game of Thrones*-style competition.

This house is just a thing. I am fortunate that I have the means to buy ten houses just like this."

Billie knew that was true. The island was studded with beachfront mansions. But this was not "just a thing." There was only one Ama's house. Only one house that had held their memories. Watched them grow. Hosted politicians and activists, CEOs, jazz musicians, and Nobel Prize–winning scientists. There was only one house that framed the ocean in just this way. No other house would have this carefully curated collection of art. You could spend your whole lifetime and you'd never be able to re-create it. The music room with its perfectly tuned baby grand piano where Glenn Ligon sat in concert with Romare Bearden. The dining room of queens walled with work by some of the best women artists America had ever known: Lorna Simpson, Carrie Mae Weems, Alma Thomas, Faith Ringgold, and Lois Mailou Jones.

No other house held their memories of being girls. No other house had their initials carved into the trees. No other mansion would smell like Ama—a heady mix of Le Labo hinoki shower gel, the leathery smell of Chanel's Cuir de Russie, and the fresh-cut tuberoses that she filled the house with each summer. There would never be another house like this one.

Billie's eyes stung with the knowledge that she wasn't going to be the one. She'd been too sloppy, too far out of the lane of love and marriage, and now she was out of the running. All she could do was thank God that Ama was still holding her, still keeping her close, had not banished her entirely.

"Just tell me now," Billie said. "It's Perry, isn't it? She's the Black Barbie and this is her dream house. Or it'll go to Olivia because she's your moneymaking mini me. I don't stand a chance."

Before he had passed, Ama and her beloved Omar had discussed who would inherit their home. Omar thought the girls might share it. But Ama had seen too many squabbles among the wealthy who were left a single, valuable piece of property. She didn't want them to feel that selling it and splitting the proceeds three ways was the only way to get their fair share. She wanted the house to have a single owner, for someone to know with every fiber of their being that the house belonged to them. "Mine, mine, mine," she had said, when at last the construction was done and the architect and contractor had left her alone in the house, one comically large brass key in her finely boned hand. She still had that key, and she wanted to give it to one of her goddaughters with the hopes that she would treasure it and the house the way Ama had.

"I have not decided," Ama said. Which was not entirely true. She had decided a long time ago but there were factors at play that were beyond her control. The girls themselves held more cards than they knew.

Billie's face was a symphony of disappointment and this was the thing Ama found the most difficult to bear. Perry, Olivia, and Billie were not her biological children, but she had woken up every day for the past twenty years and made the decision to love them. Not because she had to, but because she wanted to. She wished she could explain how that daily choice had strengthened her bond to them. She could

have walked away at any point. After their high school grad-
uations, when the checks she wrote secured that they need
never worry about tuition or a work-study job. She could
have left their lives once they were done with college,
steered them to mentors in their fields, and gently but decisively pulled away. When her husband had passed and she
began to imagine what the next phase of her life would look
like, she wondered if the girls would be a plus or minus.
Would she find loving them tiring as she got older? Could
she use a move abroad as a distancing tool so they would
not be close when she got older and sicker? Maybe that
would have been better for them. But she had decided in
the end that this was a forever love. She was in it to the
end. God had blessed her mightily, but her last request of
Him had been this: Let these girls bury her, not the other
way around. Spare and protect them. That was her daily
prayer.

Ama linked elbows with Billie and the two women began
to walk back toward the house. "There's no judgment here,
sweetheart," she said. "We all teeter. It's like that song you
all used to play by Kanye West."

Billie looked at Ama and laughed. "You mean 'All Falls
Down'?"

When they got back into the kitchen, Ama leaned over
to the device on the kitchen counter and said, "Alexa, play
'All Falls Down.'"

Billie laughed. "You know the only people who use that
technology are old people and children?"

Ama smiled. "Oh baby, that's the beauty of being old. I
am a full-time citizen in the land of I-D-G-A-F."

Billie responded by saying, "Okay. Alexa, play 'IDGAF' by Dua Lipa."

As the song blared, the two women danced around the living room. There had always been dancing at Ama's house, and as she bopped around to the pop song, she thought of all the people who had danced in that room over the decades. So many of them were gone. She missed them all, but none more than her husband, Omar. She wished she could just see him one more time, sitting in his favorite chair, waving away her attempts to get him to dance. Whoever was the next madam of the house, Ama hoped she would know that the house would never really be in its glory until its rooms were filled with people dancing.

CHAPTER 20

FRIENDS ON THE
OTHER SIDE

Olivia was back in New York. And although she had planned to spend the summer on the Bluffs, she couldn't spend one more minute surrounded by all the light-skinned privilege. They would never understand. Sure they pretended to, but they didn't. All this, "Lupita is so beautiful this," and "I love dark-skinned brothers that." Let them try to live one day in her skin. Omar, she realized now, had been her buffer. He lived in her skin. He truly understood and even, maybe, saw her beauty.

Olivia loved Le Bernardin, known as "LB" to friends. The four-star restaurant felt like a hidden gem. Entering the dining room, it almost felt like you were entering a luxurious ballroom in Atlantis. The lights were dim, the lamps cast shadows like blue-black waves across the walls. The room buzzed with activity but it was never loud. The only time the energy hit a fever pitch was when Aldo Sohm, the restaurant's famed sommelier, opened a bottle of vintage champagne with a saber, to mark a guest's special occasion.

LB had been Omar's spot. He met the chef and owner, Eric Ripert, in Cannes one year and the two men had become fast friends. Olivia had loved coming to the restaurant with Omar, loved hearing him speak French with Eric and Ben, the general manager. Olivia had studied French at school and could understand the men's playful banter. But she couldn't rattle it off the way Omar did, making jokes and sly political commentary.

Whenever Olivia had an important client dinner, she took her guests to LB. She always felt Omar's presence in the place. More importantly, she felt the confidence he had in her whenever she was there. "Walk tall," he'd whisper as he took her coat and checked it for her. "You belong here. You belong anywhere you want to be."

It was icing on the cake that the staff remembered Omar so vividly. That gorgeous summer night when Ben greeted her at the door, he kissed her on both cheeks, French style. "It's been too long, Olivia," he said. "*Cherie*, you must come more often."

He walked her to the table, a prime spot on the banquette where she sat between a woman who had just been nominated for a best directing Oscar and a man she recognized from in-flight safety videos as the president of United Airlines.

"I miss your father," Ben said as he signaled a waiter to bring Olivia a welcome gift of a glass of their finest champagne.

The LB team always referred to Omar as her father and she never corrected them.

"You look so much like him," Ben said, looking at her with genuine affection. "It takes my breath away."

Then he enjoined her to have a good dinner and he went off to take care of other diners.

When the dinner was over, and after shaking hands at the door and giving Ben a hug goodbye, she called an Uber. She only ever ordered Uber Black because, as she liked to tell Perry and Billie, "I'm not here for the world's side hustle." She was a professional woman. She wanted professional drivers. It was her extravagance, but she knew how much her mind benefited from being able to stretch out and gather her thoughts in a nice car at the end of a long day.

The car arrived quickly, and although she'd set her preferences to "Quiet, no music preferred. No conversation preferred," the guy was chatty.

"Hey, how you doing?" he said.

"Good, and you?" she murmured, in a tone meant to convey that the question was a rhetorical one. She hoped her low talking might discourage him.

"Did you have dinner at Le Bernardin?" he asked.

Why did he need to know? She ignored the question.

"I love that place," he went on. "My agent took me there when I landed my first TV gig. You might have seen me. I played a computer hacker on *Brooklyn Nine-Nine*."

She looked at her watch. It was ten P.M. and she'd been at work since eight A.M. She took out her iPad and opened the Kindle app.

"I'm just trying to finish this book," she said, with what she hoped was a chill in her voice.

The "I'm reading act" worked more often than not. But this was one of those not moments.

"What are you reading?" he said. "I'm a very avid reader."

She noted how often the opposite was true. Truly avid readers rarely advertised themselves as such. But, she thought, whatever, man.

Olivia mentioned a book she was sure he'd never heard of: "*The Yellow House.*"

But he quickly responded, "By Sarah Broom. I loved that book. Me and my mom read it in our book club."

This, she had to admit, took her by surprise. "You're in a book club with your mother?" she asked.

She looked at him then, really looked at him, for the first time. He was cute-ish. He had golden-brown curly hair, on the longer side. White. Seemed to be tall. Not her type at all. The white part, that was.

If he sensed she was annoyed at his attempts at conversation, he did not show it. He kept on.

"Yeah," he said, slowly, as if they had intentionally met up for coffee instead of the actual situation in which she was exhausted and he'd been contracted to give her a silent, peaceful ride home.

"My mom lives in Queens and she was always complaining that I never went to see her," he said. "I live in Inwood, which is a long way from Kew Gardens. So I said, I like books. She's got a book club. I said, let me join your club. I come by, first Sunday of the month. I spend some time with my mom, my aunt—that woman, what she's been through, she's a saint—and their little posse of friends. They feed me. Those women can cook their asses off. I get a good meal, a little education by way of the book discussion, and then I'm out, see you again in four weeks. It's all done in two hours, three max. And I usually catch a nice fare back to the city from JFK. Win, win, win."

"Interesting," Olivia said, not meaning it.

But the driver took her speaking words of any kind as encouragement. He said, "I know you said you like it quiet, but would you mind if I played some music?"

Olivia closed her iPad. She'd be home in fifteen minutes. She might as well let Chatty Guy do his DJ thing.

The guy turned on his music and it was far from what she'd been expecting. She would've bet good money on Post Malone. Halsey if she was lucky. The Chainsmokers as an adjacent bet to Halsey. But what he played was a cover of "Seven Nation Army" by a Black French artist named Ben l'Oncle Soul. She felt frozen. Omar loved Ben l'Oncle Soul. In fact, the last concert they had seen together before Omar got sick was Ben at the Montreal Jazz Festival.

It was more than a coincidence. It was eerie.

Olivia asked the driver, "Why are you playing this song?"

He smiled at her through the rearview mirror. "It's dope, right? It's this French dude. He calls himself Ben—"

She cut him off then. "I know what his name is," she said, trying not to sound rude. But white people trying to hip her to cool Black stuff was pretty much near the top of things that worked her last nerve.

Olivia smiled. She'd read once that smiling helped modulate the tone of your voice. Even a fake smile made your voice sound gentler and more welcoming to the person you were talking to. So she tried it and she said, in as non-WTF voice as she could muster, "I was wondering how you heard about him, as he's not super well known in the States."

The driver shrugged. "I heard a thing about him on NPR a few days ago. I just can't stop listening to him."

Olivia had, of course, met her share of white guys who tried to impress her with their affection for Black culture. There were the guys who claimed to love Walter Mosley or who claimed, however nonsensically, that Toni Morrison had changed their lives. The guys who declared their passion for hip-hop never got off the bench. But she'd learn to be wary of the jazz heads. It turned out there were few things as pretentious and boring as a white guy who wanted to lecture you on the history of jazz from Jelly Roll Morton to Jason Moran.

That said, there was something very specific about this guy. He had read *The Yellow House*. Even Olivia's friends who had bought the book hadn't read it yet.

The Ben l'Oncle Soul thing was downright spooky. Olivia had never met anyone outside of Omar who knew the singer, much less loved his work.

Which was all to say, Olivia wasn't exactly shocked when they pulled up to the porte cochere of her apartment building and the guy said, "Look, I don't mean to be forward. My name is Anderson and I think you're beautiful. I'm a comedian and I'm doing a set at the Gotham Comedy Club next Friday. I'd love it if you came."

Olivia pretended to think about it for a second and said, "Maybe. I might have to be away next weekend."

Then she said, "I'll tip in the app."

Anderson looked genuinely hurt. "I just asked you out on a date. You don't have to tip me."

So she thanked him for the ride and disappeared into the lobby, grateful that she lived in a doorman building with heavy-duty security.

Upstairs, she showered and changed into a pair of pale blue Asceno silk pajamas that had been Ama's gift to all the girls the year before. When she'd settled into her comfy sectional with a cup of fresh ginger tea she picked up her cell phone. Billie was still up in the Vineyard—the last one standing. Olivia would have given anything to be able to talk this over with her godsister on a long walk on State Beach with the sound of the waves crashing in her ears. But the phone would have to do. She called Billie and told her the whole saga.

Olivia said, "He was on the cute side. But I'm not going to go."

Billie said, "Are you kidding me? You have to go."

To which she replied, "Look, I don't have to do anything but stay Black and die."

But Billie wouldn't let her off the hook so easily. "Don't you get it?" she said. "He picked you up at LB. That was Omar's spot. He was playing Ben l'Oncle Soul, an Afro-French artist that Omar adored. Ben was the last concert you and Omar saw together. This was not an accident."

Olivia walked over to the big picture window in her living room. The window framed the Brooklyn Bridge perfectly.

"Omar sent him to you," Billie said resolutely.

Nope, she thought. "Omar wouldn't have sent me a white man," she said.

Billie sighed. "Why are you so biased?"

"I'm not," Olivia said. "I'm just saying Omar and Ama were Wakanda before Ryan Coogler was even born. They kept it blackity black black on the GP. No matter how rich they became, their circle was always solidly brown and Black."

She could hear Billie disagreeing on the other side of the phone line before she even said a word. "I think their circle reflected the time and place when they came up," Billie said. "It was about who they met socially, who they had stuff in common with, and who they trusted during untrustworthy times."

Exactly, Olivia thought. "Omar would not have trusted a white Uber driver/stand-up comedian."

But Billie wouldn't let it go. "Look," she said. "I'm in town all next week for a climate change conference at the UN."

"Dang, girl," Olivia replied. "Were you even going to give me a 'what's up'?"

"Yes, of course," Billie said. "I'm staying at Ama's. The conference ends on Thursday and I was going to go back to the Vineyard on Friday. But I'll change my flight. I'll go to the show on Friday with you. Let me suss out this Uber guy for myself. But I'm telling you now, I'm not feeling any red flags. Omar had impeccable taste."

After they'd said their goodbyes, Olivia zapped her tea in the microwave and returned, contemplatively, to her Brooklyn Bridge view. Omar, she thought. I love you. I miss you. But what exactly are you up to? Don't you know Michael B. Jordan is still single? Couldn't you have spirited him to the table next to mine at Le Bernardin?

CHAPTER 21

THERE IS NO PLANET B

That Monday, Billie also left the island for a quick work trip to New York. She knew that the off-island sojourns were not what Ama had planned. But work was work. Billie dressed carefully for the climate change summit at the UN in the guest bedroom at Ama's New York City apartment. Her usual spring work uniform consisted of sleeveless turtle-necks, long cashmere cardigans for layering (the labs were warm but Woods Hole was always icy cold because of the waterfront breezes), jeans, and boots. Ama had given all of her girls a love of dressing up and New York brought out the fancy in her youngest goddaughter.

Through her work, Billie had visited the UN dozens of times, but it always made an impression. The elegant Sec-retariat Building was thirty-nine stories and the first in the city to use glass curtain walls. Transparency, in act as well as architecture, was a priority from the beginning.

The meeting, in the North Delegates Lounge, was a gath-ering of some of the greatest minds in her field. The room, recently renovated, felt like a movie set with thirty-foot ceil-ings, dark wood walls, and chairs in a palette of navy, spruce green, and dark gray. Everywhere she looked there were translators and aides buzzing about. She said hello to a few old friends, then took a seat near the back.

During the morning presentations, Billie's head spun with the urgency of the work at hand. Global emissions were at a record high and there was no indication that the numbers wouldn't continue to spike. The past five years had been the hottest on record, and even the Arctic was heating up at a perilous rate. The sea levels kept rising. Coral reefs were the canaries in the coal mine of the environment and the news there wasn't good either. The coral reefs were dying and if they disappeared entirely, global hunger of unseen proportions was a certainty. Whole countries would be thrown into poverty and political instability. And the bees. The bees were dying.

It was so frustrating, Billie thought, to understand the facts so deeply and then day after day see and hear the climate deniers in government, who were in a position to do so much more than any one group of scientists ever could. She thought about Ama's beehives and her contributions.

At lunch, Billie ran into one of her friends from UC Davis. Jaime Molina had grown up in Miami. After they graduated, he spent three years in Florida, trying to convince his hometown officials that without immediate and dramatic action, within decades their city would be going the way of Atlantis. When that failed, he'd moved to Washington to take his fight all the way to Capitol Hill.

"How's life in the belly of the beast?" Billie asked playfully.

Jaime was wearing khaki pants, a navy blazer, and a white

shirt. She noted that he looked more like a crush-worthy high school English teacher than the Washington insider he had become.

"It's exhausting but necessary," he said. "Fighting the good fight. How's your cushy life? You still playing with aquariums and eating lobster every night out on Martha's Vineyard?"

As they made their way through the buffet line, she gave him a playful punch on the shoulder. "I don't live on Martha's Vineyard. It's Woods Hole, big difference. And as much as I would like to, I don't eat lobster every night. For one, that would heavily deplete the crustacean population."

Jaime smiled. "Oh, don't forget. I've been to your god-mother's house. I know you're not slumming it like the rest of us."

Billie grinned. Ama had thrown a graduation party for her at the house when she'd finished her master's program. She was happy that she'd gotten to share that moment with Jaime and her other scientist friends.

At the end of the day, when the conference wrapped, Jaime was waiting at the door. "Hey, do you have a sec?" he said. "There's someone I want you to meet."

He led her to a different elevator bank than the rest of the conference staffers were using. He took her to an empty conference room, and as she looked around, she wondered aloud, "Jaime, are you trying to recruit me for the CIA?"

She heard a woman laugh and turned around to see some-one Billie recognized right away, Desiree Justice Touissant.

Desiree Justice Touissant—that was her real middle name—had run a hard-fought race for a Senate seat in Texas. She'd lost but had emerged a Democratic Party star. Desiree was dressed in a belted pin-striped pantsuit with a stylishly nipped-in waist and a pair of chic pumps that would have made Ama proud. In fact, she reminded her of Ama. Desiree was in her forties and Ama was in her sixties, but Billie thought if you stood the women side by side, Desiree could have been Ama's daughter. They had the same height and slim build. They both had the same kind of Southern belle grace and yet there was that steel magnolia thing, too. They both seemed like they were fully capable of throwing down if the situation called for it.

The *New York Times* had suggested that Desiree had that Obama quality. She skewed left because of her race, but people on the right liked her, too. In a recent poll, Jaime explained, between 60 and 75 percent of Americans agreed that Desiree Touissant was a strong and decisive leader, could get things done, and—this was the clincher—shared their values.

"Those numbers are just unheard of for someone who's never held national office," Jaime explained.

Desiree gestured for Billie to sit next to her at the conference table. The view was floor-to-ceiling windows overlooking the East River and Queens.

"I'm building a team, Billie," Desiree said. "I'm exploring a run for governor of Texas in 2022. But some say I might end up on a VP shortlist as early as next year. I know what I want to do in this country, and climate is at the top of my list. We're fighting—and losing—the fracking battle in my

home state of Texas and too many states across the heart-
land. And we haven't done enough in states like Louisiana
to make sure that a tragedy like Katrina never hits Americans that way again. Solar energy in Puerto Rico must be
explored because the grids are so problematic. Jaime told
me about your work leading global sustainability initiatives.
He told me that you work with some of the smartest people
in the world on these topics. I want to start formulating
some big, ambitious ideas. I'd like you to lead that work. On
my team."

Billie was silent. It was the last thing she'd expected when
she got up that morning. She was thrilled. Desiree Touissant
might well be president of the United States one day and
to build a working relationship with her, from so early on,
would be a once-in-a-lifetime opportunity. But she also felt
scared. She'd never imagined herself in politics. Ever. And
what she'd seen going on in Washington over the past few
years had only amplified her desire to stay far out of that
particular fray.

"I have to say, I'm impressed," Billie said. "Everything
you've said underlines what we talk about at the lab every
day. The situation is dire. Scientists can't stand apart from
the call to activism indefinitely."

Desiree smiled. "I'm glad to hear you say it."

Billie asked the first thing she could think of: "Would I
have to quit my job?"

Desiree answered, "Good question."

Jaime jumped in and said, "What we suggest is a leave
of absence if the lab will give it to you, which we hope they
will. This kind of assignment raises their profile, too."

"And what's your role in all of this, Jaime?" Billie wondered, for the first time.

"Jaime is my newly minted chief of staff," Desiree said proudly. "And the first person he suggested we hire, after a director of fundraising, because the money thing is real, is you."

Billie's first thought was of Dulce. DC to Woods Hole was a long way, but the flight to Boston was only two hours. She could, potentially, come home every weekend. That could work.

As if reading her mind, Jaime said, "So this is the thing, B. We're setting up shop in Houston, Desiree's hometown, for the next three months. Then, depending on what goes down at the conventions, we'll either move to Washington or stay put."

Now Billie was more than just nervous. She felt uncomfortable. She'd never lived away from the East Coast. Houston to Boston was not sustainable for a weekend commute. Even if she could find the money and the stamina, the carbon footprint would be enormous. It would be hard to build credibility on climate change if she was regularly undertaking that kind of travel. Maybe Dulce would consider coming with her. After all, that was the great thing about the culinary industry: there were restaurants everywhere.

CHAPTER 22

SECOND CHANCES?

With Perry back in New York, there was now talk of possible settlement negotiations in her Glitch case. It seemed that the lawyers on the other side thought with Perry gone for the summer they could glide into the fall. Well think again, Counsel.

She decided that she would stop at Hudson Yards to pick up takeout at Fuku, the Korean fried chicken spot that had been one of her and Damon's favorites.

She was surprised to see Damon in line. And a sudden thought struck her: God, what a beautiful man.

"Hey, what are you doing here?" she asked, her voice more flirty than she expected.

"I miss this place," he said. But the way he said it sounded like, "I miss you."

He then added, "I thought you were up at the Vineyard for the summer."

She grimaced. "There was just a little bit of interruption to my summer in paradise."

"Tell me," he said.

And she was reminded of what a good listener he was, how good it felt to have someone who asked "How are you?" And to know that the person actually, truly wanted to know the answer.

"Be my dinner date?" he asked.

She nodded in agreement. He was her husband. There were moments when being with him felt like that line in the Minnie Riperton song: "Lovin' you is easy 'cause you're beautiful."

They'd ordered two spicy fried chicken sandwiches, Korean-style, on potato rolls.

Perry remembered that she used to think, No worries about the carbs. I'll work it off in the bedroom. Just the thought reminded her of how good they were in bed together. But was it enough? She worried that it just wasn't enough.

"We've got to get squash rings," Damon said. Perry nodded in agreement. It wasn't Fuku fabulous without the squash rings.

"Don't forget the cheesecake," she said. They always split one slice of cheesecake.

By the time the order was wrapped up and they could feel it steaming in the bag, Perry knew that Damon would come home that night. They would eat dinner together. They would hypertext through all their old arguments and just be together. It was like that Floetry song, all she had to do was say yes.

Still Damon didn't overstep. "Cool if I come home with you?" he asked as they stood at the top of the escalators in Hudson Yards.

She nodded yes.

They took an Uber to her apartment. He held her hand and beamed at her as if she was the only woman in the world, the only woman he had ever wanted and would ever want.

When they got to the apartment, he turned the oven to two hundred to keep the food warm. Then he said, "Bee stings?"

She took off her office uniform—the tartan sheath, the matching blazer—and changed into a pair of silk pajamas that had been a recent gift.

When she emerged from the bedroom, Damon had whipped up a pitcher of a drink he called the bee sting, which had become a favorite of theirs on the Bluffs—tequila, lemon juice, jalapeño for heat, and honey from Ama's bee-hives for sweetness.

She blamed the cocktails for what happened next. They'd made love on the floor of their living room as if nothing had ever gone wrong between them, which meant they loved each other again and again.

The next morning, the sound of a flurry of text messages woke them both up.

"It's your phone, Damon," Perry had said, half-asleep.

"Nope, it's yours," Damon had said, not even opening his eyes.

She'd gotten up from the mess of blankets and pillows on the floor and grabbed the phone that was buzzing nonstop. It was Damon's phone and it was a string of messages from Jeremy:

Yo bro, it's poker night. Let me know if you're in.

Text number two:

**I invited Bri. She's pregnant, but she still can't play for shit. I
plan to fleece her for whatever she's got.**

Text number three:

Your bitch wife still out of town?

Perry remembered feeling more naked looking at those
messages than she had the night before.

As Perry read the messages from Jeremy, Damon began
to wake up.

"Morning, beautiful," he murmured, his eyes half-closed.

"Beautiful?" Perry fumed. "Or 'your bitch wife'? I saw the
texts from your boy."

Damon looked first sheepish, then guilty, and finally dis-
traught.

"Come on, P," he said, his voice thick with longing. "You
can't punish me because Jeremy is an asshole."

Perry raised an eyebrow. "Oh, really?" she fumed. "Omar
always told us if you lie down with dogs, you get fleas."

Damon was standing then. He was naked, and Perry took
in how beautiful he was. He was like an African American
Adonis. Is that why she couldn't let him go? Was she really
that shallow? Was it more?

His voice snapped her out of her reverie. "Come on,
Perry," he said. "I'm not lying down with Jeremy. I'm not a
dog with fleas."

Perry wasn't sure. Omar and Ama's marriage had been

perfect. And right now she needed perfect to stand the world's chaos. She had no control of so many things. She couldn't change the polemic dynamic of the political climate. She couldn't change the fact that being brown in America meant that you were always, in some way or another, shortchanged and on guard. But she could reach for something different within the walls of her home, within the confines of her own personal life. She wanted a mighty love. She could demand it. She thought Damon was it. But he kept falling short. That's what she resented the most, the way he kept letting her down. She wanted loyalty. A ride or die. She knew that a house divided could not stand. What kind of real man, what kind of true love, would let another man casually call her "your bitch wife." The words stung like a bee from Ama's hive.

"Let's talk," Damon said.

She didn't want to talk. Omar hadn't been a talker. He'd been a doer. He'd shown Ama and his girls who he was by the quality of his character, not by how hard he could hustle with his sweet talk.

Damon shook his head. "Someday you're going to learn that nobody's perfect, Perry. Not Ama. Not Omar. We're human. We do the best we can. Jeremy is my best friend. I want him in my life. I don't have any other male friends. I just feel like I don't want to lose that connection to my past life. You are my wife. It isn't a competition. Why can't you understand that?"

He stepped into the bathroom and Perry picked up her phone. She lost herself in work emails, just longing for him to leave. The magic of last night faded.

He emerged from the bathroom, fully dressed and looking heartbroken. "I love you, Perry," Damon said. "I'm not perfect. But you are perfection to me. I hope you have a good time on the Vineyard. Just say the word and I'll be there. Always."

She hoped he wouldn't kiss her, but he approached her with the confidence of a husband approaching a wife, oblivious to the invisible electric fence she was throwing up around her heart.

He kissed her on the cheek and said again, "Whenever you need me. Just say the word and I'll be there."

CHAPTER 23

ABOUT THOSE
SCHUYLER SISTERS

After the second day of the conference wrapped up, Billie walked across Central Park to Perry's apartment. It took a little more than an hour, but she listened to a podcast on the way. It was the third season and it was about the music and rivalry of Biggie and Tupac. She was riveted. It was sunset when she showed up at Perry's apartment on the Upper West Side. The view was gorgeous and the apartment looked like the movie set of the rom-coms she couldn't get enough of, hetero-normative story lines be damned.

When she arrived at her godsister's apartment, Perry was looking fierce in a charcoal-gray Rachel Comey jumpsuit and some devastatingly intricate high heels. Billie was feeling cute and sporty in a button-down shirt and silk crepe culottes. Perry poured them both a glass of rosé and they sat at the counter in her eat-in kitchen, looking glamorous and feeling like sisters.

Billie knew that Perry and Damon were on the outs, although Ama seemed to think it was merely a marital blip. What she didn't expect was what came next.

Perry said, "So this is the thing. I want you to invite a guy up to Ama's for Fourth of July weekend and pretend he's your friend. You know, someone you met in the sustainability industry or something. His name is Nikesh and he is someone I like a lot. The whole thing with Damon is so screwed up. I just . . . I just need this."

This was a ridiculous plan, Billie thought. But she told herself she needed to be there for Perry. Billie didn't believe much in the all-knowing power of the universe, but Dulce did and it was definitely rubbing off.

Billie took a sip of her rosé and looked her godsister squarely in the eye. "You know this is a terrible, very bad, no *bueno*, plan, don't you?"

Perry sighed. "I know. Do it for me. Think about Hamilton and all that Angelica did for her little sister Eliza."

Billie shook her head. "That was a totally effed up situation. In the end, Hamilton hurt Eliza—bad."

Perry got up and topped their glasses off. "This will go better, I promise." Then she raised her glass and said, "To love. And to figuring it out."

Billie clinked glasses with her godsister and hoped like hell that Perry was right.

CHAPTER 24

GOD SAID, "MADE YOU LOOK"

On the other side of town, Olivia was also wading into unchartered territory. A date with the white Uber driver/comedian. Olivia told herself that she didn't care what Anderson thought about her, so she would not dress up for the comedy club. Besides, there was really no such thing as "dressing up" for a comedy club.

But then, somehow, as she rifled through her not tiny closet, Olivia felt . . . inspired. She threw on a vintage champagne-colored slip dress that had been Ama's in the nineties. Then she topped it with one of Omar's Ralph Lauren blazers that Ama had given her when they'd gathered on the Bluffs for a celebration of his life, the summer after his death. "Okay, Omar," she said to the air. "If you really set this date up, you might as well come along."

She added a pair of playful Sophia Webster sneakers to the mix and by the time she was done, she was so close to cute that she decided she needed to do an un-makeup makeup look to take it over the line.

She quickly dabbed on some concealer under her eyes.

Screw her work ethic. She didn't need to look like she'd been at her desk since eight A.M. She defined her brows with a Pat McGrath liner then a brush and she broke out her favorite McGrath eye shadow, the chocolate-brown one with the gold flecks.

She'd seen a video on Instagram where Lizzo talked about how you didn't need fake lashes if you took the time to build a lash, meaning you had to let the mascara dry between applications. Because Olivia had trouble following instructions and because she was easily distracted, she'd made a three-song playlist, designed exclusively around her mascara routine. Song number one: Drake's "Controlla." Song number two: Stefflon Don's "Don Walk." Song number three: Major Lazer's "Particula." (She also had multiple toothbrushing playlists but that was another story for another ADHD time.) When the last song on the lash list came on, she gave her eyes one more swipe with the mascara wand, did a quick lip with a pinkish-brown gloss, and had to admit she looked good, whole mood, feeling like soul food good.

Her extended makeup routine meant that she was twenty minutes late to meet Billie at the comedy club. Her godsister was patient, but saucy. She said, "Damn, you look awfully nice for a girl who doesn't want to date a working-class white boy."

Billie was working her usual Zoë Kravitz, street style thing. She looked amazing in a Virgil Abloh bodysuit, a denim maxi skirt, a camo jacket, and matching camo heeled boots.

"I like your outfit," Olivia said. "You setting a thirst trap for some funny people tonight?"

Billie had come out to her godsisters in college.

"Nah," Billie said, "I'm kind of seeing someone."

There was a seventeen-dollar cover charge at the door and Billie started clowning on Olivia right away. "Some date. You've got to pay for the privilege."

"It's not a date," Olivia said huffily.

When they sat down, a surly waitress approached them. She was in her mid-twenties, and both girls thought she was awfully young to be so bitter.

"It's a two-drink minimum, princesses," the waitress barked.

"I'd love a glass of rosé," Olivia said, as kindly as she could.

The waitress looked annoyed. "I'd like a foot massage from a dominatrix wearing Chanel couture who looks like Lady Gaga and smells like gardenias. But we don't always get what we want. I will come back when you have realistic expectations." Then she stomped away.

Billie guffawed. "You should hang out with me in Woods Hole more often. It would cure you of your trifling, petite bourgeoisie tendencies."

The surly waitress returned. "I've got two kinds of wine— red and white. I can mix them together using my boot as a cocktail shaker, princess. You'll have pink wine, but I'll have to charge you extra and I can almost guarantee it won't taste good."

Then she charged away again.

"What the hell did I do to her?" Olivia asked, incredulous.

"Just order a beer," Billie whispered.

"But I don't like beer," Olivia hissed back.

"Order a gin and tonic then," Billie suggested.

The waitress returned, clearly relishing in fucking with Olivia.

"May I see a cocktail menu?" Olivia asked earnestly.

The waitress stared at Billie and said, "I just hope to God that the two of you are related. Choosing to spend time with this Dionne reflects very poorly on you."

Then, as if she was wearing roller blades, the waitress glided away to help other customers. The place was busy.

"Why would she call me Dionne?" Olivia asked, regretting that she'd opted out of binge-watching *The Crown* for what was developing into an evening of insults with some wannabe New York hipsters.

Billie looked amused. "You know, Dionne from *Clueless*."

"I'm totally not a Dionne."

"Says the girl who ordered rosé in a dive bar," Billie said. "Let me do the ordering, okay?"

The waitress returned with two drinks on a small tray. She said, "A beer for you, on the house," and handed a beer to Billie. "The management takes pity on home-care workers for the mentally ill."

Then she handed a drink to Olivia. "A cranberry vodka for the diva. That'll be twenty dollars."

Olivia looked confused. Twenty dollars? For a drink she hadn't ordered.

Billie whispered, "Just shut up." Then she handed the waitress two twenties and said, "Keep the change."

The waitress seemed pleased, "I knew you were a superior-quality human being. A royal among pheasants."

Then she curtsied and skipped away.

"Did she mean peasants?" Olivia asked. "Why would she say 'pheasants'? Did I hear 'pheasants'?"

"It's not supposed to make sense," Billie said, as if she had a masters in surrealist art as well as marine biology.

Olivia looked stricken. "What have I gotten myself into?"

"Relax, O," Billie said cheerfully. "It's a comedy club. Clearly part of the game is trying to one up each other with all the crazy."

She looked at her watch impatiently. "If this wasn't a Friday, I'd be out."

"This is so good for you," Billie said. "You are wound so tight. You're starting to remind me of . . ."

Olivia said, "Don't say it."

For a moment, the tension between them was real. Over the years, they had met each other's parents. Perry's mother and father, her adoptive parents, were like the anatomically correct blacktino Ken and Barbie of the Bronx—straitlaced, middle-class, and pretty stiff. When Perry's dad made a joke, he slapped his knee as if to signal to you it was okay to laugh. When Perry's mother laughed, she covered her mouth as if she were in desperate need of dental work and/or she wanted to be super ladylike and polite. They also never missed church on Sundays or Wednesday Bible study or the Friday night teen church lock-in.

Olivia and Billie had long agreed that the reason Perry was such an undercover freak was because of her parents. There was also the X factor of her birth parents. Who knew what they were like?

Billie's dad, Mike, owned a comic book store in Manhattan. Billie had totally inherited his "weird is cool" aesthetic.

None of the girls knew much about Billie's mother. Whenever Billie asked him, he responded in an odd, distant way, like David Duchovny in *The X-Files*. "The truth is out there," Mike would say. And somehow because he seemed to be a pretty dope mix of Marvel's Nick Fury and Professor Xavier of the X-Men, Billie didn't ask questions her father didn't want to answer.

Olivia was the only one of the three who knew everything there was to know about her parents. Her mother had been widowed at a young age. Olivia was just a baby when her father died. Her father had been military, then law enforcement. Cindy Jones was sad and cold and just a little bit mean. All of the girls agreed she had serious wicked stepmother vibes and they'd wondered if she was actually Olivia's mother. Or was it a *Tangled* Rapunzel situation. Cindy was Maleficent level in her bad moods and rages, so when Billie mentioned that Olivia reminded her of someone, she had the good sense to pull back and not compare O to Cindy. That would have been far too cruel.

The tough waitress returned, just as the host was warming up the crowd. She said her name was Genevieve and that it was imperative that they order their drink before the first comedian came on. Billie ordered another beer, which Genevieve comped.

Then Olivia ordered a glass of white wine, which came out warmer than room temp and Olivia had the audacity to complain.

Billie groaned. "You never complain about the service in a comedy club. We'll be lucky if she doesn't start spitting in our drinks." Genevieve came back with a check.

Twenty-two dollars for one glass of wine. Billie was incensed.

She paid the bill and said, "Never again will I come along as a third wheel on one of your eighty-dollar dates. You're in finance. Perry is a lawyer. I'm the scientist. I'm the poor one."

Then, dropping her voice to confide in Olivia, Billie said, "I think Perry and Damon are going through some stuff."

Olivia was just about to spill the tea when the host walked off the stage and the first comedian, a woman, came on. Despite herself, Olivia felt excited. It had been a long time since she had done something so different.

The comic did a whole bit about anxiety and ended by reminding the audience, "Any pizza can be a personal one if you eat it when you're crying."

Then a guy came out and said, "My son is deaf. Which can make it hard to communicate. He's fifteen and instead of 'Good morning,' he wakes up each day and signs, 'Fuck you, Dad.' At least that's what good morning looks like when an angry teenager uses sign language."

The crowd burst out laughing. Olivia and Billie laughed, too. "Y'all don't understand. This is progress right now. Now Black kids get to be rude and we don't threaten to beat their asses."

After that, Anderson got on the stage. He said, "I know there are some white men in the audience who are looking to dip into the chocolate pond and date a Black woman. Before you do that, let me just give you a little heads-up, so you are prepared for some changes that will likely occur. For example, I was told never to touch a Black woman's hair. This is her crown. Maybe, just maybe if you get permission, and she is trying to prove to her girl that it is all hers." The crowd cheered their approval. Anderson continued, "And this is serious business, okay? Follow me. Once I was dating this fine Black woman and when we started to make out on her couch one evening, I stroked her hair. Well, if I'm being honest I went all in—I went Becky into the roots. I wanted to give her a scalp massage. I figured that would get me some. Yeah, it got me some. Some Uber charges when she threw my ass out. Date was over. You would have thought I had cursed her mama. She looked at me, cursed *my* mama, stood up, and promptly asked me to get the hell out. See, she covered that with me on date number one, but I was not listening. I won't make that mistake again. Fellas, you just touch the hairline. And like over the hair. Not 'on' the hair. Not 'in' the hair. 'Cause that shit is disrespectful. Okay?" The crowd laughed. "I also noticed that I'm also hypersensitive and woke to racial insensitivities now. The other day, I was standing in line with my girlfriend at Starbucks and this little white boy just cut us in line and I spoke up to tell him about his white privilege and entitlement. I was angry. To me, it didn't matter that he was four years old and looking for his nanny. I'm an ally in the movement against The Man." Anderson finished his set after a few more "heads-up" jokes and the crowd cheered and laughed as he walked offstage.

✳

After his set was over, Anderson came over to Olivia and Billie's table. He sat down and the waitress brought him a beer.

Billie said, "Thanks, Genevieve."

Anderson laughed and said, "Her name is not Genevieve. It's Lisa. She's such a drama queen." Then when she returned, he said, "Next round is on me. Bring these ladies whatever they want."

Genevieve/Lisa looked annoyed, which filled Olivia with some small satisfaction.

Billie said, "I liked your act. How long have you been a self-hating white guy?"

Anderson shook his head. "You've got it all wrong, my friend. I love being a white guy. I didn't go to college. I grew up in a solidly middle-class household. I still have a relatively good chance of getting rich and famous. And I don't worry about getting shot by the police. But my time is almost over. I'm an ally. I need to use my privilege for good. That's all my act is about."

Billie nodded. "I don't disagree. Question though—why are you trying to date my sister? She's Meghan Markle-ish. She's pretty and smart, independently wealthy, and likely to adopt a fake British accent at any moment. But as far as I can tell, you're no Prince Harry. What are you bringing to the game?"

Olivia grimaced. The only thing she liked less than being set up with a non-college-educated comedian/Uber driver white guy was Billie being in the mix and needling her. And yet, if she was honest with herself, she'd liked the show. It was good to be around other people her age. She'd spent so much time in business school and boardrooms, she'd forgotten what it was like to just be somewhere where they didn't serve a nice rosé and the appetizers were cheap and questionable. She'd laughed out loud and that was an improvement, too. Billie was right. She was like a superhero who didn't know if their powers would be used for good or evil. It seemed, at all times, that there was a fifty-fifty chance that she'd end up a bon vivant like Ama and Omar and an equal chance that she'd end up a rigid, well-read, profoundly discontent, proud Black woman like her mother.

The waitress returned. "Hey, my shift is ending. Guess how many Dance Dance Revolution machines there are left in the city?"

Billie smiled and said, "Two. One in Times Square and one in Chinatown."

Genevieve/Lisa said, "Want to go to Chinatown with me? We can dance and eat the food of my people."

Billie said, "Sure."

As she went to collect her coat, Billie mouthed, "You owe me."

Anderson and Olivia sat there for a few moments in an awkward silence. Billie must have begun texting Olivia furiously the minute she stepped outside because her phone kept buzzing. Then Anderson said, "You want to know what the funny thing is? Lisa's shift isn't over. She just walked out."

Olivia, who never broke a rule intentionally, looked alarmed.

Anderson waved her concern away. "It's okay. She's dating the manager. He's crazy in love with her."

Olivia said, "So she's not gay?"

Anderson shrugged. "Who knows? She's part of the no labels generation. How about your sister?"

Olivia sipped the cranberry and vodka that Lisa had dropped off before she went off with Billie. "She's my god-sister and she also doesn't like labels."

He shook his head and said, "And just so I'm a hundred percent clear. You are straight?"

Olivia said, "It's boring, but it's true."

He smiled and said, "I think you're anything but boring. Ms. I Eat at Le Bernardin and I Read Books on My Kindle to Ignore Uber Drivers."

Then he said, "I'm glad you came. Can I tell you something?"

Olivia nodded.

He said, "I never get stage fright. But I looked out from backstage. And you were looking so amazing and I almost couldn't do my act."

She didn't want to be rude but the whole "I'm a white ally" thing didn't seem so complicated, not compared to her job.

He seemed to have read her thoughts. He said, "I know it's still a WIP."

"Really?"

He said, "A work in progress. But I'm still working on my tight five."

She was confused again.

"It's that perfect five-minute set that kills no matter what the audience is like," he said. "The thing is, real comedy, the best comedy, is involuntary. You don't laugh as a favor to the woman or man onstage. When they are that good, when they are at the top of their game, you laugh because you can't help it. When I get there, when I get my tight five, my agent will start putting me up for Trevor Noah, Fallon, and Kimmel."

Olivia looked at him. "So are you one of those?"

He seemed to know exactly what she meant because he didn't shy away from the question. "One of those white guys who only dates Black girls? Hell, fucking, yes. Because I've got two eyes in my head and I know beautiful when I see it."

Olivia found herself blushing. Her mother used to say that brown girls didn't blush because no one could see the blood rushing to their cheeks.

But Anderson reached up and touched her cheek, right at the spot where it felt the most hot.

He said, "Let's get out of here."

"Are you going to drive me home in your Uber?"

The minute the words were out of her mouth, she wondered about the politics of it. Would she sit in the back or the front? Would he ask her to open the app? She was pretty sure he would drive her for free.

He said, "Oh my God. Stop thinking so much. I'm not driving an Uber tonight. But I do know where you live. I mapped it before my act. It's about an hour walk. Olivia Jones, may I walk you home?"

And it was the first thing he said that hit Olivia like an arrow to the heart. He'd said, "Stop thinking so much." And before he'd said it, she hadn't realized how much that—more than anything—was what she desperately wanted to do.

One of the downsides of being a banker was that the whole "time is money" thing got into your head. As Olivia strolled down the street with Anderson, she struggled to remember the last time she'd walked down Sixth Avenue. She loved New York. They all did. Growing up in the city under Ama and Omar's tutelage had ensured that they had all seen the best the Big Apple had to offer. But these days, Olivia either walked to work looking down lost in her thoughts about the next deal or Uber-ed door-to-door to this or that destination.

They started in Chelsea, and she had so many memories of being in that neighborhood. Of Omar taking her and the girls to Doughnut Plant. Of Omar and Ama taking the girls to see Twyla Tharp and Bill T. Jones at the Joyce Theater. Of going to see Desmond Tutu and Deepak Chopra in conversation at the bookstore in Chelsea Market when all the girls were too young to know who either of those men were. There was the old school British tea shop, Tea & Sympathy and the fish and chips shop next door, A Salt & Battery. When they got older, they sometimes accompanied Ama to the gym. She liked to frequent an old school boxing gym in the Meatpacking District that smelled of sweat and cigars and, as Olivia got older, she realized had the faintest scent of blood. They also sometimes accompanied her to an old school yoga studio, on top of a bookstore on West Twenty-First Street, that she also loved. These were precious places to her, but she rarely walked in New York, so she didn't come across them by accident.

She hadn't realized how much she'd been talking when Anderson said, "So the lady does something besides work. I'm happy to hear it."

When they reached the West Village, Anderson suggested they stop for a drink at Charlie Bird.

It was a place Olivia knew well. All of the white guys in

her firm who were under forty loved it. The chef was a hip-hop fan and the restaurant served some of the best Italian food in the city, all to the soundtrack of LL Cool J, Missy, and Common.

Anderson suggested they stop in for a drink and Olivia demurred. She knew it was expensive, and she could only imagine he was on a serious budget.

He said, "It would be my pleasure to buy you a seventeen-dollar glass of wine, Oli. But fret not. My friend, Elly, is working as a bartender here tonight. If my credit card bounces—and it's been known to happen—she'll cover me, you won't have to."

They stepped into the restaurant and Olivia, who had been there before and not liked it much, felt right at home. Anderson glided past the hostess and maneuvered them, with a quickness, to two seats that were opening at the very crowded bar. His friend Elly was a beautiful tattooed Asian girl and she said, right away, "What happened, Anderson? You win king for a day or some shit? You never pull a queen like this."

Olivia thought of how often she'd been out with Perry and no matter what the Black guy looked like, he gravitated toward the girl with the lighter skin.

Anderson seemed to think she was the prize, Lupita with an MBA. What was crazy was that Elly, who was a friend of his, appeared to think the same thing.

She was happy he'd asked her out. Happy that Billie had forced her to go to the show.

They ordered the razor clams and a couple of glasses of rosé.

Anderson told her about how his parents both died young. "I never knew them," he said. "The woman I call Mom is my foster mother in Queens."

His father, he explained, had been a cop. His mother was a junkie who his father kept trying to save. They both died in the nineties. His father in the line of duty. His mother from an overdose shortly thereafter.

Their stories were similar. It was crazy. She told him, "My father was a cop, too. He died when I was a baby."

She started to tear up then, even though she was just a baby when her father died and the truth was she'd never really known him, couldn't remember him. She dabbed her tears with the lapel of her jacket and he pulled her hand away. He took a clean handkerchief out of his pocket and handed it to her. He said, "That's a beautiful jacket. Don't cry on that."

Because she was wearing Omar's jacket and because she had come to believe that Omar had indeed put them together, she told him about Omar and Ama and he was . . . amazed. She didn't tell him about Omar and Le Bernardin, or how much Omar loved Ben l'Oncle Soul. But just the story of the Tanners and how they'd pseudo-adopted three random girls was enough to blow his mind. Especially because he'd grown up in foster care.

"It sounds like we both hit the lottery with our found families," he said, toasting her with a glass of grappa that his bartender friend had poured them for free.

She toasted back. For the first time in as long as she could remember, she felt like the lucky one and being the dark girl hadn't precluded or obstructed that luck.

After last call at Charlie Bird, Olivia and Anderson kept walking. She thought about taking him home. She'd actually never slept with a white guy—and despite being an Uber driver, she had decided, hours before, that this one could get it.

So they kept walking and talking. He said, "I know the cancel culture is bullshit. But 'Ignition (Remix)' was the song I loved most from my sixth-grade dance. But I just can't with R. Kelly. I can't."

"Wait, what kind of school did you go to that they were playing R. Kelly at the elementary school dance?"

Anderson looked at Olivia as if she were a Supreme Court judge and he was under oath. "What kind of school? Public school," he said, then he burst out laughing himself. "It made no kind of sense."

Then Olivia said something that was so out of character for her, she couldn't dial it back, even if she wanted to. She took his hand and said, "I don't want to go home. I don't want this night to end. Where should we go now?"

He smiled, a kind of "I gotcha" grin. And she hoped, only half jokingly, that he wasn't one of those crazy white guys that killed and ate people. He hailed a cab. And in the cab she texted Billie. **I'm still with him. I've also enabled Find My Friend on my phone.**

Billie's response was an emoticon with a monocle.

Olivia swore. Would it have killed her to use words to respond to the text? Sometimes Billie was so freakin' Gen Z.

The cab dropped them off at Veselka, a Ukrainian restaurant in the East Village that Olivia had never heard of.

Anderson said, "Oh, this is a good place. Comedians effing love this place."

They walked in and Olivia said, "Oh my God. What a mood. This room is so beautiful, it reminds me of *Natasha, Pierre and the Great Comet of 1812*."

Anderson signaled for the waiter and said, "So the first rule of hanging out all night. You can't speak nerd after two A.M. My small brain can't handle it."

Olivia jumped right into apology mode. "I'm so sorry. It's late and I'm talking about an obscure musical about the Russian revolution."

Anderson said, "So let's establish a baseline. You're better looking than me. You're smarter than me. You're more cultured than me. Half the things you say are going to go over my head. This is clearly a glow up for me. But I like you a lot and will treat you like the queen you are. And if it's okay, just so I don't spend the rest of the night wondering when it's going to happen, I'd like to kiss you."

He kissed her then, in the booth of a Ukrainian spot. It was all against Olivia's plan. But perhaps, all according to Omar's plan. As it was the best first date she'd had in a very long time. Maybe ever.

They spent the rest of the night at Veselka. Drinking vodka shots and eating pierogi. It was all over Olivia's head. Anderson took her home in a cab, made sure she got in safely, and then promptly fell asleep on her couch.

Olivia awoke to find herself still dressed in the blazer and vintage champagne-colored slip dress she'd worn the night before. She'd clearly made it to her bed, but skipped her routine. She peeked outside her bedroom door and could hear Anderson snoring loudly on the couch. His presence made her smile. She answered the ten texts from Billie: **Home safe.**

Olivia then texted a follow-up: **Did you smash?**

With the crazy waitress? Billie asked. **Um, no. Did you smash?**

Olivia smiled. This was not her usual conversation with anyone. **No,** she explained. **But he's still here, sleeping on the couch.**

Her head felt like a sidewalk that was being jackhammered. But it was Saturday. She didn't have to go to work, and the fact that she hadn't remembered half of the night before seemed like a very good thing because it meant that at some point, the night before, she'd stopped thinking so hard.

When Anderson finally woke up around eleven, Olivia was in the kitchen, freshly showered, in a robe.

"Good morning," he said.

She gave him a look and teased, "I see you made yourself at home?"

He looked shy then. "I dunno. Wanted to make sure you were okay."

She said, "I'm making breakfast. Want to stay?"

"Yes," he said, taking a seat on one of the kitchen island barstools.

She was cutting vegetables and cracking eggs and there was a fresh pot of coffee brewing in her fancy Nespresso machine.

Then she said nine words that she never imagined saying to a slightly funky white boy, in need of a shave and a shower, who'd spent the night on her couch. She said, "Hey, what are you doing Fourth of July weekend?"

CHAPTER 25

MEMORIES AND MEANING

These days, the sisters and Ama often flew to the Vineyard straight from Teterboro on Wheels Up. Ama appreciated not just the luxury but the privacy. When she was a kid, years before jet shares were a thing, Ama always drove. It was always the happiest day of the year for Perry because her parents let her skip school the Friday before Memorial Day. Ama would send a car to pick up Perry in the Bronx, Billie from Brooklyn, and Olivia from Queens. The three girls would meet at Ama's Central Park apartment and Omar would let them pick anywhere they wanted to eat for lunch. They always chose the secret burger place in the Parker Méridien hotel. In the lobby of the fancy hotel there was a simple red curtain. You opened the curtain and there was a dark corridor. Every time Perry drew the curtain open she felt like she was unmasking the wizard in the *Wizard of Oz*.

At the end of the hall, there was a door with a neon burger above it. Inside, the entire restaurant was smaller than Ama's New York City kitchen. Just ten tables and walls covered with graffiti. The menu had only three items—burgers, fries, and coleslaw.

The girls would talk a mile a minute and Omar would just sit there—taking it all in while he enjoyed an Allagash beer.

By the time they reached the apartment, the doorman would have loaded Ama and Omar's Escalade with their bags and they would be off.

Ama and Omar listened to jazz up front. The TV in the back could play DVDs. The girls always watched the same movie on the way up, *Parent Trap*.

By the time they were in high school, the girls had moved on. Olivia would spend the entire time on her phone, chatting with her friends. Billie would curl up with a fantasy book. Over the summers she went from Harry Potter to Percy Jackson to His Dark Materials. But Perry always watched one of the old DVDs. She loved them all: *Sisterhood of the Traveling Pants. Mean Girls. Bring It On.*

Later, Perry and Damon always drove up to the Woods Hole ferry together. Even if he had to work, they would drive together, listening to audiobooks. Damon loved James Patterson. The books scared Perry, but they made the drives fly by. She cataloged the summers by the books they listened to. *Along Came a Spider, Kiss the Girls, London Bridges, Double Cross.*

Even if Damon had to work, he drove her to Woods Hole. Then he turned around and made the five-hour-drive home. If that wasn't love, what was?

Impulsively, Perry picked up her phone and texted him—I miss you.

His reply was sharp; she could feel the blade of it even via text: **Really, Perry? Stop playing with me. Don't text me until you're ready to have me come home.**

Home. The idea of a home that the two of them shared was so far away.

Perry scrolled through her phone. Her mind drifted further away. Nikesh had sent her an article about the new company he was working with. In the picture that accompanied the story, he was wearing a lavender shirt with French cuffs and cuff links. The color looked so good against his dark brown skin. She'd saved the image to her phone and looked at it more often than she cared to admit.

So this is him, she said, texting the picture to Billie. **He's cute, right?**

Billie texted back an upside-down face.

We'll be there by dinnertime.

Billie texted back a thumbs-up.

Damn girl, don't you have a second to type a few words?

Billie's response: **TTYL**

Perry sighed. Gen Z.

✳

Billie picked up her phone and looked at her girlfriend.

"Perry is so cray," she said. "I'm sorry you won't be there this weekend."

"No big deal—I've got to work all weekend. Holidays are never a break for chefs. But you've got to promise me this is the last weekend of secret keeping. It's one thing for us not to share our relationship with our neighbors who've got Trump signs on their lawn. But family is different. You've met my mom and my bro. If this is real, I want to meet your family, too."

Billie put her arms around her and kissed her. "This is real."

She reached her arms around her waist and pulled her closer.

"Could we?"

"I wish. But I've got to go down to the wharf and pick the catch of the day. If I'm late, Gordon from Alchemy will steal it out from under me."

"Okay," Billie said, giving Dulce a quick hug. "I love you. Be good."

CHAPTER 26

THE FERRY

Nikesh arrived at Perry's apartment building at 10:30 A.M. sharp. They embraced and Perry couldn't help but notice how good he smelled. He was freshly shaven and freshly showered. She thought, Damn, it's early for him to roll in here, looking like a snack.

It was a beautiful summer day in New York, the kind that made you forget about the dirty snow, the late and filthy subways, the traffic jams and all the rest.

Perry's 2020 BMW X1 had been a birthday gift from Damon. It was a mini SUV, which wasn't great for the environment, but Perry loved the idea that if an apocalypse should ever hit New York, she could live out of the car for days, if not weeks. She had to admit, it felt funny at first to have Nikesh in a car that had been a gift from Damon. She felt like she was playing with the forbidden. Pushing boundaries. And she liked it.

Nikesh offered to drive the first leg of the trip and she had let him. Settling into the passenger seat, she thought about how much sitting to the right of a man in a car made it feel like he was yours. Perry felt instantly comfortable sitting next to Nikesh. Handsome and smart, he was her type. They hadn't even reached Ama's and in her mind she had already given up the pretense that Nikesh was there as Billie's friend. He was there because Perry wanted him there—that made her feel bad and good at the same time.

Out of respect for Damon and their traditions, she didn't play any audiobooks. They listened to a Spotify channel of comedians. They laughed the whole way.

"Olivia, my godsister, has a new boyfriend. He's a comedian. He's coming up tomorrow."

"Cool," he said. "I look forward to meeting him."

"Hmm, I hate to say it but I'm not," Perry said.

"What?" he asked, surprised.

"He's white. We've never had a colonizer stay with us in the house before. It's kind of great just being in a people-of-color zone sometimes."

"Really?" Nikesh asked. "But what about your childhood friend from the Bronx?"

He'd remembered Layla. He seemed to remember everything.

"Yeah, well, Layla is different."

"Why?"

"Because she thinks she's Black. And she has me convinced that she very well may be."

"And that's cool with you?"

"Layla is the exception to a very hard-and-fast rule."

"Got it," Nikesh said.

Even when he disagreed with her, he didn't seem to need to argue a point down. If you believed in that astrology stuff—and sometimes Perry did—Perry's zodiac sign was Leo and Damon was Scorpio. They both dug in when they felt they were right.

"What sign are you?" she asked.

"Virgo," he answered. "I can't believe I know that. But my mom's into horoscopes."

"That's cool," she said. "You're a Virgo. Let me look you up."

She tapped an app on her phone. "It says here that Virgos are organized visionaries with the capacity to dream big and the discipline to make those dreams come true."

By Woods Hole, Perry could feel her heart racing. It always felt like Christmas in July when she entered the lot where the cars were lined up to board the ferry.

The guy at the ferry booth was old school New England with a sunburn and a thick Boston accent. "Lane three," he said. "Hope you have a wicked pissah time."

Perry had booked her car ferry ticket months before. It all felt like a privilege. The beautiful car she was driving in. The smell of sea air and the ferry that would soon be filled with cars hauling bikes and paddleboards. And the house full of love waiting for them on the other side.

She looked over at Nikesh and said, "Wait till you see the island."

He said, "It's already magic, Perry."

They boarded the ferry and parked the car. Then they climbed the metal staircase to the port side of the boat and walked out onto the top-level deck.

From the moment the boat pulled out of the dock, Perry

could feel herself relax. Ama used to say, "Problems aren't problems on the island. They are challenges. There's such a big difference."

Nikesh looked over at her. "This place. It calms you. I can see it in your shoulders, in your face. Your whole body was just transformed. Thank you for bringing me here. Thank you for letting me see you in your happy place."

CHAPTER 27

INDEPENDENT WOMEN

The Vineyard on the Fourth of July was the place to be and to be seen. Young professionals tried to make sure they could align their vacation schedules around that time. Of course, old proper Vineyard families hated that time of year because of all the "infiltrators"—no one could stop talking about that year they advertised the Vineyard to all the GDIs (God Damn Individuals) over the radio. But truth be told, they were thrilled that their kids were home from college, Europe, gap years, et cetera. Dulce's restaurant saw it as a business opportunity and was planning to do a pop-up on the Bluffs on the Fourth. Billie also saw it as an opportunity to introduce the love of her life to the family.

The Monday before the long weekend, Billie asked Ama if she could join her on her morning walk. Before breakfast, Ama walked two miles every morning, setting out on the beach just as the sun lifted over the breaking waves. She always looked super chic, in a fabulous tracksuit and a simple sleeveless tee.

Every morning, as she set off, she murmured to herself

a line from one of her favorite books, *Gift from the Sea*, by Anne Morrow Lindbergh.

It had become a kind of prayer for Ama. The morning walk. The reminder to herself of patience. The acknowledgment that her home and the rich, vibrant life she had lived there, was her ongoing gift from the sea.

She thought about Carter more and more on these walks. How unlikely it had been that they had found each other, in Harlem, a part of town where neither of them lived. But Harlem was like that, it was more than a neighborhood, it was a magnet. And now, once she joined Carter in living abroad, there would be other seas: the house he had in San Sebastián, the trips he took to Brazil and Japan. The whole world was opening to her. A widow at sixty-six, it was the last thing she'd expected. But there it was. Life liked to be surprising.

That morning, Billie joined her on the back porch of the house and the two women walked down to the water's edge together. As the house faded in the distance behind them, Billie blurted out, "I'm seeing someone, her name is Dulce, and I'd love to bring her to the house for the weekend."

Ama had always known and was relieved that Billie finally felt comfortable enough to let her in. "Billie, I've known and loved you since I can remember. Omar, too. I can't wait to meet the woman who has finally stolen your heart. I am delighted to meet her." Billie relaxed her stride, smiled at Ama, and simply said, "Great, I told her all about you." As Ama walked beside Billie she thought, I've known and loved this child since she was a young girl. I will protect her and the person she loves with everything I have.

Ama knew that of all her girls, Billie was the one who most cherished her privacy. It reminded Ama of herself. Years before, Omar had shown Ama a TED Talk that discussed the idea of "extroverted introverts." It had been an illuminating moment. She never understood how she could love to entertain, truly treasure their large circle of friends, and at the very same time, crave, with a hunger that bordered on feral, long swaths of time alone. The talk explained it. There was a term for what she, and she thought Billie, were: *extroverted introverts*.

*

On Tuesday night, Perry arrived with Nikesh by car. It didn't seem necessary to pretend that Nikesh was a friend of Billie's, but she did it anyway. Olivia and Anderson flew to the island and took a taxi from the Vineyard airport. Dulce drove to the house late, after the restaurant closed.

All of the plus-ones slept in guest bedrooms on the first floor of the house. Ama was old-fashioned that way. Only spouses were allowed to sleep in the girls' bedrooms on the second higher floors. And it was rather interesting that the very sexy Dev Patel, young Sanjay Gupta was here. Ama did not quite buy the story Perry told about Nikesh being a friend of Dulce's through his parents' restaurant, but she sensed his presence was trouble.

The next morning Olivia woke early to help Ama in the kitchen. She knew that Ama would be whipping up a feast. She padded downstairs in her pajamas and her sweater-knit slippers with the marabou feather pom-poms. Ama was already in full swing in the kitchen. The hot jazz notes of Sidney Bechet's "Mandy, Make Up Your Mind" floated through the room, mingling with the scent of cinnamon, honey, and maple-cured bacon.

Olivia kissed her godmother on the cheek. Ama was already showered and dressed in a simple black cashmere tunic and sharply creased white capri pants.

"Good morning, *cher*," Ama said, pulling her middle goddaughter into an embrace.

Olivia made them both lattes and asked, "What's on the menu?"

Ama laughed. "The better question might be what's *not* on the menu. I'm making rum-soaked French toast with whipped ricotta and Queen Ama's honey butter for those who like their breakfast sweet. Chive biscuits and a platter of bacon-scrambled eggs for those who prefer savory. There's fresh pineapple and yogurt parfaits already made in the fridge. Champagne for mimosas. Peach mango banana smoothies. I'm forgetting something, I know I am . . ."

Olivia looked over at the stove. "Something in the oven?"

Ama looked relieved. "Yes, thank you. Sour cream and blueberry coffee cake in the oven. I saw the biggest blueberries at Alley's Farm Stand on Vineyard Haven the other day. They looked like marbles. They were that big and juicy. I had to grab 'em."

"Anderson seems nice," Ama ventured. What she liked was how he looked at Olivia and barely noticed Perry was in the room. Until Billie had clued her in about the girls' tuss-up earlier in the summer, Ama had not realized just how often the reverse was true.

She and Omar used to discuss colorism and how it might affect the girls. But they always felt, hoped, that it was a remnant of another era that would come to its own inevitable demise. They thought that, like the whites-only signs of their youth, colorism would eventually disappear from their lives. But Ama realized that thinking had been naive. Segregation didn't just disappear, it was *marched* out of the nation. Colorism wouldn't just disappear either.

"He's not what I expected," Olivia said softly. "But I like him. He's funny. Of course, he's funny, he's a comedian. But he's a good one. Really funny. And he's smart. And we amazingly have a lot in common."

Ama nodded. "The fact is, *cher*, we all have more in common than we differ."

Olivia reached into the cupboard for the mason jar of Ama's homemade granola. It was so sweet, made with Queen Ama's honey, that she and the girls never bothered pouring it into a bowl, they ate it straight from the jar.

"Can I tell you something crazy, Ama?" Olivia asked, leaning on the granite counter.

"Anything, my love," Ama said.

"I met Anderson in front of Le Bernardin. He picked me up and it felt like—"

"Like Omar sent him?" Ama finished her sentence.

Olivia looked surprised. "How did you know?"

Ama wanted to tell Olivia that no one in the world loved her like Omar and that there was a very specific reason why. But she and her late husband had agreed—no playing favorites with the girls. And the time had not come for Ama to tell them all she knew. So she hugged Olivia and said simply, "I believe that Omar is watching out for us. That he's on guardian angel duty for all of us."

By eight thirty, the other members of the house began to trickle in for breakfast. First Perry, followed by a clearly lovesick Nikesh. Then Billie, who held Dulce's hand proudly. Then Anderson, who wore a comically loud Hawaiian shirt, board shorts, and no slippers.

Ama looked at his feet and said, "Oh, did you forget slippers? I can leave you a set by your bed?"

Anderson smiled and said, "I'm good. It's the beach, right? Me go barefoot, mon."

Ama's smile froze and Olivia cringed a little. She'd have to speak to him later. It was a big mistake to confuse the elegance of Oak Bluffs with the "Come, Mr. Tally Man" stereotype of a Jamaican beach vacation. This was not a deserted beach island vibe. This was the Black bourgeoisie in all of its glory. And he was a colonial who had been invited to the island. These natives weren't so interested in repeating history.

They ate out on the back porch, looking out at the ocean, and made plans for the night ahead.

"I can't wait to see the fireworks," Dulce said.

"I love fireworks," Billie agreed.

"I love walking on State Beach at night," Olivia said.

"Is that the one they call the Inkwell?" Anderson asked.

Billie gave him the most subtle side-eye. She hoped Olivia's new guy didn't just have a bad case of jungle fever.

"That's Town Beach," Olivia said, noticing Billie's expression. "I'll give you a tour of the island after breakfast."

Nikesh leaned over to Perry and said, "Look at that view."

Then at the same time, they both said, "Heaven on earth."

They spoke so softly, it seemed no one could hear them. But Ama didn't need to hear what they said to know that her eldest goddaughter was being wooed by a man who was not her husband.

CHAPTER 28

THE FIFTH OF JULY

A few days later, after all the festivities of the Fourth, Perry and Nikesh drove down to Lucy Vincent Beach in Chilmark. It was one of Perry's favorite places on the island. Never crowded, with big, beautiful rock formations that reminded her of Stonehenge.

Nikesh had brought along a proper camera and he snapped pictures of her as they walked along the waterfront. She felt seen through the camera and a little bit protected by the distance the camera put between them. She couldn't seem to separate herself from him on her own.

"Do you remember when we first met?" he asked.

Perry looked up at him. "We met at your parents' restaurant that night I ate alone at the bar."

"Yes," Nikesh said, "but do you remember the day?"

She thought long and hard. It had been about a year before, maybe a little more. Damon was out of town at a conference with his bestie Jeremy (who apparently called her a "bitch wife") and their bitch plastic surgeon friend Sabrina.

She'd heard about the restaurant from a neighbor and

decided to stop by and order takeout on the way home from work.

She was sitting at the bar when Nikesh approached her and said, "Takeout never tastes as good when you get home. You should stay here and eat."

She thought about it. She used to love eating in restaurants alone in Boston, before they met. But that all changed with Damon; when he wasn't in town, she never ate out solo.

"Is someone waiting for you back home?" Nikesh had asked, ignoring the big diamond on her left hand.

When she thought back on it, she remembered that she had been uncharacteristically coy. "No," she said. "My guy is out of town."

She'd said "My guy." Not "my husband."

And maybe it was that small, flirtatious choice of words that had started all of this. If Nikesh kept leaning up against the door of her heart, could it be because she'd made it clear that—despite her marital status—that door was cracked open?

That day, when they first met, he said, "Eat here! I'll sit with you." And they sat together and talked as she ate. That made her feel good. She hadn't realized how lonely she got when Damon went out of town.

She told him that she remembered that day. But he shook his head no.

"You came in once before that," he said. "I was in the back, talking to one of my father's suppliers. My back was turned to the front door. It was a Friday night so we were busy. The door kept opening and closing. But I never turned around. When you grow up in a restaurant, you learn to tune out the distractions. But there was a moment when you walked in and the air in the room seemed to change. You were standing at the front door and you were . . . radiant. It was like there was a giant spotlight on you."

Perry felt dizzy. She sat down on a rock and stared out at the waves. What was she doing? What was happening to her life?

Nikesh continued, "You said a few words to my mother, who was standing at the front. I don't know what you were talking about but you smiled. Then you laughed and I was undone. I always thought that falling for someone was nothing like the movies. The whole 'I will see my true love, across a crowded room' sounded like bullshit to me. But in that moment, watching you laugh, you were the most beautiful woman I'd ever seen. I thought, 'There she is, my wife, the woman I will spend the rest of my life with.'"

Perry felt unhinged. She steadied herself and whispered, "But I'm not your wife."

Nikesh stared at her unflinching. "No, not yet."

The waves kept crashing in and for the first time in forever, the sound and sights of the ocean didn't calm Perry. She felt tangled up, as if caught in a net.

Nikesh said, "There's a Hindi word, you might know it, *kismet,* or as it's known in the West, kismet."

"It means 'fate,'" Perry said.

"Yes," he said. "In English that's true. But in India, the word has many more layers. We have a constellation of words that mean the same thing: luck, fate, fortune, destiny, happiness. Destination. The day I saw you, I felt like you were my destination. It was as if I'd been out in a little boat, in the middle of the ocean, alone my whole life and then you appeared, like the way this island appears as you approach by ferry. It was like you were the thing I'd been steering toward my whole life."

Perry sighed. "Nikesh, this makes no kind of sense. You're young, you're so sweet. The things you say, it's like poetry. You think this is the way you feel now. But believe me, the day in and day out of marriage changes things. It doesn't stay magical. This thing we're feeling, it won't last."

Nikesh smiled.

"What?" Perry said. "I'm turning you down."

"You said 'we,'" Nikesh explained. "You said, 'this thing we're feeling.'"

She flushed. "I did not."

He insisted, "You did."

She waved him away. "Whatever, but the fact is I've been there. I felt all the things you talked about for Damon and things changed."

Nikesh said, "Okay, when did you meet him? What was the date?"

She thought back. "It was the spring semester. Layla and I would have these red beans and rice parties at Harvard. In New Orleans, you have red beans and rice on Mondays. So it was a Monday. I think it was April."

Nikesh asked, "And what was he wearing?"

Perry was confused. "Jeans probably. A polo shirt. Why do you ask?"

Nikesh took out a little Moleskine notebook from his pocket. He opened to a page and showed it to Perry.

October 20, 2017. White turtleneck, khaki trench, a black skirt. Knee-high boots. Legs for days. And that smile. The most beautiful woman in the world just walked into my parents' restaurant and now I know. Fairy tales are real.

November 2, 2017. The goddess has a name. Perry Soto and she's a lawyer. Brains and beauty. She ate at the bar and I offered to keep her company. Married, I think. Said her husband was away on business. I get work. But who would let a woman like this ever ever eat alone?

November 16, 2017. Lightning can strike twice and here's the proof. 14 whole days since I last saw her. But she came back today. She told a funny story about a guy who'd had a heart attack in prison. He'd been legally dead for 60 seconds while the doctor worked to revive him. He was serving a life sentence. He sued the state. He said since he'd been legally dead, he'd fulfilled his punishment. Perry rolled her eyes and said, "I mean, I'm all about prison reform. But that lunatic needs to stay locked up."

Perry flipped through the pages of his notebook. In between checklists of restaurant supplies, reminders to send his mother flowers on her birthday and pick up new menus from the printers, he'd made a note about each and every time they'd met.

She handed the notebook back to him. "I don't know what to do with this."

He looked sad. "Me neither."

They sat in silence for a few moments and she said, "It's not Monday. How about I make you some red beans and rice?"

✳

The house was empty when they returned. Ama was taking a tennis lesson. Perry swore that the woman had more energy than all of them put together. Olivia and Billie had gone up island for a hike. Dulce was at work. Olivia's boyfriend had gone into town to see if he could score a set at one of the bars that sometimes had live comedy performances.

"We're alone," Nikesh said.

"Not for long," Perry said, walking quickly past the staircase that led to the second-floor bedrooms.

She suddenly understood how easy it was to cheat, how tempting the entire situation was. She could lead Nikesh up to the bedroom, undress him, and he would be inside her within seconds. If they were quick, no one need ever know. She could have him, take him, and never tell a soul.

Then she thought about the notebook, all the things he'd written about her. She lusted after him, but he seemed to think he loved her. He was enamored with her in a way that felt big and real, like he said—it was like something out of a movie. If there was a chance that he was right, that she was his destiny, kismet, then she shouldn't throw it all away for a quick romp in the bed. And if she did, she knew it would change something with Damon.

Damn it, she thought, why does life have to be so freaking confusing?

Everything in Ama's kitchen was elegant and French, but her spice rack was pure New Orleans Creole: Crystal hot sauce. Slap Ya Mama Cajun seasoning. All powerful reminders of the land of Ama's youth.

Nikesh turned on music as Perry chopped the andouille sausage into disks. She heated the oil in the Dutch oven until it shimmered from the heat. Then she browned the sausage, adding in onion, bell pepper, and celery along the way.

"It already smells amazing," Nikesh said, pouring them both a glass of rosé.

He got up and stood behind her, holding her waist as she stirred the pot.

"I could hold you like this forever," he whispered. "This could be our life together. Forget Ama's house. If you were my wife, I'd build you a palace with my own two hands."

Perry laughed and said, "Okay, you're nuts." But what she thought was, I don't want a palace. This house is all the palace I'll ever need.

Cassandra Wilson was singing on the Sonos speakers. It was her cover of Sting's "Fragile."

They began to sway to the music. Perry felt safe with Nikesh's arms around her. She couldn't deny it. His embrace felt like home.

She was wearing a pink Rachel Comey sundress with

bracelet-length sleeves and a deep V in the back. Nikesh pulled her closer to him and she could feel his erection. What was she going to do? She turned the stove down to simmer and gave the pot one final stir.

When she put the cooking spoon down, he leaned down and kissed her lightly on the neck.

She shivered.

"Nikesh," she said, "we shouldn't."

"And we won't," he said.

His lips followed the curve of her collarbone, then he ran his fingers along her back as if tracing a destination. Then his lips followed the trail of his fingers and Perry knew that whatever happened next, she wouldn't, couldn't say no.

He turned to kiss her and when their lips met, the desire was hungry and satisfying at the same time. Perry felt weak. Then she thought, If this is it, if this is everything—just this kiss, it'll be enough.

But he had no intention of stopping there. He led her to the window seat in the kitchen and sat her down.

"This is pretty," he said. And pulled her wet panties off her.

He kneeled in front of her and looked her in the eyes. She felt shy then, knowing what he was going to do, wishing they had gone up to the bedroom so she could close the shades and they could do their dirt in the dark. But it was happening here. In Ama's kitchen. The sun bright through the bay windows. The beach just steps away.

"We could get caught," she said.

"A chance I'm willing to take," he said.

And maybe it was the risk that made her pull him toward her.

He said, "Let me make you feel, the way you make me feel."

He pushed her legs apart and in an instant, his mouth was on her most sensitive spot. He teased her with his tongue, gently licking her. He traced the length of her thighs with his mouth then returned to her sex and she moaned. She was going to come so quickly, she thought. Too quickly. She tried to avert it, tried to wriggle her hips away.

"Do you want me to stop?" he asked. He looked at her, and he was so handsome. There was so much adoration in his eyes.

"No," she told him. "Please don't stop."

He continued licking her. She was going to climax. She had been with him and everything had changed.

She grabbed his shoulders and she went to a place she'd never been. She screamed with pleasure, saying his name, again and again. And he didn't stop until she stopped shaking, which seemed to them both, a very long time.

He sat next to her on the window seat and he pulled her head into his chest.

Nikesh said, "Perry, let me love you."

She didn't answer him.

A few minutes later, she heard a car ambling down the gravel driveway. It was Olivia and Billie.

Nikesh rose. "Maybe we should clean up?"

Perry nodded.

He picked up her underwear from the floor and handed them to her. "I think these belong to you."

Then he disappeared down the hall toward the guest bedroom. She turned off the stove and went upstairs to her room, to shower, to think. Was she going to turn her life upside down for Nikesh? Or could she, should she take this pleasure for a while—a summer fling, nothing more—then carry the secret of it to her grave?

CHAPTER 29

BRING HOPE WHEN YOU COME AROUND

They were all having such a good time that Nikesh and Anderson decided to extend their vacations. Nikesh had two weeks' vacation stored up so he would stay until July 18. Anderson joked that as he was "self-employed," he could put both his comedy and his Uber gig on hold to spend more time at Chateau Laveau. They spent the next few weeks in an easy rhythm of morning bike rides and tennis games, afternoon naps and swims, nighttime drinks and card games.

That night, Billie was playing Spades with Anderson and Olivia in the dining room when she got a text from Dulce. It was amazing how Anderson just kinda fit in. He even knew how to play Spades, the quintessential black card game. And he played it well. The man was full of surprises. Although he kept on walking around the house without slippers in a show of his Caucasity. Just soles out everywhere. Everyone kept on staring at his bare feet but he didn't seem to get the hint. Ama even started leaving slippers for him everywhere he walked. Still, bare feet. And now the soles were black. No one dared say anything. Billie's phone vibrated. She looked down and saw a text from Dulce.

Knocking off early. Meet me for dinner.

Billie smiled and responded: **You don't have to ask me twice.**

Then she laid her hand of cards down: "Later, peeps. I'm out."

Olivia looked annoyed. "Way to quit when I'm winning!"

Anderson winked at Billie with his black-bottomed feet on the ottoman. "You got a date, huh?"

Billie smiled and said, "Better than that, I've got a lo-vah." The summer between her senior year of high school and freshman year of college, she, Olivia, and Perry had binge-watched *Sex and the City*. Olivia and Perry had stopped saying *lo-vah* years ago but Billie still used the word with abandon.

Olivia said, "Fine. Please. Go. Call us if you need a ride."

"Thanks, O, I'm good," Billie said. She was still so grateful for Uber. When she was a teenager, she'd gotten into more cars than she cared to admit with a driver who was underage and over-intoxicated. Traditional cabs on the island were not her favorite. Too often, you called for a cab and a van showed up full of prying neighbors who would drop a dime on your indiscretion without even thinking about it. Back when she was single, Ubers were more amenable to the late-night creep, and more than any of the other girls, Billie prized her privacy.

That afternoon Dulce invited her to meet her up island

in Aquinnah. The name of that town always made them laugh. The area used to be called Gay Head because of the colorful stone in the cliffs, but it had within their lifetime been changed back to the original Indigenous name, Aquin-nah. Which was cool, but they still made jokes about the old name. When they rode their bikes up island, Billie joked, "We are entering Gay Head." And Dulce would say, "Damn straight." Which always made them laugh like adolescent boys making fart jokes.

The restaurant was called the Breaking Point. As the name promised, it sat along the cliffs and framed the water through large picture windows. Billie looked around the room, taking in the old school swagger of the place. There were, for example, more utensils on the table than Billie had seen in a long time. Another cue that they were truly in the whitest part of the island. The background music wasn't jazz or low-key R&B the way it was on the Bluffs, it was straight up orchestral vibes: instrumental classical music. It could have been Thomas Wilkins conducting the Hollywood Bowl, but it still sounded mighty white. It was not the kind of restaurant Dulce normally chose for a date.

Billie noticed that Dulce had changed out of the cute but casual T-shirt and pastel-colored overalls she wore when she worked in the kitchen. She looked lovely in a simple maxi dress with a beautiful black-and-white geometric pattern.

"Not really my style," Dulce explained. "My buddy from culinary school just became the executive chef here. It's a cushy-ass job. Can you believe it comes with an on-site cottage with water views? He invited us for dinner."

"How'd you get off from work?" Billie asked. She knew that chefs in resort towns never got the weekends off—much less a busy weekend after the Fourth of July.

Dulce shrugged. "Karma. I've covered for so many people this summer that Max took mercy and gave me the night off."

Max was the executive chef at the restaurant where Dulce worked.

"You look gorgeous," Billie said, wishing she'd upped her game from the yellow cotton jumpsuit and espadrille sandals she'd been wearing all day.

"Don't be self-conscious," Dulce said. "You're the most beautiful woman in this place."

Billie felt shy all of a sudden. Dulce was hot. Like Salma Hayek and Penelope Cruz got together and had a baby that perfectly mixed their DNA.

"I look like I just got off a nanny shift," Billie said self-deprecatingly, pointing to her casual clothes.

"Don't talk yourself down," Dulce said. "I don't like it. Your beauty is undeniable. Own it, okay?"

Robbie, the executive chef, came out then and kissed Dulce on both cheeks. Even though Billie had dated a few guys in her time, seeing a man be that friendly with her girlfriend ruffled her.

Dulce always said that to work in a professional kitchen you had to rely on your intuition. If that was true, then Robbie was intuitive. He picked up on Billie's vibe with the quickness. "Hey, nice to meet you, Billie," he said. "I'm from Harlem, but you know, a little culinary school in Paris, a stage or two in Italy, and all of a sudden, I'm kissing everybody two times, three times, like *mwah-mwah-mwah*."

Dulce looked around and said, "You know, Robbie. This is a nice place. You're a long way from that chicken-and-waffle spot you were working at when we first met."

She turned to Billie and said, "I gave him his tour when he was just a line cook applying for admission at the Culinary Institute of America."

Robbie was the definition of tall, dark, and handsome, think Chidi from *The Good Place* in chef's whites and fluent in French. When Dulce called him out on his uptown fast-casual restaurant roots he gave a belly laugh that filled the whole room. "Now she's going to start spilling tea. The next thing she's going to tell you is pretty embarrassing. So I might as well tell you myself . . ."

Dulce's eyes were dancing, and she showed a side of herself that Billie rarely saw: it was like Dulce had reverted back to her middle school self. She turned to Robbie and gleefully chanted, "Tell it, tell it, tell it."

Robbie looked around like the whole place was bugged and stage-whispered, "Oh, I'll tell it. It is not untrue that I passed out the first time we had to gut a whole fish. That class was a nightmare for me. I still have nightmares about waking up in the bottom of a well that's filled with dead fish eyes."

He shuddered, as if a brutally cold wind had just gusted through the room.

"I covered up your puke and gutted your fish for a whole semester so you didn't get thrown out of the program." Dulce smiled. "Now you're a fancy executive chef. You've got minions who do your dirty work for you."

Robbie scanned the fancy dining room proudly. "I do

have minions now. But I don't forget my friends. You guys have a nice meal. Order whatever you want. It's on me."

He kissed Billie on both cheeks and squeezed Dulce's hand. "Think about my offer," he said.

After he'd returned to the kitchen, Billie wondered what he'd meant.

"Offer?" she asked innocently.

"That joker wants me to come and work here, serving dinner to the *Golden Girls* set."

As Robbie disappeared into the kitchen, Billie thought, This is one of the million reasons why I love Dulce. I found family with Ama and my godsisters. Dulce's kitchens are like found family, too.

"Wow," Billie said, trying to picture Dulce up island. "Would it be better than the job you have now?"

Dulce rubbed her fingers together. "The job pays almost double what I'm making now. *Demasiado* coins. But there are other considerations. For one, the commute. We'd have to stay in Woods Hole for your job and in the winter, this would be a haul. We're closer to Rhode Island than to Woods Hole way out here."

A waiter came and placed two cocktails in front of them. "Mezcal margaritas. The chef says they're your favorite."

"They are, thank you." Dulce smiled.

She turned to Billie and said, "Reason number two: to not work with a friend from school. Robbie knows all of my business: the good, the bad, the cringeworthy."

Billie stared at the menu like it was a Magic 8-Ball. She kept cycling through her instincts:

Signs point to yes.
You may rely on it.
My reply is no.
Reply hazy, try again.

Dulce was talking about a job offer. It would be the perfect moment to tell her that she had recently met up with a friend from school, too: Jaime. And that Jaime had cooked up a job offer for her with Desiree Touissant.

She looked out the window. It was a perfect summer evening on the island. As far as her eyes could see, there were meadows of lavender and fields covered with a riot of wildflowers. Billie and Dulce shared a love of the natural world and often spent time challenging each other's knowledge of the names of local flowers. Butterfly weed and sandplain blue-eyed grass, swamp rose marshmallow, and seabeach knotweed.

Billie's favorite poem in the whole world was Mary Oliver's "The Summer Day." Billie thought of the poem because that was how she felt in that moment, how she felt so often with Dulce—"idle and blessed." She did not know exactly what love was, but she knew that with Dulce, it was what she was feeling all day.

It had been Billie's favorite part of graduate school, what Mary Oliver called "the art of paying attention," of realizing that she could go to school for a hundred years and never be able to name all the living things on God's great green dirt ball.

Then along came Dulce, adding common names of flora and fauna to the genus and species that Billie had in her head. The world literally got bigger every day she spent with Dulce, and if that wasn't a good life, if that wasn't what Omar used to call a "mighty love," then what was it?

Billie knew the moment was right to tell Dulce about the job offer. She should tell her. But they were not even a year into their relationship and they'd never had a fancy night out like this. Even if, best-case scenario, Dulce said, "Screw everything. I'm with you. Houston, here we come"— everything would be different. The evening would be fraught with questions and logistics, planning and weighing of options, not to mention a discussion of the politics involved in the job. Any kind of discussion of politics was bound to be fraught.

It was selfish, and maybe stupid, but Billie wanted the evening to stay simple and glorious. She wanted the sunset and the wildflowers and the big blue of the Vineyard Sound without anything troubling thrown into the oh-so-delicate mix. Her news could wait. She looked at the menu and said, "Did he mean it when he said we could order anything? Because I'm starving."

As the sun set over the sound, Dulce and Billie feasted. They ordered the raw Chilmark oysters, which were perfectly paired with a mignonette sauce and a lime granita. They were delicious. Then Robbie sent out as a "chef's treat" the grilled Katama Bay oysters with kimchi butter and crispy garlic.

Every dish was an artful blend of textures and flavors. Japanese mushrooms sautéed in brown butter with black

and white sesame seeds; fried brussels sprouts served with
a salty pistachio butter and a sweet local honey. The scallop
crudo was topped with a dollop of wasabi and served on a
bed of crispy quinoa, and the prawn ceviche was paired with
a rich jalapeño crema.

Billie could picture Dulce adding her own touch to each
of these dishes. She loved how serious and laser-focused
Dulce got as the waiter brought each course to the table.
She didn't just pick up her fork and have at the small Le
Creuset of chorizo and clams steaming in a peppery tomato
broth or the bacalao, crisp to the touch, served with a piri-
piri sauce. Dulce took the whole dish in with each of her
senses. She touched the plate to see if it had been heated
to a sufficient temperature and she tapped the fish ever so
lightly. She closed her eyes and inhaled deeply.

Ama always returned from trips abroad with catalogs
from the museums she had visited, Billie had watched Ama
study paintings from the Mori Art Museum in Tokyo and
the Louvre in Paris. Dulce studied each course, examining
the mix of colors and shapes before her, in the same en-
raptured way.

It was only when Dulce had taken in the dish as completely as she could manage, that she would raise her fork
and ingest the first bite. Billie had not known when she first
met Dulce that chefs were scientists, but she knew it now.

By the time the waiter brought the menu of sweets, they
were stuffed. They ordered just one dessert to share, a banana cake with a white coffee ice cream and two crisp glasses
of ice wine.

But Robbie sent out every dessert on the menu—so

many that the waiter had to pull over the table next to them. Their favorite was not a traditional dessert at all. It was a whole roasted pineapple served with a little bowl of peppery spices, jasmine cream, and cilantro granita. It was so good that as they devoured it, fork after fork, eye contact never wavering; they felt like there was no one else in the room. And maybe, just maybe, they had—while eating this perfectly ripe tropical fruit, enhanced by a five-star array of flavors and enhancements—let out the slightest of moans.

It was at that moment when they were making subtle sexual sounds over the dessert that Robbie came to the table and observed them with amusement. He said, "Ladies, ladies. If it's that good, may I suggest you get a room."

Billie had observed that there was an inn attached to the restaurant. She very much wanted to get a room with her lo-vah.

Dulce put both hands together and did a very subtle yoga bow toward Robbie. "You done good, kid. This meal was . . . extraordinary."

Robbie beamed and said to Billie, "You know that's a lot coming from your girl. She's a hard one to impress."

Billie looked lovingly at her girlfriend, knowing he wasn't just talking about food. He was talking about everything in Dulce's life. She was demanding, but she didn't expect more of others than she did of herself. Her levels had levels.

Billie smiled and said, "So true. Excuse me a sec. Just running to the ladies' room."

When she returned, Robbie was gone and Dulce looked . . . furious.

"What happened?" Billie asked, genuinely concerned.

"You're moving to Houston? With some guy named Jaime?" Dulce asked, her voice tinged with venom. "What? Do you have some kind of Latin fetish?"

Dulce chucked the phone at Billie and Billie caught it, just in time.

She looked at her phone. There was a text from Jaime. Mi amor, it said, followed by an emoji with heart eyes, you're not from Texas but Texas wants you anyway. Let me know when you've broken the news at work and we can start apartment hunting.

Then, as if Jaime had a diabolical plan to ruin her life, he'd added, Love you. We're going to change the world together. Bye.

Billie didn't know how to explain that the message had been misconstrued without explaining all the things she'd been hiding and the weeks she'd been hiding them.

Dulce looked so angry and Billie knew this was her girl-friend's defense mechanism. Dulce didn't cry. Typically, she took out her chef's knives and started butchering dead animals, vigilante style, with a fury that suggested the ill-fated cows, pigs, and fish on the butcher block were hapless assassins who had been foolish enough to come after Dulce and everyone she loved. Now her voice was measured and laced with disgust.

"Guess what?" Dulce said. The words came out hard, like rocks.

"We didn't just end up at this restaurant," Dulce explained. "Robbie's trying to recruit me, yes, but I set up this dinner for a very specific reason."

Billie knew better than to speak. She sat quietly. Whatever Dulce said next, she deserved it.

Then it happened, Dulce looked as if she was about to cry. She said, "I asked you here tonight to propose. I was going to ask you to marry me."

She flashed a little velvet box that she'd had hidden in her bag. Dulce pocketed the ring and said, "The bill's taken care of. I left a good tip. You should grab an Uber home."

Then she walked out. Billie couldn't move. Dulce was about to propose. She hadn't seen that coming. But instantly her mind flashed to Damon and Perry's wedding. They'd gotten married on the Bluffs, in Ama's backyard. The waves crashed against the shore as they said their vows. Billie had never pictured that kind of wedding for herself. Maybe because she was the youngest. Maybe because she'd seen herself as an athlete and a scientist, not as a "here comes the bride."

But when she closed her eyes, she could see herself and Dulce standing on the beach behind Ama's house, both of them wearing the most beautiful white dresses. She could see them sharing their vows and she could imagine the dinner under a big tent with all the food cooked by Dulce's posse of chef friends. She could see them dancing to their first song. Maybe "Thinkin Bout You" by Frank Ocean or Corinne Bailey Rae singing her version of "Is This Love?"

Olivia and Billie assumed Perry was going to get the house. She was the married one. She was the one who looked like she could have been Ama's granddaughter. She was the most like Ama in her style and tastes.

But thinking about Dulce and the life they were building together, Billie thought, Why not me? Why couldn't I be the one to inherit the house? She was, after all, the only one to build a life on the island. The other girls were summer visitors. She and Dulce loved the island. It was home.

She pictured coming home from work and walking into that house instead of the cottage in Woods Hole. She pictured Dulce cooking in Ama's straight out of *Architectural Digest* kitchen. She pictured the dinner parties they would host, the fundraisers they could throw for the causes they believed in. And for the first time she pictured having children with Dulce. How amazing would it be to raise a couple of kids on the island? They could take them to Boston and New York to go to museums and plays, but their kids could grow up in this wild and natural place, not taking subways and taxis the way she had as a kid. Their kids could grow up swimming and biking, visiting lighthouses and sailing.

If they built a life together on the island—with or without Ama's house—Billie thought maybe she could convince her father to come and visit during the summers. Her dear sweet dad, the middle-aged comic book nerd who managed a shop full of graphic novels and action figures. He still got dressed up and put months of effort into his Comic-Con costumes. He always said, "That fancy Vineyard life isn't for me." But maybe if she had a baby he would come. Maybe he would meet a nice forty-something lady on the Vineyard, a woman who loved comics as much as he did. He'd been alone all of his life. She had found love, now she wanted him to find love, too.

But had she found love or had she just lost it? Still unable to move, she signaled the waiter and asked for a gin and tonic. How could she fix it? It was just one text. One little lie of omission. Surely this wasn't the end for her and Dulce.

When the waiter returned, he put a gin and tonic in front of her. Then next to the cocktail, he put the small, baby-blue, velvet box.

"The madam says this belongs to you," he said, then he walked away with what Billie thought was a sad, wry smile.

Billie opened the box. Inside there was a ring set with a single opal and flanked with two small shining diamonds. Billie took the ring out and put it on her finger. She liked the way it looked. But even more she liked the way it felt. It felt like hope. She finished her drink and went to find Dulce.

CHAPTER 30

HOW DO YOU SLEEP?

After a late breakfast, Nikesh was helping Perry wash the dishes. She rinsed and he loaded the dishwasher. Nikesh was streaming an R&B mix on the speakers. He started singing along and Perry hummed in harmony.

"You're full of surprises," Nikesh said approvingly.

"What do you mean?" Perry asked innocently. Part of her couldn't believe that Nikesh had made it so that she couldn't even look in a certain direction of Ama's kitchen without feeling like a complete and total slut.

"I would've never taken you for an Allen Stone fan," Nikesh said playfully. "John Legend seems way more your speed."

Speaking of that sexy man, Perry had noticed that Nikesh looked awfully good that day. The plan was that he was going to play tennis with Ama before lunch. Perry thought he was looking movie-star fine in his tennis whites.

"Are you kidding me about Allen Stone? I've been down with that Seattle blue-eyed soul man for a mighty long time. 'Unaware' is my jam," Perry said. "Omar was the biggest music fan. He was always sending us links to new stuff he'd found."

Ama stepped into the kitchen and said, "Some men take up golf when they retire. Not my husband. He quit golf and became the family DJ."

Ama looked twenty years younger than the years she proudly claimed. She was dressed in a bright orange shirt and a matching orange and white tennis skirt.

"Yaaaaas, Ama, you look good," Perry said.

Ama looked down at her gams with pride. "The legs are the last to go."

Perry wanted to age like that. She wanted to build her life exactly as Ama had. But Ama was perfect or as damn close to it as a woman could get. Perry was far from perfect. No matter how well she tried to keep everything in her life in line, things kept getting messy. This thing with Nikesh and her crumbling marriage to Damon was the biggest tangle of drama she'd ever experienced. It was her deepest fear that the moment Ama found out just how screwed up she was, Ama would stop loving her.

The older woman reached into the fridge and grabbed a bottle of water, and then she went out to the porch to finish the morning paper.

As Ama sat, gazing out at the sea, she thought about the scene she'd observed in the kitchen. Why did her god-daughters ever think they were pulling anything over on her? Nina Simone had spent a drunken night singing at the piano in the living room, just steps away from where Perry now stood, washing dishes and making googly eyes at a man who wasn't her husband. Why did these children—and yes,

they could vote and drink but to Ama they were children—
think they could get away with anything? In a house that
had hosted Miles Davis, Ossie Davis and Ruby Dee, Roscoe
Lee Browne, Alvin Ailey, Diahann Carroll, and Josephine
Premice—could these children actually think they could
keep secrets from the grown folks?

Ama thought of Nina's trademark song, "I Put a Spell on
You." It had been a particular favorite of hers, having grown
up in New Orleans, the land of voodoo and gris-gris. It was
clear that Nikesh had put a spell on Perry. Maybe it was the
other way around, Ama wasn't sure. What she was confident of was that between the two of them there was some
powerful juju afoot.

Perry was married. She and Omar had clenched hands as
they watched Perry, looking like an angel in a cream-colored
Amsale gown, jump the broom with Damon.

Later, Damon strolled around the dance floor with Jeremy and his frat brothers from Kappa Alpha Psi and Perry
had spent a goodly amount of the reception with her pinkie
up with Layla and her sorors from Alpha Kappa Alpha. Then
much of the time was spent with Perry doing her demure
"I'm not sweating this blowout for nobody" dance with
Olivia and Billie. Observing the happy couple separate in a
classic display of parallel play, Omar had said, "Does it seem
like there are two different parties going on here?"

But Ama had been . . . unconcerned. Yes, it was true,
Damon and Perry had different energies. But so did Ama
and Omar. Damon was air and fire, Perry was earth and sea.
But fire needs water, like the earth needs all the nourish-
ment it gets from the sky—sun and rain and wind.

Ama had thought she was right about Perry and Damon. What if it turned out she'd been really wrong? Damn Omar for leaving her to figure this out on her own. Because the one thing Ama had learned in what was becoming a long life was when she trusted her instincts, she was rarely wrong. That was a blessing. But when Ama did make an error and ignored the evidence in front of her the results weren't just erroneous, they were catastrophic. Ama's mistakes, as rare as they were, tended to be epic and costly. That was the curse. She was sitting on her porch, looking out at the sea, and thinking on that wedding and the clues she might have missed when the doorbell rang.

The sound startled her because people rarely rang the bell in the Vineyard. Neighbors and delivery people did a hearty New England knock then turned the knob and stepped in while calling out a friendly "Anybody home?" Like most of the longtime Vineyard residents Ama kept her door unlocked when she was in town.

If the doorbell surprised Ama, it downright spooked Perry. She had been fantasizing about playing naked beach blanket Twister with Nikesh when the doorbell rang. The sound was so unusual, so unexpected, Perry knew that it must have been God sending a warning that she should take her mind out of the gutter.

They all moved to answer the door—Perry, Ama, and Billie, who had been reading a book in the living room.

Standing at the door, ringing the bell like a stranger, was Damon dressed in a simple polo shirt and khakis. He was also carrying what appeared to be an overnight bag.

"Yo, it's the whole welcome wagon," he said with a smile.

Ama thought, Speak of the devil and in he walks.

Ama glanced at Perry. Her goddaughter didn't look happy to see her husband. And if there was one thing Ama knew: Perry was a very good lawyer and a terrible liar.

They stood there, awkwardly, in the foyer for what felt—at least to Perry and to Ama—like an eternity. Perry squeezed Billie's hand in what felt to the younger sister like a death grip.

Nikesh walked into the entry foyer and looked Damon up and down, with the arrogance of a man who'd been intimate with his opponent's woman—which, fair enough, he had. Damon just kept staring at Perry as if she were a pitcher of ice-cold water and he'd just spent the last twenty-four hours slogging through the Sahara.

Ama stood at the doorway, just taking it in. Young people and all their foolishness, she thought. You spend a quarter of your life or more looking for love. Then you spend the next twenty-five years figuring out how to love. Then you spend the remaining decades knowing just how little time you have left to love. It was, she believed, a terrible equation. She wanted her girls to do better, fall in love younger and faster with more confidence and more time left to love and less time spent muddling through it. But you couldn't rush the math of humanity. No matter how hard you tried.

When it became clear that no one wanted to be the first one to make a move, Ama swooped in to save the day.

"Damon!" she said, with an enthusiasm she didn't fully feel. "Come give me a hug. It has been an age. How are you doing, *cher*?"

The expression was a relic of her New Orleans days, one

that she rarely used. It was a rich spice—like saffron or truffles—that she saved for the most necessary occasions.

Perry audibly exhaled and glanced nervously at Nikesh.

Nikesh looked like he was ready to fight Damon. Everything about his stance said a few slugs and this might decide the whole thing in minutes. Why did men break down to the most basic of instincts? Ama thought. She knew not all men were like that. But it seemed to her more rather than fewer succumbed to these coarse tendencies. She wished Omar was there to help her balance the storm that was brewing inside the precious teacup that was, for the time being, still her house.

Who's this dude? is what Damon was clearly thinking as he finally realized there was a stranger in the midst.

Reading his mind, they were still—for the time being—married, Perry said, "Damon meet Nikesh. He's a friend of Billie's."

It was a lie so lacking in muscle that it had barely made it onto the ferry. Yet here she was, trotting it out. Why? She didn't know.

The two men shook hands and their glances were so frosty that Ama could only thank God that the days of duels were over.

Perry was wearing a coral Ulla Johnson blouse with a ruffle sleeve. Even without a smidge of makeup she was beautiful. If only the young knew what to do with all that beauty, Ama thought, seeing herself in Perry for not the first time. Helen of Troy, Ama thought. A face that could launch a thousand ships.

"You look familiar, man," Damon said. "Do you live in the city?"

Nikesh loathed Damon on sight.

"Yeah," Nikesh said, answering Damon's question about whether they had crossed paths. "My parents own an Indian restaurant. It's been written up on Eater a couple of times. Maybe you've eaten there."

It was at that moment when Damon could have pieced it all together—that his wife was a big fan of Indian food, so much so that she ordered it every time he went out of town. He could have considered that he came home from work trips to find the fridge stocked with takeout containers of raita, tandoori chicken, and spinach vindaloo. But the truth was, the clues were lost to him. He didn't inspect the fridge when he came home from work trips. He didn't think about what Perry ate when he traveled. And he would never imagine that Perry would betray him.

If Damon was 100 percent honest, he didn't think about Perry a lot when he traveled. He was always front row at the TED Talk–style seminars, which were all the rage at medical conferences these days. He attended them because one of his biggest dreams was to give a TED Talk and see his thirteen minutes of genius on display. But Perry didn't know that. Perry never asked him questions about his work. She seemed to think that the big job after medical school was the endgame for him, like her job at the firm had been the endgame for her.

Lately, he'd been thinking about everything differently. They could trot along the Ama and Omar path later when they had kids. If they had kids. He always thought Ama and Omar had gotten that part exactly right. Make bank. Travel the world. Then in your forties, even fifties, be the fairy godparents to some needy kids. But Perry had disagreed with him. Every time he brought up the idea that their infertility wasn't necessarily a bad thing, she'd fight him like he was a mugger in an alley trying to snatch her purse. "I'm adopted," she'd say. "I want blood relatives. I want and need a family of my own."

After three years, Damon knew what family meant to Perry. She was the girl who never wanted to go looking for her birth parents because she loved her Bible-thumping Black and Latino bougie-aspiring parents from the Bronx so damn much. Perry was the same girl who loved Ama and Omar as if they were her birth parents. She called Olivia and Billie her godsisters, but the love-hate relationship with those two seemed as true to sibling life as any sisters Damon had ever known. Perry kept talking about family as if now the only relatives that mattered were the ones she knitted up in her womb with her own DNA. But the part that really hurt was that after all this time and as far as he could tell, he did not fit any definition of family to his wife. This was his greatest fear. He worried that nobody but Perry's biological children could fill the giant hole in her heart.

Ama stood up. "Nikesh, we should get going. I'm not in the mood for fighting one of those Edgartown biddies. Those women will squat on the court they know they didn't reserve like they're Columbus knocking Indigenous people off of Plymouth Rock. And I, for one, am not here for it."

Nikesh waved to Perry. Damon didn't notice.

Standing in the living room with Billie, Perry, and Damon, Billie felt the desperate need to get out of what was surely going to be a war zone. She grabbed her purse and Ama's car keys. "I'm going into town to meet up with some friends."

Within minutes, Damon and Perry were alone in the house. There had been a time early in their marriage that an empty house was all they needed to fall into each other's arms. Perry thought that seemed like a lifetime ago.

"Would you like a glass of tea?" she asked, knowing that there wasn't a man alive who would say no to Ama's sweet tea. Perry also knew that the secret was that Ama steeped the tea in an infusion of pureed peaches that were flown directly to Ama's house from a farm in Georgia and then she sweetened it with honey from her own beehives.

She poured them each a glass of Ama's secret recipe sweet tea. They stood at the kitchen island, sipping their drinks silently. Words had never been so hard to come to before.

"I wasn't expecting to see you," she offered. Then, lest he think she was being churlish, she added, "It's a nice surprise."

He looked around. "Ama's house is so beautiful. As many times as I've been here, it always feels like a movie set." Then in a soft, kind tone he added, "I hope you get the house, Perry. Nobody but Ama loves the house as much as you do."

She noted that he hadn't said, "I hope *we* get this house." She knew that while Damon had enjoyed his summers on the Bluffs, he had the unique ability to have fun wherever he went. He carried the party with him and it was, it seemed to her, all the same: the Vineyard, Vegas, Aspen, Maui, Cabo. Damon could have a good time—a great time—wherever he went.

The way Perry felt about the Vineyard was different. She hadn't been born here, but she knew she wanted to grow old on this island. She couldn't really explain it or understand it but this was her place. She wanted her ashes scattered here the same way they'd scattered Omar's the year after his death. She wanted her children to know the carousel and the gingerbread houses. She wanted to watch her kids jump off the famed Jaws Bridge and throw them clambakes on the beach. She wanted to give to another generation what Ama and Omar had so generously gifted her. It was all she wanted. The Bluffs were the truest home she'd ever known. That Damon didn't love it and didn't get why it meant the world to her needled her to no end.

Damon may not have understood Perry's affinity for the island, but he was her husband. He could tell when she wasn't happy.

He looked at his watch. "Look, it's almost eleven. Let's go for a drive."

He had rented a car in Boston, a little two-seater convertible.

For reasons she couldn't explain, just the sight of the car annoyed her. Only Damon would rent a two-seater, as if to gloss over the fact that she couldn't have a baby. As if a sporty coupe would make up for the fact that the car she wanted to be driving was a family-sized SUV.

Doctor car, Perry thought, as she climbed into the passenger seat. All of Damon's friends drove sports cars with vanity plates. One of Damon's friends was an orthopedic surgeon from Spain; he drove a Fiat Spider with plates that read HUESOS. The dentist that Damon golfed with drove an Audi R8 with a plate that read SAY-AHH. The nurses weren't immune, they came to Perry and Damon's holiday parties in sporty little cars with plates like INTUB8U. Damon's own car had a license plate that read LUBDUB, which was apparently the sound the valves of the human heart made.

"Lub dub! It's like the first thing you learn in medical school," he had said, cracking up. Oblivious to the fact she never thought it was that funny.

She got in the car and couldn't help but think how out of place she felt sitting by Damon's side. She felt like a character in a sci-fi novel who had stepped into a parallel world where the man she had married, the one she had promised to love and cherish in sickness and health till death do they part, felt like a total stranger.

Damon drove to Giordano's without asking. The first time they'd come to the island together they'd gone to Giordano's and picked up fried clam platters and a six-pack of beer from Jim's Package Store. Then they'd driven to Sengekontacket Pond where they'd made a picnic and proceeded to make out until their food got cold.

Perry mused, Score one for nostalgia. She always thought fondly of that day.

When they'd picked up lunch and a couple of beers, Damon parked the car and took a blanket from the trunk. The gesture touched her. He'd not only flown up to see her but he'd gotten a blanket—it was new, she didn't recognize it—somewhere along the way. He'd come up with the intention of winning her back, of reminding her how good things had once been between them.

She kissed him on the cheek and said, "I'm glad you're here." She hoped that her heart might follow her words down to a path where she actually meant the things she was saying. Because in that moment with every third or fourth breath she took, she was thinking about Nikesh. It wasn't fair how much space this new thing—could she call it a romance?—took up in her brain.

For maybe the first time Perry understood how challenging fidelity truly was. The old relationship was a soundtrack that was wired to your mainframe. You didn't really hear it, the same way you didn't really hear the lights flick on in your home or the fridge hum or the stove turn on. All the sounds were just there until they weren't. They were only noticeable in their absence.

New love, new lust, whatever you want to call it, was different. The sound of a fresh infatuation was a marching band. It was a football field full of HBCU steppers stomping it out at homecoming. From Howard to Coachella that sound and those steppers made a booming beat that was almost impossible to ignore. She did not know enough about Nikesh to promise him anything—but the pounding in her heart was a determined and unrelenting yes.

With that yes, she understood why the phrase "fool for love" had so much currency. New love, new lust, whatever you call it, wasn't bigger or better—it just had such a loud ring that it was nearly impossible to ignore. Never mind that there was no promise that the new love wouldn't fall into the old traps. You couldn't know. The decision it seemed to Perry was this simple and this opaque: leap and move forward with Nikesh or stay put and hope that the love with Damon was, like Ashford & Simpson, "Solid as a Rock."

Perry and Damon laid out the blanket. They laid out their platters of fried clams, with fries that were just okay, and a surprisingly good coleslaw that was crisp and fresh.

Damon longingly looked at Perry. No matter what went down it was clear he'd never forgotten why he'd fallen in love with her. He never doubted that marrying her was the best decision of his adult life. She was beautiful and smart, complicated and strong. He knew with a certainty that calmed him that she was the definition of a ride-or-die chick. In bad times and hard times she was the kind of woman you wanted by your side. What he hadn't expected was that the hard times would come so soon, that the bad times would sneak up on them when they were both young and healthy, with good careers and high incomes.

"I'll start," he said. "We've got a lot to talk about. But the reason I came here is to ask you face-to-face: Do you want me to come home?"

Perry chewed her food deliberately, hopeful that it would give her the pause she needed to gather her thoughts. She hadn't really known where this conversation with Damon would begin. She'd hoped it would start with Sabrina's baby shower or Jeremy and his trifling friends from medical school. For her that was steadier ground. Possibly he could have apologized.

She ate one french fry, then another, then another. The fries were already cold, totally not worth it. In the city, she would've asked them to hold the fries.

Damon was asking her if she wanted him to come home. The words came out before she could stop them: "Uh, I want a lot of things, including a child. We don't always get what we want, Damon."

Damon took a breath and tried to cakewalk around the baby issue.

"I know, sweetheart," he said. "But how are we ever going to make a human life together when we're living apart? This is starting to feel less about punishing me and more like something you want."

Perry looked away.

It had been easier to take when he was just words on the other end of a heated text exchange. But it was harder to evade Damon in person. Which was of course why he'd come to the Vineyard.

Since she couldn't lie to his face she opted for a half-truth: "I don't know what I want."

He looked crushed, defeated almost. He did not expect that answer. That was something they never told you when you got married, how much power comes with all of that love. Perry understood then how divorce blew through a life with so much wreckage and destruction. All of those months turned into years of loving Damon had been her own little enemy bootcamp. By acquainting herself so intimately with his heart she'd also been training—inadvertently—in the most precise ways to pummel it. She had two hands inside his chest now, she could feel it. Their marriage was lying on the table with a pulse that was barely detectable. She had a choice: she could either grab the paddles and try to revive their union back to life or she could turn the machine off and call time of death. It was a lot of power. Too much power. She wasn't ready for either step.

Damon's mood veered like the Vineyard weather from overcast to stormy, from vulnerable to angry.

"That's all you've got?" he asked. "You don't know what you want? You don't know if you love me? If you want to keep wearing your wedding band? What you're saying, just so we're clear: you don't know if you want to stay married."

Perry sighed. "You said it yourself. We've got a lot of things to talk about. Stay for the rest of the weekend. Let's talk."

Damon shook his head now. "I'm not going to hang out at Ama's house like it's all good. I'm not going to stick around if I don't know that we're back together and determined to fix this, come hell or high water."

It was the choice of words that threw her. If Damon didn't know about Nikesh, and by all indications he didn't, what exactly did he mean when he said, "come hell or high water"? What was the "hell" he was referring to? It couldn't have just been her anger and indecision. What was the "high water" that was barreling toward her marriage? She was fully aware of her own indiscretion, but when exactly had the levee in their marriage broken?

She steadied her voice the way she did when she cross-examined a witness, and she asked him the question that had been eating at her since the day she told him to move out. "Damon, did you sleep with Sabrina?"

His answer was the wrong answer. Mostly because it was a question. He didn't say no. What he said was, "That weekend in the Caribbean?"

He took in the stricken expression on Perry's face and tried to brush past it. He said, "The Sabrina thing. Why do you always go there? She isn't important to me anymore."

"'Anymore'?" Perry screamed. "What in the hell does that mean?"

"Okay, Perry. Sabrina isn't important to me, but I should have been honest with you a long time ago. Sabrina was my girlfriend in medical school before you. I thought I was in love with her. But the fact of the matter was it was infatuation. It wasn't real. Sabrina knew it and Jeremy knew it, too. He proved it to me by sleeping with her one night while I was studying for a final. I came back to the room and they were in bed naked together. I will never forget the knowing look in her eyes. It's as if she knew me better than I knew myself. She later said she wasn't good enough for me. But at the time, I was devastated. Until I realized I had taken what was a friendship with benefits too far in my head. We have all remained friends. At the conference, we all got too drunk and I saw men taking advantage of a situation. I took her out of that situation and carried Sabrina back to her room. She grabbed me, kissed me, and said maybe she had made a mistake about us. I pushed her away. She apologized to me the next day. I've never told you any of this because one, I'm embarrassed by my immaturity; two, I figured you would never understand; three, you would think I was a freak; and finally, I didn't want to lose my friends and my ability to go to medical conferences. And that's the truth."

Perry couldn't speak and felt chills wave over her body. She just stood up and quietly packed up the food containers. She folded the brand-new picnic blanket. All the while she thought, Fuck him. Fuck him. Fuck him for trying to gaslight me into thinking I was the cold one, the crazy one, the jealous-with-no-reason one.

"Drive me home, Damon," she said evenly, suddenly glad that they didn't have a child together and she didn't have a lifetime of negotiating with him over matters big and small. She wished it hadn't happened on the island. Up until that moment her memories of the island had been pristine.

This was no longer true of the Vineyard. Her bargain with disaster had happened right here on a pond she hoped to visit as long as she had breath, on an island that she hoped to call home for all of her days. She had crossed over now. This was no longer just the place of fairy-tale dreams and summer memories viewed through a blindfold of gauze that rendered all that was even slightly imperfect into something romantic and magnificent.

She was no longer just a tourist in this town. She was a part of this place and it was a part of her. She had the broken heart to prove it.

They drove in silence. The island looked different to her now. Perry's love for Damon felt broken and with every mile the pieces were hardening. When they pulled up to the house, he said, "Call me when you want to talk. I want to talk about this."

She fixed him with a steely glare. "Oh, I'm done talking," she said. "And screw you for making me feel like I was the one who broke us. You did this. *You* had that *fucking bitch* in my wedding. A groomslady!" She slammed the car door and Damon sat there for what felt like an eternity before he pulled out slowly.

Then she went inside and let out a wail that made the whole house shake. For fuck's sake, Ama, she wondered, could the house be hers now? She'd been married here. And now it seemed like her marriage was ending here. How else could she prove to Ama that this was her home, the only home she ever truly wanted? Since the house was empty—no one came running when she screamed—it felt so good to really let it out; she screamed again.

In high school, she'd read a play called *The Madwoman of Chaillot*. She hadn't understood it then but now she did. Insanity wasn't always a by-product of genetics or the inability to stand mentally strong against the injustices of the world. Rather, it seemed to Perry that madness sometimes lay in the divide between what the world tells you is real and what you sense in your heart to be real. When you slip between those two things and can no longer tell one from another, that was madness.

As she went from room to room letting out soul-curdling screams, there was another insight. There was more *mad* in madness than she had been led to believe. Meaning she was less crazy and more filled with a blood-boiling rage than anything else. She had asked him about Sabrina a dozen times if not more:

Had it been her imagination or did Sabrina seem to be flirting with Damon at their wedding?

Did it seem like Sabrina texted Damon an awful lot?

Was Sabrina always tagging him in photos where she was half dressed?

How had it been that Sabrina's baby shower was on the

day of one of Perry's appointments with the infertility doctor, an appointment she'd been forced to go to alone?

When she sat still, stopped screaming, and really thought about it there had already been so much loneliness in their short marriage. All the mornings she ran in Central Park alone because he had an early call at the hospital. All the evenings he had gone out with his friends to let off steam when she'd come home too tired to do anything more entertaining than take off her bra and high heels, order in food, and watch TV. She'd felt so bad so many of those nights. She was supposed to be the interesting one, the fun one, the creative one—she hadn't banked on being the exhausted one.

Now here she was adding crazy to tired. Nikesh would leave the next day. That was a good thing. She would have to find a way to explain to him that he was right, there was a real chemistry between them, but she was too broken to act upon it. He had such an idealized vision of her but she wasn't the enchanting woman he thought she was. She looked in the mirror and felt for the first time that in her heart there was something dark and twisted. She didn't know what lay ahead of her but she was confident the road would be rough long before it was smooth again.

She had screamed until her voice felt scratchy and not like her own. Her screams had downgraded to sobs until finally through a veil of tears she made her way upstairs to her bedroom. It was a big house, and as an only child she usually relished how the house teemed with life every summer. But she felt so grateful to be, at least for a few moments, all alone.

She opened the window so she could hear the sound of

the sea. Ama liked to remind them that the greatest gift of seaside living was perspective: the ocean had been there before they were born and would be there long after any of them had drawn their last breath. Perry always took comfort in that. This day was no different. Even in her grief she appreciated the luxury of the house and the haven it provided from the life she had been born into, the life she might still be living if not for Ama and Omar. As she drifted to sleep drained by the sheer output of emotion, the house felt almost like a third parent. The very bones of it seemed to be rocking her to sleep.

CHAPTER 31

OMAR'S STORY

The next day, after Nikesh and Anderson left the island, Perry and Billie went off to queue in the breakfast line at the Artcliff Diner in Vineyard Haven. Ama invited Olivia to join her at the back porch for a chat.

Ama had never told Billie about meeting Carter Morris in Central Park on a night when *the* Bob Marley was playing. But she sometimes played his music on summer afternoons when she needed to be reminded not to worry, that every little thing was going to be alright. This was one of those times. She put Marley on the Sonos and let the music transport her to a more peaceful place.

Olivia thought she was finally going to get the talking-to that she had coming. She'd brought a white boy to the house and Anderson had had a bumpy ride the whole time. She thought he was hilarious, but his "white guys drive like this" humor and no-wearing-slipper self didn't elicit a whole lot of laughs or endearment on the Bluffs. Sure, Layla had been a regular visitor over the years, but Olivia was pretty sure that if Layla ever took a DNA test she would discover there was definitely a little coffee in all that milk. Layla was different. Anderson was white-white. Olivia liked him, but she wasn't sure if she liked him enough to bring him back to Ama's. And he certainly wasn't going to help her case in trying to get the house. Ama and Omar had been Mr. and Mrs. Black Love. They were Ossie Davis and Ruby Dee. The original Michelle and Barack. Olivia remembered how they talked so fondly about their old building on 110th and Cathedral, how much it had meant for them to be in a community of creative, successful Black couples. Ida Walker and Jane Abbott still came for the last week of the summer, and it was like watching Coretta Scott King, Maya Angelou, and Toni Morrison hold court in heaven, the way those three older women carried on, hooting and hollering, slapping cards on the table and sipping glasses of Chateau Ste. Michelle. Olivia used to think that she, Perry, and Billie would be like that when they were older. But these days, she wasn't so sure.

Ama didn't want to talk about Olivia and Anderson, not specifically. She wanted to tell her a story about her beloved husband, gone four years from the world now, Omar.

"I want to tell you a story about Omar, and I think you'll understand by the end why I think it's time I share the truth."

Olivia didn't know what to think. Perhaps Omar's path hadn't been so squeaky clean. Maybe he'd gotten involved with some insider trading in the eighties, maybe even spent a couple of months in prison for white-collar crimes. That was the era when he'd made his big money. A lot of shady shit was going down on Wall Street in those days.

But she was, again, wrong on all counts.

As Ama explained, there had been more guilt and heart-break in Omar's past than Olivia or the other girls ever knew.

Omar's Truth

It was the early nineties, and Omar Tanner had been at Cra-vath, Swaine & Moore for almost twenty years. He'd made partner, married the love of his life. They'd built their dream home in Oak Bluffs and thrived within their community—both uptown in their Central Park building and on the is-land, during the summers.

Chip Brock had started at the firm the year after Omar and even after all the time in which they'd worked closely together, the two men had never bonded. Chip was the son of an old railroad family. He'd inherited the kind of wealth that meant he never had to work a day in his life. Which translated into a very loose work ethic. Chip lived in a downtown loft with wife number two, a supermodel who was pregnant with his first kid. He was a regular fixture on Page Six and often chaired galas, none of which he ever invited Omar and Ama to, although more than once, Omar had said, "Hey man, would love to support whatever chari-ties you're getting behind."

Chip always brushed him off with a "Thanks, pal. I know I can count on you."

But the invitation to join him at this or that elite social gathering never came.

Ama could never understand why Omar cared. "Give me our side's elite over those downtown jokers any day of the week," she would say.

But for Omar, it was more than a divide, it was a personal affront. No matter how successful he'd been, he and Ama were millionaires many times over at this point, they didn't see him as good enough. There was still a segment of society that would see him as other and unworthy. He didn't want to want Chip's approval, to be part of his circle. But every time he saw his colleague's photo in the newspaper or in the pages of *Town & Country*, he bristled. "Why not us? Why not me?"

In the fall of 1993, Cravath, Swaine & Moore was hired to represent the police officers union, whose pension fund had been raided. They were accusing their former finance director of embezzlement and falsifying trades to the tune of $38 million. The name of the whistleblower was being kept under wraps. So much so that Jonathan Moore, the head of the firm, kept all the documents off premises in a locker at the Yale Club.

One afternoon, Moore invited Omar to meet him at the Yale Club for drinks and a cigar. Moore was a good guy, Omar thought, and the two men met for drinks every six months or so. Their relationship was more than cordial. There was a mutual respect.

That afternoon at six, Omar entered the Yale Club and found Moore sitting in a high-backed leather chair, smoking a cigar and drinking an old-fashioned. Moore, his hair white and his figure trim in what was certainly a custommade suit, gestured for Omar to sit down. "Quitting time, my friend," he said.

Omar ordered a martini from a man who could have been his brother, they looked so much alike. The Yale Club was filled with Black men who reminded Omar of family—porters and servers, doormen and bartenders. Omar, who had grown up in a house with a single mother and a sister, always longed for the company of other Black men. It was what made the summers on the Bluffs such a gift for him.

Jonathan Moore said, "You know that union fraud case we're working on?"

Omar nodded yes. It wasn't just a high-profile case for the firm. The nature of policemen being robbed of their pensions meant that it was in the paper almost every day.

Jonathan said, "I'd like you to depose the witness."

Omar knew, in that instant, that the whistleblower was Black.

"Happy to do it," Omar said.

"We suspect that someone at the firm is colluding with the opposition," Jonathan said. "I'm trying to keep this under wraps the best I can. I'd like you to meet the witness at another location. I have a buddy at BNP Paribas, Jules D'Amboise—met him during my study abroad in France a million years ago. I trust him with my life. Their offices are at 787 Seventh Avenue. No one will know you there. I'll set it up."

A few days later, Omar took the elevator up to the thirtieth floor. Jules D'Amboise was like a French version of

Jonathan Moore, the same build, the same easy smile, the same expensively cut style of suit.

"This is quite the case," Jules said. "Your guest is already here. I have you in the small conference room."

Omar walked into the room and Chris Jones stood up. He was dressed in civilian clothes and he looked like Denzel Washington, the young Black man who was taking Hollywood by storm.

"How are you doing, sir?" Chris said, reaching his hand out to shake Omar's.

The "sir" always threw Omar. He knew that he was in his fifties, but in his mind, he still thought of himself as that young brother, new to the game.

Chris was dressed in civilian clothes but everything about his posture said military: his stance, his close haircut, the careful cadence of his words.

"Were you military before joining the NYPD?" Omar asked as he opened up his briefcase and took out his tape recorder and notepad.

"Yes sir. US Army Special Forces. Spent time in Afghanistan and Panama. My CO tried to get me to join the CIA. But I said, 'No sir, that cloak-and-dagger isn't for me.' And yet, look at me, now. A whistleblower."

The two men looked at each other. They stood at the window. They were high enough that they could see all the way out to the Hudson River.

"Thank you for your service," Omar said, gesturing for Chris Jones to sit down.

"Hey, before we begin," Chris said, "you got kids, man?"

Omar shook his head no. He and Ama had waited so long.

Then it seemed like they'd waited too long. Omar said, "No kids. Just this beautiful, brilliant wife."

He opened his wallet and took out a photo of Ama. The photo was crinkled around the edges and part of the color rubbed away from her red sweater. He had taken it out of his wallet so many times. He'd heard that some Catholics carried images of saints in their wallets. He didn't need a saint, God had gifted him the finest woman he'd ever known.

Chris Jones let out a low whistle. "She's a beauty, sir."

Then he said, "Permission to show you a picture of my baby daughter, sir?"

Omar almost laughed. "Permission granted, young man. By all means."

Chris took out a photo, taken, it seemed, in a department store photo studio. Olivia was a year old in the picture, eighteen months tops. Her hair was pulled into a tight ballerina bun on her head and she wore a pale pink sweater. Gold dot earrings shone in her ears. She was more than smiling, she was laughing. Whoever the photographer was, they had snapped the photo at exactly the right time.

"She's my whole world," Chris Jones said, putting the photo to the side. "I told my wife, Cindy, that I want to have four more just like her. I'm fixin' to make myself the first female basketball team to take over the NBA. I'm going to have five baby girls and they are going to take the world over."

Omar laughed. He liked this young man. Maybe, he thought, when this whole trial was over, he would invite Chris Jones and his family up to the Vineyard.

"Ever been up to Martha's Vineyard?" Omar asked.

"No sir, but I heard that they have a whole community of Black people living the good life up there."

"They do," Omar said. "Someday you'll have to come visit."

"Me and my whole female basketball team?"

Omar said, "Yes. The whole team will be welcome."

Omar looked at his watch. It was time to get to work. There were so many documents to go over.

Four hours later they were done. Chris Jones shook Omar's hand again and the two men exchanged phone numbers. Chris took Omar's card. Chris didn't have a card so he wrote down his name and his home address on one of Omar's legal pads.

As Omar began putting the papers he'd strewn across the conference room table away, he found the picture Chris had left of his baby daughter. He put it in his briefcase to return at their next meeting.

It wasn't a week later, when Chip Brock invited Omar to join him that weekend for a golfing trip. "Hey, bud," Chip said, hovering at the door to Omar's office. "I know this is short notice. But a few buddies of mine are flying down to Hilton Head on Saturday for a day on the links. We're going to take a jet down from Teterboro early Saturday morning, golf all day Saturday, go out for steaks, home on Sunday. You in?"

It was short notice. But Omar had waited a long time for a social invitation from Chip Brock, so he said yes. All around it was a good time and Omar finally felt seen.

That Saturday night at dinner, Chip said, "Hey, Jonathan

wants me to get involved in the police pension fund. The whistleblower's a young cop, right? I forget his name."

The words came out of Omar's mouth before he knew it: "Chris Jones. Great kid. Just had a baby girl."

It was a moment he would play back over and over again for the rest of his life.

That week, Chris Jones was fatally shot while leaving a bodega in Harlem. The police claimed he was caught in the middle of a drug deal gone bad, but Omar knew that this was far from the truth. He spoke to Jonathan Moore but it was impossible to tie the Jones murder to Chip Brock. Over the years Omar pieced it together. The banker who orchestrated the raid on the police pension fund had been an old boarding school buddy of Brock's. The two men had remained close friends, and did a considerable amount of coke together in the eighties. Eventually it was the drugs that became Brock's downfall. He was in and out of rehab so much in the years that followed, the firm was forced eventually to let him go. Brock lost everything. It wasn't enough of a payback as far as Omar was concerned, but at least he never had to see Brock's face again. The man disgusted him.

Omar carried Olivia's photo in his briefcase for weeks after Chris's murder before he told Ama the whole story. They knew they wanted to help Cindy Jones, now a widow, and her young child, but they didn't know how. They were able to dummy up a fake police pension fund in Chris Jones's name and put enough money in it that Cindy could move to the suburbs, but not so much that she would get suspicious.

When they learned that she was looking for homes in Montclair, they arranged for her to be shown a beautiful house then made a deal with the seller to slash the price, paying the difference without her knowing it.

None of it was enough to assuage the guilt that Omar carried with him. He thought of Chris Jones every day for the rest of his life. He would close his eyes and hear him say, "You've got kids, man?"

Omar kept Olivia's photo in his wallet next to Ama's, determined to find a way to do what her father had always hoped to do—give this girl the world.

When Ama brought Perry to the Vineyard that summer, it occurred to him that maybe he could have a more direct relationship with Olivia than the money he funneled in small amounts into her father's insurance policy and the college fund he had set aside for her on the day of Chris Jones's funeral. Maybe he could get to know the girl. Maybe he and Ama could be a real force in her life.

He was nervous the day he drove to Montclair to introduce himself to Cindy Jones. He had called her on the phone and asked if he could come by. He explained that he'd been in the military—which was a lie—and that he'd been stationed in Panama with Chris Jones—also a lie. But while Cindy Jones had sounded cold, she didn't sound suspicious.

All around the Joneses' living room there were photos of Chris. Omar could feel his voice catch as he took in how young the man had been when he had lost his life.

Cindy Jones caught the emotion welling up in Omar and softened. "I miss him so much," she said. "It's going to be ten years next week and it feels like yesterday. I keep expecting him to walk through that door and say, 'Where's my two beautiful girls?'"

She served Omar a cup of coffee in a mug that said PROUD ARMY WIFE and he said, "I remember he used to say he was going to have five daughters . . ."

"A basketball team!" Her eyes flashed and he sensed she hadn't smiled like that in a very long time. "When I tell you that man was a fool, I mean it. I wasn't going to have five babies so he could have a basketball team. For one, who was going to pay for it?"

Omar shook his head. "If anyone could have figured out a way, it was Chris."

Cindy shook her head, softly. "You're right. He had a 401(k) fund that I didn't even know about. That man must have eaten dollar slices and drunk Kool-Aid every day of the year to have squirreled away that much money. But that was Chris. He was a provider."

Omar was relieved she wasn't suspicious about the money, that she never asked how it could be that her investments were getting 20 and 30 percent returns.

He explained that he and his wife had never had any children, but they had a goddaughter, Perry, close to Olivia's age. They wanted to invite Olivia to visit them in Martha's Vineyard. Cindy, of course, was welcome to join them.

He gave Cindy his business card, a profile of him and Ama that ran in the *Vineyard Gazette*, urged her to call around and ask if she had any questions. But she said, "I'll keep the article and the card. But I trust you. Chris's friends were always good as gold. They come around every year on Father's Day to take Olivia to Great Adventure. You can take her for a week and if she doesn't like it, she'll let me know. She's not shy."

And that's how it began.

*

Ama put her tea down and put her arms around Olivia, who sat there sobbing. "He loved you all, but Olivia, you were the light of his life. He kept this picture in his wallet, until the day he died. He had copies made, just in case he ever lost it, but he never did. This is the original, the one your father left behind in the conference room that day."

All she felt was anger. Olivia could feel it coursing through her veins like a drug. How could this be?

Ama said, "There's something else, too. He left the house to me, but Omar left his entire estate to you, Olivia. He wanted you to have everything and never ever want for anything."

Money? Was Ama really talking about money?

Olivia sneered. "I don't want his money. That's blood money, Ama."

"Olivia—" Ama began.

But Olivia wasn't done speaking. She continued, "Not that you're offering it, but I don't want this house either. I can't even sleep here another night knowing that for all of these years, you and Omar brought me here every summer, pretended to love me, all the while keeping the truth about my father from me."

Ama sighed. "You have a right to be angry, Olivia."

Olivia looked out at the water and the crushed-shell walkway to the beach lined with hydrangeas. This view always calmed her but now she felt nothing but fury. It was like she was caught in a bad dream. She always thought this was the most beautiful place in the world, but it was a facade; underneath there was more ugliness than she could ever imagine.

"Why didn't he tell me himself?" she asked.

Ama said, "The idea was that he'd tell you himself when you were older. But he died sooner than any of us expected."

Olivia said, "I'm glad. He's a murderer. He killed my father. I'm glad he's dead."

Ama flinched. She knew that while Olivia presented herself as a woman, she was a child—a devastated, wounded child. It was Ama's job to be the grown woman in this scenario, to stand and take all of Olivia's outrage and asperity. But in that moment, Ama felt her heart cleave in two. One part of her could take it—stand strong as her heartbroken daughter pummeled her with her words. But the other part of her was a widow, still missing the love of her life. It hurt her to hear Olivia call Omar a murderer. It devastated her to hear Olivia say, "I'm glad he's dead."

Ama knew Olivia so well, had lived with the secret so long, that she had expected these very words. She thought she had prepared herself for them. But as she sat, willing her hands to stop shaking, she found herself reaching for a prayer she hadn't said in a long, long time, Father, take this cup from me . . .

But Omar was gone. He had wanted to do this. He had been ready to stand like a sentry and take it, the bluster and squall of Olivia's anger. But Omar was gone. There was no one else who could possibly take this cup. Olivia glared out at the ocean and Ama crossed herself and thought, Your will, not mine, Lord. Your will.

Ama stood up and went to the kitchen, returning with a pitcher of sweet tea. She poured them both a glass, used the sip she took to gather her thoughts. "You are entitled to your anger, Olivia. You lost your father. Murdered. You should remember that your mother believes he was killed, nobly, in the line of duty. So you might want to consider if and when you want to share our version of events with her."

Olivia thought of her mother, Mrs. Cindy Jones. For most of Olivia's life, her mother had felt like more of a distant nanny figure than a loving parent. Cindy had cared for Olivia—combed her hair, made her meals, sorted her schooling, washed her clothes—as if it had been her job. It felt to Olivia that when her father died, he took all the love out of the house with him.

All the sweetness in Olivia's childhood had come from outside of her immediate family. There were the men in her father's precinct. Those men had been there before the Tanners and they were there still. Every Father's Day, they left their own children and families to see her. When she was in elementary school, it was the annual trip to Six Flags Great Adventure amusement park in New Jersey.

Every birthday, the men sent her a card with a crisp one-hundred-dollar bill in it and they never delegated the task. Somehow, they always managed to get together and sign the card. There were always three distinct signatures: Roberto, Joey, and Jeremiah.

She had always thought of Omar as part of that constellation of stand-in father figures. It was Omar who taught

them to swim in open water at the Inkwell and who docu-
mented their annual jump off Jaws Bridge at the end of the
summer. Ama was always too nervous to watch.

"The day some kid hurts his spine jumping off of that
bridge is the day you will all stop," she'd say, with a shudder.

But Omar always said, "Fortune favors the brave, Ama.
We raised our girls to be brave. To be queen bees." Our girls.
Olivia now shuddered at the memory. How dare he.

Those memories, once her most prized possession, tasted
bitter and rancid now to Olivia. How many times had Omar
called Perry, Olivia, and Billie "our girls"? How many times
had he referred to her as his "special girl," all the while
knowing that if he had managed to keep the secret he'd been
trusted to bear, her father would be alive. If her father had
lived, her life would have been entirely different. Not lavish
like the way Omar and Ama had made it—using money to
paper over Omar's fatal error. But happier. If her father had
lived, Olivia felt sure her life would've been happier.

She told Ama, "I'm going to pack my things. I'll stay in
town tonight and take the first flight out in the morning."

Ama put an envelope on the table. Olivia glanced at it
and recognized it right away, Omar's careful script. Over
the years her heart always raced whenever she opened her
mailbox and saw his handwriting. Even though he used
email proficiently, once every couple of months, Omar wrote
each of the girls a letter. On general principle, he only used
stamps of African American luminaries: Edna Lewis, Miles
Davis, Jackie Robinson, Maya Angelou, Romare Bearden.
"I'm the last friend the US Post Office has," he would say
with a laugh.

For the first time in her life, Olivia ignored a letter from this man who she had loved like a father. She didn't give a damn what Omar Tanner had to say to her. Let him keep his confessions from the grave.

"Do Perry and Billie know?" she asked Ama plaintively. Wondering just how much of a fool she had been.

Ama shook her head no. "Nobody knows," she said. "Just you, me, and Omar."

Olivia stood up. "I'll go now."

Ama said, "Take the letter, Olivia. Please."

Olivia stared icily at Ama. She realized it was the first time she had even had the inclination to look at this woman she had adored with anything but love. Even in their teen years, when the other girls would act up and act out, Olivia remained honey-sweet. She admired Ama so much that she couldn't imagine ever being fresh or impatient with her. She gathered her courage and said coolly, "I don't want the letter, Ama."

They stood that way for a moment, in silence. Ama facing the sea, Olivia facing off against her, loaded for bear.

Ama spoke evenly, but her eyes were wet with tears. It was a rare show of vulnerability. She was from a different generation. Those women and men who were old enough to have gone to segregated schools, who remembered the tragedies of Birmingham, the lynchings, the dogs, the firehoses that were turned on peaceful protests, were not easily rattled. Ama had been born into Jim Crow and had lived to see a Black man become president. It had taken a lot of fortitude to make that long walk to freedom and possibility, to see a dream deferred become a dream realized. But this moment with Olivia looked as if it had just about broken her.

She wiped the tears away and turned to face her goddaughter. Her voice held a steeliness that was more Ama than the softness in her face. "Let me tell you something, little girl. Your father's death almost killed my husband. There were days and months when everything seemed fine, then Omar would fall into a depression so dark I feared I'd come home and find him dead—with a bullet in his head. Then you came into our lives. He went and brought you into our lives and the depression never returned, not to the same bottomless depths."

Ama stood and reached for Olivia's hand but Olivia refused her and Ama leaned against the porch railing instead. She said, "Olivia Jones, you were his reason for living in the last twenty years of his life. Not me. You, child. You. He dedicated himself to filling your father's shoes. He knew he was no substitute. I believe that if he'd had the ability to go back and lay down his life for Chris Jones's, he would have done it—a hundred times over. But that was not an option. In the wake of offering his life, he offered his love to you. You think you're angry? You have no idea how angry he was at himself. It terrified me the way he would beat the walls and how much I feared living in a high-rise. I was so afraid that he would throw himself out the window and onto the sidewalk to punish himself for his mistake. His anger at himself was soul-crippling. Because I've seen it, because I've lived with it, I hope you find a way to dial back your rage, Olivia. Not for me. Not for Omar. And not because you aren't entitled to it. But only because in the long term, that is no way to live."

Ama stepped toward Olivia once more. The instinct to hug her was so subconscious, it was like breathing. But then she thought better of it and said, simply, "I love you, Olivia. We loved you the best way we knew how."

Then the older woman turned and went into the house.

Sitting on the porch alone, Olivia felt as if the story Ama had told her had hit her like an electric shock treatment, forever altering the neural pathways of her brain. She felt her knees go weak as if someone—Ama, Omar, the both of them—had taken a bat to her legs with the express purpose of crippling her. She would leave the house as soon as she could. She had to. After brunch, Billie and Perry were planning to go to Newport for the day. She wanted to be gone before they returned.

She steadied herself on the table and looked at Omar's letter. She thought then of the year she'd turned ten. She had been in the fifth grade and a proud member of her Montclair Girl Scout troop. When spring came, she and her mother learned that the troop had an annual father-daughter dance. She hadn't planned on going. The decision hadn't felt particularly sad, but rather more matter of fact. Her father had died when she was a baby. She didn't need to go to that dance.

But then Ama had shown up at her door. Ama was holding a dress—it was apple red and with a heart cutout in the back. She also had a pair of brand-new black Mary Janes with a kitten heel in Olivia's size. Olivia's mother had let loose a deep sigh when she saw the dress and shoes. "It's . . . so . . . beautiful," she said. Cindy Jones had nodded yes when Ama had asked if she could take Olivia to the local blow-dry bar to get her hair done.

Two hours later, Omar had shown up with a corsage and a limousine to squire her away to the dance, Prince Charming style.

Her mother had looked so happy when Olivia emerged from her room, wearing the tea-length dress and her hair pinned in a simple but elegant half-up, half-down style.

"You look so beautiful," she said, her voice cracking with emotion. "You look just like your father."

It was Omar who had held her mother when she began to cry softly. "We all miss him," he said.

Olivia knew that Omar had known her father, but as a child, she'd never pressed for any further details.

In the limo, Omar had said, "You know, girls who look like their fathers are lucky."

It was as if he knew that Olivia's resemblance to her father was yet another barrier between her and her mother.

When they arrived at the dance, Olivia had reached for the car door handle, but Omar had admonished her to sit still. "No, you don't," he said. "You let the man open the door for you. That's chivalry."

In the time it took for him to exit the car and walk around to Olivia's side and open the door, word had spread all over the Wally Choice Community Center that Olivia Jones, and her dad, had arrived at the dance in a limo.

She hadn't bothered to correct any of the girls that night.

For as long as she attended school in Montclair, people believed that Omar, slightly older, always dapper, was her father.

Although he often took a backseat to Ama in social situations, he was, unsurprisingly, an excellent dancer. He twirled Olivia around the dance floor and she felt, for maybe the first time in her life, that she was the envy of every girl in the room.

The truth was she couldn't remember her father. Every memory she had of a man playing the father role was of Omar. She realized then that her fury was less about her father's murder and more about how much it hurt her to know that Omar had played a part in his death.

She thought, I have to hate Omar. What kind of person goes on loving the man responsible for her father's death?

She wished in that instant that she'd never been handed this unwieldy, unbearable truth.

And somewhere deep down, the truth that felt most clear was she'd loved Omar and he'd loved her back and this was a tragedy of heartbreaking proportions.

Olivia picked up Omar's letter and went into the house to pack.

CHAPTER 32

THE SECRET ABOUT PERRY

Perry spoke to Nikesh on the phone. He called in the morning to wish her a good day. He texted throughout the day and then they settled in for a long chat every night. Perry thought it was like having a boyfriend in high school: easy breezy.

It was early August when Layla came and joined Perry and Ama on the Bluffs. As was their custom, Perry sat with Layla near Donovan's Reef. It was sunset, the best time of day on the Bluffs, and although it was a little early, but five P.M. somewhere, they were both sipping happily on one of Donovan's famous painkiller cocktails. They found perfect seats to perch and be seen. Donovan's was a small cocktails-only stand where the line of locals and visitors stretched and snaked past Nancy's Restaurant and takeout counter, where Sasha Obama had worked the counter under the watchful eye of several Secret Service agents way down the dock. The line was always long because Donovan refused to hire any help. Every drink was made by the master mixologist himself. If you took a survey, each patron would proclaim it was worth the wait. On any given day, you could hear reggae music flowing through the speakers and see Donovan serving up his masterpiece cocktails, from painkillers to dirty bananas. Some days Valerie Jarrett would be sitting on a bench eating with friends. The entire setting was a scene. Dark blue waters crowded with yachts was the view. Laughter and old money in white jeans weaved in and out of the seats. This was casual on a whole other level. The girls were dressed up for a night on the town: Perry was wearing a strapless embossed bandeau dress and a pair of strappy sandals. Layla wore a neon sleeveless shell and a brightly patterned skirt. They took a selfie, for the 'gram, then got down to business.

"You know I used to have this theory," Perry said, sipping her drink.

Layla looked amused. "Which one? That you're secretly Beyoncé's half sister?"

Perry shook her head. "Not that one."

Layla said, "Oh, right, the one where Ama is secretly your mother, not your godmother."

Perry pointed to her nose and said, "Ding, ding, ding. I'm so sick of not knowing," she said. "I've just got to ask her."

Her friend was far from convinced, "Think about it, P. Ama's working that good Black/Gucci cute thing, but she's old. She's almost eighty. How could she be your mom?"

"She's sixty-six." Perry sighed. She loved her girl, but math wasn't her strong suit.

"Still. That's kind of old to be your biological mother."

Perry disagreed. "She would've had me at thirty-eight."

Layla drained her drink and signaled for another. "Like *that* was going to happen."

"Iman had a baby with David Bowie when she was forty-five."

Layla waved her away. "Are you kidding me? Don't talk to me about Iman. She's got that hundred-percent-African, lost-tribe-of-Wakanda blood. She's got that bionic woman uterus. Ama's too light for all that."

Perry sighed. How was it she had to take light-skinned disses from everybody? Even her white friends couldn't stop with the colorism noise.

"What about Janet Jackson?" Perry offered. "She had a baby at *fifty*."

Layla clapped her hands as if explaining something to a toddler: "*Janet.*" Clap. "*Jackson.*" Clap. "*That's some pop star poonanny, okay?*" Clap. "*That. Ain't. Ama.*" Clap.

"Look, say what you want," Perry said. "But if I've learned anything this summer is that I've got to trust myself. I'm going to ask her."

Layla looked serious. "Go with your heart, P."

"But I'm scared," Perry admitted. "I need you to be there when I ask her."

"Oh, no, that's not happening," Layla said. "I can't. That Creole woman frightens me. When she gets mad, she's got that Yoncé in the Yoruba yellow dress and swinging a baseball bat vibe."

Perry cut her eyes at her friend. She and Layla had been friends since the third grade, almost twenty years. What part of being a *ride-or-die chick* did Layla not understand?

"Ama is not going to swing a bat at me for asking an honest question."

Layla sucked her teeth. "Says you."

"Look, she knows something. I think she knows *every-thing*. It's time for me to put on my big-girl panties and find out what she knows. Are you rolling with me or not?"

Layla reached out and squeezed her friend's shoulder. "Fine. You know I got you, girl."

✳

Early the next morning, Perry got up and made a sausage-and-vegetable frittata. Chopping the vegetables calmed her. And when Ama rose and walked into the kitchen, she gave her eldest goddaughter an approving smile. "That looks de-licious. Thank you for cooking, *cher*."

Over breakfast, Perry asked Ama if she wanted to join them for lunch at the beach. Olivia had been called back to the city on account of work and Billie was spending the week with Dulce's family.

"Oooh, that sounds nice," Ama said. "State Beach?"

Perry said no. Ama was practically the mayor of Oak Bluffs; everywhere they went, she ran into someone she knew.

Perry said, "I was thinking we could go up island for a change."

Ama studied her goddaughter's face carefully. Some-thing was up. She guessed it was the house. More than any of the girls, Perry loved their summer home. At times, Ama thought it was because she was the oldest. That first sum-mer, it had just been Perry, Ama, and Omar: Neither Ama nor Omar had much experience with kids. So they over-did it that year. They hired Serena Parker, the daughter of

Bert Parker, the senator from Los Angeles, to be the girl's babysitter. They arranged for tea parties with other girls on the island and planned playdates for every day of the week. Together, they traipsed around the island like tourists. They took a boat tour to Newport, visited the petting zoo at the alpaca farm, and went go-cart racing.

It wasn't until the last dinner on the island, at the end of the summer, that Ama and Omar realized just how much they'd packed in. They had reservations at Atria in Edgartown. Ama had dressed Perry in a beautiful lemon-colored Ralph Lauren sundress. She'd brushed the little girl's hair and flipped the ends with a hot curler. Omar wore a sharp blue and white seersucker suit. Ama had joined the board of Burberry that year and one of the happy bonuses of that engagement was that the line's young creative director, Christopher Bailey, regularly sent her special items from each season's collection. An olive-colored dress with cap sleeves in the iconic tan plaid print was one of Ama's favorites. She'd been saving it for their last dinner on the island for the season. She and Omar had not expected how besotted they'd become with the little girl and both viewed the dinner at Atria as a celebration.

"So how did you like your summer?" Omar asked, once they'd ordered.

The girl, who had just turned ten on August fifteenth, grinned. "Oh my God, I loved it. I cannot thank you enough, Mr. Tanner. I'm very grateful for the opportunity. But . . ."

Ama's stomach did a flip. What was the *but*? What had they done wrong?

Omar placed a reassuring hand on his wife's hand. "Finish your thought, dear," he said. "You can tell us anything."

"Oh," Perry continued. "I was just going to say that I've had *so* much fun but I'm *so* tired. I think I'll sleep the whole car ride home tomorrow."

Omar and Ama looked at each other and laughed. It was then that they realized that the puffiness under the girl's eyes, which they had noticed and dismissed as seasonal allergies, was actually dark circles. The girl had bags under her eyes like she'd just pulled an all-nighter. She was exhausted.

Ama thought of that moment as she studied Perry's face. The deftly applied concealer on Perry's beautiful face couldn't hide the fact that her eldest hadn't been sleeping well. Ama hoped that Perry wouldn't make a rash decision about her marriage in the hopes of putting the matter to bed. Sometimes it took time, months, even years, to truly work your way out of a rough patch.

"Okay if we leave at twelve thirty?" Ama asked.

"That's perfect," Perry said.

❋

Every morning at eleven A.M., Ama had a call with Carter. He was spending the month of August at the house in San Sebastián. He had offered to come to the Vineyard, but she couldn't imagine it. Having Carter in the house she'd shared with Omar seemed like a bridge too far. This place would always be her and Omar's. If she was going to step into this new chapter, she needed to step out of this house, close the door, and not return for a good long while. She needed to let one of her girls take over and make the house theirs.

She stepped onto the porch off her master bedroom. There

were two lounge chairs facing the ocean. Sometimes out of the corner of her eye, she could swear she saw Omar sitting there in his navy-blue robe and tortoiseshell Wayfarers, just staring out at the sea.

She put her feet up and took a long sip of her coffee. In their youth, Carter was perpetually and chronically late. She'd learned that if they were going to a gallery opening or concert, it would only make her blood pressure soar if she waited for him outside. She needed to go in, get herself a glass of wine, and find a comfortable perch for people watching. Fifteen or twenty minutes after their scheduled meeting time, Carter would come crashing into the room. His hair would be a mess of curls that clearly he'd combed through with his fingers on the subway. He'd cover her face with kisses and say, "I'm sorry, so sorry. No one should keep a woman like you waiting."

Salt-and-Pepper Carter—which is what she called this older version of her young love—was different. When he said he would call at eleven, the phone never rang later than 11:02. It was nice to see the small and thoughtful ways in which he'd changed.

She glanced at her watch. It was ten fifty-five. She had a few minutes to gather herself. She hadn't told Carter about any of the secrets she needed to reveal to the girls that summer. Like the house on the Vineyard, the secrets were the provenance of her marriage. It was hard to do this telling alone. Olivia's fury had not been unexpected, but still, it was so brutal to take. As she looked out at the pounding waves, she had faith that even if the girls needed to pull away for a bit, they would find their way back to her. She was their shore and their sure thing. She had faith that this family she and Omar had built wasn't a house built on sand.

At eleven on the dot, the phone rang. Ama allowed herself to sink into the buttery softness of Carter's voice. "Good morning, beautiful," he purred into the phone. "How are you on this fine day?"

✳

Perry pulled her car into the parking lot of Our Market. She took a basket out of the trunk of her car, remembering the days when every shop on the island gave out plastic bags like the free mints at restaurant hostess stands. But the Vineyard had gotten the memo of how bad plastic was for the environment and the oceans early. Now every summer, Perry packed the trunk of her car with a canvas bag for farmers market trips and two picnic baskets, each with its own set of reusable silverware, cups, and cloth napkins.

In the store, she picked up a bottle of Whispering Angel Rosé, Billecart-Salmon Brut Rosé Champagne (just in case there was good news to celebrate), an assortment of soft cheeses, fresh fruit, and bread. The lobster they would get in Menemsha at Larsen's or the Menemsha Fish Market, depending on the day's catch. They could sit outside and watch the fishing boats while they ate, which Perry always loved to do. The picnic goodies sorted, she swung back by the house to pick up Ama and Layla, and drove out to Menemsha.

After picking up their cooked lobsters, they walked along the beach in silence to find the perfect picnic place, taking in the simplicity of the pebbled sand and gray-blue water. It was hard to believe how much of the Vineyard still seemed so wild and unsettled. Once you drove away from the down island towns, there was so much rawness and space and unadulterated beauty.

Perry had packed her favorite picnic blanket—an embroidered image of a Mickalene Thomas painting that she'd won in a silent auction at one of Ama's Studio Museum fundraisers.

She laid out the lobster, cheese, fruit, and bread on a tray and filled each of their glasses with rosé. Even midday, the sun was rarely punishing on the Vineyard. It was just another perfect summer day.

After Ama had taken a few sips of wine, she said, "I know you asked me here because you've got something on your mind. I know how much you love the house and I don't want you to stress. None of my girls will go empty-handed."

Perry glanced at Layla, who gave her friend a look that Ama couldn't read.

Perry put her glass down. "Ama, I didn't bring you here to ask about the house."

She choked on her words, then her eyes filled with tears. Her shoulders shook as she cried, and Ama, not expecting such an outburst, rushed to comfort her. Ama held her girl the way she had a thousand times before and held on to her until she heard Perry's breath even out.

Perry wiped her eyes and the two women sat, side by side, on the blanket, facing the ocean.

"Ama," Perry whispered, "are you my biological mother?"

She knew it was strange to do this in front of Layla, but she couldn't be alone when she asked the question that had haunted her entire life. Layla was her best friend. She needed her. And Ama recognized in Layla the type of friend she, too, at one time had.

It wasn't the question Ama had been expecting. Layla looked at the two women in profile. None of the girls resembled Ama the way Perry did. They had the same creamy shade of skin, their hair had the same S wave. Their noses sloped in the same way and their almond-shaped eyes were fringed with the same dark, thick lashes.

Layla polished off her glass, unsure of what Ama would say and feeling less brave about sitting here during this serious conversation.

Ama sighed and said a silent prayer: Omar, if your spirit wanders these shores, be with me now. Help me not to mess this one up.

The look on Perry's face was a jagged collage of hope, heartache, and longing.

Ama said, "Perry, I wish you were my biological daughter."

Perry gasped in disappointment and began to cry again. Ama reached out for her but Perry pulled away, embarrassed. She had been so sure. *Sooo* sure.

She braced herself for what would come next. Was her mother a drug addict or a prostitute or both? How much sadness, violence, and darkness was knotted up in her DNA? She'd never wanted to know. That's why she never went looking for her birth parents. But here she was. She couldn't put the genie back into the bottle now.

Layla moved closer to Perry and whispered, "I got you, sis."

Ama stood up and walked to the water's edge. She let the

waves wash over her hands, Pontius Pilate style. The time had come.

She turned and walked back to the two girls, took a seat facing them on the blanket. She said, "You know, the minute you said Menemsha, I should have known. I was sitting right over there, on this beach, at sunset, when your mother told me she was pregnant with you."

CHAPTER 33

LIBBY'S STORY

It wasn't what Perry expected. Ama had known her mother? Perry's eyes widened. "Ama, who was she?"

One of the things Ama had her assistant do as she prepared to give the house to one of her girls was to scan her favorite pictures into an album that she kept on her phone.

She took her phone out then and pulled up the picture of her and Libby Brooks in front of Libby's red convertible. The two girls in their brightly colored Lilly Pulitzer sheaths, Ama looking like a sepia-colored version of her friend. "Her name was Libby Brooks," Ama said. "She was my first friend in New York City and a true friend and eventually my best friend."

Perry shook a little and said, "She *was*."

Ama nodded. "She died just months after you were born. She left you a letter. She left you a lot of letters. But the most important one is in the safe at the house. I think we should go and get it."

Layla sat in the backseat of the car with Perry, who was motionless with shock as Ama drove back home. When they pulled up to the house, Ama said, "What I'd like to do is go inside and get the letter. Then I'd like to drive you someplace that was special to Libby for you to read it."

Perry nodded and whispered, "Okay, Ama."

It seemed strange to Layla that nobody was throwing fists, real or metaphorical. Why wasn't Perry angrier? How could Ama keep a secret like this for so long? Perry was always the one who said she didn't want to know anything about her birth parents. But Layla always suspected some dirt under Ama and Omar's squeaky clean veneer. Who swoops up to the Bronx and starts fairy godmothering some random kid without there being some backstory?

Ama returned to the car and handed a large cobalt blue envelope to Perry. The stationery looked expensive and the envelope felt heavy in Perry's hand. The handwriting on the outside was so carefully rendered, it looked like calligraphy. It said:

To my heart, my dearest, my Esperanza.

❊

Ama drove the two young women from the Bluffs to West Tisbury. There was a caretaker but she visited the house several times every summer to make sure all was well.

"What is this place?" Perry asked as they ambled down the driveway.

"This was your mother's house," Ama said.

Layla looked around. "But there are like three houses here."

The three women stepped out of the car.

Ama said, "This is where I first stayed when I came to the

Vineyard. The main house was the Brooks family summer home for generations. Then Libby's dad, your grandfather Chris, shrewdly began to buy up the neighboring property."

She pointed to the house to the right of the large interior courtyard. "Stratham House is a four-bedroom property where Libby's brother and his family used to stay. The building to the left is the Barn; it's a renovated guesthouse and entertaining space. Why don't we go over there?"

"Dayuum girl," Layla muttered to Perry. "You about to be paid. This is dope. She must've left you at least one of these 'lifestyles of the rich and shameless' cribs."

Ama took a ring of keys out of her pocket and let them into the Barn. The ground floor was an open-plan space flanked by glass garage-style doors. A great room flowed into a giant dining area, and to the far end of the first floor, there was a large pool table, and beyond that, the girls could see a screening room with a dozen movie theater–style chairs.

"There are three guest rooms with en suite bathrooms upstairs," Ama said, "and there's a chef's kitchen in the back."

Ama opened one of the garage doors to reveal a rectangular pool paved with black stones. Perry and Layla stood at the front door, taking it all in.

"Why don't I give you some privacy to read the letter and I'll be back in an hour," Ama said.

Perry nodded and then, out of habit more than anything else, she hugged her godmother and said, "Thank you, Ama."

Ama gestured for Layla to follow her to the door. "Keep an eye on her for me, please? I'll keep my phone close. Please text me if you need me."

Layla nodded.

When the door closed, Layla went to Perry, who sat on the oversized sofa, holding the letter with both hands. Layla was reminded of the first day of third grade. Perry had transferred into their Catholic school, the working-class parents' alternative to underfunded public school, no matter their religion. Perry stood in the front of the room, looking down. Her Peter Pan blouse was perfectly starched, her pleated navy skirt was clearly store-bought and new. It was only her socks which kept sliding down her skinny calves that gave the appearance of something short of perfection.

"Do you want to go out to the pool?" Layla asked.

"God, no," Perry said. "I already feel like I'm drowning."

"Okay then," Layla said. "Let's close the door to the pool."

She fiddled along the wall until she found the switch that lowered the giant glass door. Clearly, no one had been in the house all summer, if not longer, but everything worked perfectly. She'd noticed that about really rich people. They kept everything in tip-top shape, even if they didn't need it.

She said, "I bet there's some cold water here somewhere. Can I get you some water?"

Perry whispered, "Yes, please."

Layla found the kitchen. It was a lot like Ama's, all tricked out like something on the Food Network. The fridge was plugged in and stacked with bottles of water—still and sparkling. Layla thought, Damn it if rich people don't keep their houses stocked like a Costco.

She handed Perry a sparkling water and said, "How about I go sit in the chair by pool table. That way you can have privacy but I can keep an eye on you."

"Okay," Perry said.

Layla hugged her friend and said, "You know you don't have to read it right away."

Perry shook her head. "I've waited long enough. I can't wait any longer."

"Okay. I'm right over there."

"I don't think I could do this without you," Perry said.

She thought of Damon, how many times they had stayed up in bed talking about Perry's birth parents. "As a doctor," Damon would say, "if only for the medical history, you should find out."

But Perry never wanted to know until she couldn't not know. She had to give Ama credit. When she asked, Ama had not hesitated. She told her the truth right away.

Perry wondered if she had ever really believed that Ama was her mother. The more she thought about it, the more she realized that Ama was a safe placeholder for her birth mother. Ama was everything she wanted to be. She knew that her godmother was not perfect, but Ama was exquisite in her humanity. Perry admired it all—Ama's beauty and grace and the way she had bossed up when she was the only woman making deals on Wall Street. Perry dreamed of building a life like the one Ama and Omar had created. They were rich in love and rich in experience and then they generously, selflessly shared it all with her, Olivia, and Billie.

She never expected that her birth mother was a white woman. She also hadn't imagined that her birth mother would be dead. She'd never dreamed, eyes open or closed, that when she finally met the woman who'd given her life that she would be reaching out to shake hands with a ghost.

She took a sip of water and self-consciously wiped her

hands on her pants. The envelope was so pristine, she couldn't believe it was decades old. It was sealed shut. She opened it and began to read:

My Dearest Perry,

I cannot believe that I will not be there to tell you all of this myself. But here we are. The doctors tell me I have stage four invasive breast cancer. They say I have just months to live so I am writing it all down, as fast as I can.

I will tell you more about me in future letters, but right now, what is most urgent is that I tell you the story of you, my miracle girl.

A few summers after my best friend married her love, Omar, I also got married. My husband's name was Chip (born Chippendale Kerwin Taylor III). You'd think that having grown up a WASP, I would recognize a stinger when I saw him, but I did not.

When we married, I told Chip that I wanted a city life and the career on Wall Street I'd fought so hard to get. I was a broker like Ama; I never ascended to the heights she did but I broke a glass ceiling or two in my day.

Chip and I lived for one blissful year on the Upper West Side—Riverside and Eighty-Second. I loved everything about the neighborhood—the food, our neighbors, the life, the culture. I came home from work one day to find the apartment completely empty. Not even a hand towel in the bathroom. I thought we'd been robbed by the most efficient band of thieves the city had ever seen.

It turns out that my husband had bought a house in Greenwich and moved all of our things out there without saying a single word to me. He said it was a gift. A surprise. It felt like a trap. It reeked of betrayal.

From the beginning, I had trouble getting pregnant. Well, actually I got pregnant, I just couldn't stay pregnant. I lost baby after baby. Chip said it was the stress of my job so he insisted that if I was serious about starting a family, I should quit. Spending all day alone in that Greenwich house turned out to be more lonely and stressful than any job. My misfortune and infertility continued.

Chip's career took off and he spent a lot of nights in the city. He said he was staying at the Yale Club but I had grown up in the world of these rich Connecticut husbands. I knew the real deal. I thought, foolishly, that a baby would solve it.

Five miscarriages later, my body was a wreck and admittedly, so was my head. I wasn't any fun to live with. Our marriage was over but neither of us had the courage to leave.

If you'll allow me to give you some advice from the grave—not being in love is enough reason to split up. You don't need a punishable offense to leave. The Lord knows that a truly loveless marriage is punishment enough.

We stumbled along like that, not loving each other, not liking each other, for so long. We kept lashing out, kept begging each other to change so we could be "happy."

Then it happened: Chip was snapped at a party in a lip-lock with a young, beautiful fashion designer. It was a slow news day, and the picture ran, big, on Page Six. His private equity firm had invested in her new and very successful line.

It was the week before my fortieth birthday. Chip had planned this big party for all of our friends at Mr. Chow. We canceled the party because we both knew our marriage was over. The affair was the key that opened the latch and let us both out of our miserable cage.

What hurt was that Chip promptly sold the house and moved with the designer into a loft in SoHo. "She'd never live in Greenwich," he said, when we met to give me a check with my half of the proceeds.

It was April so I came up to the Vineyard and opened the house early.

I met your father Memorial Day weekend at the lighthouse in Aquinnah. He was the most beautiful man I'd ever seen. A tall, strong, bronze man with a warm smile. He saw me staring at him and he said, "Do we know each other?"

I apologized and said, "I'm sorry, we don't."

Then he said, "If we do not know each other then we should remedy that immediately, my name is Kofi."

He had just finished a year working for Refugees International in Washington, DC. He was spending the summer with friends who had a small guesthouse. He was studying for the bar exam and teaching SAT prep courses to teenagers who were spending their summer on the island.

He was just twenty-six. I had just turned forty. It didn't make any sense. But he romanced me and life with him was so easy. Every afternoon at five, I went to his house and we rode bikes together and hiked. He cooked me the most delicious meals in the tiny kitchen of that guesthouse—jollof rice, peanut soup, corn and cassava, and all kinds of fried fish. He was brilliant and spoke many different languages fluently, especially French and Spanish. I would practice my rudimentary high school Spanish with him. We talked about our hopes and dreams, our *esperanzas y sueños*.

When we began to sleep together, I honestly didn't think I could get pregnant. We used protection and I never thought it was more than a wonderful summer fling that extended into the fall.

Then one day, I dropped by the guesthouse and he wasn't home yet. The door was unlocked. No one locks doors on the Vineyard. There was a letter on his desk and I recognized the handwriting as feminine. It was from a girl who called herself his fiancée. There was a photo of her and she was young, pretty, Senegalese. She wrote about life at medical school in France and their future together.

What can I say? The letter confirmed all my fears that I was too old, too white, too undesirable for him to ever truly love me. He was furious that I'd gone through his things and that I didn't trust him. He said we were too new for him to break off the marriage his parents had arranged for him. I told him he should marry the woman he was engaged to and that I didn't want to see him again. Later, I would realize I was still broken from my marriage with Chip. I didn't know how to do love right after so many years of getting it wrong. I kept my distance. He wrote that he had gone back to DC— "The island is empty without you," he said—and he urged me to look him up if I ever wanted to talk.

I realized I was pregnant around Christmas. The only

person I told was Ama. I'd had so many miscarriages that I thought it was just a matter of waiting for the inevitable bad news. After the holidays, my parents went back to New York. My brother, his wife, and their kids went back to Boston.

Then the craziest thing happened, dear girl, you stuck around. I found an OB in Woods Hole. Every month I returned to her, prepared to hear the worst, and every month my doctor just smiled and said, "This one is a fighter. Listen to that heartbeat."

I started talking to you—something I'd never dared to do with any baby before. I rode my bike until my belly was too big to balance. That winter, I'd take you on long car rides around the island, blasting all of my favorite tunes. I wanted you to know this island, every stretch of it. Every morning, I'd fill my thermos with tea and honey and we wouldn't come back for hours.

In the afternoon, I'd make soup and stews and we'd sit by the fireplace. I'd love to say that I read a lot of great literature to prep your little brain. But I was so tired, alone, and pregnant. The truth is I read a lot of John Grisham and Terry McMillan.

Ama and Omar came up a lot that winter. Ama made a New Orleans–style feast and filled my freezer with gumbo. I probably don't need to tell you that she can cook her butt off. I knew they already loved you. The island was so beautiful that spring and summer. It was like Mother Nature was showing off just for you.

Then you were born—August 15, 1991. Best day of my life.

I named you Esperanza, my hope, because you are everything I ever wanted in this world.

So this is the not so great part. During my pregnancy, I noticed changes in my breasts. I had always been kind of flat chested and now they were getting pretty big. I figured it was just a part of pregnancy until I started feeling some odd hard lumps. By the time I was tested and diagnosed, I was about to give birth to you. I had planned to keep you, to raise you, on the island. I thought I'd set up an investment firm, just 401(k)s and simple funds, and commute into Boston a few times a month to meet clients. But when they told me I was sick, it all happened so fast. I went from giving birth to chemo in a matter of days.

I guess I could have given you to my parents to raise but they were already retired. They didn't even know that I was pregnant and then I had to break the news that I was going to be checking out on the sooner side.

As a biracial child, I thought the best thing would be for you to be raised by an African American couple. That is why I asked Ama to raise you. I knew that Ama and Omar would love you and guide you as their own. Ama promised me they would be your parents and someday, they'd tell you about me.

Now time is running out and there are only three things I really need you to know.

The first is that my dying wish is for you to have the house in West Tisbury. It's here that we spent the first year of your life. Because our time together is not long, I'm counting both the time you spent inside me and the time you spent in the world. West Tisbury is our home. This island is our island.

I have spoken to my parents and my brother and they have agreed. The main house will be deeded to you on your thirtieth birthday.

Ama has put the proceeds of my half of that wretched Greenwich house into a trust. If my brother ever decides to sell the Stratham House or the Barn, you will have the right to make the first offer at a fixed rate. Ama will arrange it all.

Second, I have not sorted things with your father. Baby girl, if you don't know it already, life is messy. I've got months—not years—to live. I cannot take what little time and energy I have left to find Mr. Kofi Koulibaly and explain that I hid a pregnancy, gave our baby to my best friend and her husband, etc., etc. My focus is on you—securing your legacy, writing these letters, making sure that somehow I can make it that you feel as if you know me, even a little bit.

That's all I can do with the time I have left. My suggestion is that when you are ready, you ask Omar to track down your father and smooth the path for an introduction. That man can charm the birds out of the trees. Omar will help you.

And third, really, this is the only thing I need you to know, what I need you to believe and remember for the rest of your life:

You were wanted, Perry.

You were loved.

And remember what that doctor told me every month of my pregnancy: You are a fighter.

I'm not there to hold you to my chest, but when in doubt, listen to your heartbeat.

PS: I'm not sure what happens after death. But if there's someone you need me to put a hex on, just say the word. If I'm able to, I will haunt them until they beg for mercy. Nobody messes with my baby girl.

CHAPTER 34

ALL I DO

None of it was going according to plan. Ama had hoped to have one more summer with her girls and then, at the end of the summer, when Labor Day was on the horizon and the footsteps of fall were impossible to ignore, she would hand each girl her inheritance. She had planned to tell each of them what she did not know at their age—that inheritances were complicated, that every bequest was so much more mysterious than line items in a will. The houses, the money, the beloved jewels, and treasured artwork were small things compared with the complexity of our emotional legacies. There was no section in most legal documents for the secrets and lies, the pain and the regrets, no real way to amend every physical gift with the messy story of its provenance. Yet Ama had never met a person the world called exceptional who had escaped being smeared with missteps and remorse.

She had planned the telling down to the last detail. The setting, a bonfire on their private beach. The meal, a low country boil as an homage to her beginnings replete with crawfish, shrimp, smoked sausage, corn, and potatoes. The food would not dull the hurt but she planned to make it a meal they would never forget. She planned to give each girl the packet of letters that she had held for them all these years. Everything about Ama's imaginings was designed for her to take responsibility for her failings without losing the dignity she felt she deserved.

No roses without thorns.

In Ama's fold, Perry, Olivia, and Billie had known only the roses. They were grown now, she needed to talk to them about the thorns.

Ama had left Perry's car at Libby's house and called a Martha's Vineyard taxi. The girls used ride-share apps, but she liked the local taxi services. She knew all the drivers. When she called from the front porch of Libby's home, her hand shaking, and the dispatcher said "Five minutes, Mrs. Tanner," she could count on the driver being a friendly face.

Winston Campbell pulled his white Toyota minivan right up to the front step and called out, "Good afternoon, Ms. Ama."

"Good afternoon, Winston," she said, as she slid into the front seat next to him.

"Where to today?" he said.

"Just home," she said.

That was one of the beauties of island life. She could say home, and people like Winston needed no street name or directions.

Her phone beeped. A text from Layla: **Perry wants to spend the night here. Warning. She's pretty upset with you** right now. Can you bring clothes and some food? Maybe you should avoid coming in though.

She paid Winston and stood outside the house to catch her breath. She had done her very best. She had done what she was capable of doing. She walked into the house and felt the urge to light a flame. She'd never known the depths of heartache and pain that could inspire an arsonist to such destruction. But today for a fleeting moment she thought if only she could burn it all to the ground and start again.

Omar used to love to sing that old Commodores song "Brick House" to her.

Ama looked at the house she had loved into existence from the studs up. It didn't feel like a brick house. She didn't *feel* mighty-mighty.

She went up to Perry's bedroom and opened the door. She remembered when they'd chosen the elegant chinoiserie pattern for the walls. It was as recherché and mysterious as her eldest goddaughter. Ama never tired of the dark navy-blue and coral-white pattern. It evoked the ocean outside of the window without falling trap to the tired and cliché nautical themes you still saw all over the island.

She opened the dresser drawers and packed a pair of petal-pink pajamas and a simple bright pink sundress she knew Perry loved. Then she went into the guest room and packed for Layla.

Next, she turned her thoughts to food. Libby's Barn was stocked with the basics—sparkling water and pantry staples. But the girls needed a warm, nourishing, comforting meal. She would have loved to fire up the stove and whip up a quick batch of Perry's favorites—fried oyster po'boys and a warm batch of Mississippi mud skillet cookies. But it seemed that the last thing Perry wanted at the moment was Ama's food.

She threw the overnight bag for the girls into the backseat of her car, an old silver Land Rover, and she drove to Katama General Store.

Before Ama could get to the takeout counter, she was accosted by Irene Terry, a former model turned socialite extraordinaire.

"I spy with my little eye, Ama Vaux Tanner," Irene said playfully.

Ama did not even bless the woman with a fake smile. Today was not the day.

They used to be close-ish. Ama remembered seeing Irene's pretty face on the cover of magazines like *Essence* and *Redbook* in the late seventies and early eighties. When she and Omar had built their dream home in the Vineyard, Irene and her husband, Donald, became fixtures in their summer dinner party circuit.

Those were tough times. A time when storms had hit her marriage, threatening to destroy everything she and Omar had built together. The girls didn't know the half of it. But they would soon enough. It was time.

Her mind flashed to a place she hadn't been to in years. The Union Chapel on Narragansett Avenue had been a church home for the Black community on the Bluffs since the 1870s. It had a capacity of 385. Ama was sure that more than five hundred islanders had crowded the church for Omar's memorial. She remembered so many things from that day—the tributes given by Omar's circle of friends, powerful men who had put aside their ambition and professional maneuvering to be true brothers to each other. She remembered how her girls had sat next to her in the front pew—Billie and Olivia sat on either side of Perry, tears streaming relentlessly down their cheeks. But Ama also remembered how Irene had sobbed so loudly that people kept turning back to stare. She couldn't figure out what the woman's mayhem and foolishness had been about.

What she did know was, after the memorial, she never received another dinner invitation to Irene and Donald's home. That first summer, she had been so deep in her grief that she hadn't noticed the slight. But the summers that followed, every time she ran into Irene Terry, the woman looked positively squeamish. "I wish I knew someone to set you up with," she would say, shaking her head as if it were a puzzle that had kept her up all night. Ama found the whole pretense so annoying. As if a blind date could make up for the loss of a man like Omar Tanner, as if Ama was the type of woman who needed a man to move through the world.

She hoped Irene would be brief. Her mind was on getting food to Perry then getting home to think. How was she going to face Billie after the disastrous unfolding of events with Olivia and Perry?

Irene beamed at her and said, "Donald and I want to invite you to dinner. It's been far too long."

Ama wondered who Irene had scrounged up to be her companion at the meal.

"Let's compare calendars right now. You'll have to bring your new beau," Irene said, her voice as thick as treacle.

Ama sighed. Carter, of course. The news of their romance had traveled to the island.

"Donald has two of his photographs in his office," Irene said, fangirling. "We are *huge* admirers of his work. I saw an article in *Architectural Digest* about his house in Spain. What am I talking about a house? It's practically a castle!"

Ama just turned and walked away. She didn't even say goodbye. She didn't have the energy.

Tom, the owner's son, was nearing thirty but every time Ama looked at him, she could imagine him at eighteen, tall and gangly with acne-prone skin and an awkwardly cut flat-top. There was a definite vibe to the few African Americans who lived year-round on the Vineyard. More heart, less flash.

"How are you doing, Miss Ama?" he asked politely. He'd grown into a handsome man. Married to a white girl. Twin boys with red hair and bright freckles. Ama saw them every year at the agricultural fair. He seemed happy. And she was happy for them.

"I'm fine, Tom," she said, lying graciously. "How are those beautiful boys of yours?"

"Oh, they are terrific," he said. "They'll start fourth grade this September."

"Fourth grade? How could that be? I remember when your wife was pregnant! Time flies. May I have a roast chicken, a side of potatoes, a Caesar salad, and a container of the honey-glazed carrots?"

"Right away," he said. He noted the look on Ama's face and quickly wrapped up the items.

There was a wine cooler built into the island in the Barn's kitchen, but Ama added a few bottles of rosé and two slices of blackberry cobbler to the basket anyway.

Her shopping done, she jumped into the Rover and headed

north on Katama Road toward Correllus State Forest. How many times had she and Omar biked down the trails of that beautiful expanse? She rolled down her windows as she drove by. The scent of pitch pine filled the car. It was comforting. Omar always said that legacy was planting seeds for trees you'll never get to see. What had she wrought that summer? What had she planted in revealing these truths? Would fruit ever grow from their found family tree again or would it just wither on the vine?

※

She pulled into Libby's driveway and Layla walked out to meet her.

"How's she doing?"

"She's pretty messed up."

Layla eyed Ama as if daring the older woman to take a step toward the Barn.

"I think you should just give her some space. I'll come back in the morning to pack up the rest of our things."

"Are you going back to the city?" Ama asked plaintively. She could hear her voice catch. She didn't want Perry to leave the island. Somehow she felt it would be worse if she left.

Layla shrugged. "Don't know yet. She may want to stay here for a few more days. Assuming that's okay?"

"It's her house, now," Ama said. She looked around and wished she could see her friend Libby one more time. She could close her eyes and picture Libby, her dark blond hair, her heart-shaped face, the pinkish red lipstick she wore from the time they met until the day she died. When Libby had passed away, Ama had found a makeup cabinet with a dozen tubes of the same shade, Soirée à Rio. That was Libby. Even when she was facing death's door, with a newborn infant in her arms, she had style and she had verve.

"Well, you know where to find me," Ama said finally, coming out of her reverie. "Let me help if I can."

"Sure," Layla said, walking away with the bags in tow. But the tone in her voice made it clear that she felt Ama had done enough.

Ama drove, without thinking, to the East Chop Lighthouse. It had been a favorite after-dinner destination for her and Omar. She thought of him as her lighthouse. When she was at sea, drowning in work or a messy knot of her own emotions, all she needed to do was look across the room and glance at her husband. He was her true north, her light, her navigational aid.

She sat on the rocky shore and watched the sunset, a blaze of red and orange with an improbable band of violet at the very top.

It was dark when she got home. She had no appetite to eat. She went up to the master suite, filled the tub, and lit a candle. The room filled with the reassuring scent of lavender and eucalyptus. Ama prayed regularly and she believed that God was everywhere. But she rarely got on her knees and prayed. She felt the moment demanded it so she knelt down. "Guide me, God," she whispered. "I'm laying it all down now, order my steps and guide me. Let there be light at the end of this tunnel, for all of us. Amen."

CHAPTER 35

I NEED YOU

That same Saturday night, at Libby's Barn, Perry and Layla had made a fire in the outdoor fireplace. The dinner had been delicious. They were on their second bottle of rosé. Layla looked every bit the uptown New York career girl, but her attitude was still pure South Bronx.

"I can't believe Libby asked Ama to raise you and she gave you up for adoption," Layla said. "That is messed up."

Perry nodded. It was. Perry could not understand it. She needed an explanation. At the same time, it was hard for her to imagine how things might have unfolded if she had lived with Ama and Omar full-time, if Olivia and Billie had never been a part of their lives.

"My mother, the one who raised me, used to say God has a reason for everything and that reason is benevolent and good," Perry said, feeling more calm.

Layla rolled her eyes. "Tell that to Job. God tortured him."

Perry couldn't see the ocean from Libby's backyard, but she could smell it. It was one of the things she loved about the Vineyard—there wasn't a place on the island where the air wasn't briny and sweet.

"But I haven't been tortured," Perry said. She was exhausted. She was sad. She was still a little embarrassed about the way she'd collapsed into Ama's arms, praying that her godmother was secretly her birth mother. But she didn't feel tortured.

She looked up at the house. She and Layla had found a picture album of photos of Libby, no doubt compiled by Ama. There was just one photo of Libby and the man she assumed was her father. It was an old Polaroid; the color was beautiful to Perry, it was as if the picture had been taken by a camera covered with a peachy gauze. Her birth father, that was a term she'd have to get used to, looked like an African prince in his crisp white shirt and khaki pants. Libby looked smitten, smiling at him, in a faded yellow dress with bright red embroidery.

Perry flipped through the pages of the album, getting to know her birth mother through her poses. She would've liked to have known Libby. For all the years she said she didn't want to know who her birth parents were, this was the deepest cut. This woman who smiled so broadly, who jumped into waves and mugged at every camera pointed her way, was her mother. Perry had wanted to be like Ama—to be so elegant, so graceful, to move through the world like a swan. But it seemed her inheritance was something else entirely. Her mother seemed, from the letter, from the photos, to have been a woman bursting with joy—a woman unafraid of laughing at herself or the world. The house was beautiful. She felt at home in the Barn the way she had felt at home right away in Ama's house.

There were three bedrooms in the Barn. Layla insisted

that they sleep in the rooms with the adjoining door. "I need to keep my eye on you," Layla said.

"I'm okay," Perry said.

"You're not but you will be," Layla said. "Holler if you need anything including me going over to Ama's house and beating her down."

Perry smiled. She knew that Layla had never actually delivered a beatdown to a single human being. But the threat was a well-rehearsed Bronx-girl defense mechanism; it was how they had been taught to be strong in the world.

✳

The next morning was Sunday and Layla woke to the sound of Perry laughing. She had worried that the news might send her friend into a kind of mania. She leaned against the adjoining door to her friend's room. Perry was talking to someone on the phone.

"Play it again," Perry said.

Then silence.

Perry started giggling. "'Formation.' By Beyoncé."

Silence.

"Noooo. Who even heard of some song called 'Drinks on Us.' I can't guess a song based on five seconds."

"Yes, I'm a true hip-hop fan," she said, pausing to listen to the voice on the phone.

"I won't say it," she responded playfully. "Okay, 'Nikesh is the man.' You're a mess."

Layla tiptoed back to the bed.

Perry hung up the phone with Nikesh. Ever since he'd

gone back to New York, he'd been playing morning DJ, waking her up with five seconds of a song and then challenging her to guess what the song was.

Learning about Libby, spending the night in Libby's house, had been so dizzying that Nikesh had been the furthest thing from Perry's mind when she'd fallen asleep the night before.

The next morning, at seven A.M., the phone buzzed and she knew it was Nikesh. She thought about texting him, "Bad time. Call me later." Or, "Devastating news. Can't talk now."

But to her surprise, she had picked up the phone. She had played along with his game and tried to guess the song he'd played a snippet of. The smile on her face, the way he made her laugh, was like a rainbow after a thunderstorm. The levees hadn't broken. She hadn't been carried away by Ama's revelation. She had a realization that gave her pause. With Damon, she always wanted him to fix whatever was wrong with her life. Then she was angry with him when he couldn't. But she had just received the most devastating news of her life and yet, she didn't need Nikesh to ride in and be her prince in shining armor. She just wanted to hear his voice. She was just happy with the way he made her life seem simpler. With him, she could just be without needing him to be or do anything other than who he was.

When she hung up the phone, she peeked in to see that Layla was still sleeping. That girl would sleep until noon if you let her.

She showered in the downstairs bathroom and slid into the dress Ama had packed for her. Then she walked out onto the gravel driveway. Ama's house was palatial. Libby's house was a compound. It was baffling.

She decided to drive to town for breakfast fixings. She was driving when she thought about the date. It was August tenth. She always got her period on the first or second. She was usually right as rain.

Perry turned her car onto Beach Road as if she was headed to the ferry and found a parking lot in front of Vineyard Scripts, the only pharmacy she'd ever visited that had ocean views.

Back at the Barn, she put the ingredients for sausage biscuits and fried green tomatoes on the counter of the elegant kitchen.

Then she took the bag from the pharmacy into the bathroom and began the age-old ritual of peeing on a stick. She'd purchased three tests, because it seemed impossible that one night could have resulted in a pregnancy. But as test after test came up positive, she felt like a cheerleader who'd gotten knocked up on prom night. It didn't make any sense.

She came out of the bathroom and called out softly to her friend, "Layla?"

She didn't hear anything so she headed toward the kitchen to cook. But Layla was coming out of the kitchen and bumped right into her.

"Are you holding what I think you're holding?" Layla asked.

Perry nodded.

"I thought you and Nikesh hadn't gone all the way," Layla said, sounding like the high school students they once were.

Perry flushed. "We didn't. This is Damon's baby."

CHAPTER 36

A LOST BEE

After breakfast, Perry called Ama and asked if she could come over. Perry didn't hug Ama as she usually did, she just followed her silently into the house. On the porch, Ama had prepared a pitcher of sweet tea and she poured each of them a glass.

Perry looked out at the ocean, not at Ama, as she spoke. "Ama, forgive me if I tell you I don't know how I'm going to process this in the long term. I go from being furious at you to feeling forgiveness to wondering if I can ever trust you again. In her letter, Libby wrote that she asked you to raise me as your own. But you didn't. You gave me up. You didn't fulfill your best friend's wishes." Perry turned to Ama with a look of pain so deep in her eyes. "What kind of friend, woman, mother does that?"

Ama nodded. She now understood. Ama steeled herself and said, "My type of woman, Perry. I made some difficult choices in my life. Choices that were the right choices for me. You may think they were selfish. And that's okay. It is not easy being a woman in this life. And a Black woman at that. I wanted to be free. Free to make my own way. Free to have a career. Free to live my life on my own terms. What your mother didn't know is that I had also given birth to a daughter before you were born, Perry, and I gave her up. I made that choice as well. I knew I would always keep my promise to your mother and look after you. I knew I would make sure you were okay. Actually, better than okay. But I wanted a life of financial stability, culture, fine education. I wanted freedom for you, too. And I will not apologize for my choices or how I have lived my life."

The women sat in silence on the porch, looking out at the view. Ama remembered when Omar first planted the kousa dogwoods that were now a majestic canopy over the north side of the porch. He'd ordered the saplings from an arboretum in California that, in turn, had imported them from Seoul.

"These damn trees cost more than my first apartment," she'd said, steaming at the bill.

"That's an exaggeration," Omar had said, grinning. "And we can afford it."

"Hmmph," Ama had said. "A beautiful beachfront home isn't enough for you, Mr. Tanner. You need imported, Rockefeller-expensive trees, too."

"Wait till these trees grow," Omar had said. "And you're sitting on the porch with the girls. You'll thank me then. Trust me."

She had because that's what she did—trusted him. Her beloved husband was gone, but the trees he'd planted were still there. In the spring, they roared to life with the most spectacular star-shaped white blooms. In the summer, the lush, low-hanging branches offered graceful shade. Every morning, their pinkish red fruit brought the songbirds to the house—with a sweet serenade that had become Ama's summer alarm clock.

Now the tree was shielding her and Perry from the midday glare.

"You are closer to me than my mother," Perry said. "I mean my mother in the Bronx, not Libby."

"I can't change the past, *cher*," Ama said. "But please believe I will fight for your present and your future till the end of my days."

"I'm pregnant with Damon's baby," Perry said.

"Congratulations," Ama said.

"But he lied to me about a relationship and was also deceitful. He told me. The thing is I was a little less than honest, too, and I haven't told him yet."

"Yet," Ama said. "You must never tell him."

Perry shook her head. "Oh, I have to tell him. If I've learned anything this summer, it's the power of lies to destroy us."

Ama flushed. She refused to believe she had destroyed her girls.

"Men are different," Ama said. "They confess because it's a weight off of them. They don't want to carry the guilt. But men hold resentment. That's why men start wars—big ones and small ones. Damon will never forget your indiscretion. He'll bury it and water it and it'll grow in his heart. If you love him, if you want this child to grow up in a house of love, you'll keep your secret to yourself. You carry the burden of your choices, Perry. We are strong. Stronger."

"Ama, you don't understand," Perry said. "You and Omar were perfect."

Ama pursed her lips. She had never told a soul the things that had almost torn her own marriage apart. But Omar was gone and Perry needed to know the truth.

"Omar cheated one summer, with that social climber, Irene Terry," Ama said. "It was the summer after you went away to college. I felt such betrayal when he told me. But he asked for forgiveness. And he spent his whole life trying to make it up to me."

Perry was shocked. She couldn't imagine Omar even glancing at another woman. Omar who always used to say, "Why go out for hamburger when you've got prime rib at home?"

Ama said, "Omar never knew that early on, when we were going steady but before we got engaged, I cheated, too. With Carter Morris. And if I'm being honest, Carter always had a part of my heart. I kept it. Just for me. Love is . . . complicated."

Perry thought she was going to faint. When she, Olivia, and Billie were little girls, they used to sneak around the house, making what were likely indiscreet attempts at eavesdropping. Ama used to shoo them away, saying, "Stay out of grown folks' business."

Hearing Ama talk, she realized how little she knew about the workings of this marriage, these two titans she had raised to the level of sainthood. Now she wished she could unhear and unlearn all that she'd discovered about grown folks' business.

"Ama, I had no idea. I don't know what to do. I need to think," Perry said, rising.

"Study long, study strong," Ama said. "Think but don't overthink. You and Damon have something worth saving. There's no such thing as 'the one,' my love. There's just 'the one' you decide is worth fighting for."

That evening Ama texted Billie: I need to talk to you. Meet me at the house at 9?

Billie texted back: I'll be there.

Things had been frosty with Dulce since the revelation of the job offer in Texas. Dulce left early in the morning and often returned late at night after Billie was asleep. Billie was sure that they would work it out. The job was negotiable. Her relationship was not. She knew that. She just didn't know, yet, how she could make them both work.

When she got to the house, Billie thought she had never seen Ama look so . . . unlike herself. Ama could never look disheveled, but she didn't look put together. She almost looked undone. Her hair was a bit out of place. Her clothing a bit wrinkled. Her eyes clouded. This time, Ama did not try to explain. Words had failed her so completely. She simply handed Billie a thick envelope. She said, "I'm going upstairs. I hope you'll give me a chance to talk when you're done."

Dear Billie,

It was the summer of 1995 when I first met your father. He'd made an appointment to talk to me about investing.

It was the years of the first internet millionaires, so I wasn't surprised to see a young man with brown skin wearing a *Hellboy* T-shirt, a dark hoodie, and jeans. That's how all the kids dressed back then.

I invited him into my office. Your dad, Mike, sat down and said, "Look, ma'am. I'm going to get right to it. I think you're my wife's biological mother. She's in trouble and I don't know where else to go."

I felt my body go limp. Only my mother and grandmother knew that I had given birth to a child the winter before I'd moved to New York.

My grandmother did her research and found me a spot at St. Anne's, a home for unwed mothers in Los Angeles. I wasn't showing yet when I took the train from Louisiana to Los Angeles. I wore my one good suit, a Tiffany-blue jacket with a nipped-in waist and matching pencil skirt that my grandmother had made for me based upon a McCall's pattern I'd picked out myself. The cars weren't supposed to be segregated but my car was all colored. A steady stream of young men tried to speak to me at different legs of the five-day journey, but I just brushed them off. They kept asking me if I was going to Los Angeles to be an actor, as if. As if.

I had no Hollywood aspirations. I had fallen madly in love with Beau Mason Gatreaux, a handsome white boy who looked like he could be the little brother of Paul Newman. He had the same tousled hair, the same piercing blue eyes, the same easy, generous smile. Our first "date" had been to see a revival of *Paris Blues*, but because it was New Orleans in 1969, we did not enter the theater together. You just didn't in the south back then. We purchased our tickets separately,

ten minutes apart. The movie starred Paul Newman and
Sidney Poitier as bad boy jazz musicians making their way
through the City of Lights. Then they meet Diahann Carroll
and Joanne Woodward, who are in Paris on business. I'll never
forget the moment when the movie begins and Paul Newman
first makes a play for Diahann Carroll—a handsome white
boy looking at a beautiful Black girl *like that*. I'd never seen
anything like it in my entire life. She turns him down and
offers to set him up with her friend. I almost fainted when
Paul Newman looked at our Diahann and said, "Is she as
pretty as you are?"

Beau leaned over and kissed me on the cheek. He
whispered what I had been thinking: "The world is
changing."

But that was just a movie. In New Orleans, in those
days, the wheels of change were grinding at an almost
imperceptible speed, which felt like no speed at all.

Beau and I spent the whole summer sneaking around
town. We met up in nearly empty movie theaters. We'd
wake up early in the morning on a Saturday and drive out to
Coconut Beach, walking side by side without touching until
we were out of sight of any prying eyes, then we'd lie down
on a blanket I'd brought and kiss and touch and kiss some
more.

I knew that Beau's family had money. His father was a
powerful senator. I visited his house when his parents were
out. The mantel was a gaggle of framed pictures. Beau's
parents at the White House with Lyndon B. Johnson,
drinking champagne with Kitty Carlisle, who was a NOLA
girl and starred on a TV show we all loved called *To Tell the*

Truth, on the podium on election night with Victor Schiro, who was mayor of New Orleans back then. Portraits of Mardi Gras queens.

My grandmother knew I was pregnant before I did. She called me into the kitchen and poured us both a cup of chicory coffee. Then she sat down and said, "It looks like all the running around you're doing with that Gatreaux boy has led to you being pregnant. What's the plan?"

I didn't have a plan. I called Beau at his job that day and asked if we could go out to the beach that Saturday. We were walking along and I boldly grabbed his hand.

He looked around and pulled it away. "Amelia," he said. "Anybody could see us."

I turned to him and then said, "Beau, what are your intentions regarding our relationship?"

He looked away then, staring out at the ocean as if the answer would come crashing in with the waves.

"Why so serious, love?" he asked. "You know I'm going to law school at Tulane in the fall. I'll be busy with classes, but we can still have our fun."

I knew then what I had to do.

A week later, I was on the train to California. St. Anne's was downtown, not far from what was known as Filipinotown.

I got a job working in the sisters' office as a file clerk. I got a library card and borrowed books. On Saturday evenings, some of the other girls and I would catch a bus to Mama's Fino, a Filipino restaurant we all loved. We'd share big plates of adobo chicken and flirt with all the handsome boys who came in and out of the place. We must have made quite a sight, a gaggle of women with big bellies and hot-curled hair, catcalling boys the way they catcalled girls.

When it was my time, I gave birth in an immaculate downtown hospital. I held my baby just once, then handed her over to a pretty Asian woman who assured me that the family who were adopting her would make sure she wanted for nothing. "You're very lucky," she said. "There aren't that many wealthy Black families looking to adopt babies." I knew she was right.

Then I went home to New Orleans for the summer, to work and earn a little money. I saw Beau just once that summer. It was at an afternoon showing of the Ali McGraw and Ryan O'Neal film, *Love Story*. He came in alone. Then I saw him sidle up next to a pretty brown-skinned girl. The sight sickened me so, that I left the theater immediately. I still have never seen that movie. I think I never will.

I knew that one day I'd meet the daughter I gave up for adoption. I also knew that putting three thousand miles between where I'd given birth and where I made my life made the chances of a surprise meeting less likely. Your father explained that he'd found me through the adoption agency. Claimed it was a life-and-death medical situation. To his mind, he said, it was. They broke the law. But likely saved me.

Mike went on to explain that Edie, that was what they'd named my daughter, had been raised by a prominent Black family in Southern California. The father was a successful aeronautics engineer and the mother worked as a storyboard artist at Disney. They went on to adopt three more children—

two boys, one girl. The other three children were living seemingly happy, successful lives. But Edie, Mike told me, never felt a part of that home.

She was beautiful. Tall with wavy dark hair and deep-set blue eyes, and she was smart. Her coaches thought she could become a competitive swimmer, but Edie wasn't a joiner, even for a sport where she would literally have her own lane. She was constantly drawing, and her mother tried to encourage her to go to art school. She got into every college she applied to: RISD, Savannah College of Art and Design, and Caltech.

She turned them all down. Her parents thought she just needed a year to find her bearings. But the day after her high school graduation, she cleaned out her bank account and moved to Amsterdam. Her parents didn't hear from her for weeks at a time. Their only assurance that she was alive were hastily scribbled postcards with stamps from cities across Europe—Milan, Barcelona, Prague. They read:

I'm fine. I love you.

Don't worry. I just need space. I love you.

Then one day, her little sister opened a copy of *Elle* magazine and there was Edie—lounging in a ballgown with a tattered sweatshirt tied around her waist. The caption said it was photographed at the Canal Saint-Martin in Paris.

It was the days of what the fashion industry called "heroin chic." Edie had told Mike that she had tried heroin after a shoot with a photographer and a few model friends. She said she didn't like it. Later, Mike realized it was classic Edie misdirection. She hadn't liked it. She adored it.

The nineties were a good time to be a young, pretty fashion model. Edie made a lot of money.

Mike and Edie had met at the San Diego Comic-Con. Mike told me, "There weren't a lot of people of color at the conventions back in those days. It was way before the Marvel movies and all the famous actors started coming to the conventions."

He said Edie tried to downplay her beauty in a convention hall filled with thousands of mostly white, mostly male geeks. "She wore this silly fisherman's cap, a black-and-white flannel shirt, a denim skirt, and beat-up Converse. But she was gorgeous. You could not tell if she was Black or white. She was just other. You couldn't keep your eyes off of her."

Over lunch, she showed Mike her portfolio. The thing she was most proud of was a superhero she had created called Abeja. "Abeja was a Black Latina shape-shifter," Mike said, his voice full of admiration. "She was a black belt in karate and she could sting like a bee."

The drawings, he explained, "were so beautiful. Her pen-and-ink work was impeccable. It was all so good, so ahead of its time."

Billie put down the letter. Her eyes were blurry with tears. She took a deep breath and stood by the large bay window. The story she was about to hear was unlike anything she had ever imagined.

✳

Edie's Story

Ama's letter went on to explain the world Mike described to her. Six months later, Edie moved to New York and moved in with him in his apartment in Sunnyside, Queens. "She loved the diversity of the neighborhood," Mike said. "She said it looked like the world she wanted to live in: Black, Latino, Asian, Eastern European, West African . . ."

Inspired by her bee-woman superhero, Edie set up a hive on the roof of their apartment building. "She said it would help her with her comic—and it would be good for the environment," Mike said.

Edie told him that one of the great things about raising bees in the city is that the plants in urban areas, where the bees pollinated, were less likely to be treated with pesticides. Oddly enough, honey from urban bees was healthier and more organic.

"For a while, life was perfect," Mike said. "Edie did the occasional modeling gig, but mostly she drew and cooked and tended the hives.

"Then we had our daughter, Billie—named after Billie Holiday," he said. "And life was even better."

Six months after Billie was born, Edie got an offer to go to Italy for a week to do a modeling assignment. "I didn't even think twice about it," he said. "I took a week off of work to hang with Billie and I told Edie to have fun."

At the end of the week, she called to say that some of the girls had rented a house in Corsica and she wanted to go.

"I said yes, of course." Mike sighed, taking off his glasses and cleaning them with his T-shirt, as if the gesture could keep him from crying. "My mom came up from Maryland to take care of Billie."

"When she came back, she didn't seem like herself," Mike said. "But when I asked her, she said she was jet-lagged."

The young man seemed to fold in on himself. He reminded Ama of a brown-skinned Clark Kent with his thick-rimmed glasses with black frames. "Within days, I knew she was using." His voice was quiet and thin. "I'd come home and find her on the roof staring vacantly out at the East River. She stopped tending the hives. She stopped caring for Billie. I'd come home and find our sweet baby in soiled diapers, clearly hungry and sad."

Ama could not feel her heart. It had stopped beating the first time the boy had said "heroin."

She wished Omar was there. She wondered how she could know he wasn't lying. He was wearing short sleeves and she could see no needle marks. But for all she knew, maybe he was an addict, too. She was forty-two years old, too young to be a grandmother, she thought. She had so many questions. There were too many questions.

"What do you need?" she asked, mentally calculating the number on the check she would need to write to make this nightmare go away.

He seemed to read her mind.

"I don't want your money," he said. "I've got a little comic book shop. The building is rent-controlled and we are doing well. What I was hoping was that you'd come and meet Edie. She's just out of rehab. The therapist thinks that part of her disassociation from Billie and one of the tensions under her addiction stems from the disconnect she feels from her adoptive family."

Ama wanted to say no.

She had always planned on meeting the daughter she'd given up. She had worked on steeling herself against the anger and disappointment that would surely come. But a daughter with an addiction was nothing she had prepared for. The idea that the addiction might be her fault, a direct result of Ama's abandonment, felt like a vise around her chest—the more Ama tried to breathe, the harder she felt the squeeze.

That night, the moment Omar walked into the front door, she collapsed into his arms. In the years that followed, when they were profiled in glossy magazines and photographed for one list after another, no one ever asked or guessed what they had privately endured.

They agreed to go to Mike and Edie's apartment for dinner that Sunday. The girl was beautiful and her face felt warm and familiar.

"She looks just like you," Omar whispered.

"Not me, my grandmother," Ama whispered back, missing her grandmother and the safe harbor of her tiny little bayou home.

Edie was shy and tentative. "I'm so pleased to meet you," she said politely.

"What should I call you, Mrs. Tanner?"

The formality of it made Omar laugh.

"You can call me Ama."

The baby was at the tail end of a long nap. "She went down later than usual," Edie said.

Ama and Omar peeked dutifully into the room of the

sleeping child. They exchanged glances. Neither of them were really baby people.

"I've prepared a simple French supper," Edie said. "I lived in Europe when I was younger. Modeling. They say models don't eat, but they do. At least I do. When you're lucky enough to travel abroad for work, you pick up a few dishes."

They settled down at the tiny table that seated four. It had been set with simple dishes from Ikea. The meal was, however, extraordinary. Warm goat cheese with a homemade baguette. Coquilles Saint-Jacques, which had always been a favorite of Omar's. A simple green salad with a French vinaigrette. And a homemade raspberry tart for dessert.

After dinner, Edie said, "Do you want to come see the sunset from the roof? It's the best view."

It was June. Omar and Ama had skipped their usual weekend trek to the Vineyard to meet Edie. Standing on the roof, Omar pointed to what looked like a homemade air-conditioning unit.

"What's that?" he asked.

Edie laughed. "Oh, that's my hive. I ruined the last one." She looked guiltily at Mike, who held the baby, still groggy from her nap, in his arms.

"But I'm starting a new one," Edie continued. "Bees are going to save our planet one day."

"If not these bees, then your superhero, Abeja," Mike said proudly.

Omar had loved comics as a kid. "Bee-woman instead of Superman?"

"Something like that," Edie said, smiling.

When they parted ways for the evening, Edie said, "I

really enjoyed that. Thank you for coming. I hope we can do it again."

In the car ride home, Ama commented on how struck she was by Edie. "She was so polite, warm, and well-spoken."

Omar did not mention how the girl kept tugging on her sleeves, how desperate she seemed to make a good impression on Ama.

Once a month, for the next six months, they met for dinner. Edie cooked up a storm. Omar and Ama oohed and aahed at Billie, who they admitted was the chillest baby they had ever met.

Edie showed them her artwork and told them stories about her hive.

Both she and Mike turned down Omar's discreet attempts to give them money.

"We do okay," Mike said. Omar admired both his pride and his sense of entrepreneurship.

"Let's just get to know each other," Edie said.

Omar hoped that he and his wife weren't being subjected to what hustlers called the long con.

Less than a year after they met Edie and Mike, Ama's daughter disappeared.

Mike called on a Saturday afternoon. He sounded stricken, as if he'd witnessed her death himself. "It's Billie's first birthday and Edie is gone."

He explained that she'd left a postcard that said: *This domestic life is not for me. Leaving before I make things worse.*

Omar had his law firm's investigator track her, but she was a ghost. No credit card use. She'd left her passport behind.

"It's like she doesn't want to be found," the investigator said. "And with a baby, too. What kind of woman does that?"

Omar wanted to say, "My wife."

He knew Ama's and Edie's stories were very different, and yet, there seemed to be real similarities between the two women. He knew Ama loved him, but what she loved most was her liberty. Edie seemed to be the same. Sometimes he wondered if it wasn't seeing Ama successful, out in the world and childless, that had been a bigger temptation than drugs to Edie. What she seemed to want more than anything was to be free.

Mike seemed certain that the blame lay with Ama. After Edie disappeared, he dealt only with Omar. "I don't ever want to see Edie's mother again," he said.

Omar wanted to explain to him that in many ways Ama was no more Edie's mother than he was Mike's father. Ama hadn't raised her or shaped her. But the young man was hurting, and if there was anything Omar understood, it was how powerless and angry a man could be when he was hurting.

Mike accepted just enough support to secure Billie's future. When the building they lived in went co-op, he allowed Omar to purchase the unit with a trust in Billie's name. Omar and Ama eventually bought the building that housed Mike's comic book shop and they made sure his rent stayed incredibly low. They paid for Billie's schooling and eventually Mike allowed her to join them for summers on the island.

Edie's whereabouts remained a mystery. She was a lost bee, a queen who had inexplicably abandoned her hive.

*

The envelope Ama had handed Billie contained one of Edie's comic books: *Abeja Battles the Super Menaces from the Planet Paraben*.

Billie studied the cover, trying to imagine the hands that had drawn the cocoa-hued superhero in the yellow bodysuit and black cape. Those were the same hands that had held her, and she wished she could remember what they felt like.

She picked her up her phone and typed a message: I know we're fighting. But I need you. Please meet me.

Then she gathered her things and slipped out of the house to find solace, her salve, her honey, her queen, her love, her Dulce.

CHAPTER 37

WHAT GOD THROWS
MY WAY

Dulce had asked to meet at the Port Hunter, a bar in Edgartown that served fancy cocktails and live music. When Billie pushed through the door, she saw that the cover band was playing Marley covers. As an added bonus, they were not all white trustafarians. The band was fronted by a beautiful Black woman who was swaying back and forth to the soulful reggae and doing a fine job singing "Satisfy My Soul."

Billie sat at the bar and perused the cocktail menu. She loved mezcal and was tempted by a drink that had mezcal, Calpico, cilantro, and cumin. But it was called Los Gringos and the name turned her off, so she kept perusing. She considered a cocktail with tequila and chocolate called the Empire Builder but rejected it because her mood did not call for chocolate.

She was stuck firmly in a web of her own indecision when she heard a familiar voice say, "Go ahead and order the Porn Star Martini. You know you want to."

It was Dulce.

They got their drinks—the Porn Star Martini was made

with vodka, passion fruit, and topped with a champagne foam. Billie had serious issues with the exploitation of women in the porn industry, but Dulce had been right, the drink was delicious.

They found a quiet corner booth. Dulce looked at her squarely. "My team was still cleaning up after service. You know I don't like to skip out on that. You said it was urgent."

Billie sighed. She knew that the ice in Dulce's voice had to do with the unresolved issue of her job. She had five unanswered messages from Jaime Molina. Desiree Touissant was sure to be short-listed for the vice presidential nomination and he needed to know if Billie wanted the job or not. She couldn't even think about it.

"Look, D," she said. "I don't want to talk about the job right now. I've got something else I've got to tell you. It's pretty heavy-duty." Billie sighed. She drained her glass. Her passion fruit martini was delicious but damn if the glasses weren't teeny tiny.

Dulce looked at the glass. "I think we both need grown-up-sized drinks. Wait here."

It helped to have a girlfriend who was a chef. Dulce knew how to get service in any kind of bar or restaurant. There was no hapless flagging down of disinterested wait-staff when she was around.

The Marley cover band was rolling through the hits and the woman who reminded Billie of the singer Jorja Smith was doing a sweet rendition of "Stir It Up."

Minutes later, Dulce returned with two healthy-sized glasses. "Mezcal margaritas with salt rims, good?"

Billie nodded. She looked at Dulce proudly. Nobody effed around with her girlfriend.

"Is it bad news? Are you sick?" Dulce asked.

Billie shook her head.

"Is it Ama? Is she sick?"

"No, she's okay," Billie said. "I don't even know where to start."

Dulce took her hand. "Whatever it is, I've got you."

So Billie told her the whole story, from Ama asking her to come to the house, to the letter, to her mother's comic books.

"Damn," Dulce said when Billie was done. "Do they really not know where your mother is?"

"I mean, with the kind of loot Ama and Omar had, if they couldn't find her . . ."

"What scares you most?" Dulce asked.

It was the kind of question only Dulce would ask. She was holding Billie's hand and her gaze was unflinching. No matter how tough things got, Dulce never backed down. Billie thought, I must have done something right in a previous life to have a love like this.

"I'm scared that she died a horrible death, of an overdose, somewhere on the streets," Billie said. "My dad's such a straight-up nerd, I never imagined this was something he ever had to deal with."

"What about Ama? What are you feeling about her?" Dulce asked.

Billie sighed. She didn't know what to feel about Ama. "You know the whole time we were growing up, Perry thought that she was secretly Ama's biological daughter.

She's so obsessed with being just like her. But I was never like that. I always just felt lucky that this couple who didn't have kids, who maybe couldn't have kids, picked us out of the bunch and gave us all these incredible opportunities. I never thought that we were actually related. My mother wasn't close to her adoptive family. The only grandmother I've ever known is my dad's mother."

"What did Ama say after you read the letter?" Dulce asked.

Billie looked embarrassed. "I didn't give her a chance. She was upstairs and I just bolted. I just wanted to see you."

Dulce thought about it for a moment. "You should text her."

"And say what? Thank you for lying to me for twenty years?"

"Come on, now."

"Oh, I've got it," Billie said sarcastically. "Thank you for giving my mother up for adoption and creating a hole in her heart that was so big, she had to fill it with drugs."

Dulce looked at Billie disapprovingly. "Come on, sweetie. That kind of bitterness is not you."

Billie shrugged. "Who knows what's me? I've been living with so many lies for so long."

Her girlfriend then guided her out of the booth. "Let's get out of here, baby," Dulce whispered.

Billie nodded yes.

As they exited the Port Hunter, the girl with the long braids began singing "Is this love?"

Billie and Dulce were already out on the cobblestone sidewalk. They didn't need to hear the question. They knew the answer.

✳

"I made coffee," Layla said, pouring them both a cup.

"It was one night," Perry said.

"I can't believe you find out you're the love child of an African prince one day and then the next day, you find out you're carrying a child of your own," Layla said. "That mess must run in your genes. You come from a long line of scandalous, rich white women."

Perry sipped her coffee and looked at her friend. "Only some of that is true. I'm a proud Black woman."

Layla raised an eyebrow. "Wait till I get busy and call Professor Skip Gates and he helps me find my roots. You're going to find out I'm more Lupita than you are, girl."

Perry shook her head. "You're a mess."

"Seriously though," Layla said. "You've got a lot coming at you. What do you want to do today?"

Perry said, "Today. I only want one thing. I want to go to the carousel with Olivia and Billie and I want a scoop of butterbeer ice cream from Vineyard Scoops."

She picked up her phone and texted her godsisters.

Layla smirked. "You know that butterbeer is not a real thing. It's something J.K. Rowling made up for Harry Potter and stores capitalize on it because little Hermione wannabes like you will buy anything."

Perry just smiled. "Don't hate, Layla. Appreciate."

＊

That morning, Ama woke up with a heavy heart. Billie had not even told her she was leaving the house after she'd read her letter. She made herself coffee and picked listlessly at a bowl of fruit.

She sat on the balcony of her bedroom, looking out at the ocean. She did not feel Omar's presence. She felt utterly and entirely alone. She reached for her iPad and played an old favorite album, Shirley Bassey's *Never Never Never*.

She read the paper, the physical paper, the way she liked to. Her girls read the newspaper on their phones, a thing she would never understand.

She was halfway through the book review section when her phone rang. It was eleven A.M. Time for her daily call with Carter, who was, if memory served her, in Todos Santos, Mexico.

"Good morning," she said, trying to sound peppier than she felt.

"Good morning beautiful," he said. "How are you?"

She couldn't tell him all that had transpired, couldn't begin to explain and wasn't sure how she'd ever let him in with that degree of emotional intimacy. And yet, she planned to continue this romance and she had learned that love withers without honesty. So she decided to crack the door of her broken soul open.

"I've been better," she said softly.

"I sensed that," he said. "That's why I took a flight last night from Cancún to Boston."

She sat up. Was he really that close? She would drive and meet him.

"Where are you?"

"Outside your front door," Carter said.

Ama flushed. She had no makeup on. She was still in her pajamas. It didn't matter, he was here.

She walked down the stairs and opened the front door. He was wearing a pale blue crumpled linen shirt, a pair of dark jeans, and a beautiful silver bracelet. He looked like a mirage.

"Come in," she said.

He shook his head. "I know you've never invited me here because this is Omar's house. But I've had this sixth sense that this is where I should be. I just had to see you. I was wondering if you wanted to go sailing with me."

She smiled. "Give me half an hour to shower and pack?"

He said, "Take all the time you need."

"How long should I pack for?" she asked.

He grinned. "How about forever, Ms. Amelia Vaux?" he said, addressing her by her maiden name. "Does forever work for you?"

She shook her head. Of all the eligible bachelors in the world, she had to get herself hooked to the last Black bohemian.

"I'll pack for three days," she said practically.

"I'll take it," he said.

CHAPTER 38

OLIVIA

Olivia got Perry's text asking to meet up and replied, **Sorry, girl. In New York, swamped with work.**

In reality, she had taken a leave of absence from work. Omar had left her a safe-deposit box full of letters. She was afraid to read all of them. But the second one had included something intriguing: the key to a storage unit downtown, near the entrance to the Holland Tunnel.

Anderson was the only person Olivia had told the whole sordid story. She would have never guessed that the summer would end with her confidant and lover being a white boy from Queens who aspired to be a comedian and moonlighted as an Uber driver. But she'd also never imagined that Omar had played a role in her father's death. Life was surprising.

When she told Anderson about the storage unit, he said, "No way. You're not going down there by yourself. I'll come pick you up tomorrow morning. We'll go together."

She wanted to tell him that she didn't know him like that, that she was fine, she'd go alone.

But it was nice, the way he wanted to take care of her.

And she thought he was right. Lord knows what she was going to find in that unit. She didn't know Anderson well, but she trusted him.

He arrived at her apartment, dressed in a crisp white button-down shirt, a pair of black pants, and holding a black jacket. She found the outfit confusing.

"You look like you're dressed for a funeral," she said, suppressing a laugh.

"I know, but we're going to investigate your dead father's life and I wanted to show respect," he said.

"We're not exhuming his body," Olivia said, shaking her head.

"But when we were on the Vineyard, your godsisters made fun of me for my clothes and for my bare feet," he said, looking a little hurt. "I don't want to ever embarrass you. So from now on, I'm overdressing."

Olivia smiled.

He did a *GQ* pose. "Do I remind you of Usher? Big Sean?"

Olivia shook her head no.

He did another pose. "Am I a playa?"

"No," she said. "But you're just what I need. Thank you for coming."

❈

Olivia opened the storage space with trepidation.

Anderson said, "Let me go in first."

The large room resembled a gallery in a museum. It quickly became clear to Olivia that Omar had curated a memorial to her father. The walls were lined with framed portraits of her father. A large bookcase held all kinds of memorabilia: photo albums, letters, school reports, his high school yearbook.

She held it together until she saw her father's uniform. It had been cleaned and pressed, and hung on a form inside a glass box, like a fashion exhibit at the Metropolitan Museum of Art. Seeing her father's uniform, imagining his shape in those clothes, was all Olivia could take. She started to cry and Anderson held her in his arms.

"This is . . . impressive," he said, holding her tight and surveying the room.

In a letter taped to the bookcase, Omar explained that he had spent years tracking down every significant item he could that was associated with her father. "I wanted to know him. And then I realized how important it was for *you* to know him," Omar wrote.

He had re-created her father with more precision than any of those holograms of dead musicians they had started sending out on tour.

"I'll come back," Olivia said, stepping out of the storage space. "I can't take it all in right now. I'll come back."

She and Anderson went to lunch at the Dutch and then he walked her home.

When she got upstairs to her apartment, she did something she rarely did. She called her mother and said, "Mom, would you like to come and have lunch with me in the city tomorrow?"

She had always thought that her mother was so cold. But

seeing the shrine Omar had created to honor her father gave her a glimpse of what her mother had lost. She always thought that her father was just another Black man lost to the night. She didn't know how much there was to love. She never knew how much she had been loved.

CHAPTER 39

CAROUSEL

Perry and Billie met up at the Atlantic for lunch. The Atlantic was upscale, sat at the edge of Edgartown, and boasted an expansive outside patio where patrons dined on fresh seafood and sipped strong cocktails next to a quaint private dock. The setting was tranquil and great for quiet conversations. It was about a twenty-minute drive away from the livelier Oak Bluffs.

"Ama kind of blew my mind," Perry began. "It turns out that she knew my mother."

Billie couldn't yet tell her secret—that Ama was her birth grandmother, that her mother was out there somewhere, not dead as she previously thought, but possibly very much alive and doing Lord knows what.

So Billie changed the subject. "Dulce proposed to me."

Perry said, "Really? Congrats, girl! I'm so happy for you."

"What about you and Damon?"

"I don't know. I'm pregnant. With his baby. He doesn't know. I didn't think I could get preggers naturally, and we had a drunk quickie and now here we all are. But it's all so messy. We are separated and my baby may already have a sibling. Especially if he screwed that bitch Sabrina."

Billie whistled. "Wow. That is so messy. Very *Housewives* franchise."

"For so long, I thought I wanted to be just like Ama," Perry said. "I thought I'd have a perfect relationship like Ama and Omar . . ."

Billie said, "That was your first mistake. There is no such thing as a perfect relationship. I think we all should know by now those two likely had a lot of relationship skeletons in their many fancy-ass walk-in closets!"

Perry knew it was true. "You're right, but it just seemed like everything I ever wanted—to be part of a beautiful, Black couple, to have high-flying careers in the city, and then to spend our summers here. It was meant to be perfect."

Billie knew she was the youngest one, but for the first time, she felt like the older sister. "Oh, sweetie," she told Perry. "There's no such thing."

Perry didn't seem to hear her. "I think the reason I fell so in love with this island was because I felt protected here. Like nothing bad could ever happen to me on the Bluffs. This is the last place I expected my life to fall apart."

"Oh, I think this is the best place for things to fall apart," Billie said. "This is our home. It turns out they had some pretty big-ass skeletons in their closet, but Ama and Omar made this place home for us, they brought us together and made us like sisters. That took a lot of work. That took a lot of love. This island is strong enough to handle these storms that are coming at us. You know what Omar said, 'This is sacred ground. It was here before us and it'll be here after us.'"

Perry narrowed her eyes. "Yeaah, but he didn't fully grasp the extent of climate change, did he?"

Billie shook her head. "Carousel time?"

They paid for their lunch, then drove to the carousel and bought a five-pack of tickets. The first time around, they sat side by side in a wooden carriage on the carousel. But as the ride prepared to begin again, they each straddled a horse along the periphery. They went around and around, remembering a time when all it took to make it a good day was for Omar to give them a long trail of carousel tickets. Without thinking, Perry reached up and grabbed the brass ring. Just one grasp and she had it. She looked down at it, in her palm, and wondered at the ease with which she'd gotten the thing she hadn't even been trying for.

So many times when she'd taken a pregnancy test, she felt a desperate pleading. Like a character in an old Spike Lee movie, she'd find herself praying, *Please baby please baby please.* But this time, she felt a quiet confidence that was different. She knew that didn't mean a miscarriage wasn't on the horizon. What she thought was that maybe *she* was different. Maybe, after everything, she was strong enough, sure enough of herself to handle whatever came next.

She'd trained herself to emotionally hold back until the twelve-week mark. But sitting on the carousel, thinking about all she'd learned about her brave, red-lipstick-wearing birth mother, she thought, Holding back never kept me or my pregnancy safe. She wanted to love extravagantly, the same way she'd let Damon into her bed the night he returned to New York begging her for forgiveness.

Without discussing it, Perry and Billie began walking

toward Kennebec Avenue. It had been a long time since they'd taken multiple rides on the carousel followed by a no-calorie-counting stop at Back Door Donuts.

"I need a donut," Perry said, linking elbows with Billie, the way they had when they were girls. "Then I need a butterbeer ice cream, stat."

Whatever happens next week, next month, Perry told herself. At this moment, I'm blissfully not alone. There is a life beating within me. And you know that brass ring, baby, I grabbed it for you.

CHAPTER 40

SAILING

It was just a few days away from Perry's birthday, August 15. They always hosted a big party at the house. But this year, Ama felt it was best if she left the house to the girls. Before she left, she sent a text to all three of them:

My dear girls, Carter and I are leaving the Bluffs for the rest of the summer. The house, for now, is yours to share. Perry, I hope you will still have your birthday party. You deserve it. And I hope that you will all eventually, in your heart, find mercy for me. I, too, am better than the worst things I've ever done.

On the drive to the marina, Carter said, "So it sounds like you're ready to leave the island for a bit."

Ama nodded. "Yes, I'll sail with you. Then I guess I'll go back to the apartment in the city."

The "boat" Carter had borrowed from a friend was a sixty-foot ketch, which was another way of saying it was more yacht than boat.

"Where are we going?" Ama asked.

"Are you down to just roll with me?" he wondered.

She smiled. "I'm down to roll."

He looked at her for a long time. This both was and wasn't the Ama he knew.

"I've got friends in Sag Harbor. It's a seven-hour sail from the Vineyard to Montauk. We can spend the weekend there. You must meet Bill Pickens. He is the area historian. His grandfather was one of the first Black graduates of Yale. He knows a lot of the Vineyard crowd. I am sure you will have many friends in common. Then I've got to be in Positano by Wednesday. I'm doing a commission for a hotel there."

She found herself getting excited. She had never been to Positano. In their circle of friends, people seemed to split into two camps: France people and Italy people. She and Omar had been France people.

"After that?" she asked.

He shrugged. "We'll play it by ear. Are you cool with that?"

She was.

She had been afraid of this before, being an appendage to the steam train of his wanderlust and creativity. But not anymore. She'd made her fortune. She'd sought her fame. She'd loved three girls and one husband to the best of her abilities. Now she was ready to wander and explore. She wasn't afraid of being lost in the whirlwind of Carter's creativity anymore.

She'd felt so old the day that Omar had died. She saw now that it had less to do with age, and more to do with the grief and sadness, anger and exhaustion that came with letting go of a love she had planned on resting in until the end of her days.

Now, standing on the deck of a sixty-foot ketch, gazing upon her new/old love, she felt younger than she had in years. She was ready to sail into the wind of his life and let it—and him—carry her up and away.

CHAPTER 41

NOT A HOLIDAY, BUT A
SPECIAL DAY

Back at the Barn, Perry and Billie sat around the pool and studied Ama's text with disbelief. Was she really gone? Just like that?

Layla, who had changed into her swimsuit, did laps in the pool. "I'm telling you they used to call her the Witch of Wall Street for a reason. She didn't take a plane out of here. She flew on her broom."

Billie shot Layla a disapproving look. She was not down with anyone calling Ama names, then turned to Perry. "Are you up for a party?"

Perry rubbed her belly subconsciously.

Layla whispered, "It might be the last time you're able to stroll down Ocean Park without knocking people over with your giant belly."

Perry tilted her head sideways. "Remind me why I keep you around?"

Perry walked around the patio and took in the view, the scent, the atmosphere. Her biological mother had lived here; she was still unpacking all of it in her mind. She thought of how young Libby had been when she died. Just forty-one. Perry was about to be twenty-eight. She thought she ought to celebrate every birthday, even the hard ones. She also had a dreadful thought—she better get tested for the breast cancer gene.

For now, she decided to focus on the present. Perry smiled and said, "I am up for something, that's for sure."

Billie said, "Cool, let me and Dulce handle everything."

Perry texted Olivia. She didn't know what had gone down with Olivia and Ama, but she knew that Olivia must have left the island in a huff. Hey, she wrote. **Ama's taken off with her lo-vah. Come back to the island this weekend for fireworks and birthday cake?**

Olivia wrote back, **Can I bring Anderson?**

Perry sighed.

Layla took a swig of her cosmo and said, "Let me guess, she wants to bring that not-funny white boy with her."

Billie glanced at Perry. "Can you please inform your girl Layla she's white, too?"

Layla rolled her eyes at Billie and crossed her arms across her chest. "America is a one-drop nation. I know I got me some African blood. Wakanda forever."

Then Layla turned serious. "What about Damon, Perry?"

Perry narrowed her eyes. "What about him, Layla?"

"He should be here," Layla said.

"Because I'm pregnant?"

Layla shook her head. "It's not just that, P. He should be here because he's the one. You belong together. Do you know what I would give to have a man love me like that man loves you? I was there when the two of you met. You two had the kind of chemistry you only see in movies. I know you better than anyone. And you're not letting him love you."

Perry could feel her face flush. She felt called out and it made her angry and sad. "He lied to me, Layla. I don't like it. He's always traipsing around with that wannabe playboy Jeremy and I know Sabrina is still in love with him."

"That's not your problem, P," Layla said. "Damon doesn't want her. He wants you. If I were you . . ."

Perry stood up decisively. "But that's the thing, Layla. You're not me. Let me do what I need to do."

By Thursday afternoon, the Bluffs were teeming with life. Perry and Layla left Libby's house. As Perry closed the door and felt the old-fashioned key, heavy in her hand, she whispered, "I'll be back, Mom."

They returned to Ama's, where they were met by Billie and Dulce. They sat on the patio looking out at the ocean. Dulce said, "Can't wait for your party. I'm thinking a stroll by the Inkwell to see Illumination then a late-night dinner here? I've got three of my restaurant buddies coming. They're going to make food, mix drinks, play waiter, and DJ. We're gonna turn. This. Mother. Out."

Perry smiled wanly. "Sounds good." But the things Layla said had stuck with her. Had she been too cold with Damon? Was it that he was untrustworthy or was it that she hadn't let herself trust him fully? Deep down, she had begun to fear that maybe she had done the same thing her birth mother had done, ended things before she could get hurt.

Nikesh called every day, but she knew that the first thing she needed to do when she got back to the city was let him know that it was over. She wasn't going to build a life with him. She loved the way Nikesh looked at her. She had forgotten how sweet the first weeks and months of being smitten were. She had wanted to let it carry her, the power of his ardor, the way he looked at her, the way he took everything about her in and held it up to a light, like a jeweler examining a flawless diamond. But Perry was smarter than that. After Nikesh left the island, things became clear. Pregnant or not, she recognized she was infatuated by the idea of him. She was not in love with Nikesh and did not feel the same gravity he claimed for her. Nikesh was an excuse to forget about the problems in her marriage. The salve she used to mend the wounds left by Damon. It was time to let Nikesh go.

Just the week before, she'd downloaded a book online about starter marriages and conscious uncoupling. But things were different now. Could this baby be a new beginning? Was it something he wanted? Could their marriage be saved? Would she tell him about Nikesh? Should she? What happened with Sabrina? Mostly, she relished thinking about her baby. She'd found an OB on the island who'd proclaimed, "So far, so good." For the first time in a long time, she believed it. The truth of it all was when she read the letter from Libby, the very first person she wanted to speak with was Damon. Desperately. He had always encouraged her to find her birth parents—if only to get their medical history. And he was right. Her birth mother had died of breast cancer and suffered from infertility. Surely

Ama should have known these were important medical facts Perry needed to know. And the fact that Ama gave her up for adoption instead of honoring her best friend's dying wishes? What kind of friend does that? She wanted to speak to Damon, she wanted her husband's counsel, but now was so confused. Could they salvage their marriage?

✳

Olivia and Anderson arrived that night. Olivia's skin glowed against a white shirred dress with spaghetti sleeves. Anderson looked oddly formal in a blue shirt, a navy tie, and an olive jacket and pants.

"Hey, dude, do you have a job interview?" Billie asked.

Olivia stood behind him, motioning for the girls not to push it.

While Anderson took their bags upstairs, Olivia pulled Perry and Billie into the kitchen.

"He feels bad because he thinks you guys were clowning him earlier in the summer," Olivia whispered.

"We *were* clowning him," Billie said.

"You called him Mr. Dirty Feet," Olivia said plaintively.

"And it was accurate," Perry said, her eyes twinkling.

"So now he's trying to step up his fashion game," Olivia said. "He's overdoing it a little—"

"But points on the board for trying," Perry said. Then she pulled her godsisters into an embrace. "I'm glad you're both here."

"The house feels different without Ama here," Olivia mused.

"I guess, for now, we're sharing it," Perry said.

"Yeah, right," Billie said. "O and I are sharing the house. You got a big-ass estate over in West Tisbury."

Olivia looked confused. She hadn't heard the whole story, but she would.

At that moment, the speakers blared with a familiar song, 50 Cent. The sounds of his lyrics about a special day filled the house.

The girls looked at each other and said, "Layla's back."

Their friend burst into the kitchen and ordered Perry to close her eyes and open her hands.

Perry had known Layla more than half her life. It was precisely for that reason that she thought it was unwise to do as her friend ordered.

She put her hands out but kept one eye half-open.

The kitchen door opened and Layla dragged in Damon.

"It's your present!" Layla said.

Damon smiled at her and said, "Can I stay?"

Perry teared up and nodded yes. Then she hugged Layla and said, "Thank you."

They decided to walk into town, Perry and Damon, Olivia and Anderson, Layla, Billie and Dulce. It was Grand Illumination Night on the Vineyard, that enchanted evening when the sky was aglow with paper lanterns and the tiny town turned into a planetarium, everyone gazing up into the night sky.

On the way back to the house, Perry drove Damon to Libby's place. During the drive, Damon put his hand on Perry's and the warmth gave her a comfort she longed for.

"What's this place?" he asked.

"It belonged to my birth mother," Perry explained as she turned the key in the Barn door. Damon stared at her looking shocked and said, "Your birth mother?"

Perry continued, "Yes, just listen. There is so much I need you to hear. I want to tell you about her. She was an incredible woman."

"Was?" Damon said, looking at her sadly.

"She passed away shortly after I was born. Ama knew her," Perry said. The tears came quickly then. They always did when she thought of Libby.

"Wow. I'm so sorry, baby," Damon said, holding her close. "Happy you have answers. Sorry that you'll never get to meet her. What about your birth father?"

"He's an African diplomat," she said.

"Damn," Damon said. "I always knew you were an African queen."

Perry shook her head. "You're so silly."

"I love you," Damon said, as they stood on the threshold of her family home.

"I want to love you better," Perry said, holding him close. They spent the evening talking about Perry and what this all meant for her. Before she fell asleep that night, she said a prayer feeling grateful her best friend was back.

The next day, Perry would turn twenty-eight. Maybe the next day she would tell Damon that she was pregnant. And maybe the next day she would psychologically and emotionally jump the broom with him again. But for now, all she wanted to do was reach out and grab his hand. So she did.

Back at Ama's, Olivia and Billie had built a fire in the backyard. As she walked out to join her godsisters and their partners, Perry felt a chill and looked out toward the porch. She could see the beehives in the distance. For a second, she could've sworn she saw Omar, standing there and smiling silently as he had so many times in life. And it felt good to be back at Ama's. Even without her there, it was more than a house. It was their safe harbor. It was home.

EPILOGUE:

A WEDDING ON THE BLUFFS

Billie woke up in her childhood bedroom and stood at the window, looking out at the beach. She couldn't believe it. It was her wedding day. It had been a year since Ama had dropped a bomb on each of the three girls. And while it had taken some time, they had all recovered. Perry was a little surprised and, Billie suspected, a little jealous that she was Ama's only blood relative and that Ama had given Billie the house.

Olivia had told the godsisters about Omar and her father, and they had listened with both shock and sadness. They knew in their hearts that nobody was perfect. But the mistake Omar had made had cost Chris Jones his life. Time had turned the fury Olivia felt toward Ama and Omar into compassion. It had been a terrible mistake. Ama and Omar had done the best they could to fix it. Olivia had come to believe that no matter how much material wealth she now possessed, she would give it all up in an instant to have her father back. But that wasn't an option God had given her. So she was moving on.

Billie had offered to share the house with Olivia, but Olivia had declined. "I think my time on the Bluffs is over. I'll come and visit you. But this isn't my place anymore."

That fall, Billie and Dulce had moved into the house full-time. Dulce had taken the job at the Breaking Point with her old friend from the Culinary Institute. Billie had turned down the job with Desiree Touissant. If the summer of reckonings had taught her anything, it was that she needed to make things right in her own house before she traipsed off trying to change the world. So she had accepted Dulce's proposal. They had moved into Ama's house—well, Billie's house—and started planning the wedding.

Now the day had come. Billie and Dulce were going ahead with revised wedding plans. Though they had planned for all their friends and family to participate, that just wasn't possible during a global pandemic. Instead of a big wedding, they would have a small ceremony on the beach with a few family members and close friends. As she looked outside her bedroom window, Billie saw Olivia methodically measuring the distance between chairs, making sure they were the proper six feet apart. When they weren't, Anderson would move them for her to the correct social distance. Olivia had found a good partner.

Perry, Damon, and their beautiful baby girl, whom they named Libby Amelia, were staying at their house in West Tisbury. Perry's birth father, Kofi Koulibaly, was staying there, too. He and Perry had reunited. He adored her, but what was the hidden gift was that he loved Damon. Kofi and Damon hung out on the regular. They went to Giants games together and watched futbol on TV in bars around the city. His acceptance and admiration of Damon had been a bolster to Perry's marriage, convincing her that she hadn't been wrong in trusting him. Damon was a good, albeit flawed and human, husband.

But Ama's house—they still called it that—was filled with guests. Olivia and Anderson were staying in her room. Jaime Molina, Billie's friend from graduate school, was staying in the downstairs guest room along with his two twin boys.

Ama and Carter were staying at the Nobnocket Boutique Inn down in Vineyard Haven. Billie had wanted Ama to stay with her, but Ama said, "I just can't do it, *cher*. I can't have another man in Omar's house."

But Ama promised she and Carter would be over first thing. Billie could hear Ama in the kitchen, cooking up a storm. She took a deep breath and stared out the window one more time. What was the thing Ama used to say about being patient like the sea? She wasn't patient by nature, but she wanted to move slowly into the day, to make sure that she savored every moment. She thanked God that He had given her so much—it was a messy treasure, this house, this gift from the sea. But it was hers and she would love it always.

She descended the stairs slowly and nearly tripped over a toy train. "Oh my God, I'm so sorry," Jaime's wife, Isa, said, grabbing the train. "These boys have their toys everywhere."

"It's no problem," Billie said, giving her a hug. "I'm glad you all are here."

Ama poked her head into the hallway and said, "The toys are a problem. We can't have the bride twisting her ankle on her wedding day. I know you don't know me, Isa. But I need you to pull it together with these boys."

"Yes, ma'am," Isa said, then turned in hot pursuit as one of the twins went out the back door and dashed toward the oceanfront.

"Good morning, Ama," Billie said, hugging her grandmother.

"Oh my love," Ama said. "Let me look at you. You are so beautiful."

She didn't say how much Billie's blue eyes reminded her of Beau Mason.

"Good morning, bonus granddaughter," Carter said.

Billie gave him a hug. He was so cool, his head a wild mane of kinky curls. He was dressed in a pale gray linen suit and he looked as if he had stepped off the pages of a fashion magazine.

"Anything you need today, you just let me know," Carter said. "Your wish is my command."

Olivia and Anderson were drinking coffee on the back porch. Olivia jumped up when she saw Billie.

"Good morning, sleeping beauty," she said, pulling Billie into an embrace. "Can you sit for a sec?"

Billie nodded. It was her wedding day. She wasn't going to rush a single moment of it.

Anderson stood up and said, "Let me get you a cup of coffee. Light. Two sugars, right?"

"Yes, thanks," Billie said. She noticed he wore a pair of navy-blue slippers as he padded into the house.

"I see your white boy is house-trained," Billie joked.

"You need to stop," Olivia said, smiling.

"You two are good?" Billie asked.

"So good," Olivia said. "In fact, I have some news."

Billie grabbed her godsister's right hand. On it was a simple emerald-cut engagement ring.

"Oh no you didn't!" Billie exclaimed. "I'm so happy for you. Do you want to get married here? Next summer? As you can see, the house is perfect for weddings. Perry got married here. Now me. And you next!"

Olivia shook her head. "I don't mean to break with tradition. But I think I need to find a beach of my own, someplace where Anderson and I can start our own story."

Billie nodded. "I get it. I really do."

"We've been looking at houses in Sag Harbor," Olivia said. "The community there isn't as old as this one, but it goes back more than a hundred years, a history of Black whalers settling down by the sea. And yet, there's a younger, more multiracial group of families moving in there, too. I've been looking in the SANS area—Sag Harbor Hills, Azurest, Ninevah. The community and history there is really incredible. I feel as if I have found my tribe. The houses we have been looking at are right on the beach. It reminds me of the Bluffs."

"I love it," Billie said. "Can I come house hunting with you?"

"That would mean a lot to me," Olivia said.

She knew that Omar's bequest meant that Olivia would be able to buy almost any house she dreamed of. She was sad that all three girls wouldn't be neighbors on the Vineyard. But it would be fun to have a sister in Sag. Olivia was right. They needed a new chapter in their story.

"Are you happy?" Billie asked.

"I'm happy," Olivia said.

Billie hugged her godsister close.

"Can't wait to see you in your hideous bridesmaid dress," Billie joked.

There weren't actually any ugly bridesmaid dresses. Billie and Dulce had been inspired by Solange's bridal party pics and asked their bridesmaids and groomsmen to choose simple ivory-colored sheaths, suits, and jumpsuits. Billie couldn't wait until they were all lined up on State Bridge for photos. They were going to slay in their formation.

Billie heard a baby wail and knew that Perry had arrived.

"I'll be back," she said, squeezing Olivia's hand.

Anderson met her at the door with a cup of coffee. She took it and kissed him on the cheek. "Congratulations," she whispered. "Way to lock it down."

Billie glided through the kitchen where Isa and Jaime were trying to get their toddler twins to eat breakfast and not throw it all over the floor.

Ama looked like she was going to lose it with all the mess.

"It's okay, Ama," Billie said. "Dulce and I don't mind a messy house."

Ama smiled. "It's your house now."

There was a part of Billie that still couldn't believe it.

"Thank you, Ama," she said, holding her grandmother's hands in hers.

She went into the front hallway, where Perry looked haggard and a little overwhelmed.

"Are there big, giant bags under my eyes?" Perry asked.

Billie lied and said no. Damon winked at her.

"Congrats, sis," he said, giving her a hug.

He took the baby from his wife's arms and shushed her as he walked back to the kitchen.

"I'm so tired," Perry said. "When does the glam squad get here? I don't want to look busted in the pictures."

Billie shook her head. It was so Perry to be worried about the pictures.

"Are you good?" Billie asked. "Happy?"

Perry sat down on the bench near the front door. "I could take a nap right here. I'm so tired. That child doesn't sleep."

"You should go upstairs and take a nap in your own bed," Billie said. She had left Perry's and Olivia's rooms just as they were. She and Dulce agreed. No matter what, they wanted her sisters to always feel like they had a place in the house.

"How are you so calm?" Perry asked suspiciously. "On my wedding day, I was a nervous wreck."

Billie shrugged. "I dunno. I just wanted to be really present, to really enjoy every second of this day."

"You're so zen," Perry said. "I'm a little jealous."

Billie pointed toward the staircase. "Go upstairs. Take a disco nap. You've got a full two hours before the makeup team arrives."

Perry looked like Billie had just handed her a winning lottery ticket. Which Billie surmised sleep must feel like to a new mom.

"Thank you," Perry said. And she headed up the stairs.

Just then, Billie's cell phone rang. She reached for it in the pocket of her robe. She knew that it must be Dulce.

She walked out of the house and sat on one of the Adirondack chairs sprinkled across the front lawn.

"Good morning, my love," she said. "Am I dreaming? Or is today our wedding day?"

About the author

About the book

Insights,
Interviews
& More...

Meet Sunny Hostin

Miller Mobley

Attorney and Emmy-winning multiplatform journalist SUNNY HOSTIN is the cohost of the ABC Daytime show *The View*. She is the author of *I Am These Truths: A Memoir of Identity, Justice, and Living Between Worlds*. Hostin received her undergraduate degree in communications from Binghamton University and her law degree from Notre Dame Law School. A native of New York City, she lives with her husband and two children in Westchester County, New York. ᕫ

Q&A with
Sunny Hostin

Q: *Why did you want to write this novel?*

A: As a lawyer and legal journalist, I spent the majority of my career immersed in social justice, police brutality, and systemic racism affecting Black and Brown communities. But there was this beautiful part of those very same communities that I had seen, and been a part of, that too few people knew about. As a voracious reader, and as I covered those stories, I longed to get away, to escape, at least for a little while, in the pages of a book centered on Black joy, Black love, and Black excellence. I thought about some of my happy places: Oak Bluffs, Sag Harbor, Highland Beach. Beaches and seaside towns filled with those very things in abundance—joy, love, and excellence. It was in those moments that I realized if I was looking for those stories, maybe other people were, too. The incomparable Toni Morrison said, "If there's a book you want to read, but it hasn't been written yet, then you must write it." And *Summer on the Bluffs* was born. ▶

Q&A with Sunny Hostin *(continued)*

Q: What inspired the plot?

A: I love the concept of home and sanctuary. I don't own a home on the Vineyard—I hope to one day—so my husband and I have been renting the same home for many years. I always walk past this same house (depicted on the book's cover) when I'm there and joke with my husband that one day someone is going to give me that house. And I started thinking, what if someone really did own a house and then decided that they were going to give it away? It all stemmed from the simple idea of home. Some parts of the book are also loosely based on my own personal experiences and people I know.

Q: What was the writing process like?

A: I have a bit of insomnia, so I often find myself thinking and writing late at night. I also like to write in my home office, which is my refuge away from the chaos of everyday life—it's quiet and cozy. It's where I collected my thoughts and where I found the narrative and characters for this book. I also created a pseudo writers room, where I recruited close friends to come over to my house and we would read the story aloud to get their thoughts and opinions. It helped more than I can express. It was so illuminating to get real, honest feedback from people whose opinions I value so highly.

Q: Why did you choose Oak Bluffs as the setting? What meaning does it carry?

A: I'm a kid from the South Bronx projects, and it's surreal that I vacation on Martha's Vineyard at this point. Actually, a lot of people have been going to Oak Bluffs since before the Harlem Renaissance, which is something I learned many years ago after reading my friend Lawrence Graham's book *Our Kind of People*. It was actually one of the only places where Black people were allowed to buy beachfront property. Oak Bluffs has such an incredibly rich history, and I wanted everyone to learn about that. In fact, all of the books in this trilogy will take place in the three places where African Americans were allowed to purchase beachfront property in the United States. I just thought, why not write this historical fiction so that it can educate people, but also, open up this world that I've had the chance to experience because I've been to all three places? ▶

Q: What lessons did you want to include, and what do you hope people take away from the book?

A: I wanted to explore sexism, racism, and colorism, which are things that so many people don't talk about. I just hope that readers are inspired by how these women continue to rise to the occasion no matter what they face and that they see themselves in the characters. And they really, really do. Actually, my dad read this book in two days, and my husband listened to the audiobook. I really think that it has resonated with men, too.

This book is really meant to be aspirational. In my mind, love is at the center of everything. I wanted to explore relationships. It's meant to be a light beach read, but if we are exploring the lives of Black folks, it has to be nuanced; it has to be complicated. And at its center, is our love for each other. This book is a love letter to Black love in all its forms.

Q: Who is your favorite character, and why?

A: People often suspect that my favorite character is Perry, because she too is an Afro-Latina lawyer who is married to a doctor. But my favorite character is Ama, for her complexity and her agency. I fell in love with Ama for her unapologetic nature and her fierce protectiveness of her girls.

Q: *Where will the next two books in the trilogy take place?*

A: All of the books will be set in a historically Black beach community. The next two books will venture to Long Island's Sag Harbor and Highland Beach in Maryland, respectively.

———————

I hope you are able to see yourself in the characters in *Summer on the Bluffs* and are inspired by how these women continue to rise to the occasion, no matter what obstacles they face. Whether you are an Ama, a Perry, an Olivia, or a Billie, your support of this book inspires people like me to keep telling these stories, sparking a new wave of representation in storytelling. Wishing you meaningful conversation and cherished memories as you journey through.

Hope to see you on the Bluffs,
Sunny ∽

Reading Group Guide

1. How do you feel about Ama's relationship with Omar versus her relationship with Carter?

2. What do you think of Ama moving on after her husband's death?

3. Do you feel Perry should have stayed with her husband or gone ahead with the divorce, to be with Nikesh?

4. What do you think of Olivia's apprehension with dating Anderson, a white man? Do you think she had more reasons to be hesitant than what she told her sisters?

5. At the end of the novel, Olivia buys a house in Sag Harbor, on Long Island. How do you think that will change her relationship with Perry and Billie and their dynamic?

6. Given the girls did not come from privileged backgrounds, how do you think that influences the lives they live now?

7. Do you think all family has to be connected through blood, or is it possible (or better) that people can be considered family over time?

8. Who do *you* think should have gotten the house? ◞

Discover great authors, exclusive offers, and more at hc.com.